Petty Magic

ALSO BY CAMILLE DEANGELIS

Mary Modern

CROWN PUBLISHERS / NEW YORK

Petty Magic

Being the Memoirs and Confessions of

MISS EVELYN HARBINGER,

Temptress and Troublemaker

CAMILLE DEANGELIS

Published in the United States by Crown Publishers,
an imprint of the Crown Publishing Group,
a division of Random House, Inc., New York.
www.crownpublishing.com

Crown is a trademark and the Crown colophon is a registered trademark of Random House, Inc.

Library of Congress Cataloging-in-Publication Data
DeAngelis, Camille.
Petty magic: being the memoirs and confessions of Miss Evelyn Harbinger, temptress and troublemaker / Camille DeAngelis.—1st ed.
        p.   cm.
1. Older women—Fiction. 2. World War, 1939–1945—Veterans—Fiction.
3. Loss (Psychology)—Fiction. 4. Magic—Fiction. I. Title.
PS3604.E159P47   2010
813'.6—dc22   2009034348

ISBN 978-0-307-45423-2

Printed in the United States of America

10 9 8 7 6 5 4 3 2 1

First Edition

For Kate

Petty Magic

"All witchcraft comes from carnal lust, which is in women insatiable"

1.

WITCH, n. 1. Any ugly and repulsive old woman, in a wicked league with the devil. 2. A beautiful and attractive young woman, in wickedness a league beyond the devil.

—Ambrose Bierce, *The Devil's Dictionary*

THERE ARE many misconceptions of which I must disabuse you, but the most offensive concerns the wands and warts and black pointed caps. Some of us may be wizened and rather hairy in unfortunate places, but we're certainly no uglier than the rest of you lumps.

I look grandmotherly enough myself though, for it's a rare morning I don't nab a seat on the uptown 103—and when I *am* compelled to stand, the respectable citizens around me will grouse on my behalf at the bad manners of those buffoons claiming knee injuries or feigning deafness. As I disembark I wish the respectable ones a pleasant day, and I can see I remind them of their dear great-aunties. Don't I look like the sort who bakes oatmeal cookies by the gross, slips a fiver into your birthday card? Nobody ever has an inkling, do they?

Some nights I ride the bus a third time, but you wouldn't recognize me then. I'll tell you how I do it. First I run a crooked forefinger over these travertine teeth, so when I look into the mirror over the mantel I can flash my old Pepsodent smile. Then I kick off my orthopedic shoes, say the right words to shrug off this sagging elephant hide, and in a moment I'm lithe as a teenager again. Thus liberated (and three inches taller besides), I take a long hot bath with bubbles and candles, draw concentric hearts in the steam on the mirrors, and spend an hour or more lounging about my bedroom with party clothes strewn across the unmade bed and the contents of my makeup case all over the vanity table. When I'm finally dressed, perfumed, and done up, I survey myself once more in the mantel mirror. Can't help grinning like a feline at what I see. The beldame has sharpened her knives!

So I go out and avail myself of some delicious little boy I've found at a bar I've never been to before and will never visit again. Some nights it's cinnamon vodka in china teacups and other times I'll settle for a two-dollar draft—not that I ever pay for my own drinks, mind! I don't just go for the pretty ones, either; he's got to sustain my attention for the hours it takes for three or four rounds and a scintillating tête-à-tête, a cab ride home (his place, always his), and a lively tussle in the sack.

You ought to know I never go for the ones who're already taken, no matter where their eyes might wander. Wouldn't be right. But I watch how men and women alike guard their lovers: he spots another man eyeing his girlfriend's cleavage, drapes his arm over her shoulders, and looks daggers at the interloper; she sees a single girl like me merely glancing at her man, shoots me a glare, and kisses him midsentence. How primitive it is, the way they lay claim to one another.

Not me, though. I'm only asking for the night. Not even, because I leave as soon as he falls asleep. At daybreak I find the city is at its bleakest: through the window of a speeding cab I see the flickering neon of a twenty-four-hour diner peopled with insomniacs, raccoon-eyed girls teetering home on broken heels, men too sauced to bother ducking into alleyways to relieve themselves. Even at this ungodly hour the taxi driver is on his mobile. I lean my still-smooth forehead against the frosted window, the ghosts of his hands roving under my evening garb.

My taste varies by the night. Sometimes I set my eye on a playboy and revel in my triumph when he loses sight of every other girl in the club. (Aren't I doing them all a favor? And doesn't he deserve the shame and indignation he'll feel when he rings the number I've left him and the woman who answers says, "Good afternoon, Greenacres Funeral Home"?) On other occasions I mark the loneliest boy in the room and take a purer kind of pleasure in alleviating his melancholy.

There are other things you ought to know. We don't even use our broomsticks for their ostensible purpose, let alone as a means of nocturnal transport. We do not shoot craps with human teeth. We do not thieve the peckers of men who've spurned us and squirrel them away in glass jars. Think of us as sibyls or seraphs: fearsome, oh yes, but more or less benevolent. I may use magic to retrieve my youth, but when these boys climb into bed with me, they do so unenchanted.

Blackabbey

2.

M Y FATHER lasted longer than average, and so I have two sisters. We are evenly spaced at eleven months: Helena is the eldest; then Morven, who lives with me on the Lower East Side; and then me. Helena is 151 but she still runs a B and B in the house we inherited from our great-auntie Emmeline, the house we grew up in. HARBINGER HOUSE, says the sign beneath the porch light; rather ominous, I'll admit, but the most traumatic thing that ever transpired there involved a holiday turkey that broke out of the oven. Featherless and terrified out of its last wit, our would-be dinner rampaged through the downstairs rooms and sent all the family shrieking for cover before Helena could put an end to it. Good thing our china never breaks.

Blackabbey, the town's called now: a spurious name for a place off the Jersey turnpike. There was a community of Franciscans there at some stage, but who knows why they named it Blackabbey—after all, no plague ever decimated their number. But Blackabbey is a far better name than Harveysville, which is what the town was called up until the First World War. "Harveysville" sounds like a hamletful of inbreds.

Harvey was the name of the innkeeper who supposedly put up George Washington two nights before that great man crossed the Delaware. The inn is still there, stodge central, every wall covered with plaques boasting of its one famous guest who only stopped in for a pint of ale, if he stopped at all. Even in the eighteenth century, on the surface at least, it was a dull little town full of ordinary people.

Since the mid-1950s, however, Blackabbey has been rather renowned for its antiques. Interior designers, ladies of leisure, and middle-aged friends-of-Oscar make the two-hour bus ride south from Manhattan to peruse those quaint and cozy shops, and it's the mon-eyed sort who fill Helena's B and B every weekend.

This little shopping mecca wasn't there while we were growing up, of course. Back then the mews was known as Deacon's Alley, and there were a bookbinder, a pharmacist, and a few other stores with dust-filmed windows that seemed to be open only one day a week for a quarter of an hour at a time and sold things nobody would have wanted to buy anyway. The streets were unpaved and we walked knee-deep in horse dung.

But our town has more of a sense of humor now than it did in Washington's day. The Blind Pig Gin Mill, which is almost as old as the inn, has a very official-looking plaque by the front door that reads:

> HERE AT THE BLIND PIG GIN MILL, ON THE 21ST OF FEBRUARY 1783, UPON THE SECOND STOOL FROM THE END, ALEXANDER HAMILTON GOT PISS-ASS DRUNK.

Seems we're the only ones who appreciate the change, living as long as we do.

Signposted from the main street is Blackabbey Mews, where all the shops are. If you turn the corner just after the Harveysville Inn, you'll enter a narrow cobblestone alley with cheerily painted row homes on either side, the first-floor windows full of typewriters, gramophones, and landscapes in gilded frames. White geraniums tumble from the second-floor window boxes. The alley hasn't been paved since the

Revolution, so watch out for rogue cobblestones. At the end of the lane is a confectionery-café, my niece Mira's place actually. There are outdoor tables where the aforementioned city folk sip bowls of chilled carrot-ginger soup under an oak tree that is even older than I am.

One store specializes in antique and collectible toys (a set of shiny tin soldiers lined up inside an elliptical railroad track, red painted sleds for decoration only), and others carry racks of moth-eaten theatrical attire and vintage wedding gowns; there's even a tiny haberdashery full of trilby hats. Other stores deal in fine and costume jewelry, rings and earbobs of clear green glass that throw bright spots on the walls in the afternoon light.

But there's only one spot along this row where you can find a seventeenth-century alchemy kit alongside a pack of Garbage Pail Kids trading cards, only one place where you might prick your finger on a stuffed porcupine. FAWKES & IBIS, says the hand-painted sign that swings above the door. EST. 1950. ANTIQUES, COLLECTIBLES, CURIOSITIES. And beneath, in much smaller lettering: ASK NO QUESTIONS. This one is my favorite.

Fawkes and Ibis was the first antiques store here. Harry Ibis is an Irish Jew who hasn't boarded an airplane since the close of the Second World War, and Emmet Fawkes is an Afroed malcontent who hobnobs with grave robbers and maintains an extensive collection of Victorian smut. You'll generally find Fawkes seated on a low stool out on the sidewalk, either chatting with prospective patrons or grumbling to himself about the rodent problem. When you greet him he may answer you, or he may not, and either way you mustn't take it personally. You open the door and part a heavy velvet curtain with dust bunnies flecking the hem, and as you enter the front room you're hit with the smells of stale incense, mothballs, and old men.

The window display never quite typifies the wonderland within: there might be a gilded birdcage full of Christmas ornaments, a Deco tea set, maybe a concertina or a hurdy-gurdy. Venture in, and above your head is the strangest chandelier you'll ever see, a *Leuchterweibchen,* a wooden mermaid with an enigmatic expression and antlers sprouting from her shoulder blades. I hope nobody ever buys it. The shelves behind the counter are cluttered with molting taxidermies and various items pilfered from med school labs, eyeballs and eardrums lolling about in crusty glass jars, and cork-stopped medicine bottles full of sticky brown gook (FIG CANDY LAXATIVE or HONEY-CHERRY-BALSAM COMPOUND typewritten on the yellowed labels). There are old leather-bound books in languages neither owner can read, heavy ornate keys to doors that may never be locked (or unlocked) again, gargoyles salvaged from the rubble of architectural progress. Fawkes takes especial pride in a bird he claims is the penultimate dodo.

The place is chockablock, all right, and you might even call it cluttered, but don't dare call it a junk shop. Every object in the room has a history worth knowing, if you only know how to read it. Sometimes the people who've owned the books in this shop leave little clues between the pages, and not just love notes or pressed flowers. You might come upon an unused Amtrak ticket tucked between the pages of *The Adventures of Sherlock Holmes* or a sprinkling of crumbs along the gutter inside *The Complete Engravings, Etchings, and Drypoints of Albrecht Dürer.* Makes you wonder what kind of person noshes on a salami sandwich over *The Four Horsemen of the Apocalypse.*

Browsing Fawkes and Ibis always gets me feeling a little melancholy, though I suppose that's part of why I adore the place. No, I'll never again wander through the cobbled lanes and crowded markets of the cathedral cities, never sip another green chaud in some Nouveau café with chandeliers knotted in cobwebs and flies in the sugar pots. Our psychic stamina is not without limit, you see. I could poof in and out of public loos from San Francisco to Samarkand, go antiquing to my heart's content, but then there'd be no oomph left over for taking the wrinkles out on a Saturday night. Crooked fingers, crooked priorities; what can I say?

• • •

O N THIS particular afternoon I'm on no particular errand, only
that I'm home for the weekend and haven't been to Fawkes and
Ibis in a while. It's the twenty-third of June, and the air is alive with
the scent of honeysuckle and the excitement of children newly sprung
from the classroom. The little hellions race one another down the avenue, their smooth limbs and happy faces dappled by the sunshine
through the maples, and the sound of their laughter puts a smile on my
face.

Mira is out clearing tables, and she gives me a peck on the cheek as
I make my way down the alley. There are other cries of "Auntie Eve!
How do you do?" though not all the girls who greet me are among
Helena's granddaughters. (Helena has three daughters—Rosamund,
Deborah, and Marguerite—and six granddaughters in all, and though
they are all delightful it's Vega and Mira, daughters of Marguerite,
whom I hold most dear.)

As usual, Emmet Fawkes is on his stool muttering to himself—
"Satan's foot soldiers are on the march!"—and on cue a squirrel scurries
loudly across the roof tiles and an acorn pings off the gutter spout. I
hear voices through the heavy velvet curtain, and when I step inside I
spot several things on the table beneath the *Leuchterweibchen* that
weren't here last time: a phrenology model, a pair of golliwogs (it's
here you'll find the playthings Lucretia Hartmann of Hartmann's
Classic Toys won't touch), an armillary sphere with silver contours
glinting in the sunlight.

There's another man in his eighties behind the counter, with its
bronze crank-model cash register and apotropaic doodads arranged
under the glass. He wears a bow tie and gray suspenders over a short-
sleeved dress shirt, and you'd know from his coloring that his wispy
white hair was red once. On this side of the counter there's a younger,

heavier man drumming his fingers on the glass. I can tell by the tone of his voice and the tattered Macy's bag that he's come to make a return. Make an *attempt,* that is.

"Hello, Evelyn," says Harry Ibis in his usual placid tone, which seems to agitate the man even further. "Lovely day, isn't it?" I murmur my agreement, Harry gives me a wry look over his customer's shoulder, and the man glances at me nervously before continuing his plea.

"My wife is a wreck, Mr. Ibis. She's terrified! Every time she picks up the mirror she sees someone staring at her over her shoulder. Someone who isn't there when she turns around."

Mr. Ibis points to the sign tacked to the shelf above his head:

ABSOLUTELY NO REFUNDS OR EXCHANGES.

"But *surely*—"

Harry points again, to the line at the bottom of the notice:

NO EXCEPTIONS.

"You were aware of our policy before you made the purchase, Mr. Vandersmith. Buyer's remorse is commonplace in a shop like this. It's the nature of our inventory."

"You aren't going to give me my money back?"

Harry Ibis shakes his head. "I do apologize, Mr. Vandersmith, but if I gave a refund to every customer who changed his mind we'd go out of business."

"What the hell am I supposed to do with it then? I can't bring it back into the house. My wife has already had to go on antianxiety medication!"

"I'd try eBay, if I were you," Harry replies. "You might even get more than you paid for it." Plenty of fools all over the planet willing to pay good money for allegedly haunted bric-a-brac.

The man pulls the mirror out of the bag and thrusts it into Harry's hands. "You don't believe me. You think I'm crazy. Or my wife is. But just you look in the mirror and tell me you don't see him."

"Him?"

"Just look. Just look and tell me you don't see him." Mr. Vandersmith pauses. "He's got big long sideburns and a moustache. And he's got no eyes, just . . . empty sockets."

Harry is opening his mouth to tell his customer that he really cannot countenance such a story, that he is not so patient as he looks now he's in his ninth decade of life, but I decide to interrupt. "What a lovely mirror," I say as I approach the counter. "Victorian, is it?"

Mr. Vandersmith nods, suspicious.

I rest my fingertips on the mirror handle. "May I see?"

"I don't know if I should allow you, ma'am," he replies entirely in earnest. "What you see may frighten you extremely."

"Oh, I don't scare easily. Mr. Ibis can tell you so himself. I've been shopping here since the day you opened, haven't I, Harry?"

Harry cocks an eyebrow. "So you have, Evelyn."

I raise the looking glass and angle it so I can see over my shoulder. I stare into it for several moments. "My niece had a mirror quite like this one once. It was part of a set. There were two brushes and two combs and a tray to match." I lower the mirror and place it gently on the counter. "Such a shame the mirror cracked." With a few words she'd made it good as new again, but a girl can never own too many mirrors.

Mr. Vandersmith stares at me. "You . . . you didn't see anything in it, then?"

"Have *you* ever seen anything in it besides your own reflection, Mr. Vandersmith?"

He hesitates, afraid to admit his wife might be going potty. But eventually he shakes his head.

"Tell you what: I'll give you what you paid for it. It's my niece's birthday tomorrow." I fish my checkbook out of my handbag, open it on the counter, and click my pen. Mr. Vandersmith gapes at me. Harry is relieved, though he'd never admit it.

A few moments later I follow the man out onto the sidewalk, where Fawkes is grousing about the myriad inadequacies of Medicare Part D to two passersby too young to care. I touch Mr. Vandersmith lightly on the elbow. "Your wife isn't crazy," I tell him in a low voice. "I thought it might ease your mind if I told you so."

He looks at me, flabbergasted, but I venture back through the velvet curtain before he can ask me why in God's name I bought the mirror from him.

"I'M GLAD you've come today, Evelyn," Harry says as I reenter the shop. "I've made a rather life-changing decision."

I gasp. "Tell me you're not selling!"

"Not exactly. I'm retiring, at last. *Semi*-retiring. My sister's grandson is coming down to manage the shop for us from now on."

"What! Emmet's retiring too?"

"Emmet leaves for Europe at the beginning of August—he'll be gone at least three months, I'd say—and I was on the phone with my sister last week, and she was telling me how her grandson, Justin is his name, he has a philosophy degree but he's been working in a second-hand record shop. It seemed like the right time all around. Invite the boy down, give him a chance at a proper career. I have no one else to leave the shop to, anyhow."

"Your nephew's still quite young, then?"

"Only twenty-four, twenty-five. Haven't seen him in yonks. I expect he's grown through the ceiling by now."

Hmmm. The prospect of a little summertime fling isn't exactly disagreeable, now, is it?

So I ask Harry what he'll get up to once he commences this so-called semi-retirement—fly-fishing, tai chi, might even have a go at writing his memoirs—but it's his nephew I really want to hear about.

What's he like? *Smart kid, always remember him in a black nylon cape and plastic moustache practicing his magic tricks. Went to Brown and fraternized with all the other green-haired dope-smoking hooligans squandering what little brains they were born with. Philosophy. Pah!*

Will Harry mind having him around the house? *Not a bother, he'll be staying in the upstairs apartment while Fawkes is gone.*

Now for the most important question: and when will your nephew be arriving? Tomorrow afternoon, he says. So soon! I say. Isn't that nice. I'll send over a toffee cake to welcome him. One of Helena's granddaughters will bring it over. My sister has so many, you see, that it's a rare man who can tell them apart; nor would he notice if there's one more Harbinger girl hanging about the place from time to time.

I CAN'T IMAGINE living any other kind of life. Never an abscess or fever; never a worry about a bursting bladder on a long bus journey; never short on gentlemanly affections or womanly wiles; to be, truly, only as old as you feel. Getting older is just getting wiser, so they tell me anyway. How women can live with matchstick bones and menstrual cramps, I'll never know—though I always wonder whenever I brush elbows with the ordinary shoppers in the Blackabbey mews.

When I come out of Fawkes and Ibis I see the window display's being changed at the vintage wedding dress boutique across the way. The new gown is from the early forties, with a Peter Pan collar, and the mannequin's torso is turned so we can see a line of dainty oyster-shell buttons from nape to small. The sleeves are bishop-style—full in the forearm and gathered at the wrist—and the cuffs are fastened with buttons to match. You aren't a full-grown woman 'til you've worn sleeves like that.

Dymphna—a dear old girl; she owns the shop—arranges the frilly bits and bobs atop the lid of a rosewood hope chest, then adjusts the train so it looks like a pool of creamy silk on the velvet-covered platform. She looks up, gives me a little wave, and comes out the front door to greet me properly. "Lovely, isn't it? Found it at an estate sale in Perth Amboy last week." In silence we admire it together. "Funny thing, though——"

"It's never been worn," I murmur, still gazing up at the dress on the blank-faced mannequin.

"How could you tell?"

"No strained seams or discoloration under the arms, for a start. No sign of wear at the back hem either. An estate sale, you said?"

Dymphna nods. "Bought, but never worn."

It's a certain type of girl who's out for the gowns Dymphna sells—the kind of girl who'd choose an engagement ring at Fawkes and Ibis—and this bride-to-be adores the self-conscious modesty of such a dress. Purity, propriety: they long for it, and not merely the impression of it, though no magic on earth will fashion a dress that can recover all it stands for. There's no tailor in the back, no taking in or letting out when the merchandise is this old: the dress either fits you, or it doesn't. Yet it *is* only a dress, is it not? To be worn once, then hung in the back of the closet and mostly forgotten about.

Worn twice, more like—for it wasn't so long ago a bride would save her veil for a winding sheet.

On Fidelity

3.

. . . who's to know
Where their feet dance while their heads sleep?

—Ted Hughes, "Witches"

✼✼✼

HERE IS how it goes. Girl meets boy, mutual infatuation ensues, and when boy proposes marriage girl disregards the lessons of family history. For her father left her mother when she was still too small for any firsthand memories of him, and it was the same with her grandfather before that, and her great-grandfathers too. Hardly any of her friends have ever known their fathers either. Still, there are occasional stories of long and happy marriages with ordinary men, though she disregards the common wisdom that a dame in want of a faithful husband must go candy-striping at the local madhouse. Girl also disregards the dilemma of mismatched life expectancies, for she will live at least twice as long as an ordinary woman and will age half as quickly.

Visions of a golden-anniversary soirée amid copious offspring eclipse the warnings of her mother, grandmother, and aunts, and so girl marries boy. Boy still knows nothing of her underlying nature. There may be a brief period of contentment, a domestic idyll of lie-ins and leftover wedding cake. The young bride has temporarily forgotten that she is no ordinary girl—no matter how fervently she might long to be—and for now, her only ambition is to keep a cozy home for a happy husband.

But things are *too* perfect, you see, and her man becomes distracted by vague suspicions. The house is always immaculate, his dinners delicious and served on time with a smile, yet his wife never seems to do any cooking or cleaning. She spends her afternoons in the backyard, tending the kitchen garden she's cultivated from scratch, but he cannot content himself with the homegrown tomatoes and cabbage she puts on the table. When she goes out on an errand he ventures into the garden and feels a nameless panic at all the strange herbs thriving there, plants with hard black berries, intoxicating scents, and silvery leaves.

For Christmas she might knit him a sweater, a perfect woolen pullover in his favorite color, but whenever he puts it on he feels her love closing in like a vise. And yet, for all his claustrophobia, his wife seems uncannily independent; she does not need him to amuse or console her. He might pass a long evening at a bar in town, return home expecting a shrewish tirade, and feel no relief when he finds her poring over recipe books or knitting another sweater, utterly content in her own company (and indeed, hardly aware of his absence).

The real trouble starts when she tells him she is pregnant. He is overjoyed, of course, celebrates with brandy and cigars and busies himself converting the spare room into a nursery; but when his wife offers names like Hester and Morgana and diplomatically suggests the child bear her surname as well as his, he pretty much blows his lid, and the marriage begins its inexorable decline. It rankles him, her certainty that their child will be a girl. (There is a boy child born among us every now and again, but it's not a common occurrence.)

In the end it will be something seemingly innocuous that sets him off: he might overhear another bizarre bedtime story, this one populated by sewer goblins, gnomes who live on a golf-course periphery, good-natured witches who use magic to scour the stove and take out the garbage. Those stories about Baba Yaga and her yardful of bones were vile enough, but *this*! The overwrought husband stomps off in search of his suitcase.

So it is that every few months we must ease one of our own out of a disastrous marriage. She'll arrive at Helena's house looking fairly distraught. My sister will usher her in, settle her into the coziest chair in the parlor, and venture into the kitchen to brew a cup of cinnamon tea. Helena returns with steaming mug to find our poor friend crumpled in her chair, fists full of sodden Kleenex. Helena calls the guard and we all drop whatever we're doing. Morven and I poof home for the night. We descend upon the house and listen to her stories of preposterous accusations and icy silences, how he says that when he goes he ought to take their daughter with him. (He will leave alone, though, and when he's gone his daughter will finally take her mother's name.)

We tell her we'll bind and gag him, drag him from the house, put him on a boat, and motor out for miles before dumping him overboard. But he won't drown right away, we tell her, because we want him alive while the fanged mermaids are feasting on his entrails.

She'll cringe at this, of course, and say she still loves him and wants no harm to come to him. Gently we remind her that she can now teach her daughter properly, no longer hindered by some sad little man forever passing judgment from the reclining armchair in front of the television. It doesn't matter how enlightened he might have seemed during their courtship; this devolution was inevitable.

You can believe everything I just said apart from the bit about the fanged mermaids. Not that fanged mermaids don't exist, or that we don't threaten to feed the traitorous wretch to them. We'd never actually follow through on it, is what I mean. From time to time you do hear tales of husbands gone missing, but there's always a rational explanation—stupid man went night-fishing in January or some such. And there are, of course, those stories of husbands falling in alarmingly quick succession, like dominoes, and a frequently widowed woman growing in wealth and vitality with each fresh loss. Dame Alice, the Irish sorceress, was the most infamous practitioner of such dark magic, but her power went unchecked only because her coven had no teeth.

In our coven we take a lifelong oath in girlhood—*By magic I shall do no harm, except in defense of myself or another*—but I've never heard any tales of violence in these otherwise-disastrous marriages. There may be an abundance of spite at the close of this generic tale of boy meets dame, but in no case does her husband ever raise a hand to her. She may behave foolishly when in love, but she'd never be fool enough to choose a wife beater; and besides, underneath that bravado of anger and suspicion, isn't he more than a little afraid of her?

I T MUST have happened much the same way with our parents. Our mother, Lily, had met our father at the county library, where he was a reference clerk. He had no family here, no connections whatsoever, and thus it seemed natural that he should have his family at Harbinger House just as every ordinary husband had before him. I came tumbling into the world the very day the Civil War broke out, and he left in blue uniform within days of my birth. Helena has only the haziest memories of him, and Morven none at all. I have no idea how much he knew of my mother's nature; she had ceased to speak of him by the time I was old enough to wonder.

After Antietam there were no more letters, and for months my mother lived in fear of the doorbell. The strange thing was the utter absence of portents. No puddle of spilled milk indicated his misfortune, nor robin red-breast hopping on the windowsill to inflame her dwindling hope. She could have looked into a snow globe, but she was afraid to, as any loving wife would be.

We had only one photograph of him, a family portrait taken the day of his departure—my mother holding me in swaddling, Morven in his lap, and Helena standing with her tiny hand on his knee—and I spent so many hours staring at that daguerreotype on the drawing-room mantelpiece that I would have known my father's face anywhere. He had fine and noble features that belied his humble background and the same pale cat's eyes I saw whenever I stood before the looking glass.

By the end of the war we still had no news of him, and Mother began making weekly visits to the local veterans' affairs office to lodge her inquiries. His name did not appear on any casualty list, but they presumed the worst, and she received a widow's pension.

Fast-forward a decade, to the very day I would make my oath, a bright and frosty morning. I stood at the parlor window idly watching the milkman flirt with Auntie Emmeline on the front walk, when something on the road caught my eye. A carriage was stopped on the far side of the street, and I could clearly see a man inside looking up at our house. He gazed at me with great interest, and I realized with a creeping sense of horror that the man in the carriage was none other than my dead father. I wanted to call out for my mother, for anybody, but I was frozen where I stood.

After what seemed like an eternity, I made the slightest movement away from the window. The stranger immediately put a gloved hand on the carriage door and spoke a few words to the driver, and in a moment they were gone.

That morning at the parlor window wasn't the end of it. Every few years he would reappear, always at a watchful distance, and as far as I knew it was only I who ever saw him. I couldn't tell Mother, of course, and something prevented me from speaking of it to either sister. If Morven or Helena had seen him, surely I would have known.

Once I saw him on Fifth Avenue, at the library's grand opening, but he disappeared in the crowd before I could follow him. Later on I saw him in places he couldn't possibly have been, years upon years after his life should have ended had he lived its full length; and so I came to understand that the sight of my father's face was, for me, the most sinister portent of all. Sadists, child molesters, violent drunks: I can spot them all from half a mile off.

But that wasn't the most disturbing consequence of the whole business. The notion that my father could have found in the war an opportunity to slough his old life—wife, daughters, and all—was a revelation to me. If it was true, it was utterly despicable, and yet that word did not occur to me until many years afterward. I was overcome with a new feeling, a horrified fascination: *this* was the nature of men. I had no doubt the man in that carriage was my father; I knew his face and saw the recognition in it. He knew me, too.

I came of age that day in more ways than one.

How, as it were, We Deprive Man of his Virile Member

4.

And what, then, is to be thought of those witches who . . . sometimes collect male organs in great numbers, as many as twenty or thirty members together, and put them in a bird's nest, or shut them up in a box, where they move themselves like living members, and eat oats and corn, as has been seen by many and is a matter of common report? . . .

A certain man tells that, when he had lost his member, he approached a known witch to ask her to restore it to him. She told the afflicted man to climb a certain tree, and that he might take which he liked out of the nest in which there were several members. And when he tried to take a big one, the witch said: "You must not take that one," adding, "because it belonged to a parish priest."

—The *Malleus Maleficarum*

EVERY SO often I get a craving for the kind I can't find at night. You know the sort of man I mean: a vegetarian Buddhist in thrift-store corduroys, doesn't drink, rarely pays a visit to the barber. Last time I found one I was coming home on the PATH train at half past six on a Sunday morning; he boarded with a friend, both with twelve-speed bicycles in tow. I knew I had to have him when I heard him say, "You know when you're riding down a country road and come upon the skeleton of a barn? I *love* that." He didn't notice me then, but I made sure he left his pocket journal on the train. A few days later I returned it over fair trade chai, borrowed his friend's bicycle for a ride around Prospect Park, was more regretful than usual when I left him a phony number. (Stood by the bed for a while just watching him sleep. This fellow would think of me for months afterward. Years, even.)

Now, I know what you're thinking: vain, silly Evelyn, snatching at her bygone beauty! Why can't she play with men her own age? After all, isn't that what Viagra is *for?*

First, all the men *my* age are taking dirt naps, so I'd have to raid the cradle at the local senior center over on Pitt Street. Nothing tickles my bits like a gent in diapers!

And second, I have already tried it. It's the most natural thing in the world, a libido at my age (assuming I am only as old as I look); but while these men consider their own undiminished concupiscence a sign of good health, they think a woman their age with the same impulses must be touched in the head. I arrived at the senior center one frosty Tuesday, not long after New Year's '82 it was. I challenged a certain gentleman in an argyle sweater-vest to a game of checkers, made some *completely* innocuous remarks about there being more snow in the forecast, and complimented the lemon meringue they were serving with the afternoon coffee. That was all it took: the rumors about "randy Miss Evelyn" spread faster than an outbreak of flatulence after a boiled turnip luncheon. Since then I've been to every faith-based and city-sponsored senior center on the island and was treated similarly each and every time. They're downright afraid of me.

These men aren't terribly observant, are they? When they look in the mirror, to shave themselves or what have you, they think they still see a young buck of twenty-seven, a boy in blue who can boast a girl in every port. I'm really not so foolish in comparison, am I? Besides, these are my retirement years, to be spent however I please. Would you criticize the old man who spends every morning on the golf course or the ladies who pass their evenings crossing their fingers for a bingo?

People think because they're young and stupid and I'm old that that must make me wise. I'll tell you something: you don't get wise, you get *greedy*. You go out to some posh bistro on the Upper East Side and treat yourself to a filet mignon and a glass of Margaux, in solitude, so that young couples dining around you wonder aloud if you are someone they may have read about—an heiress, or a novelist perhaps. And because you sleep by yourself, you want only the nicest bed-clothes: Egyptian cotton sheets, an abundance of down pillows, a quilted satin coverlet that reminds you of a certain Paris hotel room in 1932. You want fresh-cut flowers in every room, lilies preferably, because the older they get the lewder they smell. And yes, sometimes you do want desperately to look as you did once, when you never had to eat or sleep alone.

But don't go thinking I mind it so much—this body, I mean. After all, I've earned every wrinkle. And I must say I look quite well for my age: I dress as smartly as ever, I keep svelte because I don't eat junk, I walk up four flights of stairs to my apartment so I've still got nice gams (for an old lady), and I wear an industrial-grade brassiere so my nips aren't flapping at my ankles.

I MIGHT AS well tell you I was in love once. They say I'm lucky he didn't live long enough to let me loathe him, but I'd rather loathe a living man than mourn a dead one—and killed so cruelly!

His name was Jonah, and he'd be a hundred and six now, had he lived. On those nights I pass in my own company I often dream of him, and when I wake my pillow smells like a rained-out chicken coop.

I know it isn't right, but sometimes when I'm in another man's bed, his face only a pale smudge hovering above me in the darkness, I try my best to convince myself that face belongs to Jonah. And oh, how I wish then that I'd been born a few centuries earlier, back when a broken heart could do a girl in.

Do-Goodery

5.

WHY DIDN'T I save him?

One of the first things you learn from your mother is this: to save someone's life we must lay down our own, and we may only take a life if ours is threatened. Mind you, I'd have given up my life for him without a second's hesitation, especially since I knew full well we could never grow old together; but I wasn't there when they killed him, and by the time I found him it was too late for magic.

There is another common wisdom among us, and that is: a beldame should never become a nurse, because she feels so much more helpless than even an ordinary woman does to watch a man die in agony. A nurse of our kind may only numb his pain with the words she murmurs in the midst of his delirium. She may settle the nerves and sharpen the wits of the doctor as he enters his makeshift surgery, she may eliminate obstacles on the route so the medical convoy arrives in time, and she may bless the stretcher bearers—but she may not save the life of a man whose fate is already decided.

This is common wisdom because I happen to be the one spreading it. Now, I know what you're thinking: you, Evelyn—a *nurse*? You, who make yourself young again so you can seduce frat boys and out-of-work actors?

See, it's only in our twilight years we amuse ourselves with that petty magic. To begin with we must answer our calling just like anybody else, and we do feel we are endowed with a special responsibility to slow humanity's mad decline in any way we can. So Auntie Emmeline ran the local chapter of the Red Cross, and Helena succeeded her; Uncle Hector fought for fair trade long before it was fashionable, while Heck's twin brother was busy raising a crowd of pint-sized revolutionaries in a one-room schoolhouse in the mountains of Ecuador. Both my uncles flew bombers in the Second World War, though they're too modest to speak of it much. And Dymphna who owns the wedding boutique ran a soup kitchen in West Philadelphia (the vats of chicken noodle never ran out) before she took up shopkeeping; and so on and suchlike.

Other vocations were less humanitarian but just as necessary. Uncle Erskine, for example, was an agent with the Society for the Suppression of Supernatural Phenomena, and in the small hours he would scour the Pine Barrens in search of mutant bats, or the shores of Ocean County looking out for any mermaid skeletons that might have washed up overnight.

But no matter what they did for a living, we were always fascinated by our uncles. We envied our cousins who had dads they could learn from and look up to—after all, they were at an advantage compared to the rest of us, who hardly knew what we were 'til after our fathers' departure.

That's not to say their parents stayed married any more often than ours did; nine times out of ten they never bothered to marry at all. The Magi of old were Zoroastrian priests who studied the stars, and modern magi aren't so different: above all, they are wanderers.

At one hundred seventy-seven years of age, Uncle Heck has traversed six continents as a labor rights advocate and the seventh to show off his macho survival skills. In his retirement he has scaled Mount Everest, rafted the Amazon, and run a ring around the terrestrial

South Pole in a dogsled, using magic only when expedient. He has built and inhabited tree houses larger than most Manhattan apartments. You see why the magi make lousy husbands? Not because no woman in her right mind would consent to live at the top of a towering redwood, but because he never pauses long enough for conversation.

Which is not to say our uncles didn't find the time to play with us when we were small—indeed, they were our greatest teachers, our mothers being too concerned with telling us all the things we *mustn't* do. While our aunties showed us how to interpret our dreams and the dregs at the bottom of our teacups, how to recognize a portent (they're different for everyone, but I learned early on that blind dogs, lightning in a snowstorm, and as I say, my father's face, all bode ill for me), and how to view a snow globe at just the right angle for a clear picture of events unfolding thousands of miles away, the magi were teaching us all the fun stuff, a beldame's stock-in-trade.

For instance, there are five methods of altering one's physical appearance: invisibility is first. It requires a tremendous supply of oomph to render oneself invisible, so much so that one usually cannot exercise any other power that would make the whole business worthwhile; and besides which, the novelty wears off soon enough. To make oneself invisible does not make one able to pass through matter like a ghost. All the rules of gravity and the material world still apply. I have always found transfiguration far more advantageous. A set of wings! Now, a set of wings will get you someplace.

Some beldames (or magi) find they are more at ease in the form of bird or beast and even choose to remain that way most of the time. The transformation takes half a minute or so (depends on the animal), but it feels like you're teething all over—every bone shifting into new form, sinews stretching and contracting. Growing feathers, now that's the *really* odd part: a thousand tiny needles poking you from within. Once transformed, you have all the new advantages, and perils, of your temporary form. Birds fly high but fall fast. It is also unwise to turn oneself into an insect, as one is liable to perish upon a windscreen.

Yes, there are as many dangers as benefits in making oneself invisible and in the growing of wings or tails; a safer, more subtle option is the glamour. The art of glamoury is grossly misunderstood, for you have no doubt heard of the dabbler who plays with her mirror in hopes of entrancing a man. (Such foolery is likely to attract only the sort of men who are not worth having.) The most useful glamour is the inverse of that: to render oneself completely inconspicuous, to blend, all but literally, into the wallpaper. It was never a terribly exciting prospect when we were young, but the older we got, the more useful we found it.

The fourth option is, of course, my favorite: making yourself appear younger (or older) than your natural age. It's a simple matter, like moving the cursor up or down a slide rule.

The last involves wearing somebody *else's* face, and that takes the most oomph of all. Once the kiddies realize they fool no one when they don the their sisters' faces hoping to evade punishment for their mischief, this option generally falls by the wayside. I've only used it a couple of times myself, and only when necessitated by the most dangerous of circumstances. You can change someone else's face as well, or turn an ordinary man into a wee furry thing, but that kind of trick can knock you out for days.

Even more important than knowing how to change yourself is knowing which of the five options best serves the situation at hand, and that's where our aunties took over. The magi shared in our exhilarated laughter as we grew scales and tails and vanished into the hedgerows, but it was the aunties who tempered our glee with cautionary tales of beldames killed in foxhunts. It was the aunties who subjected us to frequent lectures on the difference between wisdom and cunning and informed us time and again that it doesn't matter where you are or what age you're living in, the sad truth is that looks are everything.

And yet mirrors are ordinary objects, quicksilver painted on a sheet of glass, and are easily fooled. The only hitch is this: if you're working a glamour and another beldame catches sight of you in a mirror, she can see you as you really are.

But in the beginning I had no notion of tricking mirrors and stealing secrets. Morven and I had grown up romanticizing the brave exploits of those medical pioneers of the gentler sex, Clara Barton and Flo Nightingale, and so we decided to devote our lives to that noble profession. We trained at the New York Infirmary, but because of our unchanging visages we could never work at any one hospital for very long.

Later on, we served in the Army Nurse Corps from May 1917 until the Armistice. There were several of us extraordinary nurses at that field hospital at Ypres, and we each had our specialty. Morven's was mustard gas burns, and mine was gangrene. Have you ever seen a man suffering from gangrene? They call it necrosis because death takes him nibble by nibble. Even the boys coming in with their limbs blown off wouldn't turn your bile quite so much as a case of gangrene.

I'll tell you how I did it. A soldier would be brought in and he'd be so bad off the doctor would plan for an amputation early the next morning. Late that night I would kneel by the bed, lift the sheet, remove the bandages, and sprinkle a bit of sulfa powder onto the rot. This was part of the standard treatment, of course, and so far the infection would have shown no sign of retreat; but I would murmur a few words under my breath and tuck a calendula flower under his pillow, and in the morning the doctor would be astounded to find the patient's foot on the mend. I could never heal it outright, of course, or somebody might have suspected.

No sense denying I was a lousy nurse, though, at least in the eyes of the doctors. You couldn't expect an ordinary doctor to understand that keeping a soldier entertained was just as important—nay, more so—than sterilizing his bandages or administering the correct level of morphine. The convalescents were sometimes in an even more precarious position than the freshly wounded, particularly if they had lost a limb, so I considered it just as much a part of my job to cheer them up, to get them hopeful for the future again.

It was then that I learned to read palms. If I saw a soldier marinating in his megrims, I'd sit down on a stool beside the bed and take his hand without bothering to ask his permission. "Do you know a girl with auburn hair and a hearty laugh?" I'd ask. "No? Well, you will."

Then I'd leave him to think of all that I'd said, to trace her profile and conjure her laughter out of the darkness; and the next morning, more often than not, I'd find a whole new man. Over time I developed something of a reputation, and the men began seeking me out for a peek at their fortunes. In exchange, I made them take me out to a field near the medical tent for target practice. More than anything else, I wanted to learn how to shoot, and learn I did. We laughed and flirted in between taking aim at empty packs of cigarettes lined up along the fence posts.

After the Armistice, while most of the other nurses were arranging for their passage back to New York (and cutting their hair short because their scalps were crawling with lice), Morven and I took the loo flue to London for a few days' holiday before we returned home to Blackabbey.

I KNEW THERE would be another war with Germany—we all knew it, the fact was plain as a tinker's mistress—and I began preparing for a very different sort of work the next time around. It was a calling to which I could apply my gifts with greater efficacy, or so I hoped, and it was this ambition that eventually led me to Jonah.

Welcome to Harbinger House

6.

But at evening she came all at once to the green lawn where the wretched little hut stood on its hens' legs. The wall around the hut was made of human bones and on its top were skulls. There was a gate in the wall, whose hinges were the bones of human feet and whose locks were jaw-bones set with sharp teeth. The sight filled Vasilissa with horror . . .

—From "Vasilissa the Beautiful," *Russian Wonder Tales*

BECAUSE THE house is haunted, Helena makes all her guests sign a waiver at check-in. The ghost is even older than we are; it seems he's fascinated, still, with the concept of indoor plumbing. The toilets flush by themselves in the middle of the night, and when a guest gets out of bed to investigate, she spots no cat slipping through the open window, no other explanation for the water gurgling in the cistern. The ghost never shows himself, but before Helena instituted the waiver, the occasional guest would try to weasel out of paying for the night because of the phantom toilet-flushing.

Of course, there are others who come here *because* of the so-called "toilet ghost." Excited middle-aged men bring EVP recorders, infrared cameras, and other devices that beep frantically just before the flush, and Helena has been interviewed on cable television more times than I can recall. People find her delightfully peculiar for the way she speaks of our ghost with fondness, for her taste in art (on the foyer walls one finds medieval woodcuts of tubby monks making merry and bare-bottomed fiends discharging Satan's deadliest weapon), and for her collection of marionette puppets scattered throughout the house.

There is at least one marionette in every room apart from the baths. Each of the five lady puppets strung above the kitchen sink is dressed in a calico frock and sensible shoes, her hair—unnervingly lifelike—worn in a bob of brown frizz, her face kind in aspect. In the parlor four marionettes hang from the fireplace mantel; three are women and one is not. The lady puppets look like Gibson girls with their bouffants, swan-bill corsets, and pensive gazes, but their broad crimson mouths and spindly fingers lend them a more sinister air than their creator had perhaps intended. The man puppet, as if for comic relief, wears wire-rimmed spectacles and a pink cravat. Come December Helena tucks each of them into a red-striped stocking, and they goggle at you like curious marsupials as you pour your whisky.

Even at a distance one discerns the careful, even obsessive craftsmanship that went into each of these puppets. They wear hand-knit Aran jumpers in soft flecked wool, herringbone trousers and tiny leather wingtips, frothy lawn dresses and off-the-shoulder evening gowns. In their little wooden hands they carry golf clubs and croquet mallets, paintbrushes and knitting needles. Draw nearer and you'll see the freckles on their noses and forearms, crow's-feet, cleft chins, and liver spots. Their eyes are full of expression: some are wistful, others mischievous. The older puppets wear hats trimmed with dusty silk flowers, bustle skirts or crinolines, wimples and rough homespun; the men wear waistcoats, bow ties, spats, and what have you. One puppet in the dining room has a dime-sized pocket watch, and if you're the first one up in the morning you can hear it ticking while you're having your breakfast.

The parrot is another subject of curiosity. Hieronymus is an African grey, a species known for its skill in mimicry. He resides mostly in the sitting room, on a perch of eucalyptus wood beside an antique lectern. Not only is our parrot literate, but his IQ is probably higher than yours (and you shouldn't feel bad about that, really, because the bird is smarter than anyone in the Harbinger clan). But he doesn't say much, since he's too busy working his way through the metaphysical poets. After that he'll be on to the Scottish romantics, and yes, he turns his own pages with a flick of his claw. The parrot takes most of his meals at the lectern—Helena spends a small fortune each month on organic flaxseed and sardines *millésimées*—and a couple of times a day he flies up two flights of stairs and through an attic window (always kept open for this purpose) for a bit of fresh air. He roosts up there, too, in a cage without a door.

You should know that the bird is entirely too proud to provide any intentional amusement. The Manhattanites who are regular guests are used to this, and so they pay him little attention even while they are having themselves a dram at the sideboard.

Which is what they're doing now, judging by the laughter I can hear through the parlor door. If they stay too long the parrot will begin to mock them. There's an old record playing on the turntable in the dining room—torch music, disgustingly sentimental—and I make my way toward the distant tinkling of ice cubes.

Each of the puppets above the kitchen sink holds a baking mitt or spatula in her little wooden hand. They sway in the faint breeze from the open window, their jointed legs clonking faintly, and seem to smile down at my niece as she chops up a spray of fresh mint and stirs it into a glass pitcher of lemonade. A lock of her lovely red-gold hair has fallen out of her ponytail, and there's a dreamy smile on her face as she watches the neighbors' children playing tag through the window above the sink. It's her forty-fifth birthday tomorrow, but to ordinary men she doesn't look a day past eighteen.

Harry'd given me a box on my way out so I could give Vega her present straightaway. I rest the shopping bag on one of the kitchen chairs, we seat ourselves at the table, and Vega pours us each a glass. But she wastes no time, that girl: "What's that in the shopping bag, Auntie?"

Seems like we are forever celebrating birthdays. I pull out the box with the looking glass inside. "Happy birthday, dear," I say as she exclaims in delight at her new treasure. "I thought it would be nice for you to have an extra hand mirror." I pause. "Just one catch."

Vega raises the mirror and regards her reflection for a moment, then tilts it so she can see over her shoulder. She frowns. "You've done it now, Auntie. Freaky bastard, isn't he?"

I cluck my tongue. "Beat his wife, I'd say."

"It belonged to her, of course." With her forefinger she traces the intricate floral engraving down the handle. "The one I've got upstairs isn't nearly as nice as this."

"Doesn't have a demon in it, either. Can you fix it?"

She casts a glance toward the foyer. Helena's guests are leaving the parlor now, clearly disgruntled. Hieronymus has made short work of them. *"It's tourist season!"* shrieks the parrot as they slam the door behind them. *"Now where did I put my gun?"*

"We'll go up to my room," Vega says, and we spend the next quarter of an hour laying the spirit in the privacy of her attic bedroom.

She raises the mirror once more, tilts it so she can see his face, and makes eye contact (or would, if there were any balls in his sockets). She doesn't open her mouth, but I can tell she's speaking to him, and from the sudden heaviness of the air in Vega's ordinarily cheerful room it seems he's not especially grateful for it. The clouds part and a muted shaft of light spills onto the hardwood floor. I see a shadow pass along the wall out of the corner of my eye, and when I look down I see faint boot prints in the hooked rug by the bed. Vega's eyes are glued to the looking glass, her mouth set in a grim line. The rest of this eldritch business passes quickly enough, though, and once the boot prints have faded she heaves a sigh, places the mirror on her vanity table, and declares we've earned ourselves another glass of the sweet stuff.

When we come back downstairs there are half a dozen gals—our friends, not the weekenders—in the kitchen helping themselves to the lemon squash, all of them looking rather glum. Our gathering ended yesterday, but the local ladies are reluctant to go back to their routines.

The covention, if you'll forgive the pun, is a twice-annual event that brings all our hundred-plus members back to Blackabbey. These weeklong events straddle the summer and winter solstices, though the end-of-year covention is naturally the more festive of the two. The covention is not merely a social occasion. There are memorials for our recently departed and rituals of welcome for babies and other newcomers, and the oath-taking for those on the cusp of adolescence. And on the extremely rare occasions when one of our members is suspected of breaking that oath, we hear testimonies, confer among ourselves, and form a judgment by consensus. It's a distasteful business, needless to say, though fortunately I've never had to witness any trials for sorcery in my century and a half of Blackabbey coventions.

Minor problems are dealt with, too, of course—we hash out our conflicts, offer up our transgressions. Mind you, we've all bent the rules at some stage, but when one of us is angling after love or money like the crassest of neo-pagan frooty-toots, with their plastic runes and two-bit spellbooks—well, then an intercession is necessary.

Otherwise, we pass the evenings with music and gossip, ribald jokes and epic card games, the tallies running year to year. We stuff ourselves with cakes and cookies, and we bawdy old broads indulge in our signature liqueurs while the children drink themselves giddy on nose-tingling ginger tonic. Those who travel tell of all the strange and marvelous things they've seen since the last covention, and among the armchair set there are recipe exchanges and reminiscences of coventions past.

Our coven has grown increasingly diverse through the generations, as hereditary members return with the progeny of their exotic unions, and as Blackabbey itself swells with those wandering beldames attracted by its reputation. Even the local coven members sleep over during the event, and the house grows another dozen or so rooms to accommodate everyone. My sister brings out the NO VACANCIES sign when there's an excess of tourists, but there's always room at covention time.

HELENA BUCKED the trend by marrying twice. Her case was exceptional, too, in that neither of her husbands left her—Henry died young and Jack lived to a ripe old age, at least by ordinary standards. Henry had some nasty kind of food poisoning; I'm none too clear on the details, but I need hardly say that Helena was blameless. Indeed, she seized upon every morbid custom by which to mourn him: she festooned the door knocker with black crepe, wore that somber color head to foot every day for two years, and during that time left the house only to visit the florist and the graveyard. To this day—and in flagrant disregard of her second husband's feelings on the matter, though his feelings matter even less now he's dead—she wears a lock of Henry's hair in a glass pendant round her neck.

Apart from that one reminder, however, she seldom gives any indication of Henry Dryden's presence in her thoughts. Helena is a pillar of efficiency, judicious with praise and affectionate in moderation. The B and B is her lifeblood now, though she doesn't do it for the income. Entertaining family and coven with tasty victuals in a spick-and-span home simply isn't enough of a challenge for her. Helena Homebody delights in finding new ways to keep her guests happy; her latest scheme consists of a system of chutes under all the guest beds, whereby an item not yet discovered to be missing is deposited in a lost-and-found box in the laundry room and returned to the surprised and grateful guest upon checkout. Yes, she revels in all the trappings of domesticity, the quilt making and the gingham aprons, the teapots and the feather dusters, the stainless-steel cookie-cutter sets and the eco-friendly cleaning products. I must look positively feral in comparison.

And of course, Helena is the only one of us three who has experienced the miracle of procreation. As I say, we reach puberty as usual but age imperceptibly from then on, which means our biological clocks keep a different time. Beldames tend to wait until they're fifty or sixty to have their kiddies. I suppose Morven had some vague wish to do so herself, but she never met the right man, in the madhouse or anywhere else. She did garner a slew of proposals at Ypres though, and she might have even accepted one had any of the men survived the hospital. The soldiers adored her—and why wouldn't they, sweet as she is? Her pointy nose and expressive mouth made her the classic *jolie laide*. Perhaps she reminded them of their mothers.

As for me, well—I did have the occasional pang of maternal desire, but I knew better than to pretend I could ever be selfless enough to raise a kiddie.

THE HARBINGERS, the Jesters, and the Peacocks are the oldest extraordinary families in Blackabbey, our ancestors having arrived among the first colonial settlers. Few were ever suspected of witchcraft, and fewer still were persecuted for it—our own Goody Harbinger, "the Harveysville Witch," being the infamous exception. Hers was the only recorded witch trial in the history of our humble burgh, initially brought about by all the haggard young mothers in the neighborhood grumbling that Goody Harbinger never seemed to grow any older. It didn't help that her hair was red and her little black terrier—her familiar, they said—would follow her anyplace she went. Subsequently she was blamed for an epidemic among the cattle, and that was that: Goody Harbinger was sentenced to die on the gallows. Though that sentence was carried out in due course, she arranged that her nine-year-old child should vanish in the crowd that bright and frosty morning, prescient as she was that her daughter would be next accused. Lily

Harbinger stayed away for a long time, nearly a hundred years, so that by the time she returned there was no one left outside the coven who might have recognized her.

Most of the people they tortured and executed in those days weren't even witches—and in those dark times you might accuse *any* woman of witchcraft. The charges were generally preposterous: if a destitute old woman was *really* a witch, wouldn't she have made herself rich and beautiful—or at least rich? (Or in the case of one-legged Elizabeth Clark, first victim of the Chelmsford hysteria of 1645, she'd have grown herself a new limb.) Ergo: not a witch.

But back then it was only men with monstrous egos and no capacity for logic who banged the gavels and built the scaffolds. They accused you, imprisoned you and seized your assets, starved and tortured you until they extracted a false confession—but that's not the worst of it, oh no! Once you were dead and buried in an unmarked grave, they sent your family a bill for the coal and wood they'd used to burn you—or, in the case of Goody Harbinger, the rope with which they'd strung her up.

It's the flying on broomsticks that *really* amuses me. The reality isn't quite so dramatic: I go by bus most days. Of course, we don't generally travel along with the unwashed masses, but I must conserve my oomph for my seductions. (For this same reason I don't, shall we say, *persuade* an ill-mannered man to give up his seat.) Our preferred means of transport is the "loo flue." Why do we travel by toilet? First, it is the only public place in which one may find a few moments' privacy. Second, your mind wanders while you're on the throne, does it not? While you're doing your business you are always thinking about being someplace else. The third reason is that toilets are fixed points: they are generally in frequent use even when their maintenance has ceased, so that it is easy to travel between them. We are never *inside* the sewer system, mind you; it is merely a navigational aid. Travel by privy is possible as well, though it's best to use them only to go to the places you know by heart, and using a loo on a train or plane is like telling a ticket agent to surprise you.

Flying on broomsticks—"transvection," those self-appointed witch-hunters called it—is only a small part of the hysterical mythology imposed upon us. They used to say we traveled in our dreams to a witches' Sabbath, where we would feast on babies and take turns kissing the devil's arse.

We have our own mythology, of course. I always found it rather poignant to read of the "Sons of Adam" and "Daughters of Eve" in the works of C. S. Lewis, but I roll my eyes whenever I hear those silly dabblers refer to themselves as the "Daughters of Lilith." *We* are the daughters of Lilith. They say she was with child when Adam cast her out of the Garden and asked for a more obedient replacement, and that Lilith, exempt from the punishment imposed after the Affair of the Apple, walks the earth to this very day. This is why we, her descendants, live so much longer than ordinary women; it is only because of our fathers and grandfathers that we are not immortal.

Now, you might be wondering how we can go on living so long without anybody getting suspicious. It's quite simple: we become our own daughters and granddaughters in the official census, and when anybody starts getting a little too nosy we distract him with a nice thick slab of ambrosia cake. We don't worry about the neighbors anymore because our families are simply too big for them to keep track of.

Otherwise, our great-grandmothers were protofeminists who engaged in frequent and often underhanded acts of social subterfuge, dropping full-strength sleeping tonics in the pint glasses of all the local wife beaters and replacing the text in the Sunday missals with demands for universal suffrage. Others weren't so subtle. Marion Peacock and Philomena Jester used to stand on dairy crates outside a millinery on Alabaster Street handing out leaflets explaining how corsetry was indirectly responsible for puerperal exhaustion and shouting things like "It is the men who dictate the fashion, for that is the means by which they enslave us." Their shrill proclamations distracted their neighbors from ever suspecting they turned themselves into great golden Labradors to frolic in the town park on Saturday afternoons.

When I said Goody Harbinger arranged her daughter's disappearance, it is the oomph to which I refer. A beldame may willingly hand her power to another, for an hour or a week, and when this is done she falls into a dead sleep that lasts until her sister's return. And in rare instances, as in the story of my ancestor, she may also hand it over for keeps.

Morven has done this for me on occasion. Well, all right: in truth, she does it all the time. I have long since ceased to ask when I might reciprocate, and whenever I make even the slightest hint she responds with a knowing but good-natured sigh. I kiss her cheek and make other expressions of blithe gratitude as she eases herself into bed. She simply hasn't a taste for boys *or* travel, which are really the only reasons one would need more oomph anyway.

But she's a great one for the needles. When a person knits, she frequently and inadvertently weaves stray strands of her own hair into her work. So Morven might knit a pair of pullovers for two old chums whose friendship is floundering, pick the strands from their brushes and weave them into one another's sweaters, and their problems will prove surmountable. This sympathetic magic works on ordinary people, too. My sister and her friends spend much of their time knitting receiving blankets for preemies and pompom caps for cancer patients. Each stitch has its own therapeutic value: diamond stitch for immune deficiencies, brioche stitch for clinical depression, seed stitch for rheumatism, and so forth. They generally do prefer to knit for strangers, as the consequences of an imperfect garment can spark a feud that wears on for decades. Back around the time the Harveysville Inn started boasting of Washington's apocryphal visit, young Lilith Peacock knit a pair of baby booties for one of the Jester girls. Poor Lilith dropped a stitch but never noticed her mistake, and when the baby died she was ostracized by most of the coven for well on forty years afterward. Grudges can form all too easily when you live as long as we do.

But don't go thinking we're as heartless as all that. Honestly, most of the time we're more Christian than the Christians. We believe in an omnipotent power, and the law of karma, and the innate goodness of humankind despite all the piles of evidence to the contrary. We believe in the immortality of the soul and in its frequent recycling. We go on, of this I am certain; but before we die we leave a little piece of ourselves in a certain object kept in the family home, so that the wisdom accrued over a long, long lifetime will never be lost.

Well, perhaps not *never*. Hard-earned wisdom is like an old leather shoe—no matter how serviceable, it outlasts its usefulness eventually. After a hundred years or two—once her children and grandchildren are old enough to follow her—an ancestor generally decides she's ready for a do-over. So she comes back, usually within the same family, though she'll have no recollection of who she was before—just like an ordinary human.

The Warrens of New York City

7.

I LIVE IN an old tenement building on Cross Street, though you may not have heard of it since my block was torn down in 1898. On the Lower East Side there used to be three streets, Anthony, Cross, and Orange, that converged into the Five Points, and the folks who lived there called it Cat's Hollow. Most of the old flophouses are gone now, in the ordinary world I mean, but our neighborhood is still called Cat's Hollow—and we, unlike its original inhabitants, will never live in the shadow of eviction.

This is precisely why we reside off the map. Rent control doesn't exceed the century mark, see, so if you want to live on an ordinary street you'll have to contend with your landlord asking pointedly after your health (and you *will* have to move in the end, lest the buzzard report you to the Feds). My bathtub's in the kitchen, the floor slopes, and I often hear spectral children whimpering in the middle of the night, but I've been here more than sixty years now and I won't be moving again. It's so much simpler to live in a reclaimed building, though it does make entertaining outside the covens rather impossible. Urban witchcraft is fraught with such mundane considerations.

There are twenty-seven under-neighborhoods on the island of Manhattan, warrens we call them, and as you'd expect they are mostly concentrated in the island's southernmost districts. We have our own shops, libraries, night schools, banks, cafés, and theaters, and all within buildings long since demolished in ordinary Manhattan.

We have converted into apartments such vanished gems as the Singer and New York World buildings. It's still possible to take a stroll through the Vauxhall Gardens on a Sunday afternoon. You can catch *She Stoops to Conquer* at the Nassau Street Theatre or diving horses at the Hippodrome. We use the old Pennsylvania Station for an exhibition space. The printing houses that put out seditious pamphlets during the Revolutionary era still produce our weekly newspapers, though if you remove them from the warren the words vanish off the page.

All our neighborhoods have retained their original character. The Pandora Securities Company is located in the Gillender Building on Wall Street, for instance; there's Boston Avenue for the swanky gals (who still throw nightly cocktail parties at the Stewart and Astor mansions), Little Hammersley for the fauxhemians, and Cat's Hollow for those of us who don't mind the lingering whiff of squalor. Oh, it's not so grim as you might suppose; only the structurally sound tenements have been preserved by the reclamation board, and they've long since cleared the riffraff out of Mulberry Bend. No one's training polecats or picking pockets these days—quieter and cleaner than your ordinary Chinatown, now, that's for sure.

Life must be easier in old-world cities, where "demolition" is a four-letter word, and so there is little need for hidden streets and all the requisite jiggery-pokery at post office and electric company. In places like London, Paris, and Edinburgh there are plenty of dark nooks where one may dwell undisturbed, where we doddering biddies of impossible age merely add to the atmosphere. European beldames have their warrens too, but they're smaller, and the buildings inside them are often a thousand years older than ours are.

Our graveyards are hidden everywhere, though—urban or rural, old-world or new—to avoid the troublesome truth that the deceased was two hundred fifty years of age. We have our own undertakers.

Now, you might be wondering how one gets into a warren, provided one lives there. We enter our neighborhoods through gated alleyways: red-bricked, ivy poking through the wrought-iron slats so you can't see in. Posh but inconspicuous, like the entrances to Grove Court or Milligan Place. There are such crannies all over the city, no matter how completely the skyscrapers and hotels appear to have gobbled up the landscape.

But where one would expect to see a lot of quaint old town houses around a leafy courtyard, one finds instead the places vanished long since: a stable yard without any horses; a tiny swath of virgin forest above a tinkling stream; or a colonial cemetery, headstones poking out of the tall grass at precarious angles and inhabitants with names like Amos or Josiah. Let's say I pass through the gate on West Houston. I'll cut through one such graveyard, full of shadows even at noon because of the apartment buildings all around it. I turn the corner at the end of the alley and I'm on Little Hammersley Street, with its brownstones gutted in fires and corner gardens lost to the concrete jungle.

In the downtown warrens especially one finds a gallimaufry of architectural styles, rustic colonial dwellings wedged between posh Beaux Arts office buildings and so forth. Some warrens are always bustling and others look deserted in the daytime. Population-wise, the only thing that sets our neighborhoods apart is that they're disproportionately female, and the absence of automobile traffic is, of course, another remarkable aspect. Otherwise, they look much like ordinary streets: chic young women sail by on vintage three-speeders and sip vanilla lattes in the parlors of old brothels; folks take a tipple at any of the clapboard taverns erected by the Dutch, with their low doorways and empty kegs lined up along the curb, those last few drops of ale ever dripping from the bungholes onto the cobblestones. Grannies thumb through leather-bound grimoires in secondhand bookshops or climb the steps into a crumbling church, now a covenstead, for a spell of quiet reflection.

We save all the churches the Christians tear down—it's the irony we relish above all else.

Now, I know what you've been thinking: Evelyn, that doesn't make any sense. How can you live in a building that was torn down a century ago? I shall endeavor to explain.

All over the world there are isolated pockets in which time and space cease to correspond, so that more than one person or edifice or what have you can be said to coexist in exactly the same location. Whether or not they exist at precisely the same *time* is still a matter of dispute among our physicists. Who knows, we might be living on the lip of a wormhole.

In the evening sometimes I look out my back window and watch the traffic on the East River, and I see awfully strange ships, boats looking entirely too old to float, furling their sails as they pull into the old slips. But I don't spend much time thinking about it. We're all of us living in the past anyhow, so what does it matter? Nostalgia poisons the present, that's what I always say—but somehow I can never seem to help myself.

The Mission

8.

The wise are of the opinion that wherever man is, the dark powers who would feed his rapacities are there, too, no less than the bright beings who store their honey in the cells of his heart, and the twilight beings who flit hither and thither, and that they encompass him with a passionate and melancholy multitude.

—W. B. Yeats, "The Sorcerers"

W E HAVE our own language, too, which we use mostly for the recitation of spells. Latin, Greek, Aramaic: all are playpen chatter compared to the words we use in secret. Our tongue is so old it doesn't have a name for itself, which is why they say it was the language spoken in the Garden.

It's also the language we speak whenever there's an international gathering of beldames. I know most European languages, of course, but back in the day we used it whenever we found ourselves in a place where the walls had ears. You must know there were *loads* of us in secret service.

They say certain personality types are naturally attracted to, and suited for, a life of espionage. Those who enter into it for material gain usually die without a farthing, though they do tend to outlast the conflicts they exploit—and that, sad to say, can't be said for the majority of their nobler colleagues. After all, the most infamous were by definition the most inept; folks tend to forget that Mata Hari met her end before a French firing squad. Jonah was one of the best, and now hardly anyone remembers him but me.

We are deviant, naturally deceitful. Lies come as easily as breathing, though not by some innate pathological defect—it's just that our nature necessitates it. No surprise, then, that so many beldames chose the life I did. We hid refugees and resistance members in our warrens and memorized military dispatches in a single glance, cracked safes with the tap of a finger and garbled enemy radio signals with a flick of the tongue. We spread black propaganda far more quickly than anyone from Morale Ops could have done, and made it all the more convincing. As I say, we couldn't change what fate had already decided, but that distinction grew so nebulous that on plenty of occasions we wound up squandering our efforts. We accomplished so much and berated ourselves for not doing more. Isn't it always the way?

Morven wasn't going back into nursing either. She scored off the charts on a series of cryptography exams and was sent to Arlington Hall early on in the war. (It was around that time she found our apartment in Cat's Hollow, though it would be years before we could actually live there.) The Signal Intelligence Service very magnanimously lent Morven to MI6, and they kept her there until V-day. She "broke"—translated, that is—plenty of codes from other beldames behind the lines, and at the end of the war they made her a member of the Order of the British Empire. She still keeps the medal in a box on her bedside table.

Yes, sir, the Harbingers pulled their weight. Uncle Heck and Uncle Hy were two of the most celebrated pilots in the U.S. Air Force; they volunteered for missions that seemed tantamount to suicide and came home again without so much as a ding in the chrome. Together they flew a B-26 Marauder all over Europe, yet the plane never made a blip on an enemy radar screen before it reached its target; the only evidence of its presence was a shadow gliding over wide green pastures in the moonlight. One could take over if the other ran low on oomph. They called them the "Immortal Duo." They really did seem invincible back then.

In many ways espionage was even more frustrating than nursing. You had very little idea how your own bit would be of value, because you were never meant to know too much in case you were captured. No matter how trivial the errand, you trusted it mattered a great deal in the grander scheme, and so you put everything you had into fulfilling it safely. Get your hands dirty without leaving a smudge: that was the trick. Every detail was crucial, no matter how minute, for a man's life was forfeit if an SS officer noticed his buttons were sewn parallel instead of crosswise. And if your luck ran out, you had to destroy the evidence and be prepared to die at your own hand. But I had all my oomph in those days—before there was a hide to slough—so there was little for me to fear in that regard at least.

As I say, foreign languages are a cinch for the likes of us. Still, I thought I might like to live in Berlin for a while, get fluent and such. I was there over twenty years but it passed like a blink: by day I studied this and that at the *Universität,* and for my living I read palms and tarot cards in a fusty parlor teeming with aspidistra; by night I drank pink champagne with kohl-eyed nancies in sequined chemises. The Romanisches Café was the best spot, the only spot. I'd drink lager by the quart before supper and tip a dainty bottle of Underberg at the finish—aids in the digestion, you know.

There was little I *didn't* do and few I didn't meet. I even ran with the socialist crowd from time to time, though I could only take their company in limited doses; they were angry men who deprived themselves of meat and drink and sex, rather like monks who'd lost their religion. The circus clowns weren't much better—they were so sarcastic they could exhaust anyone who made an effort to engage them. They would stare at you over their empty beer steins, yellow stains under the arms of their undershirts, traces of greasepaint still ringing their nose and eyes, and tell you stories of their cheerless childhoods.

But oh, the acrobats! I tell you, making love to an acrobat is a singular experience. Sarrasani was Europe's finest circus and Dmitri Nesterov—one of the aforementioned acrobats—its finest performer. I used to turn myself into a pigeon and roost on a tent pole so I could watch him perform every night high above the sword eaters and flame throwers.

And yet there was another member of the circus who was even dearer to me: the magician who called himself Neverino, a Bavarian shoemaker who'd fought in the first war and later reinvented himself as an Italian monk-turned-prestidigitator. He had gotten his stage name, Fra Carnevale, from an obscure Renaissance painter whose depiction of the Annunciation had brought him to tears as a young man in a museum in Munich. The vivid blue of the Virgin's robe had recalled the only memory he had of his mother, who had died in childbirth when he was four years old, and when he gave his first magic show that night they introduced him as Fra Carnevale. He never did tell me what his real name was—the name his parents had given him, I mean—but I suppose you could say Neverino *was* his real name.

He pulled roses out of my ears and pfennigs fell from his lips every time he laughed, and he even sawed me in half a few times when his assistant was too sauced to come on. Neverino was the closest thing to a father I ever had, and he was the only person in Berlin who knew me for what I was. He was also the one who introduced me to the members of the Centaur network, with whom I collaborated for a good few years.

Neverino and I spent many happy midnight hours in the backyard of his little half-timbered house in Werder admiring each other's tricks, me turning toad to raven to Doberman in the span of seconds, and though he wasn't able to best me there, he did show me how to play dead even more convincingly than a two-day-old corpse. He had spectacles, though he didn't need them, wore a tonsure and a rough brown robe both on and off the circus stage, and affected an Italian accent whenever it might give him an advantage.

As I say, the art of glamoury is best used to make oneself as inconspicuous as the light fixtures. I could, on purpose, drain the luster from my hair, my eyes, my complexion, and once I'd put on a drab serge suit and sensible shoes no one would ever suspect a thing of me.

In many respects it was better than being invisible, and I made terrific use of it on tours of various German munitions factories in '33 and '34. Neverino posed as a Canadian industrialist all too eager to praise the Germans' superior technologies. (Just imagine it: a native German speaking his own language with a pitch-perfect North American accent! My, but he was brilliant.)

It is a universal truth that flattery will get you anywhere, even into the belly of a Panzer. Back then the Germans had no intention of starting a war with the British—a powerful race, Aryan as theirs—and they were anxious to show off their new feats of engineering. The Germans hardly noticed the bland young woman holding a small typist's notebook, nor could they have known that the notes wrote themselves under the red cardboard cover.

For a time I was afraid our partnership would be short-lived. Hitler had seized control of the Reichstag in early 1933, and the following year Sarrasani took his circus on a tour of South America to evade the Nazi arsonists. They'd been lucky enough to stay in business after the first time the tent was torched. Neverino went too, but he promised he'd be back.

To my delight, he returned to Berlin within the month. Over a spaghetti dinner he told me that he hadn't been to South America at all, but to London. He had managed introductions with some of the people who would later head the Special Operations Executive, or SOE, and had passed along the notes we'd made on the factory tours. They'd given him instructions to set up one of the early Nazi surveillance and resistance networks, the Centaur circuit, and he wanted me to keep working for him. He paused only to laugh at the red wine rising in his glass.

And once the war started, Neverino proved himself one of the most ingenious hoax-masters for the Allies. It was his idea to plant phony intelligence memos on corpses in uniform and his idea to build ersatz military complexes out of wood and rubber to fool the German bombers. Yes indeed, Neverino was a mastermind, an inspiration. His friendship meant a lot to me, and it meant even more in hindsight. I would never have known Jonah without him.

Nibble, Nibble, Little Mouse

9.

By one of those contradictions so frequent in the Satanic realm it was the oldest and most hideous and repulsive witches who knew the recipes for the most efficacious love-liquors.

—Grillot de Givry, *Witchcraft, Magic and Alchemy*

MORVEN'S PETTY magic is as selfless as mine is not. My sister spends most of her afternoons with her friend Elsie at the Metropolitan Museum of Art, where they wander from room to room looking out for pairs of lonely people whom they might bring together by "happy accident."

For instance, one rainy Saturday afternoon two students were sketching the same gilded statue of Saint-Gaudens's *Diana* in the courtyard of the American Wing. Each was seated on a bench in good view of the statue, but perhaps ten or twelve feet from one another; they were clearly unacquainted. The girl was checking her mobile at frequent intervals (in hopes that a particular someone might have called her, so much seemed plain), and she grew more and more dejected each time she tucked the phone away. In aspect the young man was as kind—and as sad—as she. They looked to be roughly the same age but too absorbed in their own private woes even to notice one another, let alone make any overture of friendship.

"Do you mind if I sit here?" said Elsie to the girl as my sister was speaking the same words to the young man. Both gave each jolly old dame a distracted "Not at all," and went on with their work.

Several minutes went by, during which time both ladies gazed up at the statue of Diana the huntress in idle appreciation. Then, with a few silently mouthed words, Elsie proceeded to break the charcoal stick in the girl's hand, and each stick following it. The girl huffed in frustration as she rummaged through her knapsack.

"Pardon me," Morven murmured to the man beside her, "but I believe that young lady over there has just broken her last stick of charcoal." She nodded to the full box of charcoal vine at his side. "Do you think perhaps you might . . . ?"

"Oh?" he said, momentarily confused, and then: "Oh! Of course." And as he ventured across the way to offer the girl a spare stick of charcoal Elsie slipped away under some silly pretense, a coughing fit perhaps. Both ladies watched from behind a nearby statue as the boy complimented the girl on her sketch, she thanked him graciously, and they inquired as to their respective places of study, and how she smiled when he asked if he might sit beside her.

They have hundreds of stories like that one. I've been up to the Cloisters with them on sunny summer afternoons and watched as my sister stimulated three pairs of pheromones with a few carefully chosen words in the gallery of the Unicorn Tapestries, then instigated a cordial debate on the best method for the restoration of egg tempera between two pasty-faced academics—and that was only in the first five minutes.

Helena disapproves of these excursions, says it's meddling and that most lonely people have nobody but themselves to blame for it anyhow. Morven has invited me to come along again today, but I'd rather make my own mischief back in Blackabbey.

I'm not used to prowling in the daytime. The sun feels so nice on my smooth bare arms and I feel positively giddy. I shift the cake box from hand to hand as I amble down the mews, sundress flouncing round my calves. I pass Dymphna coming out of her shop and she gives me a vague smile, thinking me one of Helena's progeny, though she knows what I get up to well enough.

Picture Fawkes and Ibis in the gloom of early evening: the steamer trunks and *Wunderkammers*, the bronze busts of forgotten statesmen and voodoo poppets fresh off the bayou, the *danse macabre* carousel that plays "In the Hall of the Mountain King" when wound. The walls are cluttered with English portraits and Renaissance engravings, lords and ladies in stiff white ruffs and naked men contemplating their own innards.

I peer through the front window and see Harry's nephew bent over a game of solitaire at the counter. I can make out a long pale nose, thick dark hair in need of a cut, and a pianist's fingers as he turns a card. I get a strange squirmy feeling then. And in the next moment, as I open the door and he looks up from his card game, I believe I have just locked eyes with a ghost.

The boy has Jonah's long, earnest face—Jonah's hair, albeit on the shaggy side—Jonah's slender fingers—and precisely Jonah's look of eager expectation. It's as if these sixty-odd years have melted away in a twinkling.

A few seconds pass in this amazed silence. He is opening his mouth to speak to me when his mobile goes off—"Jesu, Joy of Man's Desiring" is the ditty—and when he gives me an apologetic look and opens the phone I finally remember myself. This is Justin, Harry's nephew, and he was only staring at a pretty girl who'd walked into his shop.

I can hear a female voice through the receiver, and he is adopting a certain tone, *that* tone, you know what I mean: "Hey, it's great to hear from you . . . How've you been? That's good . . . It's just that things've been so busy around here . . . Yeah, at my uncle's shop . . ."

Jonah had grown up in London, and he had that glorious upper-crust accent that made you feel, as soon as he spoke, that you were in capable hands; and so my first thought is that this boy's ordinary Jersey speech is just an act put on for the girl on the other end of the line.

My heart is thudding in my ears. Desperate for a distraction, I look around the room and pick out the changes since my last visit. To my relief, the horned mermaid chandelier still hangs above my head, but pretty much every item behind the counter has been rearranged and all the furniture dusted and polished. What else . . . oh! All the books are gone! There'd been no order to the book collection, just a few dusty volumes piled here and there, but now there isn't a tome in sight. Then I notice an Apple laptop open on the counter in front of him beside a stack of old ledger books. Seems the nephew—Justin—is industrious enough to attempt to bring the Fawkes and Ibis record-keeping system into the twenty-first century. Good luck to him, and he'll need it.

"Listen, do you mind if I call you back? I'm still at work . . . Yeah, see, the thing is, I'm down in Jersey right now, so I don't think I can make it out tonight . . . Yeah, okay, I sure will . . ."

Slowly I circle the casket table by the window, examining every once-sacred object on its black varnished surface as if for the first time: the reliquary carved and painted in the likeness of a girlish saint, the repoussé incense burners, the monstrance with its tarnished sunburst.

"Thanks for the call . . . Enjoy your evening . . . Uh-huh, you too. Later."

Is the girl aware she's just been jilted? Probably not, if she was stupid enough to ring him in the first place. So we have a rake, have we! Not so much like Jonah, then.

I meet his gaze again as he flips his phone shut and I feel that frisson, that very particular zing, shooting out of my quim and rearranging all my guts on its way up. Now his face is strangely blank. I look away. A length of scarlet ribbon trails over the side of the casket table, and I hook my finger through the ribbon and hold the pendant up to what daylight remains. It's a pomander, with a sprig of dried rosemary inside, but I will allow him to tell me so himself. I place the cake box on a shelf, flick the pomander's tiny clasp, and the rosemary falls into my open palm.

I can feel his eyes on me. I make a little show of putting the sprig back in the hollow pendant and fumbling with the clasp, and I hear him round the counter and approach the table.

"Here," he says gently. "Let me." Gingerly I hand him the pendant and he smiles at me as he refastens the clasp. "It's meant to ward off illness, bad spirits, and whatnot."

"Though I guess that depends on what you put inside it," I murmur.

He squints at the tiny price tag dangling from the ribbon. "Looks like it's over three hundred years old."

"The pomander itself, you mean. Not the ribbon as well, surely."

"Seems I've been telling you things you already know. You an art history major?"

I shake my head. "I'm just interested."

He looks at me as if to say *So am I*—and when he asks, "Is there something in particular I can help you with?" I am confident he isn't talking about his inventory, though his manners are technically beyond reproach.

I remember myself and pick up the cake box. "I haven't come to browse, actually." With slightly trembling hands I give him the box. "It's for you. It's a cake. A toffee cake. For you."

He stares at me, agape, and I'm not taking literary license here. After a long moment he says, "For *me*?"

"My aunt baked it. She's a friend of your uncle's, comes in here all the time. She just asked me to drop it off."

"Wow," he says. "Wow. Thank you so much." I'm touched at how touched he is.

"I'll tell my auntie you were thrilled."

He offers his free hand. "I'm Justin."

"Eve." His hand is warm, his grip hearty. "Pleased to make your acquaintance."

"Well, Eve. I'm closing the shop soon. What do you say we wash this down with a cup of coffee? Two cups, I mean. One for me and one for you."

"Can't stay, I'm afraid. I've got to get home for dinner."

"Do you live here, then?"

I shake my head. "Just visiting. I live in New York."

His eyes light up. "The city?"

I nod. "I live with my sister. We come down some weekends."

"And what do you do for fun while you're in Blackabbey?"

"We might go out for a drink. You know the Blind Pig Gin Mill?"

"Will you be there tonight?"

I shrug. "Should be."

"Great," he says with an enthusiasm that reminds me even more of Jonah. I feel a pricking round the eyes. "I'll see you there." He walks me to the door and hesitates. "Are you sure you can't come for a drink now?"

"Quite sure. My aunts will be waiting for me. Tonight then?"

"Tonight," he says, and I can tell he's biting back the urge to ask exactly what time I'll be there. "All right. Bye, then." He parts the blackout curtain and opens the door for me, and when I glance back he's still standing in the doorway looking after me.

A FTER DINNER I am playing a game of Neverending Hobscobble with Vega at the kitchen table when the doorbell rings. Vega leaves her hand on the table, ventures into the hall, and puts her eye to the peephole. "It's a *boy*," she whispers. "I don't know him. Are you expecting anyone, Auntie?"

"Not particularly," I reply, but I come up swiftly behind her and yank the door open.

"Hello, Eve." Justin pauses. "I hope you don't mind, but I asked Uncle Harry where your family lived and he gave me your address. Your aunt's address, I mean."

I usher him in and Vega looks at me as if to say, *So this is why you haven't put your old skin back on.*

I pay her no mind. "I thought we were meeting at the bar."

"We are. I mean, I was down there for a while, and then I started to wonder if you'd made other plans, so I just thought I'd come by and . . ." Justin casts a curious glance about the foyer, then remembers himself and lets out a nervous laugh.

I smile up at him. "I'll just get my purse."

OUR CONVERSATION is pleasant on the walk into town. We chat for a bit about Emmet Fawkes's European itinerary and how Justin is settling into the upstairs apartment (not exactly home, but he's getting used to the weird smells and antediluvian appliances); he tells me I have a classy name and that if it weren't on my house he'd have thought it was a stage name. I laugh as though I haven't heard this before. Like the names of all the classic film stars, ours generally sound as if we've made them up.

We arrive at the Blind Pig Gin Mill, a cozy, dimly lit pub where the blue-collar barflies and their lively sports chatter are a welcome alternative to the stodgy pretensions of the Harveysville Inn. The bartenders tease you if you order anything besides the swill they've got on tap, though the Harbinger girls are more or less exempt; I order a dry martini and the boy behind the counter nods without so much as a twitch of the mouth. Justin orders a pint of Miller Lite.

He tells me he's excited to be working for his uncle and that he'd like to travel the world "going picking." He admits he doesn't have much of a head for business, but he hopes it's something that can be taught. "Have you ever seen my uncle deal with somebody trying to make a return?" he asks, and I laugh. "He's a total hardass. I'd never be able to do that."

"You'll learn, I suppose."

Over and over he impresses me with his swiftly acquired knowledge of the Fawkes and Ibis inventory, his stories of crisscrossing Europe on a series of night trains and of the oddball customers in the second-hand record shop, and his impeccable manners. He'd held the door open for me, of course, he listens raptly to my own little anecdotes, and when my shawl falls off the back of my chair he bends automatically to retrieve it.

"How was your beer?" I ask as he drains his pint glass.

"Awful. But it's gone to a better place." He pauses. "Are you okay? You just went all pale."

That had always been Jonah's peculiar expression, from the day I met him 'til the night before he died. Whenever you asked Jonah how he'd liked his hearty lamb stew, his brandy, his just-finished cigar (on those rare occasions when there was a cigar to be smoked), he always responded with "gone to a better place"—no matter how much, or little, he'd actually enjoyed it. I've never heard anyone else use that expression except at the funerals of ordinary people.

"What is it? What's wrong?"

I take a breath to steady myself. "Nothing. I'm all right. It's just . . . I knew someone once who used to say his food and drink had 'gone to a better place.' It . . . always made me laugh."

"I thought I'd made it up," he says a little ruefully.

I sigh. "I'm sure he did too."

He has the tact to say no more. Yes, I *am* impressed.

But I can tell you one thing: no matter how innocently he may present himself, this boy's got a bag o' tricks. How can he remind me so much of Jonah, then? It isn't only his eyes, his face, his fingers. He carries himself just the same—easygoing on the surface, but watchful underneath. I had often wondered what Jonah was like when he was a younger man, but I never thought I'd get the chance to find out.

The memory of that phone call in the shop this afternoon gives me pause, and I raise my eyebrows when he rests his hand on my bare knee. "You're being rather presumptuous, wouldn't you say?"

"Hmm?"

"How do you know I don't have a boyfriend?"

He withdraws his hand with a frown. "When you came into the shop, you . . . well, you didn't look at me as if there was somebody else."

"I haven't the faintest idea what you mean. But what about *you*, Mister Kiss-and-Run?" He turns red. "I suppose you picked her up at a bar. Am I right?"

He glances away, gives a slight nod.

"Let's try this, then: why don't you show me how you did it? I find this all very interesting from an anthropological point of view."

"I don't—I didn't—"

"Don't even bother trying to tell me you didn't use some slick sort of line. Now, seduce me *exactly* as you seduced that poor girl on the telephone earlier."

"But—"

"Go on! I won't make fun."

He gives me a look, as if he can't figure out if he's walking willingly into a trap. "Well, it was her friend's birthday and she was picking up the tab. I watched her sign the credit card slip, and—"

"Ah, so you're an expert in graphology! No, no, go on, by all means. Hand me a napkin and I'll sign my name."

He plucks a fresh napkin from a holder by his elbow. I pull out a fountain pen—"Got this at your shop, by the way"—and write "Eve" with an immodest flourish at the end. I hand him the napkin and as he looks at it a smile flits across his face.

"Now, I suppose you're about to tell me the long tail on my lower-case E is indicative of my generosity? Perhaps to a fault?"

He stares at me.

"Never fails, does it?"

Justin clears his throat. "Not 'til now."

I take the last sip of my martini and pop the olive, chewing thoughtfully as I watch him fidget. "I wonder what you say if the girl's name ends in some other letter. Then again, I suppose most girls make long tails on their As and Ys as well."

He's now red as a beet. I don't treat other men this way, of course—if I made a habit of this I'd never see any action.

I feel a tingling in my fingers and toes. I've been ignoring this nagging feeling since we first sat ourselves at the bar. Running out of oomph is like running out of petrol: a smart motorist finds a fill-up station as soon as she sees the flash of the little red warning light, and I fear I'm running on fumes. You don't want to see what would happen if I were to run out: within seconds I'd be standing in the middle of the bar looking like a threepenny hoor.

"I've got to go home," I say abruptly.

"Now that your work here is done?" he says, but he is making a valiant attempt at a smile.

"I'm sorry," I say as I fumble for my pocketbook. "I didn't mean to humiliate you."

"Oh, no?"

"Well, I only meant to humble you a little. I'm afraid I overshot, though, and for that I apologize."

"There's nothing to be sorry for," he says as we exit the bar. "Can I walk you home?"

"Thank you, but your place is in the opposite direction."

"But I'd rather walk y—"

"No, honestly, Justin, I appreciate the gesture but I'm in a hurry now. There's something I've forgotten to do at home and so I've got to run."

"Oh," he says. "Well, I won't keep you. Wait—just one thing. Is there any point in my asking for your cell number?"

"There isn't, but only because I don't have one."

"Really!" He's fascinated, impressed even. "I'm always talking about getting rid of mine. There's something not right about being able to be reached at any place, at any hour. Could I have your e-mail address then?"

"I don't have one of those either."

"*What!* How am I going to keep in touch with you?"

I laugh. "I do have a telephone, you know."

I pull my pen out of my purse, grab his hand, and write my number on his palm as he's saying, "But what if you're not at home?"

"Then you'll leave a message and I'll ring you back. That's what they did in the old days, you know."

"Is this a phony number you're giving me?"

"Would I give you a phony number if I wanted to see you again?"

"Uh-oh. She's not answering my question."

"Call it and find out. I'm sorry, I've got to go." I bid him good night and hurry up the avenue toward home as that awful tingling spreads up my legs. My backward transformation is imminent.

I stumble through my bedroom door, slam it behind me, and wriggle out of my frock just as my skin is beginning to pucker. I put on an old silk robe and totter into the bathroom, where I smear on the Pond's without looking in the mirror.

The White Witch

10.

Berlin, 1930s

MY NEIGHBORS called me *die weisse Hexe*—the white witch. I had upwards of a dozen callers a day, many of whom were repeat visitors. I even felt a certain degree of affection, born of familiarity, for the middle-aged women who asked if their civil-servant husbands would receive a promotion and the elderly ladies who only wanted to know if their dear Heinrichs were still waiting for them "on the other side." If I'd grown to trust them, I might even give them a glimpse of the snow globe I kept under a knitted cozy on the mantelpiece, my very own crystal ball, where flakes of porcelain snow fell on Alpine villages inhabited by their loved ones in miniature.

Inevitably, though, there were the one-time callers I couldn't wait to be rid of, and I'll never forget the first Nazi who showed up on my doorstep asking for a palm reading.

Nazis were the original stock villains, sneering and stomping and slapping their leather gloves about, demanding to hear all you knew under pain of death when you copped perfectly well they were going to kill you regardless. And yet they loved their wives, children, and pets, same as anybody else, and experienced happiness and sorrow as keenly as you or me. We thought of them as monsters, even the underlings; but I could only regard this man as a singular creature in a hive of insects, or one of the apes who wait upon Mephistopheles.

I let him in, repugnant as I found his uniform and manner, because I thought perhaps I could learn from him. He would pay me for my services, but I would receive his for free and in perfect ignorance on his part.

"You have a secret, which must be concealed at all costs," I said. His father was half-Jewish, meaning he was a *Mischling*—rather common as far as secrets went, in those times, but to him the revealing of it would have brought ruination.

"Will I be able to keep it?"

I raised an eyebrow. "Even the safest secret can't be kept forever."

"You say I'll be found out?"

"In the end, yes. But your position will not be affected."

He heaved a sigh of tempered relief. "And . . . will I have a long life?"

"That all depends." I carefully avoided his gaze. "I can only tell you what will happen if you continue on your present course."

All at once the air in the room grew dark and heavy. He understood me. "Yes?"

"You will die in a labor camp," I said.

A long and icy silence. I wasn't afraid of him, mind, but I hated to think of the mess he might cause if it came to a scuffle. I'd rather not waste my oomph on a thing like that.

Finally he said in a low voice, "What must I do?"

On the one hand, I was rather repulsed by his determination, his primal instinct. Most folks know right from easy, but they choose the latter every time.

On the other hand, it took courage even to ask that question; he must have suspected my parlor might have been bugged or that I could have been an informant. That it was a risk he was willing to take indicated, perhaps, that he wasn't altogether hopeless.

I studied his face for a moment—the fear and uncertainty were breaking through the mask—and then consulted his heart line one more time. No, in all likelihood this man would never find the courage (or conviction) to join the resistance. It was only after the war was plainly lost that he would get up the gumption to cooperate with the Allies, thereby saving his own hide.

"An opportunity will present itself. Remember this, for it may be several years yet." I leaned back from the table and pushed back my chair, indicating the session was at an end. "You will recognize it, and you must take it. The risk will be worthwhile."

"But—but—how will I know? Tell me more!"

I shook my head, and he drew out his wallet. This time, I couldn't keep the disdain from my voice.

"No amount of money will make the future any clearer," I said as I strode to the door and opened it wide. "Good day."

H E WASN'T the last of them. Neverino's friends in the Centaur network were thrilled when they heard a growing number of bureaucrats and military drones were coming to me for advice, and they instructed me to tell the men whatever they wanted to hear. The more it pleased them, the more likely they'd be to tell me things we could use. Most evenings I'd entertain one last caller, rarely the same agent twice, and this arrangement worked marvelously for well over a year. But after my run-in with the Gestapo one afternoon at the end of 1938, Neverino thought it would be safer if I left the country for a while. So I went home to Blackabbey for the winter covention and to plan what I would do next, and Neverino went to my flat in the Chausseestrasse one last time to pick up a few books and bits of clothing for me.

He also found a bug stuck behind the radiator in the parlor. Lucky for him, the adhesive was still wet.

Legerdemain

11.

She caught his eye in a net of bright glances . . .

—Arnold Bennett, "Phantom"

PERHAPS I don't have Justin pegged after all, for nearly three weeks go by before he rings me. I'm not home, as it happens, nor is he when I return his call, and this goes on for a few weeks more. Our game of phone tag lasts so long that he eventually stops identifying himself, and all he says on the answering machine is "Bah! I wish you had a cell phone," or "If a cow laughed would milk come out of its nose?" Every time I ring him back I have doubts this time he'll return it—men have such short attention spans, after all.

It's a Tuesday evening and Morven and I are playing armchair Jeopardy, calling out the answers before Alex Trebek's through reading the questions. I'm painting my nails and Morven is crocheting another receiving blanket. The telephone rings. Altering my voice requires only a little oomph, so that's generally how I choose to answer it.

"At last!" says Justin. "When can I see you?"

"Whenever you like," I reply, and Morven rolls her eyes.

AT THE Blind Pig he starts a game of telling me all the places he's been, and all the places he wants to go, and asking me if I've been there. Sure, I've been to Vienna and Rotterdam and Berlin, but I keep the details fuzzy, say I went backpacking—which, come to think of it, is more or less the truth. He asks me what my favorite movie is and I say *Harold and Maude*. He's never seen it.

"I'm a magician!"

"Oh?"

He plucks a Guinness beer mat off the bar and holds it up between his thumb and forefinger. "I'm going to make this disappear."

I fold my arms and raise my brows. "Go on, then."

Justin shifts the piece of cardboard so it covers his palm, held in place between his thumb and pinkie. Then he brings his other hand up and claps it against the beer mat, and when he lowers his hand the beer mat is gone. "Aha!"

"That's not magic." I want to yawn but he might be insulted.

"Sure it is."

"It's an illusion. A different thing altogether."

"Not to put too fine a point on it." He gives me a wry smile. "Where's the beer mat?"

I reach forward and dart a hand into the back pocket of his dungarees. "Ooh, you naughty girl!" he says as I produce said beer mat.

"You want to see some real magic?" He nods. I pull out a pen and write "Eve Harbinger, 27 September" on the beer mat, then I place it back on the bar and cover it with the palm of my hand. I make a show of pressing my opposite forefinger to my nose—keeping my hand in plain view, you know. Then I bring my other palm down with a dramatic splat, just for effect, and when I remove my hand the beer mat has disappeared. Justin gives a hoot of admiration.

"Search me, if you like."

"I'd like nothing better. Seeing as we're still in public, though, can I just ask you where it is?"

"You'll find it eventually."

This is when he suggests we go back to the shop for a tour of the rear rooms, and of course I have to sneer.

"This time it's not a line, I swear," he says. "Have you seen the new parlor?"

FIVE MINUTES later we're standing in the front room at Fawkes and Ibis, the dim overhead light throwing weird shadows off otherwise familiar objects. "It's through here." He parts another curtain, flips on the lights, and ushers me into a room I've never seen before.

"So *this* is where all the books went." The room is a sort of parlor-cum-library, with glassed-in mahogany bookcases along the far side. The walls are covered with flocked velvet wallpaper and crammed with clocks (all showing different times and ticking clamorously), black-and-white portraits, and door knockers of every imaginable shape. Above the light switch I see an engraving of a small boy in a Fauntleroy suit dangling by a rope from a hot air balloon, legs flailing as the basket bucks against his weight. Another engraving shows a zeppelin in flight over Lake Constance, the Swiss Alps reflected in the water.

All at once I'm back sitting in a wicker chair with my nose pressed to the window; the zeppelin is passing over a *Schloss* surrounded by an evergreen forest, and we're flying so low I can see a dark-clad figure moving briskly to and fro before an open window, the quick flick of a feather duster.

I shake myself. "What did you say?"

"I said, what's the difference between a zeppelin and a blimp?"

"A zeppelin has a rigid framework—a blimp doesn't. And a blimp is smaller." I pause. "What?"

"Nothing. I mean—you're smart."

I flash him an impish smile before I take off on a turn about the "parlor." There are wedding tableaux and military portraits, photographs taken on picnics and holidays, but you'd never mistake this for a room in somebody's home. No face appears more than once.

There are two pieces of furniture in the room: a large round table topped with an ancient lace cloth and a red velvet chaise lounge flanked by Nouveau globe lights, the lamps held aloft by bronze nymphs. I sit on the chaise and lean over the arm to admire the craftsmanship of the lamps. "They're from the old Tallinn opera house," Justin says. "Fawkes went to the auction before they renovated it."

"Where is he now? Do you know?"

"Budapest. The first shipment arrived yesterday—unpacked it this morning, lots of interesting stuff. And he sends us telegrams once a week. 'Won't have nothing to do with them Internets,'" he says, affecting Fawkes's gruff tone. Justin watches me as I survey the room. "You're the only person I know our age who doesn't have an e-mail address." I have to turn away and pretend to examine a photograph on the wall so he can't see me smile.

There's but one window, with sheer curtains the color of undiluted absinthe, beyond them an airshaft of dull gray brick. Door knockers and military portraits aside, the room reminds me of a house in Paris I knew long ago—a brothel, if you must know, though my business there had nothing to do with the hippity-dippity.

"It was my idea to display the door knockers on the wall along with the pictures," he says with obvious pride. I turn around and notice a deck of tarot cards laid out on the table—quite old, probably hand-painted.

"There's another room. Would you like to see?"

In this next room a human form lurks in the darkness, and when Justin turns on the light I let out a gasp. The man wears a pinstriped waistcoat and his hands are curled around invisible bars. I recognize that face at once: the cleft chin, the rat's-hair pencil moustache, and the insolent look—rather eerie on a man made of wax. "Dillinger!" I cry. "Hah!"

"How'd you know who he was? I had to look him up on Wikipedia."

"Why, he's infamous! Robbed loads of banks, always found a way to escape from jail. They called him the Jackrabbit for the way he leaped over bank counters. He was a real maniac—dipped his fingers in acid to erase the prints." I laugh, remembering something else: "They say he sent Christmas cards to J. Edgar Hoover. To taunt him, you know." Justin gives me a weird look, but I just shrug. "It was in all the papers." Then he gives me an even weirder look and I know I've got to be more careful from here on out.

He clears his throat. "I'm partial to this one, myself," he says, and it's only then I notice the room is *full* of wax mannequins, some famous, some creepy, some both. He's touching the shoulder of a can-can girl with a ponderous bosom. Her froufy skirts are rather moth-eaten and the waxen flesh on her kick leg has partially melted to reveal the chicken-wire base underneath. For a few minutes I wander among hobos and courtesans, leaders of the free world and eighties rock stars with tight leather pants and bleached-blond mullets. "Gosh! How'd you *get* all these?"

"They liquidated a waxworks earlier this year," Justin says. "I wanted to bring your friend the bank robber up front, but Uncle Harry says we've got to keep them all back here. Says they frighten the children." He takes me by the hand and pulls me past Ronald Reagan in effigy, parts another curtain, and leads me up a darkened staircase.

I ALWAYS KNEW I'd look like a granny someday, but I swore I'd try my best not to smell like one.

What causes this fusty smell so peculiar to geriatrics? Two vices, hypochondria and thrift: we no longer open the windows for fear of the sniffles, and we don't run the air conditioner in favor of keeping the electricity bill down. Hence the miasma of Bengay, mothballs, talcum powder, and eau de toot in Emmet Fawkes's apartment. In the sitting room are a pair of tweedy brown armchairs that would give off a puff of dust were anyone to sit in them, and when I dip my hand under a fringed lampshade I notice the fingernail clippings of improbable lengths scattered on the carpet under the end table. How can this apartment possibly belong to a man who's spent his life in pursuit of beautiful things?

But that's not all, oh no: just you follow me into the bathroom! I stare, horror-struck, at the toilet seat cover of natty pea-green shag, which so uncannily matches the living room carpet, and the pile of pus-encrusted gauze on the floor under the sink. The window sash above the bathtub is painted shut—see?—though that's almost pardonable given it opens onto the air shaft. Fawkes has always been a great one for gnomic epigrams: *I don't need exercise 'cause I'm on the cookie diet; everybody knows you can see the Eiffel Tower from any window in Paris;* and the one I'm reminded of now: *One's bottom should never be dirtier than the soles of one's shoes.* With the tip of my finger I lift the lid on the toilet and find the seat as filthy as the rest of the place.

Justin comes up behind me, and we lock eyes in the mirror above the sink. He rests his chin on my shoulder. "You and Marlene Dietrich are just about the only two women who can make utter disdain look totally sexy."

I'm surprised he's even heard of Marlene Dietrich. *A country without bordellos is like a house without bathrooms.* I'd rather take a pee in the yard.

He straightens up, still looking at me in the mirror as he runs a fingertip up and down my inner arm. Then he takes my hand and pulls me into the kitchen. "Can I make you a cup of something?"

"Ehh . . . no, thank you. You haven't cleaned at all since Fawkes left, have you?"

"It's easier just to not hang out here," he replies, and I snort. "Hey, even if I were to pick up that nasty stuff on the bathroom floor, there's still not much I can do with the place."

"You could do something about the smell. Maybe vacuum once in a while."

"Fawkes will be back in a month, and despite all appearances, he really is rather particular."

It isn't just the filth that disconcerts me. That flowery fridge magnet, for instance: *There is a special place in heaven for the mother of four little girls.* Emmet Fawkes has never even married.

He starts to kiss me then, and yes it's lovely but the stink is unbearable, so I suggest we go back down to the shop and sit in the ersatz parlor. I can hear him opening and closing the kitchen cabinets as I go down the stairs, and as I arrange myself on the chaise lounge he comes down bearing a half-full bottle of crème de menthe and two freshly rinsed cordial glasses. "This is how little old ladies get drunk." He fills each glass to the brim and sets the bottle on a stack of penny dreadfuls. "Maybe Fawkes does some entertaining up there after all. Will you have some?"

So we pass the next hour finishing off the crème de menthe in the cold green glow of the opera lights. We talk of this and that, and at some point we pause in our revelry and regard each other in silence— and it occurs to me now that I cannot sleep with him tonight. I could lie here for hours just feasting on his face, but I can't let this be the only night for it.

The moment passes, and I giggle when I find myself maneuvered between boy and sofa.

"What? Oh, that. That's not mine," he said.

"Not yours?"

"It would appear that whoever wore these trousers last left a boner in them."

I throw back my head over the upholstered arm and my hair

brushes the floor, but as I laugh I feel that warning tingle starting in my toes and fingertips. He kisses my throat, and I wonder how much longer I can possibly last.

"I'm sorry, Justin, but I have to go home now."

He takes my earlobe between his teeth. "No, you don't."

"I'm afraid I do."

"I don't know why you always have to rush off," he sighs. "Feels like I'm dating Cinderella."

If I'd known how long it would be before I saw him again, I would have stayed a little later.

WHO KNEW you could drink too much crème de menthe? The following morning I am doubled up over the toilet bowl, and Morven is holding back what's left of my hair. Beldames aren't supposed to get hangovers, but this is what happens when you've used up all your oomph. "You're getting a bit old for this," says my sister.

"Truer words were never spoken." I catch a whiff of my own dragon breath and retch again.

Morven wants to return to Cat's Hollow and she knows Helena will show me no mercy, so she poofs us both home and I spend the rest of the day in bed. When I fall asleep I toss and turn, dreaming I'm locked inside Fawkes's apartment.

Not that my place is much better, I'll admit. Layers of sooty tea-rose wallpaper furl at the seams, and too many paint jobs have obscured the intricate patterns on the pressed-tin ceilings. Long, long ago, before this building was a tenement, it was the home of a merchant prince.

But the place is as clean as we can make it, it smells nice because I always have fresh flowers on the dresser, and I usually leave the windows open. (Cats from the neighborhood dip in from time to time, and if they catch a mouse I reward them with a saucer of milk. Cat's Hollow warrants the name, being so near the fish markets.)

As an added precaution against the dreaded must-and-fust, I burn patchouli incense in a little brass censer Fawkes brought back from Bombay.

I CAN'T EVEN recall the moment I realized I'd lost track of how many men I'd slept with. I sure as heck can't remember all their faces, much less their names. As I say, you get so greedy, and at some point it simply doesn't matter anymore.

Sometimes I lie awake at night listing all the men I'd have done the business with, given the chance. Wilfred Owen is always first; ashamed as I am to admit it, there's something undeniably arousing about a brilliant young man robbed of his prime. Owen was killed in the Great War, but there are plenty more poets who perished of consumption, which is almost as romantic. Oh yes, the Pre-Raphaelites, the metaphysical poets, the transcendentalists and the revolutionaries, the folksingers and the puppeteers and the actors who could make you bawl without uttering a single word. The astronomers and the sculptors, the social reformers and the satirists, the Irish playwrights and the French mimes. As for the Germans, I knew (socially *and* biblically) so many of them in gay Berlin that I have their names on a separate list.

Over time I have learned that you cannot love a man for his accomplishments, as his abilities are all too often responsible for the most repulsive aspects of his character. Such truths matter nothing on these flights of fancy, of course, and it matters little if the man, the *real* man, had rotten teeth and a nubby willie. My list is shorter than it could be, though, believe it or not. I may not be all that picky, but I draw the line at the clap.

THREE NIGHTS later the phone rings at two thirty in the morning. The machine clicks on, and when I hear "Hi, Eve" I scramble out of bed and into the sitting room. "I have some bad news" is what he says next, and I freeze. "Fawkes has had a heart attack. He's in a hospital in Budapest. I've told Uncle Harry I'll go over for him." I grip the back of an armchair to keep myself upright as his voice fills the darkened room. "I don't have any idea how long I'll be gone, but . . . well, I just wanted you to know that I'll be thinking of you, and I hope I can see you again when I get back. Good-bye, Eve, and take care."

Through the month of October he sends postcards to Helena's house. On the first postcard he tells me Fawkes will be all right, but it may be several weeks before he's well enough to fly home; Justin rises early to go picking at the flea markets and visits Fawkes at the hospital in the afternoons. On the postcards that follow he only scribbles a line or two, things like *Hope you haven't forgotten about me* and *I finally found that beer mat inside my copy of* American Gods. *HOW DID YOU DO THAT and how did you know I would bring THAT book to Budapest?!* and he doesn't sign them. Some of the postcards are from the Hungarian National Gallery. The last one has a naked girl lying in a field under a blue sky with scudding clouds, head tilted to watch a bird wheeling overhead, and on the back all it says is *This painting reminded me of you.*

No postcards at all the month of November. Fine, then; I'll just have to forget about him. Wouldn't be so besotted but for the resemblance, anyhow. I resolve to make pretty and go out again just as I used to; I shed the skin, don the heels, smile the smile, and graciously accept the drink when it is offered.

Then a curious thing happens: *I come straight home again.* Seems I've lost the taste for it.

So most afternoons I go out troublemaking with Morven and Elsie, come home and watch a game show or read a bit of Proust, and turn out the light well before nine o'clock. Then your "randy Miss Evelyn" has a nice long fiddle with her bits.

Despite my resolution, I go over every part of that night: how he smelled of Old Spice and tasted of ripe mint, his smooth hands and eager tongue, and how the chaise lounge was still faintly redolent of cigar smoke.

And when I think of that creepy wax mannequin in the next room I recall another tidbit from the lore of John Dillinger, which is that J. Edgar Hoover kept the bank robber's pokey in a jar and that it's still stashed away somewhere in a labyrinth of offices in downtown Washington, D.C.

If this rumor is true, then it seems we have infiltrated the FBI.

The Melancholy Knight

12.

Early 1939–Summer 1942

NEVERINO WARNED me against returning to Berlin, but I couldn't stomach the prospect of a secretarial job at the German embassy, sifting through crumpled sheets of carbon in the rubbish bins like a common snoop. So after a respite in Blackabbey, I resumed my palm-reading practice in a new neighborhood, using various glamours to escape the attention of the plainclothes police.

All through my time in Berlin, Morven and I had kept in touch through silver lockets we wore with one another's pictures inside— rather like mobile phones without the monthly bill. We didn't see much of each other once the war broke out. That's the primary drawback of the loo flue: it isn't safe when your destination is in a war zone. You can't land when the porcelain's just been blown to smithereens. It's even more dangerous to attempt travel between two war zones: if both toilets get bombed, you're a goner. Sounds like a slim chance, but it's not slim enough to risk it.

So even if I'd had time to flue home, I'd have to get back the ordinary way (by sea, probably, and the voyage would take forever and a day)—and how would I explain how I'd gotten to America in the first place? Living in London, Morven was able to flue home for coventions, but she was obliged to return by way of a WC in some sleepy little shire, then go the rest of the route by train.

I visited her in London once, toward the end of the Blitz, and I had to do the same thing. I wasn't used to traveling by ordinary means, and it always put me in a sour mood—howling babies and prams blocking the aisles, the jostling and the inane conversations and the stink of unwashed bodies. I so wanted to flee to the toilet at the end of the car—but when you use the flue on a moving train, there's no telling where you'll end up.

Morven met me at the station. She suggested we go for a cocktail at the Monkey's Uncle, a cozy little watering hole we'd been to a couple of times during our stopover in London after the *last* war.

"Still standing?" I asked.

"Was, as of yesterday."

The Blitz brought down dozens of buildings every day, meaning that the warrens of London were expanding at an unprecedented rate.

THE MONKEY'S UNCLE was much as I remembered it, though the shelves behind the bar weren't so abundant as they'd once been, and there were freshly printed posters on the walls reminding us all that TITTLE TATTLE LOST THE BATTLE. The clientele had shifted, too—locals were mixing with military service personnel, and posh diplomats rubbed elbows with factory workers. War is the great equalizer in this respect, at least. I had a special fondness for this place, associating its dim snugs and Cockney chatter with relief and impending homecoming.

The sirens sounded midway through my third whisky ginger. The proprietor came out from behind the bar and instructed us to make for the shelter downstairs as he locked the front door and pulled the blinds. Most of his customers, primed by routine, were already polishing off their drinks in one go before making their way to the basement door.

"How do you generally handle this?" I asked my sister, just as the proprietor hurried past our snug without so much as a glance.

"That, first," she said with a small smile. "Then I unlock the door and see if anybody out on the street needs help."

It wasn't as straightforward as she made it sound. No sooner were we back out on the street than a bomb fell three blocks up, and as we ran forward a couple of wardens in gas masks forcibly shooed us away again. The façade of a whole row of houses had been torn off by the blast, leaving all the davenports and floral-papered walls exposed like a life-sized dollhouse. Dust was rising off the rubble that spilled out into the roadway. There wasn't a sign of life anywhere.

While the wardens were busy picking through the ruins, we turned ourselves into ferrets and plunged into the mess. I followed Morven deeper and deeper, until we came upon a wrought-iron grate over a basement window. We peered in, and with our beady eyes we could see two young mothers huddled in the far corner of the basement with five children between them, clearly too terrified even to cry.

"Don't worry," Morven said, loud and clear, with that strange aplomb unique to Blitz-time Londoners. The mothers couldn't see her, but they responded to the sound of her voice with visible relief. "We'll get you out of here." I started at the shrill sound of a telephone ringing somewhere in what was left of the building.

Back on the street, we knew where to dig, and this time we paid no attention to the air-raid wardens.

"Remind me why we didn't just go to a bar in Little London?"

"The pubs are better here," Morven replied as she tossed a chunk of concrete. "At least for the time being."

ONE NIGHT in the spring of 1942, my last caller turned out to be Neverino. He checked behind all the radiators before he uttered a word. "Please correct me if I am being presumptuous," he said, "but I wonder if the White Witch isn't bored out of her gourd, doing this as long as she has?" I was, truth be told, and furthermore I was beginning to fear my disguises weren't really fooling anyone. He told me he had a new job for me, a real opportunity, the work I was made for.

"You must go back to London—tonight, if you can—and tomorrow afternoon go to this address." He handed me a card. Once I'd read it I held it to a candle, then tossed the flaming bit of paper into the grate, and Neverino nodded in approval. He instructed me to present myself as "Alice" and tell whomever answered the door that I was there to see "Mr. Robbins." He left that night without telling me whom I was really meeting or what this was all about.

The address on the card turned out to be Orchard Court, where the Special Operations Executive kept apartments for interviews. When Jonah—"Mr. Robbins"—opened the door, my first thought was that his face reminded me of an effigy, a medieval knight. His features had a finely chiseled quality, though there was nothing cold in his looks or manner. He was tall and dark, clean-cut though a bit rumpled round the edges. The man clearly hadn't been to the barber in a while—his hair was tousled like a small boy's—and he hadn't shaved in at least two days either. Still, you could tell at a glance that he inspired confidence—but more important, that his capable air was born out of acumen rather than arrogance. He walked with a pronounced.limp, but if the injury pained him much he gave no other indication of it.

He didn't tell me his real name then, of course, nor did I give him mine. He ushered me into the apartment and a sturdy young woman, his assistant, served me instant coffee using a proper tea service, an incongruity that made me grin. Robbins caught my eye and smiled with me at the joke, offered me a cigarette, and then proceeded to conduct the most banal and utterly aimless conversation I've ever had.

He asked about my family, my upbringing, my educational background, but there was no mistaking this for an ordinary interview: he would switch from German to French and back again, and I would answer in the same language. I eyed him appraisingly as he spoke; he had to be in his late thirties. No wedding ring, but I had an inkling he was married. I was eighty-one years old by this time, but I had documentation stating my age as thirty-eight, and my natural appearance was younger still. I could do this.

"I've heard a great deal about your activities in Berlin," he said at last. "We would be very much obliged if you would agree to work for us."

"Pardon me, but if I'm not mistaken, I've already been working for you lot for quite some time." I affected distance, taking slow pulls on my cigarette as he told me there would be at least three phases of training before I received my first assignment. Phase one commenced tomorrow.

I came out of that meeting feeling giddy as a tadpole, though I did my best not to show it.

THANKS TO the glowing references of Neverino and others in the Centaur network, I was able to bypass the SOE preliminary school, where they conducted introductory weapons training while weeding out the recruits who couldn't pass muster. It would have been rather silly to test me so, seeing as I had already proven myself a reliable subagent in Berlin.

I eventually found out that Robbins was something of a hero. Assigned to a resistance circuit outside Lyons in the fall of 1941, he had been betrayed, arrested, and tortured at Avenue Foch, and later imprisoned at Fresnes. After a month in solitary confinement there, he was put aboard a train—a cattle car, more like—bound for one of the German death camps. He had managed to escape from that train in the chaos of an air raid, and despite a shattered kneecap he'd made his way across France mostly on foot (though he had once been rolled up in an oriental carpet and stuck in the boot of an old roadster).

He had finally returned to England in a fishing boat in March of

1942, and among his SOE colleagues he was rightfully regarded as a miracle man. Robbins was the obvious person to instruct us in the art of keeping alive by the seat of one's pants, and so he accompanied us to Mallaig in the Scottish highlands, where SOE had a paramilitary school.

The men training at Mallaig were all adventurers and opportunists whose brains would otherwise have been squandered in the military, and the women were generally educated abroad and spoke at least four languages apiece. Something else you would have noticed is this: although they were seldom beautiful in the conventional sense (cleft chins, mousy hair, frog eyes), they each possessed that je ne sais quoi that prevented any man from ever refusing them anything. If one of these girls asked a man for a fag and he was down to his last he'd hand it to her without hesitation, even with the knowledge that his ration was up for the week. Their brains were essential, of course, but their charisma was even more valuable. Charm is not a virtue—I'd learned that the hard way long ago—but for once I could put my own to work for a worthy cause.

To call the first day of training "grueling" would be a hideous understatement. I pretended not to notice the resentful glances of the other women recruits, who saw that I was not scratched, bruised, and breathless after a daylong slog through the mountains like they were. I often caught Major Robbins looking at me too—in open admiration. No nettles in *my* hair, no dirt or blood on *my* elbows.

Over the following days we were shown how to dump sugar in the Nazi gas tanks and how to deploy an exploding candlestick without losing a hand. We scaled walls and fences and had target practice for hours on end. Much of what we were learning was already familiar to me, stealth tactics and suchlike, but even the boys grimaced at the prospect of using wire garrotes and street-fighting like a pack of rogue Chinamen. We were also presented with a prototype of the infamous truth drug and taught the various means of administering it. I didn't think I'd be needing any of that, but the knowledge still proved useful in the end.

I sailed through those three weeks. After all, my instincts were sharper and my aim surer than any ordinary recruit's. The other women agents began to grumble to our instructors that I was getting special treatment, which was perhaps to be expected—for success, quoth Mr. Bierce, is the one unpardonable sin against one's fellows. Our instructors merely answered that they would do well to follow my example— if they could.

They told us stories that were meant to keep us vigilant, if only to avoid providing them with yet another horror story to tell future recruits: the man who ordered a café noir when café noir was all they served, what with milk being rationed; the unfortunate agent who hid in a madhouse in Kraków, only to find that all the inmates were scheduled for euthanasia.

Other anecdotes were meant to inspire us: the American agent with a wooden leg who had already parachuted into Lyons and had quickly proved herself one of the SOE's greatest assets, or the ultimate determination of the Jewish agent who got plastic surgery to make his features appear more Aryan. And of course there was Major Robbins, whose bravery and razor wit had proved his salvation.

Robbins gave lectures nearly every day, and he often assisted the unarmed combat instructors. He was very fond of saying, "Don't *think* so bloody much!" whenever a recruit was slow to respond. It was the classroom time with him I relished most, though; with each new day I learned more about the circumstances of his capture and escape. "There was a second," he said. "One second, that's all I had, to leap out the open door and disappear into the forest along the track. I am only here speaking to you now because I did not hesitate."

He was informal and quick to laugh, but he never made light of the task before us and the consequences of failure. "Boys and girls, there is a reason our species has thrived, has dominated all other creatures on

God's green earth since the dawn of time. Why? Because the human survival instinct is second to none, that's why.

"Our language, our civilization—these are just the trappings. It is our instinct that preserved our distant ancestors from the beasts on the African plains, and you must trust that instinct above all else. If you recall only one thing from all your weeks of training, let it be this." He paused, gazing around the room at each of his pupils in turn. "If you hesitate," he said, "all will be lost." The excitement and admiration he inspired was very nearly palpable; they were fine words, all the more so because he had lived them.

Then someone had to go and ask what would happen if you shot a comrade by mistake. "Anybody who kicks down the door is, in all likelihood, no friend of yours," Robbins replied, and the group erupted in laughter. "Again," he went on above the snickering, "it is a matter of intuition, a matter of instinct.

"You must divorce yourself from all sentiment," he said. "There can be no tender thoughts of your mother—no thoughts at all, if you can help it. You cannot save the life of a child at the price of your associates'."

Then he told us that there was no shame in confessing ourselves unsuited to the task, and that if so our job prospects for other branches of government or military service would be unaffected. At times you could see a doubt flicker across their faces, but the majority of my classmates were to decide it was much too late to turn back now. You could only pretend to be the man or woman you wanted to become, and hope and pray you would eventually grow into it. So everyone prayed—everyone but me.

OTHER WOMEN at Mallaig were much friendlier, but they weren't the ones in training to be parachuted into France. All the cooks and housekeeping staff had given themselves aliases—Mrs. Wrench, Mrs. Pitch, Mrs. Axel, Mrs. Sledge—and they attended to our needs with jollity and a brisk sort of affection. They considered themselves den mothers as much as maintenance staff, though the head cook, Mrs. Dowel, ran a very tight operation. After all, no self-respecting beldame lets her cauldron—full of *soup,* which is *fully edible,* mind you, no bat wings or eyeballs in the mix—run dry.

Of course, I knew what they were from the get-go; if a beldame ever wants to see if there are kindred nearby, she needs only to look at the crescent moon on the base of her thumbnail. The moon will glow if there are other beldames about, as I found when I shut myself in the WC upon my arrival.

At our first supper I lifted my teacup to find a strange symbol scrawled in black ink on the napkin:

One of the other recruits had already noticed and was craning her neck to make sense of it, her brow knotted. "What *is* that?"

"Haven't the faintest," I replied coolly as I took a sip. She would tell the others, of course—but let them talk.

Mrs. Dowel was making the rounds, stopping by each table in the canteen to ask if everyone had enjoyed their meal, and on the far side of the room I heard Robbins declare her hearty lamb stew had gone to a better place. When she paused at our table to lap up the compliments, I gave her a look that said I accepted her invitation to meet her and the others that same night. They don't call it the witching hour for nothing.

L ATE THAT night I crept out of the dormitory and made my way out of the camp. There was a guard on duty at the entrance, but I briefly turned myself into something small enough to scurry under the gate. I turned onto the road for Mallaig village and walked a ways, until I found the symbol on my napkin etched into an old stone road marker. A trail through the woods was just visible in the moonlight.

I heard a murmur of female voices through the trees, but when I reached the clearing I found the only creatures in the wood were the birds convening in the branches above. I said a few words and then I flew up to meet them.

Mrs. Dowel introduced me to all her friends from the Mallaig coven, some of whom were also employed at the SOE camp. They were elderly beldames, most of them even older than I am now. Their daughters had all gone off to London to volunteer, and they were eager to hear whatever news I could offer them. And I, in turn, was curious as to how they were keeping themselves busy. Did they pass along any of their oomph to those young women cracking codes and ferreting out Nazi spies down in the capital?

The birds traded glances, so that it was obvious they were trying to decide if they should let me in on a secret. "No, nothing like that," said one of them rather diffidently. "They manage quite well on their own."

Just then another corbie alighted on a branch beside me. Dumb as it was, the bird soon realized its mistake and flew away again. "Out with it, then," I said.

Turned out they were the guardians of a huge trove of artworks, masterpieces rescued from museums in all the occupied nations of Europe. Michelangelos, Titians, Rembrandts, you name it, all of it safely kept in the attic of the old Mallaig town hall, which had been torn down in 1892. "And we brought it all through the flue!" said Mrs. Pitch with obvious pride.

Most of their gossip was art related. "Well, my Lily's in Berlin," said Mrs. Dowel, "and she told me they've taken all the statues down off the cathedral dome and dumped them in the river! Can you imagine? St. Peter and all the angels and cherubs, covered in muck!"

"They're safer at the bottom of the river," said Mrs. Sledge.

"Couldn't your daughter have hid them herself, in one of the warrens?" I asked.

"My Lily has *much* more important things to do. St. Peter is on his own," Mrs. Dowel sniffed.

Mrs. Sledge turned to me. "If you or any of your friends should ever come upon an important piece, you will send it here, won't you?"

By the time the sky was growing pink in the east, I felt as if I'd known these ladies all my life, as if my coven and theirs were one and the same. For better and for worse, the world is a great deal smaller than we believe it.

I made it back to the SOE compound before dawn broke, flying over the guard shack and alighting on a windowsill outside the dormitory. I spotted no one about before I made myself human again, but as I went to open the window I heard a twig snap behind me.

I turned round, my heart in my throat, but relaxed when I saw it was Major Robbins. The look on his face was inscrutable as he gripped me by the elbow. "They say the rook is the devil's messenger," he said under his breath. "Or is it the magpie?"

"The corbie, I think."

I stood there staring at him for what felt like a very long time. "Come on, then," he said at last. He still had a firm hold on my elbow. "We'll go back to my room."

I TOLD HIM everything. I told him I was born the day the American Civil War broke out, and I told him I would live as long as a bowhead whale, maybe longer if I was lucky. And I told him the story of Goody Harbinger, how legend said she'd outwitted the devil by switching his Book of Lost Souls for her own household ledger, but that she'd eventually succumbed to the hysteria that had claimed so many more lives up north in Massachusetts. And I told him how her nine-year-old daughter was found on a ship bound for Liverpool though her name wasn't anywhere on the passenger manifest.

He listened as I went on and on for what felt like hours, his face impassive. I couldn't even imagine what he might think of me now—after all, the only man I'd ever told was Neverino.

Eventually I stopped for breath, and there was only a brief pause before he said, "If Goody Harbinger was so powerful, why couldn't she have saved herself as well as her daughter?"

"What?"

"Surely she could have, if—"

"You mean . . . you believe me?"

"I *saw* you turn yourself from a bird, didn't I?"

We talked so long we wound up missing breakfast. I told him the story of Adam and Lilith, and he said from that moment on he would always think of me as the Wandering Jewess. And I told him about the *beneficium* pledge.

"Recite it for me," he said.

"Recite it for you?"

"Go on. I want to hear it."

I took a deep breath. "By magic I shall do no harm," I said, "except in defense of myself or another. I shall not use my abilities for mercenary ends. I shall always practice discretion and make every effort not to reveal my true nature to persons ill equipped to understand. I shall spend the prime of my life in the service of humankind, and upon my retirement I shall never engage in any mischief of a malicious nature. Furthermore, I shall always encourage the same principles in my fellows. I make this vow upon the integrity of my ancestors and by the Eternal Power to whom I owe my life and ability."

"Well, I'll be," he said at last. "It all makes sense now. Everybody else was dead tired at the end of that trek on the first day—as anybody would be—but not you. You had a rosy glow all the while, as if you were only out for a stroll. I knew you were thirty-eight—according to your birth certificate, at any rate—and yet you're no more than a girl. Your perfect aim, every time. Your lightning reflexes.

"I don't know what I was expecting when I sat up to wait for you tonight," he went on, shaking his head. "But it certainly wasn't this."

T HE AIR between us crackled with electricity all the next day. That's not to say I was distracted; on the contrary, my aim was sharper than ever. That night I made another confession, quite an embarrassing one this time—I'd never been on a bicycle—and he went off straightaway and found an old three-speeder rusting in a shed somewhere on the compound. He didn't once laugh at me, bless his heart, and I picked it up in a matter of minutes.

Over the next fortnight we would go for long walks in the wee hours. We talked of politics and military strategies, Stalin's film reviews and Churchill's bathing habits. Jonah said the prime minister conducted much of his business in bed, in an oriental dressing gown. I told him I'd heard Hitler consulted astrologers and that he was conducting a mad scavenger hunt across Europe for any artifact said to have prophetic power. After the Anschluss he'd wasted no time filching the Lance of Longinus, the spear that pierced the side of Christ to make sure he was dead. *He who holds this shall rule the world* and all that sort of rot. It was hard to get a good night's rest when the fate of the world was in the hands of a first-class lunatic.

And I learned far more about Jonah than I was meant to. He told me he had grown up in Finchley, received his undergraduate degree at Oxford, moved to New York to attend law school at Columbia, and after several years working at one of the big firms he'd come back to London to join SOE. Sometimes he grew very quiet, and I wondered what he had been like before his imprisonment at Fresnes.

He also told me that he had requested my assignment to his next mission to Paris. There was nobody else, he said, who was so perfectly suited to the task, and as he spoke a thrill went all through me.

We were accomplices now, and though we did a good job of behaving as if nothing had changed, I was a bit worried that the grumblings of the other female recruits would grow even louder. Yet the complaints seemed to have ceased suddenly; there was no whispering at all that Major Robbins had found himself a pet. The other girls treated me as warily as ever, but I made myself especially friendly and solicitous.

One night, a few days before the end of the Mallaig training, we arranged for another one of our midnight tramps; but all the physical exertion from dawn to dusk was finally catching up with me, and I slept too soundly. The next morning Robbins sidled up to me in the canteen queue and gave me a look. "I missed you last night," he murmured as he palmed an apple.

"You ought to have woken me up!"

He shook his head. "I couldn't have, even if I'd wanted to. You sleep like the dead."

But I kept my eyes open on our last night. He invited me back to his room after our walk for a "nightcap"—a swig out of his flask, which of course he could have offered me just as easily while we were out on the moor. I took a pull and relaxed as the whisky set my throat alight. As I put the cap back on the flask it occurred to me that he couldn't bring it where we were going—it was a telltale sign of his Englishness.

Then I caught sight of the monogram on the side. I noticed his initials, JAR, but it scarcely occurred to me to feel excited that I now had a clue to his real name. Come to think of it, this flask looked suspiciously like a wedding present.

He had chosen that very moment to rest his hand on my knee, but I slithered out from under it and seated myself on the far end of the bed. "Hold up a minute. Are you married?" He hesitated, and I heaved a sigh. "Just my luck."

He moved toward me and took my hand in his. "I'm not married," he said. "What I mean is, I won't be for much longer."

"You're getting a divorce?"

He nodded. "She's in New York—in the Chairborne. We'd been heading south long before we got involved in all this. The writing was on the wall, as they say."

I was relieved to hear this, but something else was nagging at me now. I had so seldom known jealousy that when it did happen I was all the more affected by it. I wondered what her name was; I wondered if she'd found another man in New York and if they were at this very moment engaged in the same conversation. Then I wanted to laugh out loud at the absurdity of all this, falling in love with a man I only knew by a phony name.

He might have been reading my thoughts. "What's your real name, Alice?"

I looked at him sidewise. "Am I allowed to tell you?" But of all the secrets I'd given up to him, my name was surely the least significant.

"You're not allowed to tell Robbins," he replied. "But Jonah Rudolfsen wants very much to know."

"Jonah," I said softly. "I like it. 'Jonah.' It suits you."

"Well, that's lucky." He laughed. "I'm sure yours suits you just as well, whatever it is."

"You want to know that badly?"

"I do." He looked at me, almost painfully earnest. "I can't make love to you without it, now, can I?"

JONAH STILL counsels me from the grave. Life is nothing without adventure, he used to say, and we *must* meet fate halfway or else our souls will wither. That said, there was no sense worrying about what might have been.

I still recall all the more trivial things he said, too—"The devil wears a toothbrush moustache," to which I replied that even Satan wasn't half so despicable as Adolf Hitler; and "You must always eat well, my darling. To abstain from good meat and wine is to squander your God-given taste buds." Not that we had all that much of either given the rationing, but when the food was foul he'd tell me about the grand old bistros in London and Paris we'd visit once the war was over.

That evening we took the Caledonian Sleeper back to London, and alack, we were obliged to sleep separately in our assigned quarters. All the recruits retired almost as soon as the train was moving—they wore us out, so they did—but I was far too excited to sleep. I had to see Jonah. I hoped I would see plenty of him in the weeks ahead—there were two phases of training left—but it might be a long time before we could be alone again.

So I came bounding into the dining car looking for him. When I clapped eyes on him, back to the door in a booth at the far end of the car, it was difficult to pretend that nothing had happened the previous night. The waiter was watching me.

I sauntered up to his booth and he invited me to sit, and the knowing glance passed in a blink. The newspaper in front of him was two days old, but the pages were still crisp. He'd been looking out the window.

And what a view it was: a valley yawned beneath the glass, and on the surrounding hills, green though rocky, sheep grazed upon vertical angles in the twilight. Wisps of smoke rose from cottages scattered along the valley floor, and beyond the brooding peaks in the distance the clouds were promising rain and plenty of it. I cracked the window and breathed in the sweet musk of peat smoke.

I glanced at Jonah, who was still gazing out at this wild and lonely scene, and he wore an expression to match it. He really did look like a knight—my melancholy knight.

The waiter brought us a pot of coffee and a plate of digestive bis-
cuits, and once he and his cart with the squeaky wheels were at a safe
distance I asked, "Why the long face?"

"The view," he said. "It reminds me of . . ."

I stirred plenty of milk and sugar into my cup as I waited for him
to go on. "Of?"

"Connemara." He took a sip of coffee—he always drank it black—
and when he paused then I knew all at once what this was about.

"Your honeymoon, was it?"

He nodded, relief plain on his face. "How did you know?"

I gave him a look.

"You couldn't ride a train through them, but Ireland has landscapes very much like this one. Tell me: would you call it bleak, or
rather magnificent?"

"I suppose it depends on your mood."

He smiled then, and the look of melancholy vanished for the moment. "Exactly," he said as a disembodied hand caressed my knee.

WHEN WE got back to London—and by London, I mean an
undisclosed location some distance outside it—I discovered I
was scheduled for two weeks of parachute training. I'd never been on
an airplane before, only a zeppelin for novelty's sake, and I didn't see
why I needed to waste any time on it when I could simply grow a pair
of wings.

"Well, of course." Jonah gave me a wry look. "How did you think
you were going to get there?" He paused. "Oh, I see." But there was no
way I could get out of it without arousing considerable suspicion;
couldn't very well explain to the F-Section leader why I didn't need it.

After parachute training came "finishing school," and there were
heaps of forms to be filled out in triplicate. I even had to make out a
will, would you believe it. *In the event of my death, I hereby appoint as*

beneficiary of any payments due me by the Special Operations Executive the following person: Miss Morven Harbinger of Blackabbey, New Jersey, USA. We women recruits were also given commissions in the First Aid Nursing Yeomanry, the idea being that we'd be allowed the rights of a soldier in the event we were captured. This last phase of training was interminable: no firearms, no long tramps across the moor, just hours and hours of "classroom instruction."

There were endless hypotheticals. What if you're being tailed—where do you go, and how do you alert your comrades without giving them away? How do you react when you're walking down the street and a car pulls up alongside you and two men jump out? How can you dispose of incriminating evidence without attracting your captors' notice? It is rather infuriating, you know, to be instructed repeatedly in matters of which you have shown blindfolded mastery since you were a mere babe. And then we were roused in the middle of the night by someone shaking us by the shoulder shouting, "What is your name? Where are you from? What is the newspaper in your town?" All that sort of thing.

I hadn't laid eyes on Jonah for the better part of a week, and as I say, the other "ladies" on the course were already working their cloaks and daggers. I was aching with anxiety to be up and away already.

At last I received a message that I should report immediately to room 217 at House Q, a redbrick building at the far end of the compound. I knocked on a door marked KING'S ROYAL RIFLE CORPS—to which some morbid trickster had added an "e" in red grease pencil—and found Jonah sitting at a desk poring over an Ordnance Survey map. A woman of forty or so poised over an open filing cabinet introduced herself as our liaison officer and invited me to sit down while Jonah briefed me on the details of the mission to Paris. Then the liaison officer presented me with papers and an identity card from the

Cover and Documentation office, as well as a plain wool suit and sturdy shoes, all French issue.

"Full moon," Jonah said as he folded up the map and tucked it in a hidden pocket in the open suitcase laid out before him. "We leave tonight."

Covention

13.

Dame, Dame, the Watch is set:
Quickly come, we all are met.
From the Lakes, and from the Fens,
From the Rocks, and from the Dens,
From the Woods, and from the Caves,
From the Church-yards, from the Graves,
From the Dungeon, from the Tree
That they die on, here are we.

—Ben Jonson, *The Masque of Queens*

IT'S MID-DECEMBER now and cold as a dead man's schlong. The mews is decked in evergreen boughs and crowded with shoppers clutching delivery receipts and bags of gift-wrapped tchotchkes. The blackboard easel outside Mira's café advertises eight-dollar mugs of mulled wine and fortified cocoa, and despite the windchill the queue is out the door. I stand at the window at Fawkes and Ibis, watching Harry putter around behind the counter, wanting to go in and ask after Justin but afraid of what he might tell me. When Harry glances up from his ledger, he notices a dark-haired girl in a fur-collared coat poring over his window display. I've taken care of myself, you see, in case he's come back.

I duck into the café, jump the queue, and beg a mug of wine to steady my nerves. I take the mug back to the sidewalk outside Fawkes and Ibis and drink it in gulps as I go on pretending I'm only window-shopping. It's almost seven o'clock and I don't want to miss Harry on his way out. Once I've drained the mug I drag myself through the heavy velvet curtain, me and my frozen sticky fingers and my yellow belly.

"So you've finally decided to pay me a visit, eh?" Harry says as I step into the room.

The *Leuchterweibchen*—may it never sell!—still dominates the room in its barbarous majesty, and the sight of it gives me heart. "I'm sorry, but I'm not actually looking to shop tonight. I was hoping you could tell me if Justin's come back from Europe yet."

"He hasn't yet, no."

"Do you think he'll be back before the end of the year?"

"Hard to say. Mr. Fawkes's doctors over there don't speak very good English." He pauses. "You're one of the Harbingers, aren't you?" I nod. "Will you take my advice then, Miss Harbinger? Justin may be my nephew, but he's a real charmer, and I wouldn't want to see one of Helena's girls in tears over it."

"Right," I manage to say. "Thanks, er—Mr. Ibis."

Harry looks at me kindly and wishes me a merry Christmas, big-hearted Jew that he is.

Now that the shops are closed there aren't many customers left at the café, and Mira is erasing the specials on the blackboard as I take the mug back to the counter. On my way up the mews I spot a mother and daughter—can't recall their names offhand, they're Peacocks any-way—marveling at all the goodies in the window of Hartmann's Classic Toys: Lightning Gliders and Flexible Flyers, Raggedy Ann and Andy, deluxe editions of Scrabble and Monopoly, a gumball machine and a yellow Sesame Street record player, Holiday Barbies in frilly lamé gowns, and tin soldiers with kepi hats and red-dotted cheeks.

I pause there, just across the way from them, and watch as the mother leans in and taps gently on the glass. The needle drops on the little plastic record player and a swing waltz begins to play. Again the mother taps the window and one of the little tin soldiers steps forward, hangs his rifle on the gumball dispenser knob, and gives a jerky bow. The little girl giggles. Her mother taps the glass a third time and the soldier starts to tap-dance, windmilling his arms and kicking up his heels. The child watches him, thoroughly delighted, and after a time the mother rests her hand on her daughter's shoulder and murmurs a few words of encouragement. The girl taps on the glass, and a moment later one of the Holiday Barbies sashays forward. The soldier extends his arm, and they take off round the window display like Fred and Ginger in miniature.

A H, MISTLETOE: "witch's broom" they called it, in a more superstitious time. People believed a sprig of mistletoe above the doorway would prevent us crossing their thresholds. We've put it up every Christmas for as long as I can remember.

The rest of the family, parrot included, has gone to bed by the time I've tacked a sprig above the sitting room door. Irony aside, I don't know why we bother, considering how few men there are to snog—and most of them related to us besides.

As you may know, Yule was one of the pagan winter-solstice festivals that gave way to modern Christmas. As with the Roman Saturnalia, our holiday is more an excuse to carouse than anything else, though it being our time of covention we do get a bit of business taken care of in between. We put up a Christmas tree, too, for the little ones. There isn't a whole lot of gift-giving though, as presents are generally only exchanged among members of one's immediate family. I have found my sisters' gifts at Fawkes and Ibis, of course: for Helena, a set of wooden *Lebkuchen* molds probably as old as Methuselah—poofed up a duplicate set for actual use—and for Morven, a red plastic View-Master I've fixed to show scenes of the future.

One of our best traditions is the gingerbread house, which we work on for an entire month beforehand. It may seem a quaint pastime by ordinary standards, but we're making a model of Harbinger House. Everything in it is made out of sugar, which can be spun so finely it's clear as glass, even the fishbowl on the kitchen counter. Family heirlooms are replicated in miniature, carved out of gumdrops or rock sugar, and all the furniture is made of Belgian dark chocolate. We use graham crackers and vanilla frosting too, of course. And who knew you could get a full palette mixing the food coloring ordinary families use for dying Easter eggs? It was our gingerbread Harbinger House ritual that inspired Mira to take the confectionery course at that fancypants culinary academy in New York.

The model is built in halves so that you can open it and peer into each of the rooms, even the ones that exist only for the occasion. We also fashion a sort of candy golem for each guest as well as ourselves; some are molded out of chocolate, others cobbled together with almonds and sultanas. Even the tabby cat is replicated in candied ginger. The house is displayed on a table in the foyer and all the candy golems arranged on the table outside the entrance. Then Helena enchants our grand creation, and the gingerbread house is a complete mirror of the real thing: candy ladies scurrying between kitchen and dining room; candy children making merry (and making naughty); the chocolate figures of all the local beldames climbing the front porch just before the real doorbell rings, and others vanishing off the tabletop just before they appear inside the WC. When we were children we could spend hours at a time giggling at every tiny chocolate dame that popped out of the marzipan toilet. On a more practical note, mothers can ensure the kiddies are all in their beds without going up two flights of stairs to check.

Our other two great traditions are the tableaux vivants—last year's was *The Thirty Heads of Princess Langwidere* (to which, regrettably, the little ones responded with more terror than we had anticipated)— and after that the puppet shows. Our puppet stage is a splendid antique.

We use the stage at every covention, because it has always been our credo that the things we love best should not be squirreled away for the enjoyment of no one. A grander stage for puppets *or* people is rarely found; indeed, it is an Odeon in miniature, with swagged curtains of festive red velvet and Atlas-like caryatids holding up the curtain rod, real footlights that cast a golden glow, an intricate ceiling panel painted to look like stained glass, and other fin de siècle flourishes. There are over a dozen backgrounds—Italianate garden, graveyard by moonlight, colonial Harveysville street scene, even one of this very drawing room—that are stored beneath the stage and may be rolled up for use with a little brass crank, as well as a scrim through which all violent or amorous scenes are obliquely depicted.

Using all the marionettes in the house, our coven's puppeteers reenact noteworthy episodes from coventions past (there's even a puppet for the Turkey Who Wouldn't Die, though his squawks are simulated), coven history (this year they're doing *The Trial of Goody Harbinger*), and reinterpretations of classic literature (in past years they've done *Paradise Lost-and-Found*, *Dante's Disco Inferno*, *Off with Her Head: A Love Story in Two Parts*, and so forth). For the little ones these puppet plays provide history lessons as well as entertainment, though the funny bits are more Monty Python than Punch and Judy.

And afterward—oh, the feast! We always have a roast goose (no turkey, never again), candied sweet potatoes and stuffing with sage and raisins, fennel sausages and rhubarb pudding and corned beef hash. Every year Helena bakes an ambrosia cake, which is something you will not find on an ordinary Christmas dining table. It is rather nondescript in appearance, but this is a product of its magic. To me it tastes like plums marinated in honey with a hint of cloves; Helena's slice tastes of pineapple cheesecake; to Vega it tastes like carrots and cardamom, and so on. And like all the other food on the table, the ambrosia cake goes on and on until we can stuff ourselves no further.

I savor the hush that falls the evening before everyone arrives, before every cranny of my childhood home is consumed in the festive chaos. They say the veil separating this world from the next is at its thinnest at the winter solstice, and if that is true then logically Christmas is the ideal time for the practice of necromancy. (You *knew* those puppets weren't ordinary playthings!)

Totems, jujus, lares—call them what you like. Late that evening I am sitting by the fire, feet up and savoring a glug of amaretto, when one of the puppets stuffed into the Christmas stockings, a Gibson girl, starts wriggling like a butterfly coming out of its chrysalis.

"You ought to have taken me off the mantel before you lit the fire," the puppet huffs as the control bar shimmies out of the stocking and falls to the hearth with a clatter.

"A happy Yule to you too, Auntie Em!" I rise creakily, pull her out of the stocking, and position the puppet on a neighboring armchair. None of the other puppets are animated yet. Auntie Emmeline always arrives earlier and leaves later than the rest, the pesky old bird.

She turns to face me and her little painted eyes glitter with shrewish shrewdness. "Don't think I don't know what you've been up to, miss."

You get awfully pushy when you're dead. Afraid of being forgotten, I suppose.

"You're asking for trouble, Evelyn. You know you are. Don't come crying to me next covention time, that's all I mean to say."

"If all you're going to do is nag me," I say wearily, "then I'd rather you kept to the ether."

She's silent for a moment, and I can tell she's softening. She'd do the same as me if she were still alive, and she'd even admit it if I pressed her hard enough. "Don't sulk, dear," she says finally. "You know I have your best interests at heart."

"You wouldn't be giving me so much grief over it if he weren't important."

"Important?" she sneers. Creak goes the hinge in her little wooden jaw. "All your men are *important* to you at the time, are they not?"

"Please tell me, Auntie Em. I'd know how best to handle it, if only I knew what it meant. Is he . . . ?" *Has Jonah come back to me?* is what I'm asking, and she knows it.

Clack, clack, she folds her arms and glares at me. This is Auntie Em for you, hoarding the secrets of the universe like a mother who hides the cookie jar from her children just so she can devour them all herself.

Which is worse, I wonder: having to listen to the overbearing opinions of all your cranky dead relatives, or how it works in ordinary families, when they come back but don't let on they're there? Oh, the things that horrify your poor old granny when you believe yourself alone!

"I hope I'll find you in a better mood in the morning," I say to the puppet, and she only harrumphs in response. It's times like this I wish she would hurry up and reincarnate already.

Before I turn the lights off in the parlor I hang an old silk dressing gown on a hook behind the door. This is not exactly a gift for Santa Claus; you'll see.

IN THE morning I'm woken by voices and bustling below. When I come downstairs I see the parrot is gone; all that's left of him's a smattering of silky gray feathers on the parlor carpet. I venture into the kitchen and find Hieronymus enjoying his first pipe of the season, wagging his hairy shin under that old dressing gown as he peruses the arts section. Some of the local ladies are already here, of course, having arrived near dawn to aid Helena in her preparations for the Yuletide bruncheon, and our departed aunties dispense time-honored culinary advice from above the kitchen sink.

I sit down by Uncle Hy and survey the scene along the kitchen counter. These are all my family and friends, so you may be surprised that I can't say I *like* all of them. Rather, I like them all but one: Lucretia Hartmann, owner of the toy shop, who has just plucked a mixing bowl from Morven's hands with the words, "But I can do it faster, dear."

Granted, when you throw a hundred people into one house for a weeklong shindig you've got to expect the occasional flare of temper; but while magic can smooth over a lot, it can't make somebody likable. There's a reason why the kiddies call her "Missus Shrew" (only "Missus" to her face, of course), and why she has a staff of part-timers to perform such distasteful tasks as interacting with the customers. Oh, she likes children well enough, but she speaks to them so condescendingly that even the smallest of babes regards her with a moue.

I've hardly had a chance to pour my coffee when Uncle Heck breezes out of the first-floor powder room, jolly as the Holly King, with a bulging rucksack full of goodies he's picked up at markets all over the southern continent. He does this every December covention, arriving to great fanfare among the little ones, who are delighted with his exotic gifts no matter how quaint the plaything or itchy the pullover. The doorbell rings over and over but no one waits to be let inside, and soon every room in the gingerbread house is crowded with our candy golems. You can see a little nougat of a newborn boy child, a Jester, fast asleep in a dresser drawer in a third-floor guest room. He'll be named tonight. Everyone's crowding the coffee and cocoa dispensers on the dining room sideboard, and from the kitchen waft the tantalizing smells of roasting chestnuts and gingerbread cookies.

After brunch we put on the tableau vivant in the drawing room. The subject of this year's tableau is Circe's Petting Zoo, and most of the girls are wearing long-sleeved leotards and pig, goat, and cheetah masks that engulf the head. (They might all turn themselves into animals proper, but why risk the mayhem?) I've made myself a girl again for the occasion, because nobody wants to see a 149-year-old woman in strappy sandals and a palla made of flimsy cotton voile. They've decided I should be Circe, of course, since I have a special flair for this sort of thing. Uncle Heck is Odysseus and Uncle Hy is one of his soldiers, whom I've just turned into a pig. The backdrop is an Aegean paradise, expertly painted by Dymphna's daughters.

After the tableau has disbanded it's time for the puppet shows, and I hurry up the stairs to the bathroom to take off my face. I really ought to put my old hide back on if I'm to enjoy the rest of the festivities; delay much longer and I might collapse into an armchair and nap well into tomorrow.

But I stand there in front of the mirror for a while thinking of Justin, and Jonah, and how this smooth young face masks a silly old hag, primped and powdered. I sit down on the rim of the bathtub and wipe at my eye makeup with a tissue—and yes, I'll admit, I do end up crying just a little. An unseen hand yanks the toilet lever and I shout, "Oh, for pity's sake!" over the loud sploshing in the bowl.

I'm startled out of my brooding by someone knocking on the bathroom door. "Eve? You haven't fallen in, have you?" It's Morven. There's a queer note of excitement in her voice, but I don't think she has to take a pee.

"Go away!"

"What are you doing in there?"

I let out an exasperated groan. "I'm flossing my cooch. Now go away!"

"There's someone here to see you," she says—so that's why she sounds so excited. "He's waiting downstairs, dear."

My heart gives a hopeful thump. *"He?"*

"Yes, 'he.' *That* 'he.' Your what's-his-name."

"Justin?"

"Yes, him. Have you . . . ?"

"Not yet."

"Lucky for you. Now don't keep him waiting any longer, the nieces look about ready to devour him."

I glance in the mirror one more time and wipe away the runny mascara. Then I hurry down the hall, pausing at the second-floor railing to look at him.

He's grown a beard, a real beard, full and black, and his perfect white teeth gleam between his perfect red lips. Vega is hovering behind him as he shrugs himself out of his coat; once it's off she whisks it out of sight, and though she looks like a nymph and smells like a rose he scarcely notices her. "I hope I'm not intruding," he is saying to Helena.

"Not at all. We were just about to sit down to dinner." My sister pauses. "Would you care to join us?" This is not like Helena at all. She is so practical and proper that her hospitable nature doesn't often benefit ordinary men, unless they're B and B guests, that is.

There isn't the slightest movement now within the gingerbread house on the hall table. Justin looks around him, in the foyer and through the doorways at our multitude of friends and relatives. "I doubt there's room at the table," he says with a nervous laugh, and this is when I start down the stairs. He glances up, does a double take, and suddenly everyone in the house is crowded around him, alternately staring at me and staring at him staring at me. This moment drags so thrillingly! I'm glad Auntie Em didn't let on he'd be here today. It's the most marvelous surprise I could have hoped for, though I don't suppose she withheld it for happiness's sake.

As my bare foot touches the first step he reaches forward and embraces me, languidly, like a romantic hero in a black-and-white film. Then he holds me at arm's length and surveys me with shining eyes. "You look like a vestal virgin," he says, and does not seem to notice the collective snigger among my assembled relations.

"What are you doing here?" I ask. "Is Fawkes all right? Why aren't you with your family?"

"Fawkes is fine. They've hired a nurse for him. My parents thought I'd be in Hungary over the holidays, so they went down to Florida for the week. Uncle Harry's gone up for a nap now so I thought I'd come over."

I glance through the drawing room doorway and see our young puppeteers standing behind the stage staring at him, marionettes dangling from their hands, our wimpled granny jujus gone limp just as if they were ordinary toys.

"But I'm afraid I've—"

"No, no, you haven't interrupted anything," I cut in. "They can finish the puppet show later." Couldn't go on with *The Trial of Goody Harbinger* with him here, that's for certain.

"Your aunt was just telling me there's room for me at the table, but somehow I doubt that."

"We don't all eat at once, silly," I say as I pull him by the hand into the dining room, and I notice that someone has draped a sheet over the mirror above the sideboard. Justin can't see me as I am in that mirror, but all the rest of them can. I catch Morven's eye, smile a smile of gratitude, and she gives me a wink. Then I skip down the sideboard piling a plate with goose liver and sage stuffing and bid him sit, put the plate before him, ask him if he'd like a spot of bubbly.

Everyone else—or as many as can fit—follows us in to dinner. The air thrums with suppressed excitement and more than a little unease. It's cruel, isn't it? All of them watching him grow too fond of a woman six times his age. He'd be horrified if he only knew. Still, Helena couldn't very well have turned him away at the doorstep, and it's not as if there's any malice in their interest. So they go on watching us, saucer eyed, wondering if the Omnipotent will take pity on poor lovesick Auntie Eve and make her as young again as she currently appears. Most of the children are too small yet to be looking at him with adoration, but they are picking up on their mothers' giddiness, acting restless and talking among themselves more loudly than they ought.

The rime on our champagne flutes shimmers in the candlelight as Justin regales us with stories of all his adventures in Budapest. He's been to a snow-globe-maker's workshop and a waxworks, and visited every open-air bazaar in the city to root through dead people's junk in search of treasure (he doesn't put it quite like that, seeing as we are in the company of children, but we get the gist). He's been to arcades with pitched-glass roofs and ridden in rickety wrought-iron elevators, gone to public baths crowded with fat men in Speedos, seen *Così Fan Tutte* at the Hungarian State Opera (*With whom?* I wonder darkly), and eaten hazelnut torte at the old café of the secret police. The little ones pepper him with silly questions and he answers them all with good cheer.

Helena puts out the ambrosia cake on a china pedestal—she hasn't eaten with us; she's always in the kitchen but you'd be hard-pressed to find her eating a morsel—and at the sight of the cake Justin's eyes light up. "Ooh, what kind of cake is that?"

Emboldened by the bubbly, I lean in and pinch his knee. "What's your favorite kind of cake?" He frowns, confused at first that I haven't simply told him it's a carrot cake, but then I say, "Wouldn't it be funny if it were the same kind of cake this is?"

He pauses for a moment. "My grandmother used to make the best cake in the world. A spice cake, for Hanukkah."

"What kind of spice?"

"Nutmeg, I think. And a bit of cinnamon and ginger. There was chocolate in it, too."

"Well, isn't this a delicious coincidence! That's exactly what this is. A nutmeg cake, with a chocolate crust."

"You're kidding me!" he says, and I cut him a slice as the children around us giggle at the secret to which he isn't privy.

"Oh God," he says as he takes the first bite. "This is amazing. Even better than my grandmother's. Did you make it?"

This is one of the few times in my life I've wished I were domestically inclined. I have to shake my head. "Helena made it."

"Helena?"

"Er—my auntie."

Vega appears at his side, thermal jug poised above the china cup at the edge of his place setting. "Coffee?"

"Yes, please!"

"Milk? Sugar?"

"No, thanks. I take it black."

He takes it black! Justin smiles at me over his steaming cup as I gulp the rest of my champagne.

Once he's finished his third slice of ambrosia cake he glances up at the doorway, where another load of curious relatives are still hanging around staring, and says, "Oh! I guess we'd better make way for the next sitting, eh?" He picks up his plate and silverware, the dear boy, but Mira takes them out of his hands on her way back to the kitchen, so we rise from the table and make our way through the hungry throng. I feel his breath hot on my neck as he murmurs, "Is there someplace we can go? To be alone for a little while?" and my heart skips three beats in a row. "But I don't want to keep you from your family," he says quickly.

I take his hand and we hurry up the stairs amid the whistles of the few adolescent magi present. They're relishing this opportunity for an open display of impudence toward an elder (and I suppose I'd do the same in their place, so I can't complain). Justin lets out a nervous laugh.

I close my bedroom door behind us and hastily stuff my discarded dress and pantyhose under the pillow as he pulls a small beribboned box out of his pocket. "Oh, Justin, I didn't—"

"It's all right," he says as I tear off the ribbon. "You weren't expecting me, anyway."

The necklace inside the box is just what I would've wanted, had I known such a thing existed: a silver Janus pendant, with a face on either side. "Found it at one of the markets in Budapest," he says. "Thought of you."

I turn the pendant—heavier than it looks—over and over in my palm, grinning from ear to ear. It is the perfect gift. How did he know?

"Can I put it on for you?"

"Oh, please do!"

His arms encircle me and I feel his breath on my neck again, his fingertips tickling my nape.

"Do you have any idea how old it is?"

"It's hard to say. Late Victorian, I think. Made in England."

"I'll treasure this," I tell him, and his cheeks redden with boyish pleasure.

"I don't want to keep you," he says softly. "We should go back down."

"I suppose we should," I reply, but I make no move to the door.

"I was thinking . . ."

"Yes?"

"Maybe we could meet up in the city sometime soon?"

"I'd love to."

"Great. Name the day."

"Friday?"

"Oh. No sooner?"

"What day were you thinking?"

"How about the day after tomorrow? Maybe we could go to a museum. How about the Met?"

I nod. I'm smiling so hard my face might fall off.

We come down and when I say, "I'll get your coat," Mira and Vega protest most volubly. "Stay a while longer," Mira says as Vega nudges him into the drawing room, where an alternate puppet show is about to take place for his benefit. The marionettes are still inert, of course, so the children are working their wires and putting rude words in their mouths. Auntie Emmeline proclaims herself a "big smelly meanie" and Goody Harbinger sings, "A noose, a noose! I'm bruised on my caboose!" They know they will be scolded for this once Justin's left, but they're having far too much fun to care.

"Those are the most amazing marionettes I've ever seen," he says, and wants to know where they were made.

I plop down in the middle of the sofa to keep the girls from sitting beside him, and as he settles himself he glances at the photograph of Morven and me in our ANC uniforms on the end table. He does a double take. *Shoot!* I ought to have hidden that.

"Is this your grandmother?" he asks. "She looks a lot like you."

I'm not pressed to lie, though, for the ongoing jollification distracts him: the naughty children are making Uncle Erskine tell Auntie Emmeline that her mother was a hamster and her father smelt of elderberries, pausing only to ooh and ahh out the drawing room window at the falling snow; in a nearby armchair Cousin Tabitha, having imbibed too much mulled wine, hiccups and giggles alternately, quite comical seeing as she's even older than I am; the catnip mouse Uncle Heck draws from his rucksack sends the tabby into paroxysms of ecstasy on the oriental carpet.

Justin's looking about the room in idle enjoyment, when suddenly he frowns and starts darting glances at the faces in the crowd. "How odd!"

"What is it?"

"Nobody wears glasses in your family. Not even your great-aunts . . . and I see a few who look like they could be in their eighties."

I shrug. "Good genes, what can I say?" Morven rolls her eyes.

Night is falling and at last he thinks he'd really better be going now. I see him to the door and he kisses me full on the mouth, but my euphoria is short-lived. I reenter the drawing room and the ancestors launch into their reprimand: *For shame, Evelyn! You have no business— no right—oh, the indecency of it!* Clickety-clack go their little wooden jaws. The children take this opportunity to quit the drawing room en masse in search of further refreshment, and everyone else fidgets in their chair.

Helena appears in the doorway, still wearing her apron. "That's enough!" she calls out. "She's done no harm."

"No harm *yet!*" the puppets cry in unison.

"The boy's only after a bit of fun himself. And so I see no harm in it." She catches Uncle Heck's eye then and nods. My uncle draws his old ibex headdress out of his pack and puts it on while the sulking puppets seat themselves on the end of the stage. Heck produces his tin whistle and plays a few notes. The children hurry back into the room in a stampede, trailing cookie crumbs all over the carpet. Faced with this wild new getup, the younger ones hide their faces in their mothers' bosoms, believing him the bogeyman.

THE KIDDIES go to bed before the meeting commences. It's one of my favorite childhood memories of winter covention: being snuggled up in bed and hearing murmuring through the floor punctuated by occasional laughter, and if you got up for a glass of warm milk you would arrive in the doorway of a drawing room gone strange in the cozy gloom, your mother's face silhouetted in the lamplight. You knew it was the same old room you passed your days in—but late at night, in the darkness, and with all the ladies and their big words and only faintly familiar perfumes, the room acquired an air of preternatural excitement. You expected there was a tremendous secret to which you'd shortly be made privy.

But what did I tell you about nostalgia? A sweet distraction before it bites you in the rump.

The first part of the meeting is uneventful, and I am too busy thinking of Justin to pay much attention. The boy child is named Erskine, after his grandfather, and the young people make their *beneficium* pledge. Many of the ladies knit through it all, and Olive Jester, Dymphna's daughter, sits in the corner embroidering a tiny blouse. (She inherited the workshop over on Alabaster Street from Uncle Dickon, who, when he got old enough, sat down and made his own juju.)

Olive's daughters appear in the doorway and listen with wide eyes as the last couple girls take their oaths. "Mommy, may we have some milk?" Two mugs appear on the end table at her elbow as Olive continues at her needlework, and the two little girls stand there in their footy pajamas with their noses in the gently steaming cups.

Then, as usual, Helena says, "Are there any matters of conduct to be brought to our attention?" to which there is always a brief silence before Morven says, "Right then, I'll bring in the tea tray."

Morven is opening her mouth to say just that as Lucretia Hartmann raises her hand. "I have a charge."

Helena starts. "A charge?"

Lucretia rises from her chair and smooths her skirt before speaking again. "It is my unfortunate duty to declare that I have come into possession of documents suggesting that you, Helena, had a hand in the death of Henry Dryden."

Gasps, gaping mouths, snorts of incredulity. My sister, a murderess? Helena Homebody? Preposterous.

"Surely you can't be serious, Lucretia," the ladies are saying.

"I assure you that I am. And if this evidence is to be believed, the consequences for this coven will be profound."

I stand, trembling, and face her. "How dare you," I say. "How dare you accuse my sister in her own home!"

"How dare *you*, Evelyn! How dare you suggest your family is above the rules of this coven!"

"Lucretia is right, Eve," Helena says quietly. "She may be mistaken in her accusation, but I must prove my innocence according to custom."

The ancestors are of little help, being too busy arguing among themselves. Their limbs clash against one another's as they argue, clackety-clack-clack. "It isn't true. We know it isn't," says Uncle Dickon, but what can a ghost offer in the way of tangible evidence?

"This is nonsense and you know it," I cry. "Everyone knows it. Where's your proof, you spiteful old cow?"

"Eve, *please!*" Morven tugs at my sleeve. "Hush now. We'll sort this out."

"You are the worst hypocrite there ever was, Evelyn Harbinger. Look at you, vain as a peacock, strutting around as if—" She cuts herself short, flushing quite deeply, for it has only just occurred to her that a third of the people in this room are Peacocks.

"Pea*hen*," Vega sniffs.

"And peahens don't strut," her sister says impishly. "They haven't the plumage."

"Be quiet!" Lucretia's face has gone rather purple. "The way she's bewitched that poor boy is positively criminal, and as I see it you're *all* to blame for your complicity." She huffs and glares at all the ladies seated around her. They avert their eyes and clear their throats. "Call me all the names you like, Evelyn," Lucretia says, "but your house is made of glass."

Morven implores me not to retort as Lucretia fumbles for her purse—a great brown thing that resembles a mound of offal more than a fashion accessory—and pulls out a neatly binder-clipped sheaf of photocopies. She's been *planning* this, the sour old prig!

She hands the sheaf to Helena, who skims the first page with a dispassionate eye (as only Helena could, the poor dear). "I found these letters in my mother's papers. These are facsimiles, of course. Her correspondent laid out the case against you, Helena, and it is lamentably convincing."

"Who is the correspondent?" somebody asks.

"Miss Belva Mettle, a native of this town." Lucretia turns to Marguerite. "Your father's secretary."

"An ordinary woman?"

Lucretia nods. "Not that it matters."

Dymphna clears her throat. "Naturally, we must have time to review th—"

"Yes, of course," Lucretia says. "Will we reconvene in one month's time?"

Helena looks up from the papers in her hands and nods slightly.

With that, Lucretia Hartmann slings that horrid handbag over her shoulder, lifts her chin, and marches out of the drawing room.

Nobody speaks. I fall in a heap onto the sofa beside Morven. Olive's children, thoroughly oblivious to the kerfuffle Lucretia has just kicked up, have been rummaging through Uncle Heck's knapsack in the corner of the room. The elder of the two is monopolizing the bag, however, so her little sister has moved on to her own mother's sack; Olive, like most of the rest of us, is too busy staring at the floor in troubled rumination to notice what her kiddies are up to. With a small cry of delight, her younger daughter pulls out a string of three unfinished puppets and carries them across the room to the sofa where we are seated. "Look, Aunties!" she says. "Look what I found!"

I lean forward to see her better—what a sweet little thing she is, Shirley Temple curls and a milk moustache drying to a crust on her upper lip—and I take the marionette she offers me.

It has no clothes or hair yet, but its face is freshly drawn, and as I look upon it I am dimly aware of Olive demanding her daughter bring her back the puppets at once. It's a girl puppet, of course, with pale cat's eyes, arched black eyebrows, and a bowed mouth painted crimson.

Olive rushes forward, plucks the puppet from my hands, and stuffs it, clickety-clack, back into her workbag. "I'm so sorry, Auntie," she mutters. "I never intended for you to see it."

Schemes and Counterschemes

14.

There is no such thing as a dangerous woman; there are only susceptible men.

—Joseph Wood Crutch

꿈

"**R**ATHER PREMATURE, wouldn't you say?" I'd said drily once someone had poured me a generous glug of brandy. "I might live another sixty years, you know."

"You might," said Olive.

"Mind you, Auntie Emmeline was two hundred and twelve. Uncle Elmsford was nearly two forty-three. And Dorcas Harbinger lived to be over three hundred!"

"You don't know that for certain," Olive replied. "Sorry, Auntie, but you Harbingers do have a tendency to exaggerate."

I turned to Morven, who didn't seem aggravated in the slightest. "Aren't you offended?" I asked. She said no, and I replied, "Why not? Don't forget, you've got almost a year on me."

The covention was spoiled, of course, though Lucretia had the sense to hide her face the rest of the weekend. I took pleasure in none of the old New Year's customs, not even the Enchanted Gingerbread Man's annual prophecy. (At least it wasn't any more ominous than it usually is.) Nobody had the heart to man the Grey Mare, so the horse's skull sat idle on the drawing room mantelpiece, the well-worn cape trailing down the side of the fireplace. Vega put two votive candles

in its sockets and we—only the Harbingers left now—sat in the darkness, watching the light flicker where its eyes used to be. Helena kept
to herself.

Until now I never truly understood how a small-town feud could
drag on for generations, how children could so willingly inherit the
grudges of their grandsires. For days afterward my blood roared in my
ears whenever I thought of the toy shop proprietress going about her
daily business, doling out Robitussin-flavored lollies with every purchase in between plotting the ruination of the Harbinger clan. Why
must we defend ourselves against her ridiculous accusations? Anyone
can see she's mad as a wet hen!

T HE DAY after Christmas we hold a family meeting. The Peacocks
and the Jesters and all the rest had offered sympathy in abundance, but none of our friends could possibly offer a solution. So we
kept our conference to ourselves.

"There's not much to tell beyond what you all know already." Helena is seated at the head of the dinner table, dignified as ever. Her
daughters pepper her with questions.

"Have you read the letters?" Rosamund asks. My sister nods.

"Who was this Belva Mettle, anyway?" Marguerite says. "I never
heard anything about her."

"She wasn't your father's secretary for very long. I don't remember much about her myself—only met her a handful of times . . ."

"Well, *I* remember her," I put in. "She had the most unremarkable
face I've ever laid eyes on, which is in itself the only reason I would
have remembered her. She was utterly nondescript."

"I do recall she was very studious, very accommodating," Helena
says. "Perfectly willing to work until ten o'clock at night any time
Henry was on one of his big cases."

"How is it *you* remember her, Auntie Eve?"

"Oh, your father was handling some small legal matter for me, so he asked the girl to bring the papers round to the house on a Friday afternoon. She was a strange little thing, too. Birdlike. Ill at ease." The image of her hovering on the kitchen threshold, eager to be away, comes to mind now as readily as if Henry had only died this morning. When she turned to go I'd noticed crooked stocking seams over a pair of shapeless calves. "Shifty-eyed," I say. "*That's* what I'd call her."

"She wanted Daddy for herself, I suppose," Marguerite remarks tonelessly, and Helena starts in her chair. "It *is* the most logical conclusion, Mother."

"Perhaps it is," Helena says in a queer voice.

"If that's so, then it's easy to see why she'd leap to suspicion. What was Lucretia talking about when she said the letters had proof?"

"It isn't *proof,* per se. The 'evidence' is all very circumstantial." Helena pauses.

"Mother?"

"*Yes,* dear, I'm just trying to think of how best to explain it."

"Why don't we hear it from the horse's mouth? Marguerite, you read it."

Deborah hands Marguerite the sheaf of photocopies and she begins reading at the top of the page. "*March 1, 1950. Dear Maud, I hope all is well with you and yours, and that baby Michael is fully recovered from his bout of colic. Life in Blackabbey is uneventful, though I am sorry to report that Henry is not looking well.*"

"'*Henry*'? They were on a first-name basis?"

"I don't think so," Helena replies. "She would have called him Mr. Dryden to his face, I think."

"*Something is amiss at Harbinger House, of that I am certain.*" (Here, a collective rolling of the eyes.) "*Maud, I feel I must confide in you, not only to ease my own anxiety, but in case something horrible should happen—*" Marguerite interrupts herself with a sigh and her sister takes the opportunity to ask, "Where is Belva Mettle now?"

"Dead, I expect, or else Lucretia would have spoken to her and told us all about it."

"Dead," I reply. "How convenient."

"Will I keep reading?" Reluctantly we nod. *Henry is clearly ill and yet he seems utterly unconcerned, though you would expect as much from a man, wouldn't you? Especially one so busy and important as Henry.*"

I let out a groan. "Will the silly mouse get to the point already!"

Marguerite is scanning ahead. "She comes to it soon enough, Auntie. *I have noticed something very odd. Some mornings Henry brings his coffee in a thermos from home, and other mornings he goes down to the diner with his newspaper and drinks it at the counter. I have observed that on the afternoons when Henry has had his coffee from home, he spends more time in the toilet than could be considered normal, and when he emerges he is almost deathly pale.*

"*Unbeknownst to him, I have taken the liberty of contacting a chemist in town to ask if he might test a sample of leftover coffee from Henry's thermos. Of course, the idea that Henry's wife could be poisoning him is shocking in the extreme. Though she is unfailingly polite and considered a pillar of feminine virtue by all who are acquainted with her, I cannot dismiss my suspicions. I am visiting the chemist's again tomorrow evening and will relay to you everything there is to report.*"

"I take it the chemist found something in the coffee," Morven says dolefully.

"Every trace chemical he found is present in an ordinary cup of coffee," Helena replies. "And yet Henry did die of it."

Her daughters and nieces respond with a chorus of gasps and "*What!*"s, and Helena holds up a weary hand. "I am getting to it. On his doctor's recommendation, Henry drank only decaf. Now, there is a chemical called methylene chloride that is used to strip the caffeine from the coffee. It is that chemical that is toxic in larger doses, and it was an extraordinary dose of that chemical the pharmacology professor found in Henry's thermos."

A long and eloquent silence follows. How can Lucretia *possibly* expect us to prove Helena's innocence more than sixty years after the fact?

We cannot ask Henry himself because he was, alas, an ordinary man. There is no earthly way to prove or disprove any of it, and yet a pall will hang over this coven until we achieve the impossible. There are unearthly means, of course, but they are too frightening to contemplate. We have not reached that level of desperation just yet.

"There's only one thing to be done," I say at last. "We must discredit Belva Mettle."

"I'D LIKE to research a person," I tell the teenage boy behind the desk. I might as well mention I've gone girlish for the afternoon. I've been to the digital reading room at the Blackabbey Public Library before, and I have observed who gets the most help from the all-male staff. Chicks trump grannies every time, blast them. "A resident of Blackabbey in the 1950s. How would I go about doing that?"

"Is it, like, for genealogical purposes?"

I glance at Morven and she flashes a grinchy grin. "It is indeed," I reply. "My great-aunt. Her name was Belva Mettle. I'd like to look through the old microfiche of the *Blackabbey Gazette* for a wedding announcement and what have you, but I was wondering if there's a search engine for the whole archive."

"Yup." He rounds the desk and leads us to a row of computers. "I can show you how it's done, if you like." I turn to Morven and roll my eyes. He'd never have offered to help *her*. These cocky young blokes think we're too feeble to understand how a computer works, that we should just stick to our typewriters and home-shopping channels. "I'll put in your aunt's name and we'll see what comes up," the spotty-skinned junior librarian is saying. "Belva Mettle, you said? B-E-L-V-A M-E-T-A-L?"

"M-E-T-T-L-E," I reply, and he, oblivious to my frosty tone, types her name into the search field.

"The results will come up in reverse chronological order, as you can see," he says, pointing to her obituary notice at the top of the screen. "Died in oh-three, is that right?"

"Uh—yes, sounds about right."

"Don't expect there'd be many other Belva Mettles around here," he says with a wink. "Anyway, there's a lot more here. Over thirty hits. You can search other newspaper archives too. The *Times* and whatever." He points to a long list on the left side of the screen. "So just make a note of the newspaper issue dates, and then you pull the microfilm canisters out of the drawers over there. Don't worry about putting them back. We'll do it. Just let me know if you have any other questions," he says, and finally leaves me be.

I scan the search list: other people's wedding announcements mostly, and her father's death notice at the very bottom. "You know what would be *so* perfect," Morven sighs. "If she'd done time at the Manor." The local asylum, she means, where there are iron bars on every window and the inmates eat Jello with their fingers.

"Let's not get our hopes up, dear. I'd settle for a charge of perjury." I pull the film canisters from the drawers at the end of the room and load the first spool, oldest news first, into the winder. Morven seats herself beside me and does a bit of typing. "I've just done a broader search on Lucretia."

"Good thinking. 'Glass house,' my took."

I start reading her father's death notice. It isn't an obituary like I'd expected—it's a *news* piece. "*Aha!* Her father was murdered."

"Murdered? Really? I'm sure I would have remembered that."

"Well, he died mysteriously, anyway. And you wouldn't have remembered; it was during the war. Here, read it."

Julius Mettle, head botanist at the Blackabbey Botanical Society and veteran of the Great War, died yesterday at his home on Pearl Street. The Blackabbey Police are investigating the nature of his death, which the coroner believes was not accidental . . .

His sixteen-year-old daughter, Belva, has been left in the care of extended family.

The details are annoyingly vague, and as it turns out, this is the only article of note in the lot. I've grown fussy as a baby, tired of our mission and eager for a dram. The boy behind the desk stares at me as I wriggle out of my mohair sweater.

But I can't quit yet—we've only begun! So I do a *Times* search, and the only hit for "BELVA AND/OR JULIUS METTLE" just so happens to be from the spring of 1939, when Dr. Julius gave a lecture at the Brooklyn Botanic Garden. Jonah was married, in Manhattan, in the spring of 1939. I pull the film canister and spool it nimbly.

I've seen pictures of Patricia Rudolfsen before, of course—this isn't the first time I've pored over their wedding announcement—and every time I see her photograph my initial impression is reinforced. She was no great beauty—didn't even have that je ne sais quoi I could have grudgingly admired—and when I met her in New York after the war I saw she wasn't any prettier in person. It was her brain Jonah had fallen in love with, and I loved him all the more for that.

I am dimly aware of someone seating himself to my immediate left, but I am too busy reading about the exotic provenance of the lace on Mrs. Jonah Rudolfsen's wedding gown to give him a glance.

"Research?"

"Justin!" With shaking fingers I advance the film so he can't see Jonah's picture. It's too strange, seeing his black-and-white likeness on the microfilm screen just before he appears beside me in the flesh. "Shouldn't you be at the shop?"

"Uncle Harry's working today. I stopped by the house and your aunt said you were here. I just wanted to make sure we're still on for tomorrow."

"We certainly are."

"Great!"

"But I'm going home tonight, so shall I meet you at the museum?"

His face falls, but he quickly recovers himself. "Sure. How about eleven o'clock? We can have lunch there."

"Perfect. I'll see you tomorrow."

It belatedly occurs to me that if my sister catches wind of our visit to the Met tomorrow then Justin and I will never see the back of her, but when I glance over she seems completely engrossed in the article on her screen. With any luck she never noticed he was here.

"Find anything juicy?" I ask as I lean over her shoulder.

"Perhaps. And have *you* come up with anything?" my sister says, arching an eyebrow.

All right, so she saw him. The Met is humongous, though—it should be easy enough to avoid running into her. "We do have time to deal with this," I say as I appraise the state of my manicure. "Rome didn't fall in a day, you know."

"Don't be glib, Eve! Remember, Helena's reputation is at the stake."

I look at her sidewise, but she doesn't seem to have noticed her own little slip o' the tongue. She forwards the film to the next entry on her list, a front-page article from the *Blackabbey Gazette* entitled "Orphan Shocked by News of Father's Murder." We both lean closer to examine the accompanying photograph and gasp in unison.

I T IS my heartfelt opinion that anyone who spells "magic" with a K ought to be nettle-whipped for a small eternity. All those tree-hugging "neo-druids" and their new-age twaddle, chirping "Blessed be!" every time somebody sneezes. If you are all that you claim to be, what need have you to advertise it?

"Belva was a dabbler!"

This revelation doesn't have quite the dramatic effect I was hoping for. I glance round the dining room table to find my nieces all looking up at me expectantly. "You know what I think?"

"No," says Helena, "but I have an inkling we're about to find out."

"I think Lucretia has it all wrong. I think *she* killed him. Belva. Oh, maybe she didn't *mean* to. But it makes sense."

"How do you know she was a dabbler, Auntie?"

"Oops, I skipped that part." I pull out a photocopy of the microfilm so they can all see the picture. "Her father was murdered while she was still in her teens—"

"Oh yes," says Helena. "I remember. Poor Julius."

"And while they were interviewing her in her uncle's kitchen, they took this picture." I lay the photocopy on the table before the girls and they all lean forward to examine it. "Notice what she's wearing round her neck."

It's a hag knot on a silken cord, worn snug like a choker, and the top two buttons on her blouse are undone as if she wants to show it off. There are two reasons to use a hag knot and two diametrically opposite types who would employ it: it can be a knot tied around a peculiar sort of stone or scrap of iron, one with a natural hole in it, and worn around the neck to ward off evil intentions; or it can be worn by one who *has* evil intentions—*maleficium*—and wants to protect them against benevolent counter-magic. (Dabblers have no inherent powers, being ordinary women, and they tend to think they can compensate by stirring up bad juju on anybody they don't like.)

The thing about her neck is useless, of course, and this photograph was taken years before she could have fallen in love with Henry Dryden. But the nature of the knot is unmistakable, and it is unmistakable proof of her dabbling. To a keener pair of eyes the girl in that black-and-white photograph is the classic schoolgirl obsessive, one who would readily resort to meddling in things she knows nothing about, heedless of all consequence.

"Well," Helena sighs, "it's something, anyway. We'll bring it up at the meeting."

The Devil's Snuff

15.

Paris, 1942–1943

T HE CATACOMBS of Paris were an ideal meeting place for the Resistance. New recruits were spooked by all the bones in the walls, but the old guard greeted the leering skulls as friends, gave them nicknames, and even pretended to offer them a fag or a bite of dinner. You'd never get through this without a bit of levity once in a while.

The Ossuaire Municipal connected every warren in Paris, and of course the only truly safe houses were those torn down years before. Now, I know what you're thinking: if a warren is a safe haven, why couldn't you gals hide the whole so-called "civilized" world in all your old tenements and opera houses to wait out the war?

Here's the rub: if you let too many ordinary people into a warren, it starts losing its magic. How many is too many? Nobody knows for sure, but it seems you near the tipping point when the number of ordinary visitors nears that of the native population. Words disappear from books, beldames start suffering from arthritis and myopia, cats go dying in the streets. A warren stripped of its magic is dead space, like when you ride the loo flue to a place that's just been bombed, and soon it isn't only the cats. Believe me, you'd be better off living in central London in the heat of the Blitz.

Another problem with hiding folks in the warrens was the possibility, in Paris at least, that one might become hopelessly lost in the labyrinth of passageways. Say a man lost his way. If he lit a match he'd come face to face with a leering skull (or fifty), and it would be all he could do to keep his wits about him. These chambers and passageways were only a matter of meters from the streets and lampposts and bistros of ordinary Paris, yet he wouldn't know it in this perfect silence, the darkness broken only by the hissing of the match about to burn his thumb and forefinger. One time the *maquisards* found a soldier who'd somehow wandered out of a Nazi bunker in the Sixth Arrondissement and apparently died of fright on the cold stone floor. Best way to go, all things considered.

Of course, it wasn't always silent down there. You could often hear footsteps, muttered conversations in adjacent corridors, the rustling of maps, and the squeaking and scurrying of rodents—and, on occasion, the unmistakable sounds of *la petite mort*.

That said, I spent most of my time in Paris aboveground. After we returned to London for the last phase of training, Jonah himself briefed me on our mission. It was common knowledge, he said, that a prominent SS officer frequented a certain brothel on the Rue de Suffren. This man had knowledge of the locations of at least half a dozen Kuhlmann chemical plants owned by Vichy industrialists. It was also well known that this SS officer's taste in whores was far more eclectic than the average customer's, and so he would almost certainly be eager to engage a new arrival. The SOE agent would pose as a prostitute, working in cooperation with those *femmes de nuit* who were members of the Resistance. She would loosen his lips using one of that newly developed arsenal of truth drugs in order to discover the locations of the plants. The agent would probably not be required to play the role to its consummation, but she should be prepared for it nevertheless.

And she would be accompanied by another agent from SOE, Monsieur Robbins, who would pose as a clerk in the Australian embassy—which maintained diplomatic relations with both the Vichy government and the Free French—and transmit those coordinates back to London via wireless telegraph, the end result being the obliteration of each of the chemical plants by the RAF. Jonah knew I could do it without any need for "truth drugs" or other machinations, and he'd convinced the head of F-Section that I was the girl for the job.

Here is how it went—for we carried it out plenty of times, on nearly every German officer who passed through the doors of that brothel, and each time was more or less like the first:

He was rather young for his rank, with typical Teutonic good looks. Normally those blandly handsome men would blend into the wallpaper, so this would take a fair degree of acting on my part. "Is it true Hitler eats no meat?" I asked with a casual air.

I had draped myself over the bed in a black silk negligee and little else; he was unbuttoning his shirt and taking care to hang it neatly from a hook behind the door. "So they say."

"No meat at all? What kind of a man is that?"

"It is not wise to talk so of the Führer, *Fraulein*."

"He is not my 'Führer,' *monsieur*."

"Pah!" He went on muttering in German as he shrugged off his suspenders: "I suppose you cannot read a newspaper. Likely cannot read at all."

I had to feign ignorance, of course, though it steamed me. I put on a colorless smile as I reached for him.

"*Pauvre cher homme,*" I murmured, stroking his fine blond hair. "You have been so busy that you talk and talk and forget when it is time to hush."

He reached out a hand to grab my arm, but I pulled away and gave him a teasing smile. "But no. I have a little something for you first."

The Führer frowned on the use of recreational drugs, in particular that white substance they called "the devil's snuff," but his officers indulged whenever they could. It wasn't the real thing, of course, but a powerful hypnotic formulated by a beldame chemist in Research and Development. It only looked and smelled like cocaine. I pulled out my snuffbox, opened the lid, and held it out to him. His eyes lit up.

"Will you have some?" I picked up a hand mirror off the vanity table and laid it on the bed between us, conjuring a razor blade from behind my back and dipping it into the box.

He did two lines in quick succession, then held out the box and looked at me inquiringly. Before I could answer, though, his eyes rolled back in his head and he slumped onto the pillows, the powder spilling all over the counterpane.

"Christ, that took long enough," Jonah said as he swung a leg over the windowsill. With a disdainful glance at the figure in the bed, he seated himself at the vanity and opened the small suitcase he'd brought with him, taking care to undo the clasp as quietly as possible. He produced a fresh tablet of paper and laid it on the table. "How long do you expect this will take?" he whispered.

"Depends on how much he knows." I laid my fingertip on the man's temple, closed my eyes, and took a deep breath. In another moment the words would surface on the page, ink welling up out of the paper like blood from a hidden wound; sure enough, in another moment I heard Jonah's muffled exclamation. I didn't turn to him or open my eyes because then the writing would have stopped. The data scrolled across my consciousness and would have overwhelmed me if I let it, but I didn't try to make sense of any pieces as they appeared, I just let the ink do its work. I'd turn it off like a faucet once the pertinent information gave way to litanies of boyhood humiliation.

Eventually I heard a soft rustling sound as Jonah pulled out his pocket watch. "Twenty minutes," he whispered. "And I think we have all we need. How do you stop this thing?"

I opened my eyes as I withdrew my hand, then climbed into bed beside the sleeping Nazi. Jonah opened the false bottom in his suitcase, tucked the tablet inside, closed it again, and with one final knowing glance—"lucky bastard," he whispered—he slipped out the open window as stealthily as he had come.

Then came the only really distasteful part of the operation—I had to trick his mickey into thinking it had actually seen some action. I turned back from the window and got the shock of my life: in the span of a blink, the soldier's face had changed into another I knew all too well. A beldame doesn't traumatize easily, but that day I came closer than I'd ever done.

THANKFULLY, AFTER the second or third round, that particular portent ceased to appear. (It wasn't as if I needed the warning; a Nazi in a brothel isn't exactly long on virtue.) We kept on like that, two or three Jerries a week, for eleven months in total. It was brilliant. As I said, Jonah had been given a clerkship at the Australian embassy at Vichy, but he only had to turn up for "work" a couple of times a week. I slept in the attic at the brothel, and some nights Jonah would stay with me, though the circuit organizer would have been horrified if he'd ever discovered it. But I never found out where he kept the radio or where he passed the nights I slept alone.

In our circuit were many of Jonah's contacts from his first mission to France, and they treated him—and, by extension, me—like a trusted friend. One of his old associates, Simone, was a beldame from Brittany who was working as a courier between the Maquis outside Lyons and Resistance leaders in the capital. We became thick as thieves immediately upon our hellos, and Jonah finally realized with a look of wonder just what she was.

Occasionally we had respites near Lyons, where we met the agents who were just parachuting in, and those were the nights we lived for. Provided the landing went off without a hitch, we were free to pass the

night in some isolated farmhouse with conversation sprinkled with all
the news from London along with heaps of food, fresh bread and goat's
cheese and sausage and omelettes. After a given night, we'd likely
never see those agents again. Not that they were doomed, necessarily—
an agent's chances of surviving the war were fifty-fifty, believe it or
not—but for the security of our own circuit we could never associate
with them again once we'd seen them to their safe houses. We never
traveled back to Paris by train; it was much too dangerous. Instead I
took Jonah by flue to a WC on the outskirts of the city, and we made
our way back on foot.

As I say, we'd been directed to cooperate with those harlots who
worked with the Resistance, but I didn't actually have much to do
with the other girls in the house; there weren't any patriots among
them, and so I spent my afternoons in basement cafés trading secrets
with Simone and her friends, many of whom were engaged in the same
work at other brothels around the city.

We might have gone on that way—drugging goons in uniform
and relieving them of their secrets until the liberation—but in the fall
of 1943, as Italy declared war on Germany, SS officers started turning
up dead in brothels all over Paris. Their superiors showed up to investigate, and more than a few terrified madams were summarily arrested.
Within two weeks the "trade" had dried up all over the city; now the
only remaining customers were Parisian businessmen, none of whom
were any use to me. We were soon recalled to London.

The Fine Art of Troublemaking

16.

This in my dreams is shown me; and her hair
Crosses my lips and draws my burning breath;
Her song spreads golden wings upon the air,
Life's eyes are gleaming from her forehead fair,
And from her breasts the ravishing eyes of Death.

—Dante Gabriel Rossetti, "The Orchard-Pit"

THE GREAT spruce Christmas tree still towers in the medieval sculpture hall, dozens of terra-cotta angels tucked among the boughs. Behind it stands a choir screen of gilded wrought iron appropriated from some Spanish cathedral. "Wow," Justin says, his eyes wide and shining like a child's. Then he remembers himself and glances at me. "I've never been here over the holidays before."

We wander off in separate directions, he to inspect the terra-cotta angels and I to revisit one of my old favorites, a Flemish altarpiece near the hall entrance. Five wooden panels tell the story of Godelieve, patron saint of Flanders, who raided her parents' larder to feed the poor and was later imprisoned for—get this—*witchcraft*.

Out of the corner of my eye I see a petite figure edging closer to view the scene at the bottom of the fourth panel: the strangling of poor St. Godelieve by a pair of thugs in jester suits. The person at my elbow is impolitely close now, which means the stranger is either severely myopic . . . or my sister.

"Hallo, Evelyn!" She's grown a ridiculously large nose today—to keep Justin from recognizing her, I suppose.

I let out a groan, and when I turn to look for Justin I find Elsie at my other elbow, her eyes twinkling behind the dusty bifocals she wears as part of her own "disguise." "My my, Evelyn—you're looking well."

"*Please* don't. I just want to have a nice afternoon out. No funny business, for once."

"You could have gone to any other museum, you know," Elsie says.

"But he wanted to come here."

Morven holds up an admonishing finger. "You might have suggested the Frick."

"But you didn't," Elsie puts in.

"So don't go blaming us for your own carelessness, Eve," my sister says. "This is *our* spot, and if you don't like it, you can take him somewhere else."

I hurry away from them and rejoin Justin at the foot of the Christmas tree. "Do you think we might go over to the MoMA in a little while? I'm more in the mood for modern art today, I think."

Justin scans his museum map and points to a doorway to our right. "Modern, eh? Why don't we head upstairs?"

I lead him away by the hand and he casts a glance over his shoulder. "We just paid ten bucks to get in here and now you want to go someplace else? Have you seen someone you know?"

I look back but Morven and Elsie are gone—for the moment.

THE EUROPEAN painting galleries upstairs are just as packed; the borne sofa in the Monet room is crowded with elderly Japanese women dozing openmouthed, and the guards are constantly having to ask the rubes not to touch the bronzes.

"Why does everyone have to walk around taking pictures?" Justin grumbles. "Why can't they just *look* at the pictures?" For a while I make a game of stepping into the viewfinder just as some potbellied fool in a baseball cap has lined up a shot, purely for Justin's amusement.

I was here the day this museum opened to the public, and over the years I've grown so familiar with its figures in stone and oils that I can greet them as old friends: Degas's dancers and Renoir's bathers, Burne-Jones's melancholy maidens, the milky matrons of Sargent and William Merritt Chase. I just wish we could have them all to ourselves. I lean into him and whisper, "What if I could snap my fingers and make everyone in this gallery disappear?"

"Wouldn't that be nice," he replies as yet another tourist elbows him aside. I *could* make it happen, but he'll never know that.

Justin pauses at a mostly unremarkable portrait of a portly man in advanced middle age, quill in hand, at a desk by an open window: *Herkimer Harvie, Signer of the Articles of Confederation, Writing His Memoirs.* "I wonder if they're any good."

"If what are any good?"

"His memoirs."

"I daresay they're out of print."

"I want to have the kind of life that warrants a memoir," Justin says as he turns away from the painting.

"Oh, but you—I'm sure you will." I pause, then offer brightly: "I'm working on mine."

He looks at me sidewise. "What, did you neglect to tell me you're in recovery?"

"Oh, no, nothing like that," I say with a toss of my head.

We amble up to another favorite of mine, Bastien-Lepage's Joan of Arc: she stands in a wooded farmyard, rapt, as those saintly apparitions glimmer in the trees over her right shoulder. We linger before it in appreciative silence, marveling at its naturalism and the extraordinary face of the future maiden-warrior, the wide eyes and the sensitive mouth.

"What a wonderful painting," he says at last.

"She was only nineteen when they burned her at the stake, you know."

"Wow. I didn't know she was that young."

"But they never accused her of witchcraft. Do you know why?"

He cocks an eyebrow—just as Jonah used to.

"The Duchess of Burgundy examined her before the trial," I say, "and told the court she was still a virgin. They wanted to charge her with witchcraft, but they couldn't—on that technicality." Just think of it: a three-minute gallop with a handsome young farmhand and history would have treated her entirely differently.

THE HEATHEN and the abstract don't interest me so much. If I were to come back after closing time I'd find the occasional possessed object, a bogey mask or a bug-eyed totem, clanking furiously against the glass case, but after the initial fright there'd be nothing to do but tap the glass and send the spirit on its way. We tour those other galleries full of weavings of parrot feathers and brass roosters left on the altars of dead African queens, intricately carved elephant tusks plenty big enough for a human shish kebab, but none of it captures my imagination.

We snag a bench in front of a war-painted canoe and Justin takes my hand, but we're soon interrupted by a commotion behind us. A little old lady, I don't have to tell you who, has just spilled the entire contents of her purse, and two young people are helping her pick up the scattered objects—three Altoids tins, an orange, at least a dozen aluminum crochet hooks, and a ball of rubber bands as big as a baby's head—amid her copious exclamations of gratitude.

My sister crouches spryly on the floor gathering up stray tissues and peppermints in cellophane wrappers. The two do-gooders, having exchanged a crackling electric shock while brushing hands on the floor, are now engaged in quiet but animated conversation.

Morven snaps the latch on her purse and approaches our bench. I glare at her, but she pays me no heed as she plops herself down right next to Justin and brushes a strand of hair from her eyes with a loud contented sigh. Out of nowhere Elsie materializes at my elbow and we find ourselves hemmed in, the two troublemakers leaning over and speaking in stage whispers across us.

My sister glances at me and clucks with approval. "What a *lovely* girl. She has a very *old-fashioned* beauty, wouldn't you say, Elsie?"

"She's cutting a dash, all right. Prettiest girl in the whole museum, and no mistake."

"She certainly is." Morven meets Justin's eyes and leans in conspiratorially. "Is she your girlfriend?"

Justin reddens, then remembers himself and sits up straighter. "I'd like her to be."

"Oh, but I'm sorry to hear that, dearie. She looks like a bit of a heartbreaker, that one."

Plainly he can't decide if he should be amused or annoyed by this, but in a moment he's decided on the former. "What makes you say that?"

I cut in before she can answer him. "Excuse me, Justin." I stand up and brush the folds from my skirt. "I've got to use the ladies'." I stride out of the gallery and Morven hurries after me. "Lovely to meet you, young man!" she calls, and follows me into the bathroom.

"Pyoo! It stinks in here."

"It *is* a lavatory, Evelyn."

"Your nose is so big it has ceased to function." I yank her into a stall, slam the door and turn the latch behind us, and point to the toilet. "You're going home. *Now.*"

"Hah! Just you make me."

I have to admit I've been bested.

I⊤'s something of a novelty for me, this opportunity to observe a man in broad daylight, and of course I find myself looking for signs of Jonah. Justin carries himself with all the confidence and fearlessness of youth, and that in itself is unfamiliar to me, but if I'd met Jonah fifteen years earlier, I might not have recognized him either. When I do catch some small familiar tic—the way he absently scratches the nape of his neck with his forefinger, how he cocks his eyebrow, or that distant half smile as he's examining a painting—it's like seeing the ghost of a ghost.

An elderly gent drops his hat and Justin bends automatically to pick it up for him; whenever he approaches a new painting he glances behind him to make sure he isn't blocking somebody else's view. He won't be chasing skirts forever—and to be fair, I don't once catch him looking at another girl's cleavage.

We pause for a spell in the Greek Sculpture Court, the benches around the marble monuments crowded with harried young parents and old folks watching the world go by. A man in a tweed jacket sketches a family grave stele, and passersby gaze over his shoulder with murmurs of admiration.

Justin gasps. "It's those little old ladies again!" I glance round and he says, "Over there. No, don't look, you'll encourage them."

I can't help laughing out loud. Morven's gaze snaps to me in an instant, and she grins like the Cheshire cat.

Meanwhile Elsie is gazing up at a statue of Apollo. "What's this, then?" she says loudly, jabbing a gnarled finger at a strategically placed fig leaf.

"They tacked that on afterward, you know," my sister replies.

"Fig leaves!" Elsie huffs. "Always spoiling the fun."

"Oh, but they couldn't leave his rude bits hanging out for all the world to see, now, could they?" Everyone in the immediate vicinity is tittering away now, but the two troublemakers pretend not to notice.

"Sure they could," says Elsie. "One doesn't see them nearly often enough."

"Speak for yourself!" Morven cries, and the crowd erupts in laughter. I watch the frown lines melt from the foreheads of those harried young mothers and consider that perhaps the two old dames aren't wasting their time after all.

The walls of this museum are positively dripping with concupiscence; I don't need Morven and Elsie to tell me that. In a glass case outside the hall of armor, a two-tailed siren in bronze sings her irresistible song; the melon-breasted nymphs and gyrating Natarajas in sandstone and granite, the bridal pairs in rapturous embrace; the beautiful boys, heroes and demigods, trapped in marble and plaster; all the period rooms where one might tarry for a moment, with a hand resting gently on the velvet cord, and envision another life in another, more decadent time. Ignoring for a moment the inquisitive schoolchildren and the electric lights flickering in the candelabras, you imagine how you would fall asleep every night under a ceiling all done up like a wedding cake, in a bedstead festooned with petit-point tapestries that cost the eyes of a hundred Flemish women, the putti on the walls paused in their merriment to witness your lovemaking. In one such room he catches my eye and smiles a secret smile.

WE STAND in front of a glass case filled with trinkets of the tragically frivolous, gilded powder pots and diamond-studded snuffboxes. "Do you ever look at these things and figure what they're worth?" I ask.

I glance at him—he's looking a trifle sheepish. "Sometimes," he says.

I move on to the next case—an array of tacky Sevres vases. "And I wonder how often your uncle has picked up things at estate sales he's bought and sold already."

"It happens," he admits. "Boomerang pieces, they call them. Fawkes seems to think it's awfully funny, but Uncle Harry is embarrassed."

"Not too embarrassed to turn another profit," I say archly, and Justin shrugs.

Take the average woman who comes into the shop, someone who might spend several hundred dollars on a piece of charming old jewelry. Does it ever occur to her that the contents of her drawers may very well wind up in a jumble on a flea-market table, that her grave may be "excavated" and those precious rings slipped from her finger bones? Does she ever imagine that, should she purchase a bauble today, the thing may be on display again inside that very case fifty years hence— or under museum glass a hundred or a thousand years from now?

Every item, down to the tiniest gilded gimcrack, is irrefutable proof you can't take it with you. And yet the lucky ones live on in their portraits and busts; their likenesses will be remembered even if their names are not.

After several hours in this place one finds one's sense of wonder dulled by the abundance of it all; truthfully, one gets rather tired of all the enameled fripperies and Spanish lusterware, the rooms upon rooms of ditch-water landscapes. Shamans and sphinxes, fearsome Assyrians and flat-footed pharaohs, no longer impress the visitor who has stayed too long.

THE GREAT HALL is bathed in wintry twilight, the cloakroom queues snaking endlessly. "Looks like we'll be here for a while yet," Justin sighs, and I wish I had oomph to spare so I could retrieve our coats at once.

"Pardon me," comes a cheerful voice from behind us, and we turn around to find—who else? "Are those your coats?" Elsie says to Justin, pointing to a couple of jackets slung over the velvet rope.

"So they are!" Justin exclaims. He picks up the coats, hands me mine, and pulls the plastic coatroom ticket out of the back pocket of his dungarees. "I ought to complain to somebody about that."

"You ought," I say. "But I'm hungry."

"Ooh, going out for dinner, are we?" Morven asks, and I grab Justin's hand and whisk him away toward the door.

In another moment we're trotting down the great stone steps into the filthy slush on the street, Justin exclaiming over and over how uncanny it was that those mischievous biddies should deliver us our belongings.

THERE AREN'T any decent restaurants within walking distance of the museum, so we take a cab downtown to some Italian bistro Justin says has the most incredible pistachio ice cream. Over a bottle of house red he tells me all about his plans for the shop once Harry starts to give him a bit more leeway, and he talks like he's forgotten that Emmet Fawkes is a stubborn old crank who'll undoubtedly put the kibosh on any innovation whatsoever. He won't be bedridden for long; men like Fawkes always live three times as long as they've a right to.

"Oh God," I say with a laugh. "You're *so* young."

Justin frowns. "Why—how old are *you?*" He gives me an appraising look. "You can't be more than a year or two older than I am."

Now I double over.

"What are you talking about? And why do I feel as if I'm being condescended to?"

I just keep giggling helplessly.

"Are you really older than I am?"

"Just a bit," I reply. "Just a bit."

"How old *are* you?"

"A hundred and forty-nine."

"You may be older than you look," Justin says, "but you're definitely too young to be getting coy about your age."

"How was your steak?" I ask. "No, don't tell me. It's gone to a better place."

. . .

"COME HOME with me," he says on the train back to Blackabbey. "I'd like nothing better. Where are you living now, anyway?"

"Found an apartment above one of the other shops on the mews," he replies. "Convenient, eh?"

Suddenly I feel a little queasy. "Which shop?"

"The toy store. Why?"

"Have you already paid your deposit?"

He nods. "Why are you acting so funny? What's wrong with the toy shop?"

"Your new landlady," I say gloomily, for it's too late to keep him from moving. "She's a witch, you know."

"She's anal, all right. Insisted on first and last months' rent *plus* a deposit. But she's pleasant enough otherwise. I only moved in yesterday."

"You haven't signed a lease, have you?"

He shakes his head, his expression curious and slightly worried. "Month to month, for the time being."

"Good."

"What's all this about, Eve? What's wrong with Lucretia Hartmann?"

"Your home is not your own with the likes of her taking the rent," I sigh. "Believe me, I know. But we'll say no more about it. You'll make the best of it, and then you'll move."

"Look at you, planning my life out for me," he says with a smile, though there's a subtle note of discord in his teasing. I'd better nip that in the bud.

"Oh, Justin, I don't mean to boss you. It's just that my family has . . . well, a *history* with her. I know her better than I would have cared to, you see. I just don't want you to be unhappy with where you're living. That's all."

The smile he gives me is reassuring. "It's sweet of you to be so concerned." He draws me in and puts his arm around my shoulders. "I'll tell you what. If I find she's breathing down my neck, I'll look for another place."

The rest of the journey passes very pleasantly indeed, with few words exchanged.

I'M A little disappointed to see that Justin's apartment has a private entrance on the street—I was rather hoping I'd have the opportunity to poke around in Lucretia's office. I've never noticed this door before, with a transom window marked 13A in blue stained glass.

He doesn't show me around the apartment, just leads me to his bedroom and pours two glasses of water from the kitchen sink. It's difficult to get a sense of him from the few things in the room, seeing as he hasn't settled in yet. There is one item of interest on the nightstand, a five-by-seven framed photograph of a family vacation at Niagara Falls. His parents have kind faces. That picture is a good sign.

But when he returns with the water glasses he seems restless, even nervous. He walks over to the window and looks out over the mews, as if there'd be anything to see this time of night. After a few moments I stand up from the bed and lay my hand lightly on his shoulder.

"The truth is . . ." He turns around to face me. "Well . . . I'm a little afraid of you."

"Why should you be afraid of me?"

He doesn't answer; he just keeps gazing at me with an inscrutable expression.

"Honestly," I murmur. "I want to know."

"We've waited a while for this, haven't we?"

I laugh and say, "You have no *idea* how long it's been." He pulls back slightly and looks down at me, his face colored by flattered confusion.

"And to think that I was so sure I didn't have a chance," he says softly.

From then on everything seems to happen in slow motion. Every gesture shows a tenderness unwarranted by our relatively brief acquaintance, and I keep wondering if he feels it, the strange momentousness of it, because right now I have all the confidence in the world that he was Jonah, is Jonah. I run my hand over his unmarked flesh, his perfect kneecap.

And so we thump and shimmer, like a pulsar. I fancy we are glowing through the bedclothes.

A good while later we collapse in a sweaty knot of limbs. There's a long contented pause. Happily he yawns, and feeling my eyes on him, he lifts a lid. "Was I worth the wait?"

When I say yes I very nearly call him by the wrong name.

I WAIT UNTIL Justin falls asleep before I put my clothes on and wander into the sitting room. It's a pleasant enough space, full of boyish bric-a-brac and secondhand furniture in good condition, but I immediately notice something odd. One of the armchairs is drawn up against a door with a heavy-duty lock on it. My toes they are a-tingling, but I figure I have a few minutes yet; I shall have myself a snoop.

The lock gives me no trouble, and when I venture down and open the door at the foot of the stairs I find myself in Lucretia's office.

It is preternaturally tidy, not an invoice out of place. There are stacks of crates along one wall, all neatly labeled KEWPIE or ATARI or HOLIDAY BARBIES 1988. I poke around her desk for a bit, but I'm beginning to think I won't find anything interesting. Then I look up, and gasp.

There are marionettes leering down at me, dozens of them, hanging by the handful on metal ceiling hooks. They aren't any ordinary marionettes, either—it's perfectly plain they're Olive's handiwork. I don't actually recognize any of the faces this time, but what does that matter?

I don't like it—I don't like it at all.

Good Juju

17.

Aꜰᴇᴡ ᴏꜰ our marionettes have never roused, never uttered a word out of their little wooden jaws, and my mother's is one of them. Perhaps it has something to do with the circumstances of her death—Uncle Dickon hadn't even begun to think of crafting her juju; she was that young. That's the only reason he could offer.

We weren't in Blackabbey when it happened, Morven and I—we'd just begun our nurses' training at the infirmary in New York, and no one told us of her disappearance until a week had gone by. Auntie Emmeline, still in the flesh, mentioned that Mother had gone off with the swans, saying she might not be back for a few days.

As I say, that had been precisely seven days before, and I felt sick when I thought back to the events of the previous week. There had been snow and lightning that night; I remembered telling Morven as we ducked into the ladies' WC at the infirmary that I was awfully glad we didn't have to slog home in all that mess. I had only had this portent—lightning in a snowstorm—once before, the night my favorite spaniel died, and I could only hope it would prove insignificant.

I was afraid, but I didn't let on. As far as anyone else was concerned, this absence wasn't necessarily cause for alarm; Mother had grown less interested in keeping house in the years after our father had gone, and Helena had long since stepped into her shoes where domestic matters were concerned.

For weeks we waited for her to come back. The winter covention came, and Goody Harbinger and all the rest of the ancestors reassured us that she hadn't joined their number. The summer covention came, and again they told us we had plenty of reason to hope. But at the next winter covention Uncle Dickon arrived bearing her juju, and though we said the words to give it life, the puppet hasn't stirred from that day to this.

It has always been a bit of a sore point between us Harbingers and the branch of the Jester family that makes the marionettes. We have always felt obliged to say *It couldn't be a fault in the craftsmanship, no, of course not*—but what other reason is there? Other beldames have died too soon, but *their* puppets have come to life just like all the rest.

So the very next morning I drag Morven down to the workshop on Alabaster Street, where Olive has evidently been turning out marionettes for the profit of Lucretia Hartmann. We are going to confront her.

The shop is just as it was in Dickon's day: sawdust all over the floor, an unfinished doll head sticking out of the vise on the workbench, the shelves stacked neatly with cans of tole paint, spools of thread arranged in rainbow order on a rack behind the sewing machine. Olive doesn't seem annoyed by the interruption; she even offers us a cup of tea. "No, thank you," is my brisk reply. "I suppose you know why we are paying you a visit today?"

"I hope you're not still upset about your jujus."

"Well, yes," Morven concedes. "*She* is, I mean. But she'll get over it."

"Honestly, though, Uncle Dickon always used to get them started *decades* ahead of time."

I stomp my foot. "That is not what this is about!"

Olive smiles wryly. "I take it you saw my puppets in the toy shop window, then."

"And why might I find that so objectionable?"

"I don't know," she replies, which is of course a prevarication. "I've been selling these puppets at trade shows for years, and you never had a problem with it."

"Now you listen here, Olive Jester. Doing business with Lucretia Hartmann is nothing short of a betrayal."

"I know she's not exactly at the top of your last will and testament right now, Auntie, but would you try to see it from my side? I'm a single mother who needs to make a living, like anybody else. What do you want from me?"

There is nothing more we can say. She's just so aggravatingly reasonable.

THIS ISN'T the first time my holiday gemütlichkeit has given way to panic and paranoia, and I resent the reminder as much as I do that silly Olive making plans for my headstone. There are some memories I would rather not revisit.

I never did let on why I quit Berlin in such a hurry the first time. It was mid-December 1938, and I had taken the flue down to Nuremberg for lunch with Neverino and a bit of a browse at the *Christkindlesmarkt,* the greatest in all Germany. From there I would flue home to Blackabbey for the covention, and I wanted to arrive with my arms piled high with toys and gingerbread so I would be everybody's favorite auntie.

It was a perfect winter evening, crisp and clear. The lights were twinkling on the great Christmas tree in the square, and on the steps outside the Frauenkirche a choir was singing "Adeste Fideles." A warm gust of cinnamon thrilled my nostrils whenever I passed a stall of roasted candied nuts.

I wandered up and down the cobblestone lanes clutching a mug of steaming Glühwein. Most of what was for sale could be got at dozens of other stalls—little wooden boats and shiny railroad cars, tree ornaments that bobbed and glittered in the lamplight, figurines with faces painted on dried plums or walnut shells—and I was looking out for something different, something odd.

Finally I found it: a puppetmaker's stall. Most of the toys were rather simpler than our jujus at home—red-dotted cheeks and yarn for hair—but there *was* one proper marionette in lederhosen and suspenders, with a tiny feather tucked in the brim of a green felt hat. He was just like something Uncle Dickon would have made.

I needed another marionette like I needed a kick in the head, but there was something about his face—the broad forehead, the wide gray eyes, the bulbous nose—that made me think he was a trustworthy sort of fellow. The countenance of the lady running the stall, however, was not so kind. "That one," I said. "How much?"

"That one is not for sale," the old woman replied.

I gave an incredulous laugh. "Well, why ever not?"

"It is merely to show the consummate skill of the craftsman," she replied with a haughty wave of the hand.

This was awfully strange, but who was I to argue? I gave my little friend one last regretful look and went on my way.

A few minutes later, I was perusing a display of hard candies in glass jars when I noticed a man watching me. What had caught my eye was this: he had sidled up to a high table at which marketgoers are meant to enjoy their mulled wine while standing up, but instead of purchasing his own, he had picked up an empty mug and was pretending it belonged to him.

I had no doubt the Gestapo had a file on me back in Berlin—owing to the nature of my livelihood, you know—but why here? I was a stranger in Nuremberg, but so was most everybody else at this time of year.

So I did what one generally does when one suspects one's being tailed: I bobbed and weaved in the crowd, turned corners and dodged back again, and each time when I looked back, I found him no farther behind. He had the most expressionless face I'd ever seen, even for a Nazi—there wasn't a trace of vicious anticipation. And *that* was what frightened me.

I began to run. So did he. I hadn't the faintest idea how I was going to get out of this, short of sprouting wings in front of hundreds of people—which, of course, is never actually an option.

As I ran I noticed I was passing by the puppetmaker's stall once again, and when I looked at the marionette in Bavarian dress it hit me that *he was looking back*!

"This way!" he said as I noticed out of the corner of my eye that the sour old woman was nowhere to be seen. "There's a *wasserklosett* behind the baker's counter, in there." He pointed to a shop just beyond the last row of stalls that was reachable through a narrow space between them.

"Vielen dank!" I whispered, and ducked between the stalls. In another second I was taking the baker by complete surprise, and a second after *that* I was doubled over on the rim of the upstairs bathtub, catching my breath. So much for my triumphant candy-gingerbread homecoming.

That poor dear juju saved me a lot of grief. I wonder what ever happened to him.

THE FOLLOWING Saturday the Harbinger House doorbell rings soon after breakfast. A middle-aged woman in a serge suit and sensible shoes stands on the doorstep, but instead of a suitcase or duffel bag she carries a brown clipboard.

"Good morning," the woman says crisply. "My name is Rose Smith. I'm from the Board of Health."

"On a *Saturday*?" I mutter from midway up the stairs, and the woman on the step glances up at me with a look of mild disdain.

"Oh my." Helena puts a hand to her chest. "We weren't expecting you for another two months."

The inspector gives my sister a pinch-lipped smile as she strides into the foyer. Helena accompanies Rose Smith to the kitchen, where at once she busies herself reading the thermometer inside the refrigerator, peering into the oven and up the ventilation hood, and inspecting the rubber seals on the sugar and flour jars on the counter, making notes all the while and muttering "hrmmm" at regular intervals. She confirms that the chopping boards are all made of hard maple and that the industrial-grade dishwasher conforms to the standards outlined in title 10, section 36 of the State Board of Health regulations.

From the kitchen they take the service stairs up to the guest rooms while Morven and I sit sipping our tea, and when they come down again by the front stairs Vega's look of proud satisfaction tells me the inspector has found nothing amiss. But her face falls when the inspector enters the parlor and gives a "Hmmph!" of disapproval. "You keep a *parrot?*"

"Why, yes," Helena replies. "We've had him many years now. None of the other inspectors seemed to mind . . ."

"And look: it's molting on the carpet! That's an additional sanitation issue, Mrs. Harbinger."

"*He,*" Helena replies politely. "The bird is male. It's normal for him to molt when he's anxious."

"Well, a parrot flying loose in a bed-and-breakfast is *not* normal. You can get away with this sort of thing in Europe, I suppose, but here in America we have standards which *must* be adhered to if you wish to remain in business."

"He *is* toilet-trained," Helena says, and the inspector snorts by way of reply. "Truly, Ms. Smith. Hieronymus is meticulous in his personal hygiene."

"Please, Mrs. Harbinger. Don't be absurd."

I glance at Uncle Hy, who is giving the inspector a gimlet stare.

No doubt he'd like nothing better than to peck her eyes out; too bad he hasn't the beak for it.

Helena puts her finger to her lips, urging him not to mock her, and in response he turns claw so that he's facing his lectern. As he flips a razor-thin page Rose Smith's eyes widen, and she clutches the clipboard to her chest.

"As I said, he is a *very* intelligent bird," Helena says mildly.

"Ahem. I have yet to inspect the breakfast room." Rose Smith turns and exits the parlor and we all follow her into the dining room. During covention time we have that grand old mahogany table to feast on, but the rest of the year the room is filled with small tables for two or four people and topped with white tablecloths, condiment trays, and fresh flowers.

Fruit bowls and Tupperware cereal bins line the sideboard, and the inspector pokes through the oranges and bananas to ensure the produce at the bottom isn't furred over with mold. Then, with an air very nearly bordering on triumphant, she points to the flip-top spout on the granola bin. Vega gasps. *The lid is open!* One of the guests must have neglected to close it, and my niece overlooked it when clearing up after breakfast. The Harbinger girls hold their breath as the inspector writes on her clipboard.

"I'm sorry, but I'm afraid you have failed this inspection."

We all start talking at once:

"You're closing us down over a lousy granola bin?"

"Look, we've told you the parrot is toilet-trained!"

Rose Smith holds up a hand to silence us. "Did you happen to read in the papers late last month that a dead mouse was found in a cereal bin by a guest at an establishment down in Cape May?"

We can only stare at her, mouths agape.

"Now." The inspector tears the pink sheet off the bottom of the inspection form and hands it to Helena. "One of my colleagues will arrive in one week to perform a complete inspection for a second time. If you pass that inspection you will be permitted to reopen."

None of us are panicking yet, for this is all fully reversible: with a few simple words the marks will shift on that inspection sheet, and Rose Smith will say *You run a very fine establishment, Mrs. Harbinger. Congratulations on another stellar inspection report,* all the while blinking like a barn owl. Vega is raising her forefinger to do just that when Helena holds up a hand in gentle restraint. Her granddaughter looks at Helena incredulously as Rose Smith strides from the room, but she does not argue. Nor do I, as I'm too stunned even to open my mouth.

"We can reopen in a week," Helena says to Vega once Rose Smith has left the house. "And anyway, dear, it's high time you had a holiday."

A Spot of Black Magic

18.

She was shunned, and at the same time cringed to. People feared to fear her.

—Mary Wilkins Freeman, "The Witch's Daughter"

ALL THE local coven members gather at Harbinger House exactly one month after Lucretia's accusation. The meeting is preceded by a potluck lunch, during which everyone converses about the weather and other innocuous topics intended to conceal their uneasiness at our postprandial business. None of us mention our unexpected visitor, though I'm so angry I can't look Lucretia in the eye. Uncle Hy is absent, as he has been sulking in the attic for three days straight. No one discusses plans for the summer covention, which strikes me as rather odd, and when I bring it up someone hastily changes the subject.

By the time we've proceeded into the drawing room and Helena has called the meeting to order, the collective dread is very nearly palpable.

Dymphna begins by asking us if we have all read the letters. We have. I rise and ask permission to present our view of the facts, namely:

One, that Belva Mettle was far from an impartial observer and was in fact in love with Henry Dryden and would have seized upon any indication, however scant or imaginary, that Helena was less than an ideal wife; and

Two, that the unnatural substance found in Henry's coffee thermos is by no means conclusive proof of malicious intent.

I take it upon myself to state my sister's case to all assembled. On the first point, I show the room the photocopy of Belva's picture in the *Blackabbey Gazette*. Judging by their expressions, most of them seem to agree this picture goes quite a way in discrediting hapless Henry's secretary.

Now for the coffee. "The substance found in that thermos is necessary to decaffeinate the coffee, and though it is certainly toxic at the levels found in the thermos, we believe the fault lies with the coffee manufacturer." I cast a smug glance Lucretia's way. "It is reasonable for us to suppose that the coffee beans Helena used were improperly processed. Of course, there is no way to prove or disprove this sixty years on."

"Was anyone else in your household afflicted?" someone asks.

"Henry was the only one who drank decaffeinated coffee." As Helena speaks the afternoon light glints off the glass mourning locket round her neck. "I threw out the can after he died."

Lucretia clears her throat. "Forgive me for interrupting, Helena, but why would you do that? I am aware that you did not open your B and B for many years afterward, but surely you, being the consummate hostess, would always have decaf coffee on hand for your dinner guests."

"I'm not sure I can answer that question to your satisfaction, Lucretia. The coffee was old. I threw it out."

Dymphna breaks the awkward silence. "We have conferred among ourselves—"

"*We*?" I ask. "Who is 'we'?"

"The elders of the coven," Dymphna replies patiently. "Mind you, we have no intention of reprimanding you in any way, Helena, especially considering the lack of conclusive evidence. I agree with Evelyn that it would be virtually impossible to prove anything so long after the fact. Having said that, though, we thought perhaps it would be best for everyone if you were to . . . well . . . if you were to take a break from your leadership role. Only for the time being."

Helena says nothing, and that makes me all the angrier. *"What!?"*

"Please let me finish, Evelyn. This would be a temporary leave—"

"But she hasn't *proven* anything!" I shout, and everyone knows I am speaking of Lucretia. "Don't you see what this means? This means that *any* of us, for *any* motive whatever, can accuse another member of anything, absolutely *anything,* no matter if there's no evidence to support it. We can all go on taking our turns ruining each other's reputations until there's no coven left!"

Dymphna sighs. "Evelyn, dear—don't you think you're being a tad melodramatic?"

"Lucretia has accused our sister of murder," Morven replies in her reasonable way. "It seems to me that the situation is inherently melodramatic." Most of the others nod in sympathy.

"Listen to me, Dymphna. You can't say you're not reprimanding Helena in one breath and in the next tell her she's got to retire as coven leader. You *are* reprimanding her. You all know as well as I do that Helena is not the retiring type."

"Be that as it may," Helena says, "I can't blame Dymphna for suggesting a leave, and in the end perhaps it will be the best thing for me. I won't argue the point."

The room erupts in anxious questions, mostly from our side:

"How could you have made this decision *before* this meeting?"

"When will she be reinstated?"

"Does this mean we'll no longer gather at Harbinger House?"

"Belva was a dabbler! Doesn't that mean anything to you people?!"

Dymphna holds up a hand, and the room goes silent. Clear enough who the *elders* chose to replace my sister! "Any other special meetings will occur at the Peacocks' house, for now. But I hope there will be no need to choose a new hostess for the next covention," she says. "I expect we will have settled this matter well before the summer solstice."

"Settle it? Settle it how? You've already admitted there's no telling what happened to that coffee!"

"In the coming weeks we will discuss other avenues," Dymphna says, and the room reacts with a stunned and fearful silence.

Morven's eyes widen and her little red mouth forms a perfect O. "Oh, no," she says. "Oh, dear."

O NCE THE others have gone, the washing-up does itself as we all sit round the kitchen table with our heads in our hands. All but Helena, that is; she sips her tea with all her usual composure, staring into the middle distance.

"We'll put a pox on her," I grumble as I pour a glug of whisky into my tea, and Morven says, "Now, *really*, Eve. That isn't helpful."

When the invisible hands have completed their work there's only one item left on the counter: a harvest-mustard casserole dish, the sort of sturdy, ugly thing you would've got for free with any five-dollar purchase at the local Shop 'n Save in 1964.

"That's odd," says Vega. "Somebody's forgotten their casserole dish."

"Who brought a casserole?"

"What? There wasn't any casserole."

We all trade looks and eye the dish with suspicion. Vega gets up from the table and lays her fingertips lightly on the ceramic handle. "It's Lucretia's."

G IVEN THAT back in the day the hoi polloi blamed any childhood misfortune on the ire of the local crone, I am not at all comfortable in the presence of ordinary kiddies. I may enjoy watching them from a safe distance, but I try my best to avoid them at close range. Ordinary children are very much like wild dogs: when you are afraid,

they will sniff it on you and behave accordingly. So you can just imagine how much gumption I have to muster to walk inside the toy shop
on a Sunday afternoon.

The place is crawling with blue-eyed monkeys, the aisles littered
with discarded playthings. "Morven—Evelyn—what a pleasant surprise." Lucretia, naturally, says this with all the sincerity of a game
show host.

I plonk the dish on the counter. "Why did you leave your casserole
dish in our kitchen?"

"What do you mean? I left it quite by mistake."

"That is *utter* bullshit, Lucretia. You brought cookies to the meeting. Why would you bring cookies in a casserole dish?"

"I would appreciate it if you would mind your language in
my store," Lucretia replies placidly. "These children are very impres-
sionable."

"Answer the question, Lucretia."

"You're telling me I left that casserole dish at your house yesterday
as a sign of"—she remembers herself then and leans in so none of the
browsing parents can hear her next words—"a sign of . . . *maleficium*?"

I fold my arms and give her the stink-eye. "That's right."

"Well! I won't dignify such a preposterous accusation. I can't say
I'm surprised, though. You Harbingers have always been known for
your arrogance."

"Better arrogant than spiteful!"

"Now, really, Lucretia," my sister says. "You can hardly speak as
though we've been thumbing our noses at you for the last century
when you only moved to town ten years ago."

"Why are you doing this, Lucretia? It's not as if you could inherit
the coven."

"This has nothing to do with me," Lucretia replies loftily. "But if
you'd rather paint me as some sort of self-interested schemer so you
can avoid dealing with this like adults, then who am I to stop you?"

"You are scheming, and you're only insulting our intelligence by denying it. Don't think we don't know who sent that bloody health inspector over to the house last week, *two months early*!"

Lucretia seems taken aback for only a moment; then she remembers something, and her eyes gleam in triumph. "Two can play at your game, Evelyn. Don't you dare deny you were snooping around my office last week."

"What tosh!"

In silence and out of nowhere, Lucretia produces a Ziploc bag that contains only a strand of long black hair. She opens the baggie and pointedly draws out the hair, and it dangles from her thumb and forefinger for a moment before she lets it fall onto the counter.

I put a hand to my snow-white coif and flash her a look of satisfaction. "Oh, Lucretia, you *are* silly. I can only wish that hair came off my head." I smell something funny then, and when I look down I notice a towheaded kindergartener—half-sucked lolly in his fat little fist— gazing up at me with an expression of fascinated disgust. "What are *you* looking at, arsebite?"

"Eve!" Morven hisses. "For heaven's sake, keep your mouth shut!"

His eyes as wide as his face, the little boy is too shocked even to call me a nasty old fogy. After a frightened pause he runs to the door and out onto the mews as the bell above the jamb gives an agitated tinkle.

"Out," says Lucretia. "Out of my store, if you please."

"We *don't* please, you *troll*—you scurrilous bovine—you treacherous fink!"

"I shall have to call the police," Lucretia says to the room, flashing a stiff smile of apology at her customers as she reaches for the cordless telephone; but for their part, they are gazing at us in bafflement, their mouths twitching with suppressed laughter. Won't they be telling their husbands all about this geriatric catfight at the dinner table tonight!

Morven grabs me by the elbow. "Let's get out of here," she whispers. "I think this hole is deep as it will go."

. . .

THAT EVENING I return to the mews in much better form. While
I'm waiting for Justin to finish up his work, I start poking through
a cardboard box of unsorted knickknacks on the front counter.

"We got that box from a guy who just moved into a house on Pearl
Street," he says as he fills out a deposit slip. "Found it in the attic. I
gave him ten bucks for it."

There are strange things in this box, valuable for their very
strangeness. I draw out a set of tiny tribal figurines carved out of ivory,
each of them with an exaggerated nose or lips or bosom; a mortar of
pale pink marble with runic carvings on each side; and a pile of jewelry, turquoise and crystals peeking through a tangle of silver chains.
A peculiar stone attached to a blue silken cord catches my eye, and as I
untangle it from the rest I realize I have seen it before. "Well, I'll be a
monkey's uncle!"

"What?"

"It's Belva's necklace!"

"Who's Belva?"

I remember myself. "Oh, just this lady I used to run errands for
sometimes. She passed away."

"Maybe it was her house he moved into."

"Hmm, maybe." I hold the hag knot up to the light. Yep, it's definitely one and the same. He tells me I can keep it.

THERE'S A light on in the kitchen when I get back from Justin's,
though it's well past midnight. I find Helena alone at the table,
staring into a cup of hot cocoa. At first I think, *Oh goody!* since Helena
makes the world's most delicious drinking chocolate (she never uses
powder, only a square of pure chocolate melted into a cup of steaming
milk). And then I notice her face.

After Mother went away the others in the coven whispered how it was a good thing Helena never took after her. The house was always in perfect order, and all the children in it were happy, well fed, and properly tutored in magic. But the look on my sister's face . . . it's the same look I sometimes found on my mother in an unguarded moment. Eyes empty, jaw clamped—it frightened me almost as much as a child as it does now.

Helena starts, and not only because she wasn't expecting me. I have a queer feeling in my chest, but I pretend nothing is different. "I know, I know," I sigh as I sink into a chair beside her. "I look like a trollop."

She gives me a wry little smile. "Would you like some cocoa?" A steaming mug appears at my elbow, the spoon stirring itself.

I pick up the mug, hesitate, and put it down again. "I just want to say that . . . no matter what happened in the past, or what happens from here on in, I want you to know we're all behind you. No matter what."

She gives me a fond look, more amused than touched. "Thank you, Eve." I pause, hoping she'll tell me how she's feeling and how I can help, but all she says is "Everything will work out. You'll see."

I slip my hand into my pocketbook, find the hag knot, and run my thumb along the smooth cold stone. Should I tell her I've found it? For what good? Belva Mettle has already given her quite enough trouble for one lifetime.

I'm not sure why I want to keep it; I guess I have a hazy notion that it will someday be of use. So I leave the hag knot at the bottom of my bag and promptly forget all about it.

Effing the Ineffable

19.

France, 1944

. . . the very *diablerie* of the woman, whilst it horrified and
repelled, attracted in even a greater degree. A person with
the experience of two thousand years at her back, with the
command of such tremendous powers, and the knowledge
of a mystery that could hold off death, was certainly
worth falling in love with, if ever woman was.

—H. Rider Haggard, *She*

YOU COULDN'T think about how useful your work might have
been in ending the war, or how many lives were spared
through your intervention, because then you'd have to face the
truth of all you couldn't do. Millions of people suffered and died all
over the world, and to think that without us perhaps we might have
lost a million more is no comfort. This magic, these powers—what
good were they?

A lot or none at all, depending on the day. Even at my age I can recall that first heady thrill of my adolescence, discovering my birth-
right: growing wings for the first time and flying all the way to the sea
and back, which from Blackabbey is a good forty minutes' drive; and
even then I was rather preoccupied with looking older or younger. On
one occasion I convinced my mother (for a good three minutes any-

way) that I was the headmistress of my day school, an ordinary woman sixty years of age, come to recommend me for early promotion to the eighth grade.

Being what we are makes our limitations all the more frustrating. You come to the realization, on the brink of womanhood, that you're just a bird in a larger cage.

THE SECOND mission to France was probably the happiest time I spent in SOE. This time there were four of us: Jonah, the organizer; Marcel, a radio operator recruited from the Free French; Fisher, an American demolitions expert who knew all of about five words *en français;* and yours truly, the "aider and abettor," a girl Friday and the other six days as well. In those months just before the liberation Jonah and I devoted ourselves to sabotage, demolition, and arming and training the local Maquis.

And in the very early morning, in haylofts and attic rooms, we devoted ourselves to each other. I hadn't paid all that much attention the first night we were together—isn't it always the way?—but the more nights we spent together, the more I wanted to know the stories behind the strange scars I kept finding all over him. I don't mean the thick bands of scar tissue round his wrists and ankles where the irons had cut into his flesh, or the lash marks on his back, although he had those as well; they had shattered his right kneecap, and there were mottled red protrusions all over his feet, from shin to sole. I thought of our first meeting, how he'd shown no discomfort at the knee injury, but now that I'd seen the full extent of it I was amazed he could walk without wincing.

When he finally told me what had caused those marks on his feet, I felt foolish for not having guessed. The scars were almost perfectly round—just as if someone, or several someones, had used his feet to put out their cigarettes.

"How would you know?" he asked. "It would never occur to a normal human being to do a thing like that."

"Did it hurt very much?"

He paused. "I don't remember."

"Was this in Avenue Foch?"

He nodded. Then he didn't speak for a while, and I thought perhaps it would be easier for him if he told me just what he was remembering. So I asked.

"I got delirious. It was almost as if I'd stopped caring what would happen to me. I thought of Patricia, I thought of my mother, but they were distant thoughts . . . their faces flashed before me, but I felt no emotion. I was aware of the pain, but it had become something separate from me. The only clear thought in my head was that I must not talk, and yet I had an acute awareness of the absurdity of my situation. I started thinking mad thoughts, utterly mad thoughts . . ."

"What kind of thoughts?"

"I remember wishing I could treat him like any schoolyard bully."

"Kick 'im in the goolies and run the other way?"

He laughed softly. "And I would have, too, if they hadn't chained my feet."

"The cigarette burns . . . do you know who ordered it done?"

"It doesn't matter now."

"It matters to me," I said. "I'll cut out his tongue."

He smiled faintly. "I thought you weren't supposed to use your powers for violence."

"What powers? All I need is a good sharp knife. Or a rusty one, better yet."

He pulled me into his arms then, stroked my hair and kissed my forehead, and when he pulled away a bit and looked down at me fondly I could see a thought of Patricia flit briefly across his face. Revenge wasn't something that ever would have occurred to his wife, not in a hundred lifetimes.

This was something I wasn't used to: growing as familiar with someone else's body as I was my own. I could put out my fingers in the

darkness while he was sleeping and feel his wiry biceps, find that
funny little knob of flesh behind his right ear.

Not that he ever *really* slept—sometimes I'd wake up and find him
in a trance, dozing with his eyes open.

T HERE WAS a blur of safe houses, so many that I couldn't possibly
remember them all. Some who sheltered us were more willing
than others. A few times we spent the night with the *maquisards*, the
guerrillas of the French Resistance, and I much preferred it to the
farmers' grudging hospitality. The mood in their camp was much
the same as it was in the Ossuaire Municipal: the better your jokes, the
more your comrades respected you and appreciated your company.

When they played cards Jonah sometimes bet his pocket watch—
which had belonged to his father—and he never lost. Once the game
was over, he might challenge one of the losers to pick a card out of the
deck, and he always knew which one it was. Like any self-respecting
magician (save Neverino, who told me everything), Jonah only ever
responded with a wink when I asked him how he'd done it.

Our freedom fighters were headquartered in a "haunted" château
ten miles from Lyons. It looked thoroughly uninhabitable from the
road, which I suppose was why the Germans hadn't requisitioned it.
The elderly couple living in the gate lodge would have given them up
in a heartbeat had they known, but fortunately they were so superstitious that any sounds or lights in the middle of the night were taken for
paranormal activity. The *maquisards* had come up with an ingenious
method of redirecting the smoke from their kitchen fire through an old
sewage pipe that stretched to the woods behind the house, so that they
were able to have hot food at night.

Our friend Simone had fallen hopelessly in love with one of the
young Frenchmen, and as a consequence the men knew more about us
than I would have liked. It was Maxime and his twin brother, Pierre,
who had jury-rigged the chimney pipe. They had also built a series of

oubliettes in the woods, wide and deep enough that escape was nigh hopeless. It was a wonder neither of them ever fell for their own trick.

They handed us tin mugs of grog they'd distilled themselves. I took a polite sip, gagged, and spat it back into the cup. "That will put the hair on your moles!" Maxime cried merrily.

I eyed him with distaste, and when I met Simone's eye she gave me a small sheepish smile.

"Do you know the reason you were called away from Paris?" he asked. "The reason all those officers were found dead in the brothels?"

I looked at him.

"They say a girl, a young Breton girl, called them back."

"Called who back? Back from where?"

He leaned in and said, in a stage whisper: *"The girls."*

"For heaven's sake, *what* girls?"

Simone reached over and pinched Maxime's lips together. "I will tell you."

What happened was this. A ship was dispatched carrying Parisian girls for the entertainment of German soldiers stationed on the isle of Jersey. There was a storm, and at the island's southwesterly point, La Corbière—a treacherously rocky headland where black birds gather—the ship capsized, and all on board were drowned.

Four days later a French beldame, a Breton girl not more than seventeen, passed the lighthouse on foot and climbed down the jagged rocks to the shoreline. She said a few words, and within moments dark heads began to break the surface of the water. Their skin was pale as putty and the light had gone out of their eyes.

It is possible for a beldame to revive the dead, but to restore them to life it must be accomplished within three hours of the last breath. If you say the words after those three hours are up, what comes back to you won't be human.

So the dead girls made their way back to Paris by boat, by train, on foot, and by donkey cart, and everyone who encountered them wanted nothing more than to be removed from their presence posthaste. They stank of mold, and water dripped from their skirts long after their clothes should have dried.

They could still speak, and remember, and reason—to a certain extent—but when they slept they looked like the corpses they were, and they required no sustenance besides revenge. When they returned to their former houses of employment, the madams were too afraid to turn them away, and so the girls retreated to rooms with heavy curtains and used even heavier perfume. Attracted by the aura of mystery thus acquired, the German soldiers would venture into their darkened boudoirs. Those few soldiers who lived to speak of it told of rotting flesh in intimate places and were convinced to the point of madness that they had contracted some horrible new venereal disease.

And I would have been afraid of them, too, had I ever encountered them; calling the undead is a mighty tricky business. Even if you bring them back for the noblest of motives, they're liable to turn on you.

Jonah had been riveted all the while Simone was talking. "What a tale," he said when she was finished.

"Oh, but it isn't a tale," she said. "The girl was a cousin of mine."

"Was?"

"Is, was." She shrugged. "I don't expect to see her again, in any case."

"So," said Pierre, turning to me. "Do you fly your broomstick every night, or is it only on special occasions?"

"That's a myth, Pierre. We don't fly on broomsticks."

"No?"

"*No.*" I tried to give Simone a dirty look, but she wouldn't meet my eye.

"Then how do you travel to your black Sabbath?"

"Let's get this straight once and for all, shall we? I do not traffic with the devil. We are not on a first-name basis. Indeed, I have never met him, nor do I wish to. I do *not* fly a broomstick, I don't have warts, and I don't eat babies. Got it?"

"Got it," Pierre echoed. For a moment he looked lost in thought. "All the same, I think your powers will be very useful for us. Aerial reconnaissance. Hah!"

I glowered at him.

"What happens when someone makes you angry? Do you put a pox on them?"

"Don't tempt me."

Pierre let out a nervous titter, and the rest of them laughed outright.

"Answer me this, then . . ."

"Yeah?"

"Who's Hitler got?"

"I beg your pardon?"

"What kind of spooks has *he* got?"

"I'm not a spook," I said frostily.

"Yes, yes, you are not a spook. But I have heard they have werewolves."

I rolled my eyes.

"Do they have witches?"

"No such thing as witches."

"What about you, then?"

"I'm—well, never you mind what I am. I'm a lady and that's all you need to know."

"And what about you, Renard?" (Among the *maquisards*, Jonah was known as "Fox.")

Jonah took a swig of grog from his dirty tin cup. "What about me?"

Pierre leaned in closer. "Are you a he-witch?"

"A he-witch?!" Jonah laughed and laughed.

But oftentimes they could put their vivid imaginations toward entertaining rather than irritating us. Pierre told a story about a city at the bottom of the sea where every drowned sailor and frogman wakes up and discovers he's grown a set of gills and webbing between his toes, and that each of them marries a mermaid—not a fanged mermaid, mind; those are a separate species altogether—who shares a face with the girl he left behind.

In turn, I told them another of our old legends, one of those classic cautionary tales your mother related in your adolescence hoping to scare you from making the same mistakes she had made. Cordelia Wynne, who had resided in Harveysville at some nebulous point in the distant past, had such an obsessive love for her poor husband that when he contracted scarlet fever she absolutely refused to let him die. He was positively ghastly to look at, and when he finally did die—through no consent of *hers*—she cut out his heart and put it in a rosewood box, and every day she would open the lid and talk to it. The coven had tried to talk some sense into her, but she eventually shunned them entirely. In the end some concerned beldame had found her on her kitchen floor, a good week after she had died; the open box had toppled over onto the floorboards, and an unspeakable stench permeated the whole house.

Simone was nodding with a look of faint amusement. *"Oui,"* she said. "We have a tale like that as well. Only the box is made of sandalwood."

Before we parted the next morning, she took me aside. "Beware," she said. *"Les boches* know about us. They'll shoot at any bird that lands on the windowsill. Especially the black ones. Be smart and stick to pigeon."

AFTER THE fall of France, the Germans positioned their V-1 storage depots and launch sites in Calais, poised and ready to terrorize the people of London yet again. Before the RAF could bomb the underground storage depots or transit routes, they had to know where they were located. Where, precisely, were they hidden? When and by what routes would the V-1s be transported from their secret testing facilities in Germany? It was our job to find out.

I say Fisher, the demolitions expert, was part of our team, but we only saw him to pass along the maps and schedules. He'd then go off and plant his explosives on the roofs of train tunnels at the appointed hour.

It was the French workers at these storage depots who supplied us with most of the intelligence, though it had to pass through several pairs of hands to reach us. Some knew what they were doing, and others were unwitting accomplices. Messages could be tucked inside bicycle handlebars or toilet-paper rolls; coded directions were written in invisible ink on silk kerchiefs and embroidered on swaths of fine linen. Rendezvous were sometimes arranged via advertisements and memorials in the local paper.

And the commonest place for a rendezvous was a church, though one priest in particular was making it increasingly difficult to escape the notice of the Germans. We attended Sunday Mass once—oh, how it gave me the willies!—and from the pulpit Père Bernard began with the words of their savior: *Blessed are those who are persecuted for righteousness's sake, for theirs is the kingdom of heaven.* He even went as far as to say that "the agents of evil are in our midst."

"Good God, man," Jonah muttered to himself. "You'll be on a cattle car before the week is out."

"I am desolated if I have caused you any trouble," the priest told Jonah behind the locked door of the sacristy after the service. I was listening from a rafter, well out of sight. "But I cannot remain silent." And Jonah said he understood.

The priest then told him, in not so many words, that he had something for us. "If you do not find me at the church tonight, seek Monsieur Boulanger. He will give you what you need." He said no more, and I assumed Monsieur Boulanger to be a sexton or custodian of some sort, one who would be there at any time of the day or night.

That evening we made our way back to the church, but I froze when Jonah hopped the graveyard gate. "I've got to go round by the front," I said.

"But it's quicker this way."

"I can't go in there."

"Don't be silly."

"We have our legends, same as you," I told him. "One of them says that in the darkest corner of every graveyard there's a portal to Hades. I don't want to find out if it's true."

Jonah stifled a laugh. "Have it your way," he said. "I'll meet you at the front gate."

So I went the long route. The massive oak door gave a terrific creak as I pushed it open, and a little old woman kneeling in a pew at the front of the church turned to glare at me. I smiled serenely as I passed her, and she hastily turned back and bent her head to resume her devotional charade. (I never understood all this Catholic malarkey. They drink the blood of their savior—or like to think they do—and they call *us* heathens? And here's what really gets me: carving up the corpses of their holy men and distributing heads, thumbs, and earlobes all over the world in boxes encrusted with jewels! Which church gets all the naughty bits, that's what *I* want to know.) Anyway, I conjured a set of beads out of my pocket and twirled them like a skipping rope as I walked, just to get her goat. From behind me I heard a gasp and an angry mutter, and I grinned to myself.

After a cursory tour of the church and its two small side chapels, and no sign of anyone but the old crone and her rosary beads going clickety-click, I resolved to wait for Monsieur Boulanger in the last pew. Eight, nine, ten minutes went by. The candles on the altar were burning low.

Why hadn't he come? I was growing anxious. We were never meant to wait for anyone longer than five minutes, though admittedly that rule had been given us as regards assignations in the cities.

I let my mind flit above the battered wooden pews like a moth, past the altar and into the tiny sacristy. Without leaving my seat I could take glimpses of darkened corners and disused rooms, and through a grimy windowpane in a second-floor storage closet I could see Jonah sitting on a stone bench beside the town fountain, seemingly engrossed in whittling a chess piece. He glanced up as if he could sense my eyes on him, though of course I wasn't actually there; he stood up, pocketed his knife and carving, and ambled toward the side door of the church. I returned my attention to my immediate surroundings, blinking, as Jonah held the door open for the little old woman, her rosary beads still swinging from her fingers.

Still no sign of Père Bernard. Boulanger had to be late—whoever he was. But something was nagging at me; I had the distinct feeling that it was *we* who were missing *him,* and not the other way around. Jonah slipped into the pew directly behind me and whispered, "Let's go."

I held up a finger and sprang up from the pew, striding toward the altar.

"Eve—"

"What is it?"

He nodded to the book on the broad high table. "Are you sure you should be touching that?"

I shrugged. "I won't go up in a puff of smoke or anything."

He looked at me, brow furrowed in doubt. "Have you touched one before?"

"Sure I have."

He held his breath as I reached for it. "See?" I held up the heavy book with both hands and waved it about, and Jonah exhaled with an uneasy laugh.

"It's only a book," I said as I lifted the gilded cover. "Same as any other." I felt for an opening along the leather edging, then did the same for the back cover. I paused. "It isn't here."

After another moment's thought I closed the book and hurried back to one of the side chapels I'd only glanced in before. To my left, more kneelers before a gaudy shrine alight with flickering votives; behind a wrought-iron gate to my right, a semicircular alcove with simple stone memorials stacked like filing cabinets up to a round, rather crudely formed hole in the ceiling. The nooks were too small to hold anything but cinerary urns, unless the bones were reinterred here—not that I wished to find out for certain either way.

I tapped the gate lock and it swung open noiselessly, and I stepped into the narrow opening and began to pore over the names on each memorial. The masonry had been scraped away around one stone near the floor, and when I crouched to read the name I sighed with relief. "Monsieur Boulanger," I said. "We meet at last."

Carefully I eased the stone from its place, laid it on the floor, and reached a tentative hand into the darkness. "'Dead drop,'" Jonah murmured to himself. "Hah." My fingers met something cold, made of metal, rectangular—a box—and I put my other hand in and pulled it out. I didn't need to open it to know that what we needed was inside. I tucked the box in my satchel and fitted the memorial slab back into the wall.

As we stepped through the gate and Jonah closed it behind us, I wondered what had happened to the mortal remains of Monsieur Boulanger. Men like him were often more useful than their living, breathing counterparts. After all, they couldn't betray you.

We never saw or heard from Père Bernard again. I found out much later that they had arrested him that very afternoon and shipped him off to Natzweiler the following week.

THAT MORNING, after we had passed the contents of Boulanger's metal box along to Fisher, we lay together in the tiny attic room of our safe house.

"Behold, the spear of destiny!" I said in a loud whisper.

He threw his head back and laughed. Then I got quiet for a moment, thinking of the real "spear"—the Lance of Longinus. "It's hidden underground someplace, a place he thinks is safe . . ."

"You don't really believe that old legend, do you?"

"How funny. You men have such a way of saying 'I believe this' or 'I don't believe in that,' as if the truth could alter itself to suit you." He rolled his eyes as I went on. "Anyway, they'll find it—*we'll* find it—and on that day he'll die, just as the legend says."

"How would you know that?"

I gave him an impish little smile, and he said, "Touché." Then another pause. "If you can see all that," he ventured to ask, "can you see when it will end?"

I shook my head. I only knew it might be years yet, but what was the point in telling him so? "I'm sorry I mentioned it. Now, where were we?"

W E'D HAD three successful sabotage operations in March of 1944. The consequence of this was, of course, that Lyons was positively infested with Gestapo. It was only a matter of time before we came face to face with them.

Jonah very rarely left his safe house in the daytime, but on this occasion it couldn't be helped. He'd been betrayed before, remember, and this time he was determined to err on the side of caution in all dealings with his fellow agents. This particular afternoon he was going to confront one whom he suspected of careless talk. He wasn't carrying his pistol, because in the daytime it was best to travel without anything that might incriminate you. That illusion of innocence would protect you far more than a firearm would. He was driving a wagon full of milk cans, ostensibly to market, and I had made myself a barn cat, sitting on the driver's seat beside him twitching my tail as if I hadn't a care in the world.

On the outskirts of Lyons a checkpoint appeared out of thin air. A German officer strode out into the road and held up a hand. "Documents, *s'il vous plaît*."

Jonah nodded and pulled from his breast pocket the sheaf of papers drawn up for him by the C&D office in London. They identified him as Michel Durand, a farmhand from the village of Pérouges, excused from military service on account of a fractured knee. Of course, it was the Gestapo who had given him the bum knee in the first place. The Nazi could find no fault with the documents, but he signaled to two other officers, who forcibly removed Jonah from the wagon. I jumped off the seat and disappeared round the nearest corner, but only to turn from cat to bird. I remembered what Simone had said and stuck to pigeon.

He was handcuffed and put in the back of a truck, and I alighted on the roof and rode with him to the police station. There he was led into a whitewashed room, where they turned out his pockets. They checked for blades in the heels of his shoes, and I prayed they wouldn't demand he undress. Those scars on his feet were practically a calling card from their comrades in Berlin; they would know at once what he was about. They didn't strip him in that room, but it was inevitable. I had to get him out of there before that could happen.

Once he'd passed from that prison anteroom I lost sight of him. They were basement cells, with narrow barred windows at street level, though the street was more a dingy alleyway. That would be to our advantage. Thank goodness we hadn't been rounded up in Paris. Liberating him from this podunk police station would be relatively easy.

I spent the next few minutes flitting from window to window and found him easily enough. He was on the floor in a cell by himself, lost in thought. I flapped my wings agitatedly to get his attention. He got up and came to the window.

Nothing stirred in the alleyway, and there was no one to see me as

I resumed my womanly form. I crouched on the cobblestones and could just barely make out the contours of his face. "Here," I said. "Come closer."

"Did you get the key?"

"Don't need it—I'll make you small enough to fit in my jacket pocket. Come closer."

I reached between the bars and placed my hand on the crown of his head.

"This is going to feel a bit strange," I whispered. "Try not to make any sound."

Half a minute later a field mouse looked up at me in utter bewilderment. I petted him briefly. The mouse skittered up my coat sleeve, and I put my hand out of sight as I came out of the alley onto the street so he could venture out again into the safety of my pocket.

I SHOULD HAVE known he would make himself distant over the days that followed. He could no longer go out of the house at any time of day or night, but that wasn't what was bothering him. Once we were ensconced in one of the safe houses in town and I was able to turn him back into a man, he gave me a long look—grave, tender, and a little resentful. He understood that if it hadn't been for me, he'd have been halfway back to Gestapo headquarters on Avenue Foch by now, déjà vu all over again. Jonah had managed to free himself once before without anyone else's help, but fortune might not keep a second appointment. Furthermore, not every man in his situation had a girlfriend who could get him out of it, and it was for their sakes, too, that he resented my help.

"What does it feel like?" he asked once, a few nights before the balloon went up.

"What does what feel like?"

He paused. "Being you."

How could I possibly answer that?

"Knowing you'll survive this," he went on. "Knowing you'll out-live the rest of us by a hundred years."

I felt a lump in my throat and a sting in my eyes. "Please, Jonah—please let's not talk about it."

"I've bested them twice," he said. "The first time by sheer provi-dence"—I made a noise of gentle derision; "providence" had much less to do with it than his own bravery and good sense—"and I owe you for the second time. From here on I'll be tempting fate, Eve. No, I mean it."

He was silent for a few moments and hardly responded to my hand on his arm. "In your file it says you were quite the fortune-teller in Berlin."

"I have a file?"

He laughed, then went silent for a moment. "Why haven't you ever offered to read my palm?"

I looked at him sidewise. "Because I don't want to know. And what's more, I don't think you do either."

There was another pensive pause. "You believe the future is fixed?"

"I wish I could say I don't," I replied. "But it's hard to deny when there's a portent everywhere you look."

"Don't you ever see one of these . . . portents . . . and seeing it causes you to change your plans, thereby eliminating what you were warned of?"

"It happens."

"But not often?"

I regarded him sadly. "Not often enough."

Maxwell Faust

20.

I DON'T EVEN have a photograph of us. What I would give for a single dog-eared snapshot, sunburned arms round each other's shoulders and heads thrown back midlaugh! I wouldn't care if it was only the size of a business card, water stained and criss-crossed in Scotch tape. What I would give for some small proof of all those happy memories we never got the chance to make.

It's marvelous, the resemblance. Sometimes I just sit there staring at him until he starts to look at me funny. Of course, they aren't alike in every respect—Jonah didn't have any freckles but Justin has loads of them, and we spend so much time together that I've begun to pick out the constellations on his arms. He's got the Pleiades on a right-hand knuckle and Cassiopeia just above his elbow.

But the similarities are so striking that I believe if I can find some quirk of Jonah's in Justin—something even more uncanny than a confluence of hair, build, and features—that perhaps I can prove it to myself beyond all doubt. There was that weird little knob of flesh Jonah had behind his right ear, and one night when I ventured to touch a soundly sleeping Justin in that same spot, I found precisely what I was hoping for.

The next day I told Morven all about the ear knob. "He *is* Jonah," I said. "I'm sure of it." Morven rolled her eyes as she picked up my hand and guided it to her face. She pressed my fingertips to a spot behind *her* ear, and she's got a knob there as well.

"You'd think I'd have noticed that long before now," I'd sniffed. "You didn't grow it just to spite me, did you?"

"Unlike *some* we know, I do not squander my energies on such petty things as growing squishy bumps behind my ears for the sole purpose of spiting my sister."

So I would need something else to prove it, and one Saturday night in February I decide on a new test.

Some nights we go into Manhattan and other times we just spend the evening at the Blind Pig, but either way I've got to make my exit before the oomph runs out. On this particular evening we've eaten at a darling little trattoria in the Village and come home early. In his room above the toy shop I watch his eyelids grow heavy. He gives me a sleepy smile. "Will you stay the night?"

"Sure I will."

"You never do. I wish you would. I'd like to wake up beside you."

I smooth his hair away from his face and he smiles with his eyes still closed. "Oh, you dear, sweet boy." I watch his face, the face of a grown-up cherub, as his breathing gets slow and even.

Death is somewhat easier to meet when you believe, as we do, that to end is to begin. You will learn to walk and speak again, lose your teeth (but hopefully only once), bite into apples, count stars lying on your back in the dewy grass—and you will know, again, what it is to lust and to love. It will be a different face you turn toward the sun, and that someone dear will call you by another name, but there are many other things you go on remembering even when you can no longer recall their meaning.

I look at Justin and think, *But sometimes your face stays the same.* I murmur his name, loud enough to rouse him.

"Hmmm?"

"Do you believe in reincarnation?"

"Hmmmm."

I wait for a minute or two for a more complete answer and, receiving none, I venture, "Are you mulling it over?"

"Mmm rmm shleep," he says.

"Justin," I murmur in his ear. *"Mein Schatz . . ."*

"Hrmmph," he says. "Shleep."

"Weisst du noch?" I whisper. *"Bist Du zu mir zurück gekommen, mein Liebling?"*

No answer.

"Sometimes," I whisper, "sometimes I *swear* it's you, but then you have to go and do something foolish. And then I think, *How can he be Jonah? Jonah was never a skirt chaser and only hung around in bars waiting for loose talk.* But you—you watch football games and stuff your face with beer nuts." I pause. "But to be fair, you're a lot younger than you were then."

Then I hear a low growl from deep in his throat, and I begin to fear I've said too much. *"Lass mich schlafen!"* he barks, and rolls over with an emphatic squeak of the bedsprings. I lie there for a while longer just staring at his back, jaw hanging. *I was right!* I'm positively tingling with excitement.

Alas, not excitement. Toes a-tingle, I put on my coat and let myself out.

FULLY RESTORED after a good night's sleep, I go down to Mira's early the next afternoon and find Justin reading the paper over coffee and a pastry. He looks up at me petulantly as I take the chair opposite. "You didn't stay."

"I'm sorry."

"I had horrible dreams. People were beating me up. And then I was rotting away in jail for something I didn't do." He shivers to himself, then looks at me accusingly, like it's my fault he slept poorly. All right, so maybe it is.

"Justin, do you remember what you said to me just before you fell asleep last night?"

"I remember you were babbling a lot. Do me a favor and don't do that again, all right?"

I dismiss his irritation with an excited flick of the hand. "You don't remember you spoke to me in German? You said, *'Lass mich schlafen!'* Isn't that marvelous?"

"Not possible," he says. "I don't know any German."

"Aha! You don't *think* you know any German. I'll have to tape-record you next time. It's all in your subconscious, see. You do remember it."

"Remember it? I'd have to have learned it first."

I try to gaze at him meaningfully but he just rolls his eyes, smiling, and then he sighs and checks his watch. "I've got to go up to Emmet's now. His nurse took the day off and Uncle Harry wants me to check in on him."

"Can't they send a replacement?"

"Not on a Sunday," Justin sighs. "Not for a crank like him, anyway. Will you come along?"

JUSTIN RINGS Fawkes and takes down a short food list—milk, bread, eggs, coffee—and I go along with him to the grocery store. Against my better judgment, I also accompany him to Fawkes's place. Justin knocks on the bedroom door and opens it just wide enough to stick his head in. "Have you had breakfast, Emmet?"

The old man perks up at the rustling sound of a brown paper grocery bag. "Who's there?"

"I brought Miss Harbinger along with me."

"Can she fry an egg?"

Justin pulls his head out and looks at me with a cocked eyebrow. "Sure," I say, and Justin ducks in again to tell him so.

"Good," says Fawkes. "I'll take four. Should be some bacon left in the fridge. And I'll have a cup of coffee too." Justin leaves the bed-room door ajar as we make our way down the dingy corridor to the kitchen. "If it's not too much trouble," Fawkes calls after us, but with a definite insinuation that if it *is* too much trouble then we are nothing but a couple of lazy hoodlums.

"Eighty-odd years on Earth and he still hasn't learned to say 'please' or 'thank you,'" I grumble.

The kitchen is far tidier than I remember it, and I make a remark to this effect. "The nurse gets overtime for doing the cleaning," Justin says as I pull a frying pan off the drain board. The whole place still has that sickroom stink, but no help for that I suppose. Justin spoons the grounds into the coffeemaker while I crack the eggs. They turn out better when they fry themselves, but I haven't the oomph to spare.

I pause in the doorway while Justin brings in the breakfast on a plastic cafeteria tray he found under the sink. Fawkes looks up at me for a moment but does not greet me. I lean against the jamb with arms folded and gaze idly about the room. Besides the bed, its principal fur-nishing is a massive rolltop desk piled high with books and newspaper clippings. The crossbar on a front-wheeled aluminum walker by the window is draped with discarded undershirts. The nightstand is cov-ered with soiled Kleenex and empty juice boxes.

The old man takes a sip of his coffee, grimaces, and spits it onto his fried eggs. "Bog water! What *is* this?"

"It's regular coffee. You asked for regular," Justin says.

"It's *Crapwell* House," Fawkes snarls.

"Maison de Merdewell," I say cheerfully. "Maxwell Mousedrop-pings. Maxwell Faust, as you'd sell your soul for something better . . ."

"You didn't tell me which brand to get," Justin says patiently.

Fawkes picks up his plate and tilts it so the spit-up coffee runs down the mounds of fried eggs and drips back into the mug. Justin eyes the old man in abject disgust. Fawkes reaches for his wallet among the dross on the nightstand. "Why don't you make yourself useful, girl, and pop down to the shop to get me a decent cup of coffee?"

I throw Justin a look—as if frying his stinking eggs and bacon wasn't enough!—before I say with exaggerated cheeriness, "For the price of your immortal soul?"

"Here's a dollar," he says. "Now get going."

WHEN I get back from Mira's Justin is watching television in the sitting room. I knock on the bedroom door and enter without pause, hand Fawkes his coffee, and take the tray off his lap and make room for it on the nightstand. He mumbles a thank-you and I fight the urge to smirk at him.

Fawkes takes a sip of his coffee as I have a seat at the great messy desk by the window. I pluck one newspaper clipping, then another. I recognize many of the names in the headlines. Some of them were neighbors.

"These are all obits," I murmur, and turn to the figure in the bed. "Are these all people you knew?" He doesn't answer me. I read the headline on the next clipping I pull from the pile and my heart gives a queer thump. "Why did you save Henry Dryden's obituary?"

"Awfully fishy, the way he died. Always thought I might just be able to piece together what really happened to the poor fellow." Given the stacks of obituaries on the desk, it seems he found a *lot* of local deaths worthy of suspicion. (I flip through a few more, coming upon Julius Mettle's, but oddly enough I don't find one for Helena's second husband. Jack was the manager of an abattoir two towns over and came home every night with blood on his collar.)

"What made you suspicious, Mr. Fawkes?"

"There was talk of him running around with his secretary. Plenty can go wrong when a man strays—seldom doesn't."

"That's my family you're talking about, Mr. Fawkes. Gossip doesn't make fact no matter how many times you repeat it."

"Well, yeeeeeah. I remembered too late that he was your granddad. Sorry, kid. He was still a good man and all though," he adds quickly.

I brush his words aside and fix him with a stare. "Did you know his secretary? Belva Mettle? I see you have her father's obituary here as well."

"Dr. Julius," Fawkes says with a sigh. "He was a good man too. Used to pay me to do odd jobs around his house when I was a kid. Paid well." He pauses. "I'll tell you one thing—them two deaths was linked somehow, I just know it."

The gooseflesh rises on my arms. "You mean you think the same person murdered them both?"

"No, no, not saying that exactly . . ."

"It doesn't seem likely," I say. "They died almost ten years apart."

"That don't matter."

"And what about Belva? Did you know her?"

"A little," he says with a shrug. "I can say this about her: she wasn't so meek as she pretended. Not much to look at, but Lord, she had *something*. I saw her work her charm on a man once. Never saw anything like it. Uncanny."

"Which man? Henry?"

Fawkes eyes me with renewed suspicion. "Why d'you call your granddad by his given name, anyway?"

"*Grandpa* Henry. Happy? Now tell me whom she bewitched."

"Don't know. Some fellow down at the Blind Pig. It was long after Henry passed."

"Did you hear any talk about Hel—my grandmother? His wife?"

"What kinda talk?"

"That she might have been implicated in his death."

Fawkes frowns in thought, then glances out the window, distracted by the laughter coming from the mews below.

"Think, man! You said it was suspicious—now whom was it you suspected?"

"If I knew, I might have gotten somewhere," he says with an exasperated swat of a hand. "He *was* murdered. No question in my mind." He pauses, and I catch a malevolent glint in his eye. "But with a family big as yours, I guess you've got more skeletons in your closets than average folk do."

"*You*, talking of skeletons! Now there's a gem." I hold out my right hand and wiggle my fingers so my ring glitters in the sunlight. "Do you recognize this?"

Fawkes shrugs.

"I bought it in your shop. Mr. Ibis told me you'd gotten it off the finger bone of a French aristocrat."

"I've never robbed a grave in my life," Fawkes says darkly. The look he's giving me very clearly says *If I weren't infirm I'd be making you mighty sorry right now.*

"That may be, but does it matter if you paid some local scag to do it for you?" I give a little shrug of triumph. "By rights, I'd say you deserve to have your own grave looted a hundred times over."

That remark seems to soften him up, though I can't say how. He chuckles and says, "More'n a hundred, I reckon."

Fawkes takes another sip from the paper cup, and after a short silence I tell him I'd better wash the dishes. I leave the dirty tray on the kitchen counter and venture into the sitting room. Justin looks up from the TV. "I needed a break," he says.

"Can't say I blame you. What's he going to do for dinner?"

"Uncle Harry's bringing takeout. I guess we can go now." He switches off the television and goes back to Emmet's room. I turn to the pile of dirty dishes with a sigh. Not enough oomph.

"There's something odd about that girl," I hear Emmet saying as I turn off the faucet. "Can't put my finger on it."

"Emmet, please. Not everyone's as deaf as you are."

"Come again?"

"She can *hear* you, Emmet!"

"It don't matter," he says as I come down the hallway. "She *knows* she's odd."

"Right," Justin replies as I pause in the doorway. "We'll see you later, Emmet. Take care of yourself."

"Hah! Life ain't worth living once you can't wipe your own bottom."

"Amen to that," I call over my shoulder with a laugh. Justin gives me a funny look as he holds the door open for me.

B UT IF Fawkes's words have sparked some doubt in him, he doesn't show it. I'm only passing time between the evenings we spend together, and when I see him again I can sense he feels the same. Some nights we get tipsy and I sing for him, mostly bawdy old pub songs. Later on he starts talking the most marvelous nonsense, things like *I could have been a rocket scientist if I'd only applied myself* and *Humility is the one true religion.*

"I thought love was the one true religion," I say.

"Who knew you were such a softie!" he says as he tousles my hair.

He tells me about this lodge in backwater Alaska where they serve fillet of defrosted mammoth at two thousand dollars a plate. He swears up and down that two of his college buddies visited such a restaurant, though naturally they could not afford to try the dish themselves.

"Brings new meaning to 'free-range organic,' " I say. "And what do they serve on the side? *Oeufs moulés du* pterodactyl?" We laugh and laugh over the silliest things—dare I say it?—*just as we used to.* And whenever we go out to eat, he finishes the meal with the same five words he always has.

Yes, the days with Justin pass so happily that it's all too easy to half forget my sister is, essentially, on trial for murder.

Curious Kitties

21.

CURIOSITY, n. An objectionable quality of the female mind.

—Ambrose Bierce, *The Devil's Dictionary*

THE GILLENDER Building is an odd little skyscraper, a mere twenty-five feet wide. It was erected in 1897 and torn down only thirteen years later, and at twenty stories it was, at the time, the tallest building ever demolished in the history of New York City. Pandora Securities Limited has occupied the entire building since its reclamation. Twenty narrow stories might seem like insufficient space to store all the secrets of the witching world, but we make do.

Skyscrapers are rare in the Wall Street warren—most of them were too ugly to bother saving—and so the Gillender rises against the sky like a frosted ladyfinger. We reach it through a broom closet of the Bankers Trust Company, and when we venture back into a different lobby than the one we'd entered we find an expanse of fine black marble and brass filigree. High above the porter's desk a moose trophy snores tremorously. The man behind the counter is absorbed in a crossword, immune to the noise it seems, and he doesn't even glance at us as we pass.

Pandora Securities provides more than just a place to stash your hookahs and nudie postcards. There are cozy soundproof cubby rooms on each floor—oak wainscoting, oriental carpets, big leather arm-chairs, Tiffany reading lamps, all very old-money, you know—and each room is equipped with a combination of ashtray, phonograph, film projector, television, and/or high-powered magnifying glass, all so that one may dally with one's secrets in perfect privacy.

But first, of course, one must access the secrets in question. The vault—a long, narrow room lit with Nouveau chandeliers and tiled in milky green marble—looks a bit like a vast card catalog, with row upon row of little brass-plated boxes set into the walls on either side. Each box has an ornamental sphinx holding the number between its paws. There are no keyholes.

Once we've signed our names in the registry book on the second floor we proceed to the ninth-floor vault. We locate box 91153 and Morven taps the number plate with a forefinger.

The eyes of the little brass sphinx swivel to meet hers. "Please provide the full names of your maternal twice-great grandmothers, in order of birth," it says in a clear, slightly tinny voice.

We turn away from the lock head and put our hands to our mouths to compose our answer. Morven frowns in thought. "Was Lilith or Theodora first?"

"Lilith" is my firm reply.

"Right." Morven turns back to the sphinx.

"Answer, please," says the sphinx.

"Lilith Harbinger, Theodora Harbinger, Margery Moore, Gillian Peacock," she says, enunciating carefully.

The sphinx doesn't tell us we've given the correct answer, it just goes on to the next question, and the second and third are as easy as the first—list, in chronological order, your daughters' names and birthdays; what is the name of your tabby cat? Indeed, they are simple enough that any member of Helena's family could easily access her box at any time. This we find a little bit odd. Not that Helena shouldn't trust us, but . . .

"Access granted," announces the little sphinx, and after a brief sound of clicking gears and popping hinges the drawer slides forward.

We pull it out and proceed to one of those cozy little rooms down the hall to explore the contents of the box. At the top we find a sheaf of official documents, her own will as well as Henry's, and beneath those a plain wooden jewelry box full of heirloom gems she lends her granddaughters on special occasions.

Underneath all this stuff you'd expect to find in a safe-deposit box, we come upon something not so ordinary: a book, thick as a telephone directory and wrapped in a sheet of protective plastic. We pull off the plastic and find a leather cover dotted with mold, the title embossing obscured by years of wear. This book is at least three centuries old, maybe more. Morven looks at me with profound anxiety.

I crack the cover and cough with all the dust that flies up. I turn to the title page and we gasp in unison:

DYVERS EXPERIMENTS IN THE BLACKE ARTS:

A Treatyse by An Anonymus Wytch

Printed by Howatch & Brayburn, London, 1699

The book is jammed with inserted pages—well used and annotated, though not in Helena's hand of course. No beldame would ever need or want a book like this.

"Eve! For goodness' sake, don't *read* any of it!"

"Relax," I reply as I thumb through the first chapter. "It doesn't make you evil if you only read a line or two."

> *Shoulde another woman be made the wife of the man*
> *thou lov'st, a Needle slipp'd inside her bedde will see her*
> *in the ground before the yeare is out . . .*
>
> *To glympse thine enemy from afar, conceal the eyes of*
> *a Fish or Lyzarde within the chamber in which she is most*
> *inclyn'd her secrets to reveal . . .*

"Oh, bother," Morven sighs. "This does make her look a little bit guilty."

WE TAKE the loo flue back to the first-floor powder room and confront Helena in the kitchen, where she is beating a cake batter by hand. That in itself is fishy, as she only bakes the long way when she wants to distract herself from some unshakable unpleasantness. "I want to tell you both something," she says without turning round. "I've decided to give up the B and B."

"*What?*" Morven gasps.

Helena puts down the whisk and turns to face us, and I put on my best schoolmarm demeanor. "Why in heaven's name do you have a copy of *Dyvers Experiments in the Blacke Arts* in your safe-deposit box?"

"I didn't want it in the house," Helena replies reasonably.

"You aren't annoyed that we opened your box?"

She sniffs. "If I had anything to hide, don't you think I'd have made the questions harder to answer?"

"But you did have something to hide, Helena! What are you *doing* with that thing?"

"I wasn't hiding it, I was storing it—and it should be perfectly apparent that I am not doing anything with it," she replies. "It's been sitting in that safe-deposit box since the day I got it."

"But what did you even buy it for?"

"I didn't buy it."

"Who gave it to you, then?"

She turns away on pretense of pouring the batter into a baking pan. "I couldn't say," she murmurs.

"This isn't the time for secrets, Helena," Morven says gently. "Surely you of all people know that."

Helena puts the mixing bowl down and drops into a kitchen chair with a sigh. "The plain truth is that I don't know who gave it to me. It came in the post one afternoon, years and years ago. It was addressed to me, but I had no way of knowing who'd sent it."

"Of course you could have found out who—"

Helena shakes her head. "Whoever sent it didn't want me to know. And how could I get rid of it? It may be a dabbler's book, but I still couldn't risk burning it. And it wasn't the sort of thing I could ever try to trade in at a secondhand store, now, was it?"

We have to concede that point.

"I was stuck with it. So I stowed it in the safe-deposit box and figured none of you would ever feel the need to open it."

Helena was always very good at shaming us without appearing to try.

T HAT NIGHT I go over to Justin's apartment, but I'm still feeling out of sorts. I keep thinking about *Dyvers Experiments in the Blacke Arts* and wondering if I know my own sister so well as I thought I did. I'm angry at myself for doubting her, angry with us both for having doubted her before we'd found any real cause to. But now we have, and I've got a wormy feeling that something has begun to unravel.

"I want to travel with you," he says dreamily. We are lying on his bed, *déshabillé*. "I want to hike the Inca Trail with you, and go bird-watching in the Galápagos, and rummage through the market stalls at Marrakesh. I want to drink Turkish coffee with you, and eat rice and beans for dinner with our fingers, and walk up and down the Great Wall of China. I want to go diving at the Great Barrier Reef . . ." Eventually he shakes himself out of his reverie and eyes me eyeing him with amusement. "Am I scaring you?"

"Not a bit."

"Tell me what you're thinking, then."

"I can't," I say sadly.

"What is it?" he asks. "Is it that time of the month?"

Hah! Haven't been on the rag since the Nixon administration.

"Eve?"

"Hmm?"

"Why d'you always have to be so cagey about everything?"

"Why did you have to get so serious all of a sudden?" I roll away from him and make for the loo. "Nobody likes a spoilsport. And here I thought you were perfectly plastered—"

He grabs hold of my arm, pulls me back onto the bed, and rolls over so he's on top of me. He puts his face an inch from mine and looks into my eyes. I squirm but he clamps his hands on my cheeks so I can't look away. "I mean it, Eve. You won't tell me what you do, or where you went to school, or even how old you are."

"I've already answered you on all three."

"Yeah, right: 'retired spy, St. Hildegard's, and a hundred and forty-nine'? I wish you'd stop playing with me, Eve. I Googled St. Hildegard's—there's no such school anywhere in the state."

"I told you, it closed years ago."

He holds me fast, his face colored with frustration. "Stop lying to me."

"I'm not lying to you, and don't you dare ask me to prove it. If you can't take me at my word, then you need never see me again."

I see a flash of desperation in his eyes. "Why don't we ever go to your place?"

"You know I live with my sister."

"So? Don't tell me she never brings anybody home."

I wriggle out of his grasp and sit up. "Actually, she doesn't."

"How old is she?"

"Eleven months older than I am."

"Oh ho, your parents were busy. How come I've never met her at your aunt's house?"

"She doesn't come home as often as I do."

"You won't bring me home, then? Home to New York, I mean?"

"I can't, Justin. I'm sorry."

"Where do you go the nights I don't see you?"

No place, I should say. *Stay at home. Don't even leave the chair.* But when I shrug and say, "Oh, no place, really," he can't take me at my word.

"But what do you *do?*" he cries.

Sudoku. Crochet. Dr. Scholl's foot baths.

"Tell me you're not seeing other guys."

"Is it the truth you want or a bit of reassurance?"

"Does that mean you are?"

"Why should I tell you I'm not if you won't believe it anyway?"

"I haven't gone out with another girl since I met you."

This revelation downright startles me. "Really?"

"Really," he says.

"Not even in Budapest?"

"Not even in Budapest."

"Hah! Who'd you go with to the opera, then?"

"I didn't go with anyone," he says, clearly affronted. "I went alone. Eve . . . I don't want you to see anybody else either."

"That's fine. Because I'm not."

"Swear?"

"I'll swear on the grave of your choice."

He seems satisfied at this, but after a pensive pause he adds, "Promise me you'll travel with me. Even if it's just for a weekend."

I hesitate.

"Eve?"

Well, all right. He hasn't specified when or where or for exactly how long. I can put him off. "Okay," I say. "We'll do it."

B ACK IN Cat's Hollow the following evening, Morven seems un-usually restless, taking up her knitting and setting it down again with a sigh. She picks up the red plastic View-Master I gave her for Christmas and starts flipping through the stack of paper disks with a definite sense of purpose. She chooses one, drops it in the slot, and holds the viewfinder up to her face. "Hrmmm."

I look up from the Colette novel I'm only half-reading. "What are you up to?"

"I thought perhaps if I . . ." She pulls the disk out of the slot, turns it round, reinserts it, and looks into it again. "Ah! Here we go."

"What are you looking at? Let me see that." She hands me the View-Master, and when I raise it to my eyes I see our brother-in-law sitting on the sofa in his office opposite his secretary.

"I figured I could make it work backward if I just flipped the slide."

"Brilliant, Morven! Now maybe we can get to the bottom of this. I don't suppose we could make the pictures move?"

"You tell me—you're the one who fixed it in the first place."

"Hmm." I murmur a few words, tap the plastic two times, and suddenly I can hear their long-ago conversation, their voices small and tinny. Eagerly I raise the View-Master to my eyes.

Henry's law degree in a mahogany frame hangs on the wall above a large fishbowl, in which two goldfish are sucking face above a little ceramic castle. I can't see the window, but I can hear the hustle and bustle of downtown Blackabbey. All the lights are on. It's too late; they shouldn't still be at work. Oh, but they're not working.

They're such a cliché, the pair of them: the silly little minx looking for someone to take the place of her father, and the middle-aged man too flattered to resist her attentions. As I watch this scene I keep shaking my head at the magnitude of Henry's stupidity. I'm hard-pressed to understand the attraction; she's too thin, too birdlike, and there's an eagerness and a hunger in her manner that by rights should repel him. She can't hold a candle to Helena, not in a thousand lifetimes.

"I can't help feeling as if I've ruined you for all other men," Henry is saying. I roll my eyes.

"There are no other men, Henry."

"There will be."

"There's only you."

"Oh, Belva. You shouldn't talk that way."

"Why not?"

"You know why not. I have a family. I have a wife."

Belva scowls as he mentions my sister. "You're afraid of her. I know you are."

"Afraid? Of Helena?" In Henry's look of genuine surprise I can see the signs of illness—he looks so pallid, so worn out.

Belva nods, her thin lips pursed in defiance.

"This has nothing to do with Helena." He pauses, then says almost ruefully, "Helena is perfect."

"She'd like you to think so, wouldn't she?"

Good Lord, what did Henry *see* in this pathetic girl? I glance at the fishbowl and notice something in the doorway of the little ceramic castle that definitely should not be there: an eyeball the size of a marble.

Henry shakes his head. "She knows, Belva. She knows everything—and yet she's willing to forgive me." He regards her with a look of tender sadness.

What he's about to say is already written on his face, and Belva reads it as plainly as I can. Her look of horrified panic is priceless. "No—Henry—"

"You'll be all right, Belva. I'll find you another position in town, with better hours. I promise."

Here it comes: she's turned on the tears. "I like working late," she sobs.

He pats her on the knee, a gesture of awkward affection. "You like it a little too much."

"No!"

"This is what's best for you, don't you see? The sooner we end this, the sooner you'll find a man who can offer you everything I can't."

"No, Henry!" She launches herself into him, throws her arms around his neck. "You have no idea all that I've lost, just to be near you."

He holds her at arm's length and scrutinizes her face. "What do you mean by that?"

"It doesn't matter. I love you, Henry. I love you more than she ever could."

And so what little resolve Henry possessed melts away in the blink of an eye—just like a man!—and as they embrace I decide I've seen quite enough of this.

I lower the toy from my eyes. "Did you hear all that?"

Morven nods grimly. "I'm just glad I didn't have to see it. Poor Helena!"

"There *is* something you should see, though." I hand her the View-Master. "Look at what's inside the fishbowl."

"It looks like an eyeball. It's . . . *watching* them."

"Exactly. I bet you anything Helena put it there. I saw it in the grimoire when I was flipping through it—"

"No!" Morven drops the View-Master so she can clamp her hands on her ears. "Don't tell me!"

"How to use fish eyes to spy on somebody," I shout, so she can hear me through her hands.

Morven lowers her hands. "But I don't see the harm in that—anybody would do the same in her position."

"Yes, but she told us she never used the book. Why would Helena lie to us?"

"Maybe it's a coincidence. Maybe she found out about that trick some other way."

I lift a brow as she hands me back the View-Master. "I'm going to advance to the next slide, all right?"

"It'll likely take you backward," Morven replies.

"Maybe that's just what we want." I press the orange tab a few times to advance the images, and then I see a much younger Helena chopping carrots and myself seated at the table talking to her as she works. "I'm in the kitchen with Helena. Looks to be about 1950." I tap on the plastic to set the scene in motion. ·

Helena pulls a codfish out of a greasy paper wrapper and leaves it on the counter to stare at the Eve of 1950 with its big googly eyes. "I don't like that fish," says young Eve.

Now Helena is busy flaying a giant parsnip. "Oh, are you staying for dinner now?"

"It's *looking* at me."

With an exaggerated sigh Helena drops the fish on the cutting board, draws a cleaver out of the knife block, and decapitates said codfish with an oddly triumphant flourish. Then she guts the fish, scoops the innards into a bowl with her bare hand, and sets the bowl on the floor for the tabby cat.

"Why do you have to do all that the long way? If I were you I'd be on the couch right now listening to *The Armchair Detective*."

"Henry might see."

"Tosh. It's three o'clock in the afternoon!"

The tabby cat sashays into the kitchen and briefly rubs itself against Eve's bare legs before heading for the goodie bowl on the floor.

"He hasn't been feeling well lately. I've been asking him to take an afternoon off."

"Hah! Henry will never take an afternoon off."

"I know," Helena says darkly as the Eve of 1950 watches her pry the googly eyes out of the fish head with a teaspoon and drop them in a lowball glass on the counter. *Plink, plink.*

"Ick. What did you do that for?" (Meanwhile old Eve is thinking, *Fish eyes, eh? Sometimes a two-bit spellbook is worth more than you paid for it.*)

Helena turns away from the counter, mucky teaspoon in hand. "Why *don't* you go sit on the couch and listen to the radio?"

"I could chop something," Eve replies, suddenly eager to be helpful.

"No, thank you," Helena says crisply. "It's done now." And as my sister turns back to the counter in her spotless gingham-check apron, the Eve of 1950 rises from her chair and leaves the kitchen with a look of mild affront.

Meanwhile, the Eve of today has just caught sight of something she had failed to notice at the time: the open canister of decaf Maxwell House on the counter by Helena's elbow. I gasp, and Morven grabs the View-Master and holds it up to the light.

"Do you see what I see?"

"Yes, Evelyn, I see it," she sighs.

"It was just like I said. She was harvesting those fish eyes. There they are, in the glass. And what about the coffee can?"

"You always did like a cup in the afternoon from time to time," Morven points out as she hands me back the little red toy.

"You know I don't drink decaf. I'm going to click to the next scene, all right?"

We're back in the kitchen at Harbinger House. Helena is sitting at the table opposite a man I immediately recognize as Belva's father, Julius Mettle—as slight and birdlike as his daughter, with that weight-of-the-world air about him. He always seemed like a decent enough chap, but I can tell even before I tap the plastic that he's there to make some trouble.

As always, Helena is playing the perfect hostess. "Would you like a slice of cake, Dr. Mettle? I just made it this morning."

"No, thank you, Mrs. Harbinger."

"Tea?"

"No, thank you. This is not a social call, Mrs. Harbinger. I had better make that clear straightaway."

"Oh?"

"I have come to discuss a matter that has troubled me greatly. It concerns my daughter, Belva. She has recently taken up with a group of wayward girls, who have encouraged her in behaviors I find completely inappropriate."

"I'm sorry to hear that," my sister replies, leaving the rest unsaid: *But what does your unfortunate situation have to do with me?*

"I have found things in her room, horrible things no young lady should ever have in her possession. Dead things in boxes—frogs, spiders. Strange pieces of jewelry. Occult symbols in the margins of her school notebooks."

Helena is listening with a patient attitude and raises her eyebrows when Mettle indicates that he expects her to respond. "Well—that is certainly strange. Have you considered taking her to a specialist?"

"I was rather expecting that *you* could provide some insight into the situation, Mrs. Harbinger."

"*Me?*"

"I am given to understand that you are Blackabbey's foremost practitioner of witchcraft."

"Dr. Mettle, I understand you are upset, but I can assure you that I do not keep dead vermin in my house."

"And what of the rest of it? You are a witch, are you not?"

"Have you spoken to your daughter? Has she implicated me in any way?"

"She refuses to say."

"Then what gave you to think I have anything at all to do with your daughter's activities?"

"I won't stand for this!" he cries. "You can't sit here and tell me you have no idea the influence you have over these girls!"

"Influence?" Helena lets out an incredulous little laugh. "I have never conversed or corresponded with your daughter. And seeing as my daughters have all left the high school, I doubt that any of them have ever spoken with her either. Your daughter has never been inside this house. Frankly, I'm not sure what it is you expect me to refrain from doing."

Mettle seems to be formulating his next move, so Helena goes on. "I hope you won't take offense at what I'm about to say, Dr. Mettle. I know that your daughter lost her mother at an early age, and you must not underestimate the difficulty that motherless children face as they move through adolescence. After all, one cannot expect even the best of fathers to fulfill the roles of both parents." Helena reaches for the ambrosia cake and cuts him a slice. "I must say I admire your determination to do right by your daughter. I lost my own father when I was very young."

"And just how long ago *was* that, Mrs. Harbinger?"

"I was only three years of age. It was a long time before your family arrived in Blackabbey."

"A *very* long time, I think," Dr. Mettle replies with a meaningful glare. "And if you don't mind my asking, what was your family name?"

"I really wish you would have a slice of cake, Dr. Mettle. Let us be civil."

The botanist shakes his head. "I know how you lot do things around here. I've watched you. You're all too skilled in the art of distraction, and I tell you, I won't be waylaid by food, conversation, or anything else you try to ply me with." Mettle leans in, pointing a finger. "I know what you are!"

Helena shrugs, still smiling pleasantly. "Positively nonplussed?"

He pounds the table with his fist. "I'll expose you."

"Are you threatening me, Dr. Mettle?" Helena speaks as if she's asking if he would like another cup of tea.

"If you don't keep well away from my daughter, believe me—I won't hesitate."

"That is easily done, as I've said, since I have had no contact with your daughter in the first place."

Without further comment Dr. Mettle rises from his seat, puts on his hat, and stalks out of the house.

"How odd," Morven says as I place the View-Master on the sofa between us. "She never told me Dr. Mettle came to see her."

Fawkes's words come back to me now, try as I might to suppress the memory: *Them two deaths was linked somehow, I just know it.* I don't say anything, I just look at her. Morven stows the View-Master in a drawer on the end table, purses her lips, and resumes her knitting.

Some Dread Malady of the Soul

22.

Autumn 1944

AFTER THE liberation of Paris they claimed there was no more work for us. They even tried to shoehorn Jonah into a desk job. There was no need for new agents in Cairo, Istanbul, or anywhere else, they said. I couldn't begin to imagine Jonah on his took shifting papers all day—and more to the point, neither could he. I saw how it maddened him to be sidelined like this, but I felt sure a new opportunity would present itself; I could do as I liked, of course, but I didn't want to go back to Germany without him. No matter how fluent we were, or how well we could claim to understand the quirks and customs of the German people, a mission to Nazi Germany was tantamount to suicide. At least that's what the Brits said.

The Americans, on the other hand, were willing to try it.

We were only cooling our heels in London for a couple of weeks, but to Jonah it felt like the better part of a lifetime. At the end of that fortnight, we found ourselves in a snug at the Monkey's Uncle, where he got so pickled he said they'd have treated him better if he'd died in a death camp.

I'd had a dream the night before that three old men were playing a card game under a green lamp. One had a cigarette tucked behind his ear, out of which sprouted a little thatch of gray hair; another tapped his feet to a tune he heard only in his head. The game ended and one of the losers stood up and threw his cards on the table. "That's the last time I play a game with you, Charlie. You're a fink."

"See you tomorrow, Ed!" Charlie called gleefully after him.

Well, when my dreams come to pass it means I can expect a tall dark stranger within the hour. The old men set up their card game as Jonah drank his whisky, and Ed told Charlie to shove it in just the words he'd used in the dream. I told Jonah to hush, that I'd had a portent and I felt sure our luck would turn on a dime.

He frowned. "Turn on a dime?"

"Turn on tuppence, then."

I heard a coin drop nearby, and a man bent over to pick it up just beside our snug.

When he straightened up I saw a bespectacled gent, somewhere past forty, wearing a Fair Isle waistcoat under his jacket. He might have been a professor. "Did somebody drop a coin?" he asked in a Boston accent.

I smiled as I shook my head. "Do sit down," I said. Jonah was looking at him with great interest, his empty whisky glass, thankfully, forgotten.

"Name's Howard," the man said as he slid into the booth. "I took the liberty of ordering another round of whisky sodas."

THE GRIMM brothers got most of their fairy tales from the Harz mountains, where even the sleepiest villages had their Walpurgisnacht parades of "witch" masks and mock sacrifices of rag dolls and china babies. But it wasn't all fiddle-faddle; every so often I'd hear a tantalizing rumor of a ring forged of Harz silver that could render you invisible. You'd slip it on your right-hand ring finger with the stone turned inward, look into the mirror and touch your hand to your throat, and if you couldn't see the ring then you couldn't be seen at all. Would've made a great shortcut.

Here, too, was a fortress inside a mountain where machines were made that could obliterate whole city blocks. Oh, how I wish I could say it was only another one of those horrid fairy tales—but the ogres who ran this death factory were all too real. The Allies had found their first complex on the Baltic Sea, where the V-1 buzz bombs were made, and blown it to smithereens. So they'd built this new subterranean plant, Mittelwerk, on the southern fringe of the Harz—and it was bomb-proof. Our objective was the same as it had been at the V-1 depots in France: to learn the supply routes and transit schedules and bomb the hell out of the railway lines, so that the new generation of rocket bombs, the V-2s, could never reach their targets.

With the mission to Germany we were starting afresh; we were under a new authority, and our code names for radio and courier transmissions, aliases, and cover stories were all reassigned. My code name was Marvel—rather fitting, and I don't mind saying so. My alias was Uta Braun, age thirty-two, widow, no children, formerly employed as a governess in Quedlinburg, and I'd been given the name and details of a local family that had left for Switzerland. As I say, we were in fairy-tale country now, ironically enough. Whenever we would pass a shop window full of witch ornaments whittled out of wood, each hooked nose topped with a huge knob for a wart, Jonah would laugh and say we'd arrived at my ancestral home.

Howard had also brought on board our demolition man, Fisher, but we had a new radio operator: Hans Grüssner, a German in his middle thirties recruited from the socialist workers' union in London. His wife and two daughters were living in a one-room flat in Brixton, and he fretted endlessly about how regularly they could expect to receive his OSS salary. I had my doubts about Grüssner—he was just the type to shriek if he spotted a mouse—but Jonah was so eager for departure that I decided to say nothing.

. . .

WE PARACHUTED blind into a field outside Quedlinburg in October of 1944. Once we'd arrived in town Hans was meant to
bring us to his cousins' house, where he hoped we might stay while we
got our bearings. His cousin, however, coldly informed us that she
could only shelter Hans, and after a night in the choir loft of a church
down the road, we three—Jonah, Fisher, and myself—had to scramble
for a better place to hide.

At midday I decided to find us a temporary safe house by way of
the local tavern, where I felt sure I would encounter someone we
could trust. I spotted a man with my father's face here and there and
had to wait until they'd finished their beers and left the place before I
could make any overtures. Finally I struck up a conversation with an
elderly man, a farmer, seated at a table beside me and found him willing to shelter us for a few nights in his barn. Through him Jonah
began to make contacts with other locals disaffected with the Nazi
regime.

He hadn't yet had a chance to get word to Hans of our whereabouts, and it was a good thing, too, for later that week I learned from
a shopkeeper that Hans had been arrested. The radio was more than
likely discovered as well. The life expectancy of a radio operator was
six weeks; Hans had lasted six days. I wondered if that statistic took
into account the time one spent in prison.

Howard had told us that in a pinch we could rely on a man named
Hoppe, whose brother was working as a translator at Bletchley Park;
the only problem was that the Hoppes' farmstead was on the far side
of the mountains.

Getting all three of us there posed a considerable problem. I
couldn't work more than a pair of shape-shifts at a time, and as I say,
riding the loo flue in a war zone is out of the question unless one's life
depends on it. If it had been only Jonah and myself, I could have
turned us both to owls so we could fly the whole way, but the chances
of Fisher making it to Bad Harzburg on his own were, as he put it,

"piss-poor." So I decided to risk the train, with a mouse in either pocket. The Nazis wouldn't suspect a woman traveling on her own.

In retrospect, it wasn't such a good idea. The conductor greeted me as he took my ticket, but as he returned it I caught him looking down at my coat pocket with a frown. There was a chance I could pass myself off as an eccentric who kept mice for pets, but Jonah's life was literally in my hand if I took him out to make such an explanation to the conductor. The man might bat him out of my hand and crush him underfoot. So I laid my hand over the twitching wool as casually as I could, and he nodded at me as he left the compartment.

But a minute later I ducked my head out the door of our compartment and spotted him conferring with an SS officer down the corridor. Right then, we'd have to take the flue. There are some times it's worth betting on the wild card that is a moving toilet, and this was certainly one of them.

I ran toward the WC on the far side of the carriage, and a second later the SS officer was in pursuit. I closed the door, flipped the latch, pulled the mice out of my pockets, and in a twinkling there were three of us crammed into the tiny stall. Fisher was swearing like a sailor with his hands over his eyes. Jonah glanced down at the train tracks passing swiftly beneath the hole at the bottom of the toilet bowl, then looked at me doubtfully. The latch groaned as the Nazi threw himself against the door.

"The general vicinity of Hoppe's Farm, Bad Harzburg, please," I said, and took the hands of both men in a firm grip.

I AWOKE IN the morning to a cock's crow in the distance and a crisp breeze wafting through an open window. I opened one eye and found Jonah seated in the corner of a sparsely furnished bedroom, the fluttering curtains occasionally hiding his face. He was gazing at me as if something had gone horribly wrong.

I sprang up in bed like Finnegan's corpse. "What is it?" I hissed (for I had no idea yet how safe we were). "What's happened?"

He didn't answer, just sighed and rubbed his eyes.

Then I had an inkling. "How long have I been asleep?"

"Three days, Eve." Clearly he'd been bursting to scold me for the last seventy-two hours. *Three whole days.*

"Oh. Is that all?"

"This isn't the time for levity. I was afraid you wouldn't wake up."

"I can't help it, Jonah. I get so tired."

"Tired? You were comatose!"

I rolled away from him and faced the wall, where a birch tree cast dancing shadows on faded floral paper. "I should have rolled you in a carpet and stuck you in the boot, just like they did to you last time," I grumbled.

He rose from his chair, sat down on the bed beside me, and reached for my hand. "Oh, Eve, you know I'm grateful for all you've done. But . . ."

I turned over and looked at him. "Where are we, anyway? And where's Fisher?"

"He's safe. He's staying at a farm up the road."

"You mean we're here?"

He nodded. "But not without a fair bit of trouble, I can tell you that. We landed in some farmer's outhouse thirty miles southeast of here, and you were in a heap at our feet. I had to stay with you in the woods while Fisher found a car. It was a small miracle there was enough petrol in the tank to get us here."

"Oh, that won't be any trouble now that I'm awake."

He only glared at me in response.

"I did try to tell you, you know."

"I know you did." He stroked my cheek. "But I couldn't have woken you if our lives depended on it. That concerns me."

"It's my tragic flaw," I replied with a twitching mouth. "Every heroine has one." He gave me one more reproving look before he got up from the bed and left the room. There was fresh water in the bowl and a sliver of lye soap on a washstand in the corner, and I splashed my face and lathered my forearms before I followed Jonah downstairs.

No one else was in the house; I could sense that as soon as I opened the bedroom door. I made my way quietly down a narrow wooden staircase, through a bright kitchen with a massive hearth—he'd left a slab of bread and butter and a steaming mug of something for me on the broad butcher's-block kitchen table—and into a sitting room where Jonah stood looking out a window into the yard. The place smelled faintly of pipe smoke. There were photographs lined up along the mantelpiece, and a needlepoint sampler lay half-finished in a wicker basket on the floor by an armchair.

And on the wall above the chair was a framed embroidery, a marvelously intricate scene of a midnight tryst between a knight and a golden-haired maiden. *Tristan und Isolde* read the embroidered caption.

I laughed quietly, and he turned around and looked at me. I decided not to tell him why I was laughing. We were damned lovers if ever there were.

I T TURNED out our new home had been forcibly abandoned the year before. No one in the area knew what had become of their neighbors, but nobody expected them to return. People were afraid of the place, so they stayed well away from it. It was the perfect safe house.

Albrecht Hoppe lived with his mother and eight-year-old daughter, Adelaide, a quarter of a mile from there. We arrived on his front step at nightfall and were quickly ushered inside. Jonah had met them three days before, and it was Albrecht who had helped him settle me into bed upstairs at the empty farmhouse.

The future of his farm seemed bleak indeed; that year's harvest had been confiscated to feed the Wehrmacht, and the family had very little to live on. Albrecht's youngest brother had been killed on the Russian front, and his other brother, as I say, had long since fled to London to work for the Allies. Hoppe had been brought in for questioning on multiple occasions, and each time he'd said, truthfully, that he'd had absolutely no contact with his brother since his departure. Owing to his family's sacrifice, the Nazis were inclined to believe him. There was a portrait of Hitler on the sitting room mantelpiece, and on that first visit it was all I could do not to spring up and cast it into the fire. "It's only for show," Jonah told me later that night. "Just try not to look at it."

I found an opportunity for a new cover in Albrecht's elderly mother, who was suffering from an eye infection so acute that I found it difficult to look at her directly. The skin round her eyes was covered in sores. When I asked, Albrecht told me that the condition was chronic and that she was often in a great deal of discomfort.

I suggested she might benefit from the services of a private nurse, and Frau Hoppe looked at me dubiously. "But do you have any experience?"

I supposed there was little use trying to make her understand that I would be *posing* as her nurse, and that it was her dumb luck I happened to be trained. "Actually, I do. I was trained at a hospital in the city."

"Berlin?"

It was only a tiny fib. I nodded, and she was satisfied. Despite her ailment, Frau Hoppe was quick to laugh and generally in high spirits. Between outbreaks, she would sing as she went about her work in the kitchen, and over the two months they sheltered us I grew quite fond of her. I sometimes made an ointment that would ease her discomfort, plucking all the herbs I needed from her window box as if they'd grown there without my help.

Jonah spent that first day exploring the outbuildings on the vacant farmstead and found several places where we might hide the radio. There was a tiny crawl space above the milking shed, accessible only by a trapdoor in the corner stall; we thought that might prove useful at some point.

Though the house was isolated, we thought it best to sleep in the stable. It was a massive structure, with two stories, and the whole place still had that pleasantly musty smell of hay and leather. There was a row of windows on either side of the loft, so that during the day the great open space was flooded with dust motes twirling in the sunlight. There was a door to the loft on the upper story, but the outside staircase had been removed so the wood panels on the side of the building were discolored where the stairs had been. The owner, rest his soul, had nailed several planks across the door on the inside so that no one could open it by mistake.

The Hoppes were starved for company, Adelaide and her grandmother especially. First the child sought us out in the daytime, then her grandmother began to linger after she'd brought the food basket. She'd sit and watch us eat our dinner, and it wasn't long before she was telling us about the family who would, in all likelihood, never return there. They had had a child about Addie's age, she said. She hoped he was safe.

A FTER HANS's capture, Jonah served as organizer as well as radio operator—through Morven's locket, I'd been able to arrange for an arms drop that also included rations and a new radio. Unlike Jonah, I could afford to do much of my work by day. Frau Hoppe was fond of napping in the afternoons, and once she was sleeping soundly I would make myself into a hawk to observe the activity along roads and railroad lines in and out of the mountains. If I wanted to eavesdrop, I would turn myself into a barn cat or a pigeon. I gathered still more intelligence from members of the resistance, though they would never have identified themselves as such.

There was a limit to what most men were willing to do, and some nights it drove me mad. Hoppe came to the stable one night with our dinner of sausages and boiled potatoes, and we invited him up to our humble table in the hayloft for a spot of whisky. He was plainly uncomfortable, but Jonah was making a heartfelt effort to put him at ease.

Perhaps I shouldn't have, but I pressed him. The next time he went into town, I said, he should keep an ear out for any talk of *Werwölfe*.

He was astonished. "Werewolves?"

"Die Bandenkämpfer," I said. "The Nazi guerrillas. They are expecting an Allied invasion, so there are men preparing for it now up in those camps in the woods." I suspected most of the "werewolves" were little more than schoolboys, but it was better to err on the side of overestimation. "I'd like to know how many they've recruited."

Albrecht didn't answer.

"Will you listen out for me?"

"People don't talk of such things. Not at the market. Not anywhere."

"People always talk of such things."

"You are mistaken, *Fraulein*."

I slammed my mug on the table, folded my arms, and glared at him. *"When?"* I said, rather more loudly than I ought. *"When* will you resist?"

Jonah took hold of my arm, and I yelped like a startled hound. "Remember yourself, Uta," he said in English. "This man is sheltering us." After a moment he said more gently, "He *is* resisting."

Over my shoulder I looked at the farmer seated on an overturned milk crate. He was staring at the floor as he swished the last drops of whisky around the tin cup in his work-worn hands. He couldn't have been more than forty-five, but suddenly he seemed ancient as a prophet. I wanted to rage at him, to make him understand that it wasn't enough to keep his fist in his pocket.

"Everyone capable of active resistance is dead," Jonah said quietly. He paused. "Or will be, shortly."

"*He's* capable."

"No, he's not." Jonah spoke with the patience of a schoolteacher. "And you've got to accept it."

Things were awkward between myself and Hoppe from then on, though he seemed to bear me no ill will. The next time I visited his house, the portrait of the Führer had disappeared from the mantelpiece.

OUR FIRST success came in late November, when Allied fighter planes bombed a train carrying forty V-2s from the Mittelwerk plant. All the rockets were shipped back to the factory for scrap.

I'd never seen Jonah so energized, so full of purpose, though that's not to say he wasn't well aware of the danger we were in. There was a blind dog, a Saint Bernard, at the next farm up from the Hoppes', and whenever I laid eyes on the poor thing I knew there'd be a German direction-finding car out that night. On those nights Jonah couldn't use the wireless telegraph set, and I warned the Hoppes well in advance to keep their radio hidden. They assumed I had come by the intelligence somewhere in town that day and didn't question me.

I would come back after midnight, and once I'd given him my report—and provided there'd been no portent that day—Jonah would pull out his wireless case and set to work. I fell asleep listening to his nimble forefinger making a soft *rat-a-tat-tat* on the transmitter. Sometimes we'd climb up onto the roof of the stable and watch the sunrise, bundled up together in a scratchy wool blanket.

Our conversations inevitably hinged on our families, our ambitions, our regrets, all the choices that had led us to this very moment: perched precariously on an old tiled roof that might give way anytime, in the freezing dark of a hostile country. We looked up at the great celestial wilderness, and I told him which stars were dead and which were dying.

"How can you possibly know that?"

I shrugged. "I just do." I'd dallied with an astronomer in Berlin, and when I started pointing out which stars I believed were dead, he'd looked into his telescope and told me I was right.

Other nights we'd see the Allied planes flying in formation on their way to Berlin, and when the moonlight caught the tinfoil they dropped to jam the German radar, it looked like a meteor shower on the horizon.

It would have lent a nice shape to this story if I could tell you he promised to marry me someday, but he didn't. It wasn't the thought of Patricia that kept him from it, or the knowledge that we would not age in tandem. I suppose part of him just *knew* somehow that he wasn't going to live long enough.

He asked me one night if I'd ever wanted children. "Not especially," I said. "I have enough trouble taking care of myself, you know." He laughed at how true this was. "Why—did you?"

He nodded. "We tried for a few months before I left."

I felt a wave of nausea at the thought of Jonah making love to another woman hoping for a child. To me Patricia was a spectral figure, ever the dark shape at the foot of the bed—provided there was a bed to sleep in.

He drew out his tobacco pouch and began to roll a cigarette. "Of course, looking back on it now, I'm glad it didn't happen. That's the problem with marriage," he said as he licked the paper. "It's only after the fact that you become intimately acquainted with one another's faults. I have my share, Patricia has hers. Some faults you can live with, and others . . ." He lit the cigarette and handed it to me.

"And others, you can't," I said.

He looked at me and nodded.

"What are the faults you can't live with?"

"Patricia is . . . well, she's exceptionally bright. Bookish, you know." I handed it back, and he took a long, pensive drag.

"What's the good of knowing half a dozen languages if you never use any of them?"

"That's it, exactly. She belongs in that office with all her maps and card indexes." He paused. "All brains and no guts."

"Surely you knew that beforehand."

He looked sad. "I thought it wouldn't matter."

"Or do you think perhaps you weren't cut out for it?"

"Not cut out for marriage?" Plainly this notion had never occurred to him.

"Halves one's rights and doubles one's duties, you know."

"No," he said. "It's not that I wasn't cut out for it. I loved Patricia—I still do—and I can't say our marriage was a mistake. But . . ."

I didn't press him there; there was no need to say any more.

"I wonder about you sometimes," he said after a brief silence.

"What about me?"

"You've no nerves at all. You never cry, you never panic." He paused. "How can I be so in love with a girl who seems so inhuman?"

I sat up abruptly, shivered, and turned away from him so he wouldn't see my face. "I *do* feel," I said, looking up at the sky. It had grown so cold all of a sudden. "I feel plenty."

"Oh, darling," he said as he reached for me. "I didn't mean it—I know you do. You just don't show it, do you?"

"Be fair, Jonah. It has been known to happen, on occasion."

He smiled sympathetically. "Like now?"

I didn't answer, just stared out at the forest and the mountains and the blooming light in the east. "I'll never understand it," I said finally. "How you can sit here thousands of miles away from your wife and talk about her the way you do. What's the difference between how you love me now and how you loved her then?"

"I don't know."

"Is it different?"

"Of course it is! But why are you so hurt? You've loved other men."

"I didn't love them," I replied. "Flings are one thing. Marriage is meant to be for keeps. You must have thought you knew, when you married her."

"This is different," he replied. "I know it now—because of Patricia." He didn't say anything for a while. "Just think of it: if I hadn't jumped off that train, I would never have known you." He pulled me tight and tucked my head under his chin. I felt his heart beating against my cheek. "*This* is for keeps, Eve."

So you see, he never asked me to marry him. But he didn't have to.

A s THE nights got colder Frau Hoppe started inviting us to pass some evenings with her family. Would we care to listen to the BBC?

Two German soldiers had passed through a few weeks back and had offered some of their rations in exchange for milk and bread. Addie showed me two packages of *Lakritzen*—ropes of salty licorice—and four fifty-gram bars of phony chocolate.

"It is foul stuff," she told me, and I couldn't help laughing. "No wonder the soldiers are so bad tempered. Before the war Papa used to bring us real chocolate from Berlin. Will we ever have real chocolate again, Frau Uta?"

"Yes, Addie," I said. "I'm quite sure you will. Say, why don't you go over there and look in my knapsack? The front pocket, yes, that's right."

The little girl was thrilled to find a stash of Cadbury's ration chocolate, all the labels removed of course.

Jonah looked at me in amazement. "Where did you get that?"

"A warehouse in Kent," I whispered back.

"It's real chocolate, Oma!"

"It can't be. Let me taste a little." Frau Hoppe broke off a piece and popped it in her mouth. Her eyes rolled back in her head, her eyelids fluttered, and she let out a little groan of pleasure. Addie giggled and reached for the wrapper, but her grandmother slipped the rest of the chocolate into her apron pocket and swatted the little girl's hand away.

"You mustn't have any more, Addie. It is bad for your teeth."

"You can't fool me, Oma," the little girl said good-naturedly. "You want it all for yourself."

Her grandmother broke into a guilty grin before relenting, and between the two of them they devoured the bar in seconds flat.

"Is there any more?"

"Addie!" her grandmother hissed. "Don't be rude, child." But Frau Hoppe caught my eye, and plainly she was wondering the same thing. I nodded to Addie, who eagerly plunged her hand into the rucksack pocket once more.

"How did you fit all that chocolate in there?" Frau Hoppe cried in delight as she tore off the foil wrapper.

When their sweet teeth were satisfied at last, Addie pulled a string of marionettes out of her little toy chest. The pride of her collection was a girl puppet with a dirndl dress and blond ringlets made of real hair. It wasn't a juju, but the craftsmanship was admirable all the same. Addie amused herself, and Jonah, by seating the pretty puppet on his knee and making cooing sounds. But when her father began pacing in front of the sitting room window, we knew it was time to go.

A NOTHER NIGHT, soon after that, Albrecht let Jonah use his razor. We were in an upstairs bedroom that hadn't been slept in for a long time; there was dust on the furniture and the colors of the patchwork quilt on the bed were all too crisp.

Addie had brought up a bowl of hot water, and there were a large mirror, a badger-brush, and a cake of soap on the dresser. "Do you ever wonder what you'll look like when you're old?" I murmured as I watched him lather his cheeks.

"Sure I do."

I watched him for a while more as he passed the blade over the contours of his face. "Would you like to see?"

He paused midstroke and turned to look at me. He looked positively boyish then, returned to the time in every person's young life when one is desperate to know, *now now now*, how it will all turn out.

I bade him turn back to the mirror, and with a few words I began our transformation. I made myself, too: the skin round my eyes grew thin and fragile as rice paper, and the color faded from my hair until it was white as snow. I even sprouted a few chin hairs for good measure.

Jonah was giggling like a schoolgirl—the hair grew out of his nose and ears, and his eyebrows became thick as caterpillars. His face had changed, too: despite the sagging flesh, its chiseled lines were becoming even more so. Then he tried to bare his pearly whites and discovered he no longer had any. "Hey! What happened to my teeth?"

I laughed, and at that moment we both heard a board creak on the landing outside. I turned around to find the door ajar and Addie standing in the hallway staring at us. She had seen our faces in the mirror, and she was terrified.

"Don't be afraid, Addie. Nothing has changed—I'm still your friend."

She hesitated. Fear and wonder fought for mastery of her sweet little face. "Are you a fairy?"

I felt Jonah's eyes on me as I knelt on the floor and grasped her hands. "Yes, dear," I said gravely. "I'm one of many. We are trying to help end the war."

Addie looked confused. "But fairies don't live in *our* world," she said earnestly.

"Who told you that?"

"Oma did. Oma says there's a magic tree on the mountain with a little door at the bottom and that's how you come here. Is that so?"

"No, dear."

"Oh. Which world do you come from, then?"

"This one, same as yours," I said, and when I glanced at Jonah I had to wonder what he was thinking. Addie was looking at me expectantly.

"You don't believe me?"

She shook her head.

"I come from America," I said. "I came across the ocean."

"I knew it!" the little girl cried. I only realized later that she had probably never laid eyes on the sea. She pointed to the mirror. "Can you show me?"

"Show you?"

She paused. "Will I . . . will I be pretty?" As she said this she cast a quick glance at Jonah and turned back to me, blushing like a girl twice her age.

I laughed as I petted her hair. I couldn't afford to indulge her—shouldn't have been playing with the mirror to begin with. "Of course you will, *Schnuckelchen*. We don't need to trick a mirror to see that."

I HAD SWORN Adelaide to secrecy, but I ought to have known better; there's a reason why children make the best spies of all. They've no inkling when it comes to the consequences of their rambling stories, their eagerness to share and be praised for it. Addie had been taught that the Nazis were bad men and that she should never speak to them—we could only cross our fingers and hope she'd never be tested—but she couldn't help confiding everything in her Oma.

The next evening Addie arrived without the dinner basket. "Papa says you're to come to our house for dinner tonight," she said breathlessly. "He says to ask for your help. Oma is sick."

"I knew it," Frau Hoppe breathed as I ventured into her bedroom. The fug in the room was terrible. "I knew your pocket couldn't hold so many bars of chocolate," she said as I opened the window. "It was magic. I *knew* it."

"I haven't the faintest idea what you're on about, Frau Hoppe." I turned from the window to look at her then and gasped. The candle-light flickered over her long pallid face. She'd had an outbreak of sores, and I could hardly see the whites of her eyes. It must have been unbearably painful just to open them.

I made her close her eyes and said I'd be back in a moment. Ten minutes later I sat down on the bed beside her with a jar of freshly made ointment.

She was agitated, fidgeting excitedly as I dipped a clean cloth into the mixture. "Is this the magic unguent which gives the fairy sight?"

They may have found me out, but I had no intention of satisfying their curiosity. After all: *I shall always practice discretion and make every effort not to reveal my true nature to persons ill equipped to understand.* "No," I said shortly as I dabbed round her eyes. "It's kitchen lard."

THE HOPPES passed their days in silent dissent, but many other German families were still living fully inside the illusion. The fac-tory complex on the Baltic Sea had been entirely self-contained, with housing estates and schools for the families of the scientists and engi-neers employed there, but there could be no such arrangements made in the bowels of a mountain, so the wives and children of Mittelwerk em-ployees were quartered in towns along the outskirts of the Harz. Many families were living in Wernigerode, a charming town of half-timbered houses painted in cheerful colors; it was as safe, or unsafe, a place as any. In Wernigerode we would carry out our most dangerous mission yet.

The Nazis had taken over the *Schloss* overlooking the town, mostly for administrative use, but now they were planning a soiree on New Year's Eve for the engineers and their families. If we could infiltrate this party, locate the most important men, and open their heads as I had done to all those Jerries back on the Rue de Suffren, we had a shot at shutting down the complex and liberating all who were enslaved inside it. I felt sure, then, that the war in Europe would be effectively over.

Here is how we would do it. On the thirtieth of December the Allies would bomb the Nordhausen railway line, the primary supply route to Mittelwerk. There would be twenty-four casualties on that afternoon train, among them two Nazis from the Armaments Ministry, a Dr. Schafer and his secretary, who had been en route to Wernigerode. A beldame from Berlin would pass along their identity cards and documentation, and another Resistance member would send a telegram to Wernigerode SS headquarters explaining that Dr. Schafer and his secretary, Fraulein Gross, had been delayed in the capital and would arrive instead on the following afternoon. It would be two days before Wernigerode could be notified that the doctor and his assistant had actually died on that train. We would impersonate them at the New Year's Eve ball at the *Schloss,* and if we carried it off it would be our biggest accomplishment yet.

Lord of the Slippy

23.

> They baptized their toads, dressed them in black velvet,
> put little bells on their paws, and made them dance.
>
> —Grillot de Givry, *Witchcraft, Magic and Alchemy*

O NE MORNING in early June I happen upon an advertisement in the *Little Hammersley Courier* for Nieuw Amsterdam's 384th Annual Summer Solstice Masquerade. We've attended it only once, a very long time ago, and I wonder aloud if it isn't time we blew the dust off our dancing shoes.

"Are you thinking of taking Justin?" Morven asks.

"I was thinking of taking *you*."

"Hah! Fat chance."

"Come on, it's only one night. Just think what a bunch of sad sacks we'll be at the Peacocks' house that weekend, with all the preparations and all the fun snatched out from under us. Won't you be glad of a distraction?"

In the end I persuade her, of course, and then I ring Justin and tell him to rent a tux. These balls are always full of ordinary men—otherwise whom would we have to dance with?

J USTIN MAKES charmingly stilted chitchat on the cab ride uptown. "Funny how we've only just met, isn't it, Morven? Eve's told me hardly anything about you."

"Oh?" She's promised to say as little as possible tonight. I don't want her letting on they *have* met before.

"How come you weren't there at Christmas? I thought for sure I'd meet you then."

"Oh, I was there. I think Eve was doing her best to keep us apart," she replies with a not-so-convincing giggle.

Justin sidesteps that one. "So what do you do?"

My sister turns to me and whispers, "What do *you* do?"

"He knows I'm a lady of leisure," I reply.

"She told me she's retired," Justin says, eyeing me warily.

"And you're wondering if that's a euphemism, eh?" Morven yelps when I pinch her bare arm. "I'm . . ." She pauses. "I work at an art museum. Human resources."

"Really! That's so cool. Which one?"

"Which one what?"

"Which art museum?"

I shoot her a look.

"Oh. Uh . . . the Frick."

"I haven't been there yet, but I've been meaning to go. Well anyway, I'm sure we'll have plenty to talk about. I'm an antiques dealer."

"I know," says she.

The Astor mansion—Astor mansion number *two*, that is—is so ideally situated on Central Park East at Sixty-fifth Street that ninety years later the beldames of Boston Avenue still laugh at the folly of the men who tore it down.

These urban manors of the Gilded Age were built with the same degree of forethought that goes into the making of a sandcastle, and knocked down again with that same fickle impulse. They've thrown Nieuw Amsterdam's Annual Summer Solstice Masquerade here since the mansion was demolished in 1926.

We get out of the cab a block from the manse, and I draw a blindfold out of my evening purse. "What's this for?" he says as I tie it over his eyes. "Are we partying with the CIA?"

"Humor me," I say as I kiss him on the cheek. "It's more fun this way." Temple Emanu-El currently occupies the site at 1 East Sixty-fifth Street, but we can't have Justin thinking we're going to a party at the synagogue. Morven and I lead him to a gated side entrance. A strange little man, suspiciously simian in appearance, silently takes our tickets and opens the gate for us.

In the foyer we can hear the strains of a six-piece orchestra, and once I've pulled off the blindfold Justin looks around him in awe. The place is a trove of oil paintings, oriental carpets, and figures in bronze—though of course all the great gilded mirrors have been removed for the occasion, so that nobody can spoil anybody else's fun. But Morven manages to catch her reflection in a piece of tabletop glass and gives it a tiny disbelieving smile. "I feel so . . . *exposed*," she says, though her dress shows very little cleavage. It's her own face she isn't used to, all the lines and spots erased for the evening. Morven hasn't looked so young since she *was* this young. I even had to show her how to lose the geriatric gait. My own frock is vintage, of course—a low-backed gown of luminous peacock-blue velvet—and round my neck is the Janus pendant Justin got me for Christmas. Arm in arm, the three of us stride into the ballroom, the hem of my gown rustling against the doorjamb.

Oh, how the chandelier shimmers and the wall sconces glow, and how slow and languid the movements of the dancers. I look at Justin, and for a moment a pang of sadness mutes my delight. I nearly have to bite my tongue to keep from asking if he can recall the last time we found ourselves in a ballroom. Better for him if he doesn't.

Motes of glitter catch the light as they fall on the crowd. Justin eyes the hapless young men in codpieces and tricorn hats and murmurs in my ear, "Was I supposed to come in costume?"

"If I'd told you to wear stockings you'd never have come," I reply as we follow Morven to the banquet tables.

And the food! Even I've never seen such a spread in all my life. There are so many platters of roast fowl—goose and quail and pheasant and even peacock, with feathers reattached!—that one can't help wondering if the chef raided the aviary at the Central Park Zoo. Stranger still is the carnival grub: the illuminated signs above the popcorn and cotton candy machines, girls in satin corsets and pillbox caps handing out boxes of buttered popcorn and whirls of cotton candy on wooden sticks. There are brass fountains of champagne and dark chocolate and crystal bowls heaped with strawberries big as your fist, trays upon trays of canapés and bonbons and fancy Italian sausages, oysters dripping with white wine and butter, glistening slabs of braised beef in aspic. There's even a three-foot Ferris wheel made out of carrot sticks and bell peppers—and it moves! Justin stares at it, open-mouthed, the rest of the food forgotten in his childlike wonder. Eventually we heap a few plates high with hors d'oeuvres and find a half-curtained alcove from which to people-watch.

After a few minutes' critical survey, I conclude that we look as well as anyone here. There are more than a few like us, of course, but at a party like this, where nobody knows you, it doesn't matter what you look like during the day. I'm sure some of the loveliest girls here are past the two hundred mark, and lucky for them you can't tell who's who. It's quite a thrill for us old birds, cashing in on chips we've lost long since.

At one point I leave the two of them chatting in the alcove so I can get some more munchies, and when I come back I linger behind the curtain so I can hear what they're saying about me.

"Oh yes," Morven is saying. "Eve always had a lot of beaux. You might well be one of the nicest. I wouldn't know for sure, since I never get the chance to meet most of them. Yes," she says with the disapproving sigh of a maiden aunt, which of course she is, "life is all a great drama to Eve. Want to know the first word she spoke as a child?"

I can't make out Justin's reply.

"'Mine,'" Morven says. "That was her first word: *mine*. Then there was the time she sat on a wild turkey . . ."

Justin nearly chokes on his chicken skewer. "What?!"

"No. I just said that for the benefit of our *Eves*dropper."

I part the curtain, plop down on the sofa between the two of them, and give Morven a piece of my elbow. That's the last word she'll say to him tonight, if I've got anything to do with it.

The hours pass in a blur of waltzes, hook-nosed masks, and trays of fizzing champagne flutes bobbing and weaving among the crowd. Justin tells me over and over how he's having the time of his life, and he gives me another thrill of happiness every time he politely declines to dance with another girl. Morven dances a few, too, with borrowed partners, and I can't help tittering when I spot her with a man in a foofy pirate blouse. We drink and we eat and we dance some more.

Sometime after midnight the buzz begins to subside, however, and we wrinkle our noses at the sounds and smells of excess. The food trays look picked-over, the cotton candy machine has gone dark, and the tablecloths are smeared with grease because the beldames who put on this party are more than likely using their magic for other purposes now. Even the carrot-stick Ferris wheel looks like someone's been gnawing at it. I begin to notice the glazed expressions of the gay young men I laughed at a few hours ago, the awfully pointed eyeteeth of the girls leading them by the hand into those cozy curtained alcoves.

"You know something?" my sister murmurs in my ear. "This is hardly more dignified than a Roman orgy."

"Or any other kind of orgy, for that matter."

I am reminded of why we ordinarily never go to events like this. These balls are great fun, don't get me wrong, and reveling in the opulence is always amusing for an hour or so. But I feel increasingly uneasy in the presence of these men, these hapless pretty-boy ninnies, because this party has turned into one tremendous joke at their expense. Every one of these men is going to wake up alone in his bed tomorrow afternoon with the most painful headache of his life and only the haziest memories of tonight's revelry.

I decide I do not wish to know, do not like, the women who organize this ball every year; yet when I look at Justin, who has already consumed two full bottles of champagne and wears the court jester's grin to prove it, I see I am no better.

"I've met the nicest girls just now," he says as I begin the discreet process of pocketing various finger foods in paper napkins. (I tell you, a bottomless purse is a girl's best friend.) Morven drains one last glass of punch, then rolls her eyes when she notices what I'm up to.

"Oh?" I say lightly as I slip a handful of *gougères* into my purse. "As nice as me?"

"Not nearly as pretty, but much more appreciative," he says, and I freeze with my hand hovering over the mortadella.

"Justin, I think we'd better be going now."

"But we only just got here!"

"We've been here four and a half hours," Morven says patiently.

"Can we stay just a little bit longer? There are some girls over there who want to give me an award!"

"Oh, dear." Morven leans over and points to where the hostesses are standing on the grand staircase holding a gaudy brass scepter and conferring among themselves. One of them points to us, and two others start down the stairs. "They want to crown him Lord of the Slippy!"

Each year as the ball draws to an end the organizers announce the winner of a sort of beauty contest, in which all the young male guests have been unwitting participants. The most desirable man among them is called up to the front of the ballroom and his many masculine virtues are volubly praised as tittering beldames bedeck him in a crown of olive branches and a long velvet cloak trimmed in ermine, and put that ridiculous scepter in his hand. Then he is pulled rather *un*ceremoniously in the general direction of the master bedroom, and *he is never seen or heard from again.*

The disappearance of a man no one would be seeing again in any event is not necessarily cause for alarm—no doubt he'll quite enjoy whatever it is they plan to do with him—but it is still rather unsettling the way they drag him up the stairs.

"Lord of the Slippy?" Justin says dubiously. "I don't know what that is, but I don't think I want to be it."

"Well put." I take him by the hand and feel a thrill of anxiety as we hurry through the ballroom doorway and out into the hall. As far as we know, no one has ever refused to give up her date before. If we don't hightail it out of here there could very well be blood.

"The park!" Morven says breathlessly as we hurry down the steps of the mansion. "They won't follow us." There were other boys nearly as good-looking as Justin, after all. Next year we'll be black-listed, of course, but I can't say I'll care much.

At the park entrance Justin turns and gapes at the cheerless façade of Temple Emanu-El. "We . . . we weren't . . . we couldn't have been in a party in the synagogue!"

"Of course not." I take his hand and pull him away, into the park. "We were in a building behind the synagogue."

"But we just came down the steps straight onto the street!" he cries, still glancing over his shoulder.

"I'll explain it when you're sober," I reply, though naturally I haven't any intention of doing so.

The surface of the duck pond looks like quicksilver in the moon-light. We clamber rather awkwardly over a wrought-iron fence and up one of those giant boulders overlooking the pond, and Justin stumbles up behind us.

We settle ourselves in a small circle on the rock, folding our legs beneath our swishing skirts. A warm wind rustles through the trees all around us, our view beyond hemmed by all those posh old high-rises with windows still lit here and there. Justin pulls off his bow tie and swings the white strip of fabric around and around, and he laughs when it slips from his hand into the darkness below. He looks at me with gleaming eyes. "Is this the meeting of a very secret society?"

"This is the Very Secret Society of the Late-Night Snack." (Which, we hope, will sober him up *tout de suite*.)

I start drawing folded grease-spotted napkins out of my little black bag and each time Justin giggles like a small boy, then devours whatever's inside without further ado. At some point he remembers himself and asks, "Want some?"

As if on cue, my stomach gurgles ominously, and Justin laughs. "It's nothing," I say. "Mild dyspepsia."

"Or a bellyful of lies," Morven mutters. I pinch her arm and she stifles a shriek.

Justin turns to her. "What did you say?"

"Nothing," she replies meekly.

"Did you have a good time tonight, Morven? Eve tells me you aren't really the partying type."

"This right here is my idea of a good party," she says, gazing out over the trees and high-rises. Absently she runs her fingertips over her face and throat and smiles to herself.

"It's great, isn't it?" he says with a happy sigh. "A midnight picnic."

"Oh, but it's *well* past midnight, dearie," I reply.

When Justin wrinkles his nose he looks uncannily childlike. "Don't call me 'dearie.' "

"Why not?"

"It makes you sound like an old lady."

"So?" I watch him gobble up the last sausage *en croûte*. "We'd better get you on a train back to Blackabbey soon."

"Why can't you just take me back to your place?"

"We've been over this before, Justin."

"But I've met your sister now. She likes me, doesn't she? Don't you like me, Morven?"

"Of course I do," Morven yawns.

"Then why can't we just take a taxi back to your apartment and I'll go home in the morning when I'm sober?"

"When you're *hungover,* more like."

"Answer the question, Eve."

"Has anyone ever told you what an aggravating drunk you are?"

"Come on, answer the question."

Morven puts her lips to my ear. "Look, I'm not sure if we really have a choice at this point. There are no more trains back to Jersey until a quarter past five, and it's only half past one now."

"Good point, sis," Justin says loudly.

"*Fine* then. We'll take a cab. But I'm putting you on the train first thing in the morning." I snap open the clasp on my evening bag and pull out another grease-stained napkin.

"Feta tartlets!" He pops one and is still chewing as he exclaims, "I thought they'd run out of these!"

"They did," Morven replies drily. He polishes off the rest in seconds flat.

"I managed a partial bottle of Grey Goose as well," I whisper to my sister. "He's too drunk to wonder where it came from, don't you think?"

"Are you cracked?" she says. "Why would you want to give him any more alcohol?"

"Hair of the dog," I reply as I pull out a can of V8.

"That purse is bigger than it looks," Justin remarks as I produce the vodka.

"Sorry," I say. "Forgot the celery stick. And the hot sauce. And the black pepper."

"It will do," he replies as he reaches for the bottle.

"Better save it for the morning," says my sister—who has never had a hangover in all her life—so I pull out a bottle of Evian instead.

Once Justin has fully refreshed himself, we clamber down the rock, toss the rubbish in a wastebasket along the path, and hail a cab off Fifth Avenue.

"Worth and Baxter, please," Morven tells the cabbie.

Justin nuzzles my neck. "You didn't tell me you lived in China-town."

Morven and I exchange a glance over his head and she looks posi-tively frightful with anxiety. Playtime is fast running out—we've got to get home and get Justin to sleep before our faces can betray us.

W E D O it, but barely. Drag him through the courtyard and up the four flights to our flat, and no sooner have we dumped him on the sofa and locked ourselves in the bathroom than we are made prunelike as ever.

"What if he wakes up before you're restored?" Morven asks as we smear on the Pond's side by side in the mirror above the sink.

"I'll just lock the door and sleep as late as I please. The fridge is full and the TV works. And if he asks why I didn't let him sleep with me"—I gaze at my wizened face in the glass and can't help a wry smile—"I'll tell him I was afraid he'd heave on the sheets."

"Wouldn't be a lie," Morven remarks as she pops the cap off the toothpaste.

"What'll you do in the morning?"

"As to keeping up the illusion for the benefit of our houseguest? Tut tut. I don't think so. No, Elsie and I are going to the museum tomorrow. I'll be gone long before he gets up."

I PAD INTO the sitting room at a quarter past one the following afternoon, face in place and Bloody Mary in hand, and what do I find but a dozen cats crawling all over him! He's still sleeping, and when they lick his face he stirs, smiles, and murmurs gibberish. I grab yesterday's newspaper off the coffee table, roll it up, and thwack as many feline bottoms as I can.

"Scat!" The cats make for the window as Justin jerks up.

"What? What is it?" He puts his hand to his cheek. "Why is my face all wet?"

I point to the open window, where a brazen black cat sits on the sill gazing at Justin and licking a white forepaw. "Scat!" I cry again, and it gives me one last resentful look before it leaps out onto the fire escape and away.

"Sorry, I shouldn't have left the window open."

"Why did you leave me on the couch?"

"I was afraid you'd puke in the bed."

"Oh," he says, considering this. "Fair enough." I hand him the Bloody Mary and he takes a grateful drink.

Then he notices the double doors that open into my bedroom are ajar. "Can I see your room?"

"What for?"

"You can tell a lot about a person from their bedroom."

"Hah! That's what I'm afraid of."

He stands up and makes a move for it, but I hold out my arm. "Just give me a minute, okay? I don't want you to see my dirty underthings all over the bed."

"Don't see why it matters," he replies. "I've been seeing a lot of your dirty underthings lately."

I close the doors behind me so I can hide pretty much every photograph on my dresser, including my two stolen pictures of Jonah. I'm just about to head for the nightstand to hide his pocket watch when Justin opens the doors and pokes his head in. "Hey, what's the big deal? I wish you'd have let me sleep in here. I've always wanted to sleep in a four-poster." He hops onto the unmade bed, picks up a pillow, and buries his face in it. "Smells like you," he says with a smile. Then, just as I was afraid of, he notices the pocket watch on the table beside him and picks it up. "Where did you get this?" He pops the clasp and examines the clock-face, then shuts it again and stares at the initials engraved on the lid: *JAR*.

"Found it at a junk shop in Paris," I reply rather too casually.

He looks at the watch, then at me, then back at the watch.

"What?"

"Nothing." He places it back on the nightstand, hesitates, and picks it up again, holding it to his ear so he can better hear the ticking. "It's still keeping perfect time."

I want to tell him he can keep it, but sentiment wins out. If I give it back to him now, I've got one less thing to remember him by.

We decide to go out for brunch, but there's still the sticky question of how to get him out of the warren without his noticing the cockfight ring or that old shack with MRS. PRIGG'S FRESH HOT FISH PIES above the doorway.

In the end I've got to blinker him, which is to say I give him memories to fill in for the things he shouldn't see. Once we're out the front gate, all he'll remember is the dingy tenement stairwell and the crooked cobblestones of an ordinary courtyard.

In Which Evelyn Resolves to
Make a Decision

24.

E VERY BELDAME needs a circle. We are gregarious by nature,
but more to the point, we require comrades to support us in
times of trouble, to rein us in lest our baser impulses get the
better of us. A dame without a coven is a suspicious character, like a
knife sharpener with all ten of his fingers. We have a name for a beldame like that: a hysterix, after the porcupine genus. Porcupines are
solitary creatures, after all, and little wonder, but there's no hide of
quills to keep their witchy counterparts from socializing with their
neighbors. Who knows why they forgo the comfort and safety of the
warrens?

Anyway, when we meet again to discuss Helena's case it is univer-
sally agreed that proof is impossible to come by, but the elders are unwilling to leave it at that.

"Fine!" I cry in exasperation. "Hold the bloody séance then. It
doesn't matter. She's got nothing to hide."

"It is a very serious undertaking," says Dymphna, "and one that
will probably cause considerable distress for each of us. But I see no
other way."

We generally take dirty business like this outside the coven, and
that's where the hysterix comes in. Our regard for one another is

strained by default: the hysterix is polite but perceptibly disgruntled at having her psychic stores thus intruded upon, and we are rather sniffy toward her since we can't help taking her decision not to join our cadre as a personal affront. What's in it for her? Some dark and stormy night she'll be needing *our* help, and as they say, life is long and memory is longer.

So Dymphna rings the only hysterix in Blackabbey, a woman named Clovis who's moved here in the last few years, and we arrange to pay her a visit. The hysterix mentions no restriction on the number of callers, so we decide that Morven and I plus all of Helena's daughters will also be in attendance. This is a meeting of introduction and preparation only.

The hysterix lives in one of those awful condominiums built recently on the edge of town, a little purgatory of numbered parking spaces and balconies furnished with white plastic patio chairs.

I have a definite idea of what the hysterix will be like, though it bears little resemblance to those few I encountered years ago in Germany. I'm expecting a hag straight off the Scottish moors, or at least a straggle-haired hippie with a parlorful of hookahs, but I am disappointed on both counts. Clovis is astonishingly young and as ordinary looking as the complex in which she lives. The interior of her apartment betrays the life of a beldame in only the most subtle ways—the candles on the end tables crusted with drips of dried wax but tall as when first lit; an apothecary's chest in the kitchen labeled with names of rare herbs—but she has not bothered to replace the wall-to-wall carpeting or the vertical blinds that go clackety-clack when the air conditioning kicks on. The furniture is mod in style, probably inherited, and the pictures on the walls don't quite appeal to the imagination. It's not at all like *our* house, or the houses of the Jesters or Peacocks.

Marguerite proffers an ambrosia cake wrapped in wax paper and Clovis offers us each a glass of iced tea. The subject is broached after a brief interval of sipping, compliments, and inquiries as to the brand of tea and ratio of sugar used. "All I ask," says Clovis, "is that you do not question my methods."

"Of course, of course," says Dymphna.

"We won't have to exhume him, will we?" I ask.

Helena sniffs. "Don't be absurd, Evelyn. I'd never allow it."

"But, Mother, your reputation!" Deborah cries.

"Certain things are more important than one's reputation, respect for the dead being first among them." Helena pauses. "Clovis?"

"It really won't be necessary."

My sister sighs in relief.

"But I will need two or three of your husband's possessions, the dearer or more frequently handled the better. Do you have a lock of his hair, by any chance?"

Helena raises her hand to her neck and lifts the glass locket so Clovis can see it.

"Good. And the last thing I need is a handful of grave dirt. Will that be a problem?"

My sister shakes her head. "He's buried in town."

"Good. But don't bring it to me in Tupperware or plastic of any kind, understand? Use a tin cup."

WE GO home again so Helena can gather a couple gardening tools and a tin measuring cup from the kitchen cupboard, but they all leave again without me. As I say, I never set foot in a graveyard if I can help it.

Vega's left a pitcher of lemonade and a quarter of an ambrosia cake on the porch table, bless her heart, and I sit on the swing with the daily Sudoku sipping the sweet stuff and occasionally writing down a number. After a few minutes I look up and see Justin coming down the street. It's too late—he's already seen me. I glance down at myself as if I don't already know I'm not the Eve he knows. But he can't have found me out—he's *waving*!

"Mrs. Harbinger!" he calls as he comes up the front walk. "How are you?"

Confusion gives way to relief. He's mistaken me for Helena! That's fine, that's just fine—so long as they don't come back from the graveyard before he leaves.

"Hello, Justin." I've assumed my most grandmotherly intonation. "Would you like a glass of lemonade?"

"That's very kind of you, thanks," he says as I pick up a clean drinking glass that wasn't there a second ago and fill it to the brim.

He seats himself on a wicker chair opposite me and I expect he'll ask if I'm home, and if not, where I am, but he throws me for a loop. "I'd like to talk to you about Eve," he says.

"What about Eve?"

"What I want to say is—I think she's *it*."

"Pardon me?"

"Well. You know," Justin says, growing considerably red in the face. *"The one."*

Oh dear. Oh *no*.

"I was hoping you could give me some advice, Mrs. Harbinger. And maybe you could arrange for me to meet her parents?"

"Her parents are dead." As I say these words I wonder for the first time what my mother might have thought of him. She'd never have approved, I know that much—just as she'd never have approved of Jonah. What surprises me most is that he's given me no inkling this was coming; he's never expressed any desire for me to meet *his* parents.

"Oh. I guess I should have known," he says slowly. "She never mentions them."

I steel myself for the words I wish I didn't have to say. "Will you take my advice, Justin?"

He nods.

"I know that you and Eve have been enjoying each other's company very much over these last few months—"

"Nearly a year."

"Pardon?" (He's been keeping track! There's a thrill.)

"We've been dating nearly a year. That's a lot more than a 'few.'"

"Just so. But, Justin, you mustn't talk of marriage."

"But she loves me. I know she does."

"It isn't a matter of love. She simply isn't free to marry."

"Not free to marry?" He stares at me. "What, is she married already?"

"It isn't that." I'm growing rather exasperated here. "But you must trust me, Justin. Enjoy her company, but don't ask for any more than that."

"I don't understand you, Mrs. Harbinger. I thought you approved of me."

"My *dear* boy, it has nothing whatever to do with you. But you must understand: oftentimes there are obstacles in life that we simply cannot surmount, no matter how determined we may be to live a happy life. I regret that I cannot explain further." I reach for the pie knife with trembling fingers. "Now. Would you care for a slice of cake?"

JUSTIN LEAVES soon afterward, hurt but trying not to show it. I wander inside and pour myself a dram at the parlor sideboard, though I can't bring myself to drink it. I just stand there for a few moments, trembling and teary. Uncle Hy has moved on to the Irish Renaissance and is too engrossed even to notice I'm in the room. Nor does he notice that one of the jujus hanging from the mantelpiece is struggling to get down.

"I *told* you it would all end in tears, didn't I?" The summer convention is technically over, but Auntie Em does tend to stay longer than the others.

I plop into the armchair by the fireplace and hide my face in my hands. "Kick me while I'm down, Auntie—that's real classy."

"Oh, Evelyn," she says, now with a bit of sympathy. She's managed to free herself from the hook, and with a considerable amount of clonking and squeaking of hinges, she seats herself beside me in the chair and pats me on the knee. "You know I only ever want what's best for you, don't you?" I glance up at the fireplace, where my mother's juju has hung lifeless since the day we put it there, and a wave of despair leaves me in full-blown tears.

"I know you *think* you know what's best for you," Auntie Em is yammering on, "but you don't and you never have. Never in my life, nor after it, have I known a girl so reckless as you. No, you've only known what's best in the present moment—but as a wise dame once said, 'The ephemeral pleasures of life grow more fleeting by the hour.' "

I shake off her little wooden hand. "Oh, shove it." Then I pretty much lose it, and to her credit Auntie says no more. I'll take her tiny wooden shoulder over none at all.

B Y T H E time the girls have returned I am back on the porch swing and more or less recovered. Helena clasps the tin measuring cup full of grave dirt in both hands as she comes up the steps. If you didn't know better you'd think she'd just hit up a neighbor for some extra coffee grounds. (Ugh, coffee grounds! This whole business makes me want never to drink another cup as long as I live.) Dymphna says she will return at a quarter past nine for our rendezvous with the hysterix.

"Wouldn't we all be more comfortable doing it here at home?" Rosamund asks as they file through the front door. "Her sitting room could hardly fit us all."

"It isn't a matter of comfort, dear," Morven explains as they disappear into the house. "It's just that unwanted company is harder to get rid of when it's your own kin."

Someone takes the cup from Helena to stow for safekeeping, and she sits down beside me on the porch swing as Vega pours her a glass of lemonade. Once we're alone, I consider asking her why she told us she never used that spellbook when everything we saw in the View-Master proved she had.

But truth be told, I don't really want to know. So instead I say, "Are you sure you want to do this? You're not looking so good. You don't *have* to go, you know."

"All will be well," she replies, though it seems like she's only trying to convince herself.

All is not well, as it turns out: when Dymphna arrives at a quarter past nine, mad-cow Lucretia is with her. Morven puts a restraining grip on my arm. "With all due respect, Dymphna, I'm not sure Lucretia's presence is appropriate," she says. "This matter is so sensitive that I would be afraid any tension among our group would have an adverse effect on the outcome tonight."

"That is a fair point," Dymphna replies. "But I am willing to risk it. You all should know that I asked Lucretia to be here. This way the matter can be thoroughly laid to rest."

Some of us walk and some of us take the loo. "Oh," says Clovis as we file first out of her powder room, then through her front door. "There are even more of you this time. It may be a little snug." She leads us into her dining room, where the candles are already lit. There aren't enough seats around the table so Lucretia has to sit in a spare chair in a corner, half-hidden by the bulk of a china cabinet, and her scowl would put any gargoyle to shame.

Helena's daughters place Henry's belongings at the center of the table—comb, cuff links, fountain pen, grave dirt—and Helena unfastens the glass locket and lays it down with exaggerated care.

"Are we ready to begin? Now. I want you all to close your eyes and fix in your mind the face of Henry Dryden. If you did not know him, just visualize any photograph of him that you may have seen."

After a minute I open an eye. I haven't been to many of these, I'll admit, but this first part never gets any less boring. Clovis jerks her head and looks at me and I quickly shut it again.

"I summon the spirit of Henry Dryden," she intones in that very old language, "from the far reaches of the Unknown, so that we may learn the truth of his demise. In this way, we hope to lay his spirit to rest at last."

From the darkened sitting room beyond come a mechanical-sounding pop and a blue flash of light, as if the television has been switched on. We open our eyes. A shadow approaches the doorway between the rooms, and when it reaches the dining room threshold it grows lighter, comes into focus.

"Hallo, Henry," I say. Everybody gasps. He gazes at Helena and she looks positively terrified. There are soft cries of "Daddy!" and more than one of us begin to weep.

His physical presence is a little hard to describe. Let's just say he looks like a bad photocopy, only three dimensional. We can see straight through his waistcoat and tie.

"Spirit of Henry Dryden," Clovis says. "We humbly ask that you tell us if you died by the hand of another and, if so, that you name your killer."

Without taking his see-through eyes off Helena, Henry opens his mouth and begins to speak . . . *but we can't hear a word!*

We just stare at him in bafflement for a few moments. Then somebody says nervously, "There's no audio!"

Dymphna turns to the hysterix. "Is there any way to fix it?"

"I seem to have misplaced the remote control," Clovis replies tartly.

Then we hear a second popping noise, this time right above our heads. A wheel takes shape out of a ball of unearthly light, then another, then a chair, then a person inside the chair. And she, like my unfortunate brother-in-law, doesn't take notice of anyone else in the room. "Henry! Oh, Henry, how I've missed you!"

The girls turn away from the image of their father and eye the newcomer in consternation. "Who is *that?*"

Helena regards the apparition with distaste. "Belva Mettle."

"How did *she* get in here?"

Good grief—the hag knot! I've got to get rid of it. But she might not go away if I only make it vanish out of my pocketbook into the nearest trash can; I've got to undo the knot, separate the stone from the cord. Nothing good can come of an interview with Henry's dead mistress.

Aside from the glowing blue permanent and a rather impressive wattle, Belva doesn't look much altered from the scene inside the View-Master. "Oh, my dear, dear Henry!"

Henry, meanwhile, doesn't even notice Belva in her spectral wheelchair hovering above the dining table. It's like the spirits in the room are on two different channels. He holds his hand out to Helena, lips still moving, looking at her mournfully all the while.

Belva holds out her skinny bird-claw hands, waving frantically. "Henry! Henry! Can't you hear me?"

"*We* can hear you," Vega mutters. "And we wish you'd go back to whatever circle of hell you've just sprung from."

The ghost of Belva slowly swivels to look at my niece sitting at the table next to me. "How like a Harbinger," she says slowly, "to invite a gal to a party and once she's there make her feel like she's crashed it."

"Nobody asked you here," Vega retorts. I'm fumbling in my pocketbook for the hag knot while maintaining the picture of innocence above the table. Clovis shoots me a look but says nothing.

"*Some*body asked me here, or else I wouldn't *be* here. Why are you all so heartless? Isn't it enough that I've had to live and die without my Henry? Why show him to me now, why make him blind and deaf to me?"

"He's not *your* Henry," Helena replies. "And he never was."

I slide my fingernail under the knot, loosening it little by little. Belva glowers down at my sister, her wattle quivering with animosity. "You'll be sorry, Helena Harbinger."

I've almost got it now, but I can't help laughing out loud. "What are *you* going to do to her?"

Belva ignores me, wagging her finger at my sister like she's reprimanding a small child. "You may be a beldame, but you'll pay for your sins just like anybody else."

"Like you're paying for yours?" my sister replies as I finally manage to get my forefinger through the slackened hag knot and pull it out of the stone.

Belva's eyes widen, and as she holds out her hands to the specter of Henry it's like some cosmic vacuum is pulling her back to wherever she's come from. She gives a small shriek as her wheelchair hurtles backward, vanishing into the picture window. Lucretia jumps up from her perch in the corner and peers out into the night.

We turn back to the apparition in the living room doorway. Henry is still talking, still holding out his hand to his wife. Helena sits frozen in her chair, her eyes locked to his. "Read his lips!" somebody cries, but the apparition fades before we can even try.

Lucretia turns away from the window with a frown. "I find it very perplexing," she says, "that we inadvertently called the spirit of Belva Mettle. How could this possibly happen?"

Dymphna turns to my sister. "Perhaps Belva gave your husband one of the objects you brought tonight?"

Helena shakes her head. "I gave him all those things."

It's a mystery to everyone but me, though naturally Lucretia is the only one unwilling to let it go. As we rise to leave she gives my sister a look almost as mean as Belva's. Cut from the same cloth, those two.

Tonight didn't turn out at all the way Lucretia hoped it would. Helena got the last word, and that's got to count for something.

I go with the party taking the long route home and bring up the rear. This way I can throw what's left of that stupid hag knot into an overgrown azalea bush without anybody seeing.

· · ·

LATER THAT night Morven and I go back to Cat's Hollow and walk the old streets in the moonlight, chuckle at the bawdy jokes traded among the revelers outside the Dutch tavern, and buy a carton of milk to feed the strays. I'm restless when we get back to the apartment, picking up novels and puzzle books and casting them aside again with heavy sighs. Morven is working on yet another charity blanket with her supersonic crochet hook, seemingly unperturbed by the events of the evening.

I clear my throat and Morven pauses. "I've come to a decision," I say.

"Regarding?"

"Justin."

"Oh." Morven puts down her hook and folds her hands over the mound of wool in her lap. "Well? What is it?"

"I've got to end it."

Another pause. "I think that's wise."

"And well overdue, I'm sure you'd like to say."

My sister shrugs. "How will you do it? And when?"

"Soon. Next week." I pause. "There's just one thing."

Morven sighs. "You want your last hurrah, is that it?"

I nod a trifle sheepishly. "I keep telling him we'll go to Europe for a long weekend," I venture, and Morven rolls her eyes. "I'm not even asking for a weekend though—just a night. Only one night."

"And what happens once you've had your one big night?"

"I won't see him again. Cross my heart."

"How will you explain your reasons?" Morven gives me a sharp sidewise glance as she resumes her crocheting. "You will break up with him properly, won't you?"

With a forefinger I draw an X across my bosom. "And after that," I say sadly, "it will be easy enough for me to disappear."

Morven picks up the View-Master off a stack of old *Life* magazines on the end table, puts it to her face, and clicks once, twice. She puts it down again and gives me a long, sad, pitying look. "All right. I'll help you. But if you don't keep your word, I'll kick your took."

A T TEN past seven the following evening I knock on the front window at Fawkes and Ibis. Justin looks up from his neat piles of personal checks and fifty-dollar bills on the counter, grins like a schoolboy, whisks the money into the safe, and comes to the door to unlock it for me. When he kisses me I don't want to think that the times our lips will meet in the future are numbered.

No sooner am I through the door than I catch sight of a new item on the casket table by the window and gasp. "Where did you find that lamp?" It's a strange piece: a gnome crouching under a toadstool in cast iron with a faded green lampshade, the cord—with a clunky British plug—dangling off the edge of the table.

"Which lamp? Oh, the one with the dwarf? Estate sale. Why?"

"Where? Where was it?"

He gives me a funny look. "Upper East Side. Why?"

"How much is it?" I murmur as I lift the price tag. "I want it. I'll buy it right now, in fact."

Justin laughs, though I can see he's a little disconcerted. "You can buy it in the morning, if you like it that much."

He stares at me curiously for a long moment, until finally I feel compelled to say, "It has sentimental value."

He laughs again. "How can it have sentimental value when it's never belonged to you?"

"I only mean that it reminds me of someone—something." *Tell me you remember it. Tell me you remember your mother switching it off every night when you were small.*

"It's a little creepy, don't you think?"

I turn away from the lamp and throw my arms round his neck. "If I thought it was creepy, do you think I'd want so badly to buy it?"

He kisses me once, twice. That's two kisses less. "I don't know," he murmurs. "I stopped trying to figure you out a long time ago."

Now seems like a good time for it: "Let's go away this weekend."

"*Yes!* Where to?" He leads me into the ersatz parlor and flicks on the opera lamps, then approaches the old globe in the corner. "Should I spin it?"

"If you like," I say. "But the world has changed quite a bit since that was made."

"Some lines have been redrawn, but the continents are all in the same places." He spins the globe half a dozen times but every time it stops his finger is pointed someplace entirely unsuitable, like Siberia or the Indian Ocean.

I drop onto the chaise lounge and catch sight of a woven basket on the end table crammed with old postcards. "Oh. Are these new?"

"Uncle Harry's been collecting them for years. There are some really old ones in there." I pluck a card, a hand-colored etching of Notre Dame circa 1900, and when I turn it over I find the postmark is still crisp enough to read.

When I pick up the basket to flip through it on my lap I notice the tag marked *$5/each*. "Five dollars! Hah! Have you found anyone foolish enough to pay five dollars for a used postcard?"

"People like to frame them," he replies with a shrug. "They're worth more because they're used."

I sit up straight on the lounge and pat the cushion beside me. "Let's read through them together." I pass him a handful of cards. "Whatever postcard strikes our fancy, that's where we'll go." Justin thinks it's a great idea.

After a while I stop reading the messages, all of them tedious litanies of routes traveled and souvenirs purchased. Big Ben, Great

Wall, Eiffel Tower. Athens, Knossos, Giza. A few naughty burlesques thrown in for variety's sake. And—aha!—here are a few old-fashioned etchings of fairy-tale castles, medieval alleyways, Gothic cathedrals born of the sweat of a thousand men. But most of these quaint ones hail from Germany, which is the one place to which I've no interest in returning.

Then, *naturally:* "How do you feel about Germany? Found a very nice one from Bad Wimpfen." He rattles off a list of places and I nix every one. Nuremberg? Can't go back to Nuremberg without feeling like I've got to look over my shoulder at every turn. And then there was that time in Oberammergau when I came upon a public auction of porcelain and silverware; the self-appointed auctioneer had looted the house of a Jewish family who'd just been dragged off to the death camps. I made myself a vulture, roosted on a lamppost, and went on shrieking until there wasn't a soul left in the *Marktplatz*.

I need to go someplace new, someplace untainted by morbid recollection. "I don't want to go to Germany," I say as I shuffle through another stack of cards. "If you don't mind."

Something in my tone gives him pause. Out of the corner of my eye I see him open his mouth to ask, then think better of it.

As I flip through the postcards I find myself thinking of that ride back to London on the Caledonian Express, Jonah's melancholy and my wish for a honeymoon of our own. In a way, it isn't too late.

But we can't go to Scotland—too many memories there, though they aren't unhappy ones. He had been to Connemara with Patricia, and yes, it would have made sense for us to go someplace else, someplace new to both of us. But that longing in his eyes hadn't been for Patricia or the honeymoon itself; it was for the landscape, the stark and heathen beauty of it.

As I'm mulling this over, I come upon another Irish postcard in the stack—not another quaint thatched cottage or sheep-crowded road captioned *rush hour in Ireland,* but a simple shot of a bar-front with a shaggy dog dozing in the open doorway. MURTY COYNE'S, says the sign above the window.

"You haven't been to Ireland yet, have you?" I ask him.

"No. Always wanted to though. Have you?"

I shake my head. I flip the postcard and at the bottom left is printed *Coyne's pub, Tully Cross, Connemara*. The postmark is smudged, but judging by the quality of the photo on the front I'd say it's thirty-five, forty years old. It is addressed to a Miss Eugenie Pryce of 622 Greenwich Street, New York, and though the message is not signed, the scrawl is obviously a man's.

This is the best pub in all the world, it reads. *There's only one thing missing.*

I hand the postcard to Justin and as he reads it a broad smile spreads over his face. "When can you leave?"

The Goblin Ball

25.

December 31, 1944

"I will tell you everything you have forgotten. We loved each other—ah! no, you have not forgotten that—and when you came back from the wars, we were to be married. Our pictures were painted before you went away. You know I was more learned than women of that day. Dear one, when you were gone, they said I was a witch. They tried me. They said I should be burned. Just because I had looked at the stars and gained more knowledge than other women, they must needs bind me to a stake and let me be eaten by the fire. And you far away!" . . .

"The night before," she went on, "the devil did come to me. I was innocent before—you know it, don't you? And even then my sin was for you—for you—because of the exceeding love I bore you. The devil came, and I sold my soul to eternal flame. But I got a good price."

—E. Nesbit, "The Ebony Frame"

I T'S WELL past sixty years since I've seen it, but I often dream of that castle with its spires and crooked turrets on a mountain wreathed in evergreens, ominous clouds gathering overhead; it was just like a picture in a storybook. In the dream I'm riding through the forest in a posh car, an armored Mercedes, and when I meet the pale cold eyes of the driver in the rearview mirror the recognition sends a tingle of horror down my neck.

The road zigzags up the mountain. I look out the window and see figures, skeletal figures, coming out of the gloom of the forest, and they line up along the road and stare at me as the car passes. I press my palm to the glass, but what can I do for them?

The armored Mercedes pulls up to the archway and I glide noiselessly up the stairs in a black velvet gown. I pass through the chapel gallery on my way to the party and when I look down at the altar I see a corpse there in a mahogany coffin. It's Jonah's. Terrified at the sight, I run across the gallery and through the doorway into the banquet hall. The crowd of dancers parts so I can see him there at the far side of the room in his brown dress uniform, now striding toward me, smiling like he's lived to see the end.

S o we came out of the station waiting room at half past three on New Year's Eve, having spent the last quarter of an hour checking that our visages and uniforms were all in order. We didn't have to have every detail perfect; after all, no one in Wernigerode had met these two before, and I didn't want to waste any oomph making sure Jonah's new nose was just so. We only had to resemble the pictures on their identity cards.

We did ride in an armored Mercedes (sent by the *Oberst,* the colonel in charge of SS headquarters in Wernigerode, to meet us at the train station), but the ascent wasn't as smooth as I later dreamed it. Seated in front, the colonel's secretary told us we would be staying at the castle, but only for the night.

The wind set the trees to whispering, and I began to feel rather anxious. Every time I glanced at Jonah he looked back at me through the face of Dr. Schafer, and I had to fight to reassure myself that he *was* my Jonah, same as ever. He gave my hand a furtive squeeze, and I realized he must have found my face just as disconcerting. It began to rain.

The road led through a gate and skirted the castle mount as it climbed. On the left we saw a stretch of half-timbered houses and provincial shops, several of which offered more of those heinous little witch figures. To our right the castle loomed.

Soon we passed through a second gate, and the Mercedes slowed to a stop on a wide stone terrace with a pepper-pot tower and a panoramic view over the mountains. Jonah and I weren't even out of the car when a couple of porters disappeared with our suitcases. We looked up at the castle, the turrets and spires and tiny dormer windows poking out at odd places along the roof. Rough medieval masonry was set against towers of tidy brick and mullioned windows; this and other charming quirks indicated that the castle complex had undergone a spell of "improvement" every century or so.

We were ushered through a doorway and up a spiral staircase, and a knight glared at us from a niche halfway up. We reached a landing and passed through a door into an inner courtyard. Here all the architectural periods in the castle's history converged—medieval, faux-medieval, and quaint half-timbering—so that if I hadn't known better I'd have thought I'd stumbled into a warren unawares. Vines of ghost ivy snaked across the stone and wood façades, and griffin-headed gutter spouts high above our heads unleashed the rainwater in roaring cataracts onto the cobblestones. The whole place would have been very charming in summertime, but that night, the last night of the year, the narrow windows reflected nothing but the storm clouds.

I looked down at my thumb in my coat pocket and was greatly relieved when the crescent didn't glow. I'd never before met a beldame in the service of the Führer, and I hoped I never would.

A small staircase flanked by stone grotesques led to a doorway in a round tower, and I counted nine steps as we followed the colonel's secretary inside. Nine steps, that was a good sign; we'd carry it off tonight, I knew we would. I reached down to pet the dragon on the banister and felt it purr ever so slightly beneath my hand.

Our wet coats were whisked away and we were given a brief tour of the public rooms. There were gargoyles and demons everywhere we looked—on the banisters, the wainscoting, the mantelpieces. It was as if this castle had been custom-built for the men who'd taken it over.

Swastika banners were hung on either side of the heraldic stag rearing above a side doorway in the banquet hall. The walls were paneled with tableaux from local history, processional pomp and men in tights and bloomers, but these scenes were obscured by great oval mirrors taken from elsewhere in the castle, no doubt hung there to make the room seem larger than it already was. I met my reflection in each mirror I passed and felt a burst of confidence in the security of my disguise.

Beyond the banquet hall was a series of reception rooms paneled in faded red and green damask, furnished with chaise lounges, ottomans decorated with intricate needlepoint, and chess tables with pearl inlay. In the first reception room beyond the hall a great evergreen tree stood, glass icicles and silver bells glittering on every bough. The party wouldn't begin for another three hours, and there was a hush as we passed through all these rooms, an air of expectancy.

We went through another maze of corridors before we reached the guest wing, and there the secretary left us to our rooms. I'd hardly opened my suitcase when a maid arrived with a light supper tray. This Schafer chap must've been quite the big fish.

I hung up my uniform and climbed into bed in the twilit gloom. There was a great horned chandelier poised directly above my head, and if I looked out the tall windows on the opposite wall I could see the evergreens vanishing into the fog on the horizon. The rain had given way to snow.

Within a few minutes Jonah had slipped in beside me. There wasn't much need for caution; half the SS were sleeping with their

secretaries anyway. There was no telling when we might be interrupted, though, so we had to keep to our disguises. Mindful of this, he
buried his face in my neck.

Afterward he slept. I put my hand to the locket round my neck and
whispered, "Happy New Year, sis."

"Good news," Morven replied. That disembodied whisper in the
darkness never failed to spook me a little. "I just talked to Helena. The
Gingerbread Man says there'll be peace in the spring."

"Spring is centuries away," I sighed. I glanced over at Jonah and
found him sleeping with his eyes open.

I WORE A simple black gown, and Jonah was back in SS uniform. We
had to pass through the chapel gallery to reach the banquet hall, and
for a moment I paused at the handrail to look down on the altar, bereft
of all sacred trimmings. Looted or hidden for safekeeping, who could
say? There were voices and laughter coming through an open doorway on the chapel's north wall, and a brief silence before the clicking of
billiard balls and the thump of ball in pocket. Putting the *Billiard-
zimmer* right next door to the chapel seemed gauche even to me.

We passed into the banquet hall, where men in and out of uniform
were milling about. The chandelier was blazing, and it was reflected in
the long windows and all the mirrors hung about the room to marvelous effect.

The great mantelpiece in the corner was flanked by yet two more
bronze dragons and festooned with fragrant boughs. Jonah presented
himself, and then me, to the *Oberst,* and as the men took turns asking
him about our trip from Berlin and grilling him for news, I wandered
into the reception room. There were children kneeling at the foot of
the great Christmas tree, picking up packages and shaking them for
clues. Others were staring at the lavish spread of meats and sweets,
held back out of politeness by their mothers, who were eyeing the food
with just as much desire.

I stared at the plates piled high with frosted *Lebkuchen,* and my first thought was of the covention I was currently missing. *The Gingerbread Man says there'll be peace in the spring.* I looked again, and the sight of so much food made me nauseous. The German people had little but last year's potatoes, and the death camp inmates, slave laborers, and prisoners of war got nothing but soup made of the peelings. This party food was all part of the illusion that the Germans' victory was close at hand.

The cook appeared, looking jolly in a clean apron, and for a second I fancied her the German counterpart of my dear Mrs. Dowel. Would that she were! She bid us all eat and started the children singing "O Tannenbaum." I didn't touch a morsel.

When I returned to Jonah's side a light was shining in the musicians' gallery up above, and three officers had struck up a rather desultory waltz. Someone took me by the elbow. "Why, Fraulein Gross," said the colonel, "you are a very fortunate young lady."

"Oh?"

"Aren't you aware that had you taken the train yesterday as originally planned, you would most likely be dead now?"

I glanced from the face of the *Oberst* to Jonah and to the faces of the other men in their circle, as if I hadn't the faintest notion what he was talking about.

"The train we were meant to take yesterday." Jonah spoke as if to clarify some simple point to a small child. "It was bombed by the British." He turned to the SS colonel, and for one terrifying moment I lost all sense of him behind that bland mask of self-satisfaction. "At first I thought it best not to tell her," he said. "She rattles so easily— as you see." Then he laughed. "No use fretting, my dear. Let's have a dance."

As we whirled about the room I kept catching glimpses of myself in the mirrors, and this time I was surprised despite myself to see the face of the dead secretary gazing back at me. As I say, mirrors are mere objects, easily deceived, and I was the only beldame in the room—yet I half expected these mirrors might betray me.

I looked up at Jonah and he pressed the small of my back. I cocked my head as if to say, *Now, which of these Nazis knows what we need to?*

At that moment the colonel tapped Jonah on the shoulder, and Jonah gave me a wry look. *There's your answer.* It was up to me now.

"May I cut in?" he was asking, and Jonah gave a gallant half bow as he retreated.

The next time I glanced in the mirror I was struck with horror at what I saw: every person in the room, save Jonah, was wearing my father's face. I saw that same proud, remote visage on women in evening gowns as well as men in SS uniform. It was as if his image had been fractured by a kaleidoscope turned over and over again in the light. Even the children lingering in the doorway gazed up at me with his cold hard eyes. Up to now I had only ever seen his face on one snake at a time, and the effect of seeing it gazing back at me on all the hundred people in the room sent me almost to the brink of madness.

The waltz went on and on, though it now sounded as if the musicians were playing underwater. I turned back to the *Oberst,* who had my hand and waist in a viselike grip, and he glared at me as if to say my birth had been a mistake he was ready to correct.

Frantically I looked over the bobbing shoulders for Jonah and spotted him in the middle of the floor. He was gazing back at me behind the bland features of Doctor Schafer, heedless of the evil that surrounded him. When I glanced in the mirror I saw—or *thought* I saw—my own frightened face, and I turned back to the SS colonel with a stab of certainty that it was all over. They had found us out.

But my father was gone, and beyond his shoulder I perceived that the room had been restored, festive and ordinary. "Are you unwell?" he was asking me, and it occurred to me that his grip had tightened merely to keep me from falling. He led me out of the hall and into the chapel gallery, where he sat me in a pew and petted my hair as Jonah handed me a mug of Glühwein.

"It is all too much for her," Jonah was saying. "The poor lamb."

I took a sip of the hot sweet wine, and the memory of that horrible hallucination dissipated as quickly as it had come.

I met Jonah's eyes—*Are you ready?* they seemed to say. He thought this was all a pretense! Jonah handed the colonel a second mug and ventured back into the banquet hall.

"That's better," I said with a cheerful sigh. "A nice hot mug of mulled wine never fails to lift my spirits." The wine had restored me to my wits, but on the colonel it was having the opposite effect; Jonah had slipped a packet of the truth drug into the steaming cup. The door leading to the banquet hall slowly creaked shut, as if by a draft.

"We have no reason to celebrate," he said, staring with dull eyes at the steam rising from his mug. "I only tell you this because I know—instinctively—that I can trust you, Fraulein Gross."

And over the next twenty minutes he would entrust me with descriptions of the landmarks that indicated entrances to the Mittelwerk factory. He babbled that he had resolved to make contact with the Allies, that doing so was the best thing for both his family and the fatherland.

Finally he moaned that he'd had too much to drink and begged me to accompany him back to the guest wing. Jonah reappeared, and we led the colonel down the corridor and into bed. He shrugged out of his uniform jacket and promptly fell asleep.

JUST PAST two o'clock, an unmarked Volkswagen pulled up to the castle gate, headlights switched off. It was still snowing, but the driver dared not use the windscreen wipers. I caught our reflections in the backseat window; the masks were fading from our faces, but feature by feature, so that my hair was black and my eyes were my own again but my nose and mouth were still the dead secretary's. I shuddered as Jonah opened the back door and ushered me inside. We knelt on the floor, sandwiched between the seats with a wool blanket thrown over our heads in case we were stopped, but we weren't.

"You did well tonight," he whispered. In the darkness I raised my hands to his face and drew my fingers along his brow, his cheekbones, his nose and jawline—he was fully Jonah again. "Happy 1945," I said. Silently he kissed me.

Fisher drove carefully and without comment, and when we got out of the car half an hour later it was snowing still more furiously. We trudged down the lane that led to the abandoned farm, and Jonah's face was pale as the fourth horseman's in the moonlight. I reached for his hand, and for a few wonderful moments I could pretend we hadn't a care in the world apart from the chill in our toes.

Back in the hayloft of the old stable, Jonah hung the drapes and lit a candle as I opened a steamer trunk to find the rations Albrecht had left for us. Suddenly I was ravenous. The beef was tough and the cheese was hard, but I tucked into my share with little thought of how long it was meant to last me. My pockets would be brimming with chocolate again just as soon as I'd gotten some sleep. "Aren't you hungry?"

"I'll eat later." He was busy setting up the radio; the matchbox and lighter fluid were poised at their usual place on the edge of the table.

I took a sip from the milk jug and almost dropped it at the sound of thunder. A flash of lightning broke through a crack in the curtains. "Jonah, you can't use the radio tonight."

He didn't answer me for a long moment, just helped me onto my pallet and tucked the blanket under my chin.

"It isn't safe, Jonah. Not here, not tonight."

He sat on an overturned dairy crate, put his elbows on his knees, closed his eyes, and pinched the bridge of his nose with his thumb and forefinger.

"I mean it. Promise me you won't."

"Confound it, Eve! I've got to transmit what we've learned tonight as soon as possible!"

I was losing my grip on consciousness, but I managed to give him a reproving look.

"How do you know?"

"There's a direction-finding car out tonight."

"But it's New Year's!" He paused. "Did you see that Saint Bernard again?"

I shook my head.

"Well, then—"

"Snow and lightning always bode ill for me. *Always*, Jonah."

"But how do you know that's what it means?"

"I just do. There was lightning in a snowstorm the night my mother died."

He sighed. "When, then?"

Lightning illuminated the scene outside the window once again, and I held up a finger as I waited to hear how long the rumbling would last. "Tomorrow night," I said. "But after midnight."

What haunts me is this: why didn't it happen sooner, while I still had the strength to *do* something about it? Maybe there were portents falling like a hailstorm all around me and I was just too thick to notice, or maybe I never got a clue because I couldn't be trusted not to run from it.

I turned my head on the pillow and saw him duck beneath the tent that kept the light in. I wanted to warn him one last time not to use the radio, but then sleep rose up and swallowed me.

I BIT BACK my panic when I didn't wake up where I'd passed out, on the pallet in the stable loft. I was curled up under a wool blanket in a dark and narrow place, so cold I couldn't feel a thing apart from the hideous crick in my neck. Sunlight shone through the slats in the wall, illuminating every dust mote. I'd been there quite a while.

Jonah wasn't nearby—I could feel his absence as acutely as the hollow in my stomach. I noticed something in my hand and brought it up to my face to examine it in the dim light: a pocket watch. *His* pocket watch. Then I noticed something sticking into my side, and I raised myself up on my elbow and looked down to find his dagger in its leather sheath. On the overturned milking pail by my feet I spotted the little metal case containing the radio crystals. I felt space beneath me, as if I had been hidden away on the highest shelf in a cupboard.

All at once I knew where I was, and an awful feeling crept over me, cold, slithering, as if something had happened that was irreversible.

A Night in Connemara

26.

I love the smell of a graveyard . . . 'tis a sweet and peaceful smell.

—John B. Keane (screenplay by Jim Sheridan), *The Field*

A FEW NIGHTS later, on a Friday evening, I ring Justin's doorbell with a pocketful of euros. While I'm waiting for him to answer I take a look at Lucretia's new window display. It features two of Olive's marionettes inside a toy stage that, while not half as nice as the Harbinger family heirloom, will nevertheless make quite a splendid Christmas gift for some lucky tot. I stand by that talking-to I gave her for selling her puppets to Lucretia, but I can't help marveling at her handiwork: the puppet on the left is dressed as a court jester, all gaudy stripes and jingling bells, with a pointy nose and cleft chin, and on the right is a fabulous Renaissance angel in a gold lamé gown, with shimmering papier mâché wings and a tiny lute, strung and varnished, fastened between her hands. The workmanship is exquisite.

I'm clad in dungarees and a light jumper, but when Justin opens the door he looks at me just as if I were wearing my gown of peacock-blue velvet. Then he remembers himself, looks down at the sidewalk by my feet, and frowns. "Where's your suitcase?"

"We're only going for the weekend," I reply with a shrug and a laugh. "I pack light. It's the European way, you know."

"But you don't have any luggage at all! Not even a backpack!"

"I'll be fine" is all I say, and he looks at me doubtfully.

"When's the shuttle coming?"

"What shuttle?"

"To take us to the airport? You said you'd call for a shuttle."

"Oh, yes. It won't be here for a while yet. Let's go upstairs and wait for it."

Inside the apartment I spot his heavy-duty hiking pack, studded with patches from a dozen countries, on the hallway floor all ready to go. Won't be needing that. I make straight for the bathroom, not paying any attention to Justin calling after me to wait, and when I open the door I let out a gasp of horror.

"Toilet's backed up," he mumbles behind me, oh so helpfully.

"Oh, no." I turn round and find him lurking sheepishly in the hallway. "Don't you have a plunger?"

He shakes his head. "It just happened and I figured I didn't have time to borrow one before you got here. If you've really got to go I can give you the keys to Fawkes and Ibis . . ."

"But we don't have time!" I moan. "I need a toilet that works!" Then I remember that mysterious door in the sitting room. I must be smiling a grinchy grin, because Justin looks alarmed.

"There's a bathroom downstairs," I point out.

"You can't go downstairs—that door is locked," he says as I walk across the sitting room toward the door with my hand out for the knob. "Come on, I'll open the door to the shop. If the shuttle comes it'll wait for us."

I mutter a few words and the knob yields with only a little creak. "See, it isn't locked. I'm not doing any harm, just using the toilet. It's a cosmic law that only one toilet at a time can ever clog in any given building. Come down with me if it makes you feel better." If I look particularly mischievous he'll surely accompany me, which is exactly what I want him to do.

"Just don't touch anything, all right?" he says as he follows me down the darkened stairwell. "You said it yourself, Lucretia Hartmann is a stickler."

I laugh. " 'Stickler'—ha! I'm quite sure I used a more colorful word than that."

We open the door that brings us to Lucretia's office, and I lead him by the hand to the loo and flip the light switch. Potpourri on the top of the cistern, for Pete's sake, and a plunger in the corner that looks like it's never been used.

I shut the door behind us and draw the Connemara postcard from my back pocket. "Um, I don't need to watch," Justin says.

"Don't worry, dearie." I squeeze his hand. "You won't remember a thing."

A FEW SECONDS later he knocks his head against the wooden door of a toilet stall. We can hear the strains of bladder relief and crude masculine laughter coming from the far end of the room, and cigarette smoke wafts through the narrow window at the top of the wall. We're here! I've been through the loo flue a million and one times, but I still get a thrill every time I go someplace new.

"Didn't bump your head too hard, I hope," I whisper.

"I'm all woozy. Where . . ." He pauses to mull over the vague memories I've just blinkered him with: of a shuttle ride to Newark, a long flight, and a bus trip with views of rolling green countryside through a fogged-up window. "Hey, why did you follow me into the stall?"

"Couldn't bear to be parted from you for even a moment. Shh, we can't let them know we're in here." I relax as I hear the door slam and the voices recede. "Okay. We can come out now." Seems the WC is in an alley behind the pub. I lead him inside and down a narrow hallway toward the front room. We edge past Irish folks of all ages chatting in twos and threes, and I nod at everybody whose gaze I meet.

We stand on the threshold of the pub's main room, a cozy little space with an open turf fire and a group of crusty old men nursing their pints along the bar. I lift a finger to get the bartender's attention and flash a winning smile. "Two pints of Guinness, please."

I look about the room, at the rusted tobacco ads on the walls and the rosary dangling from a shelf lined with bottles of Jamesons and Tullamore Dew. I wonder if Jonah ever came here—and if he did, was this place the same then as it is now? I glance at Justin, who is also looking about the room with all the delight I feel.

One of the old men standing at the bar turns round and looks me up and down. "Is that an American accent I hear?"

"It is," say I.

He takes a sup from his pint glass and eyes me thoughtfully. He wears a tweed cap and a jacket with elbow patches, and the hand that holds his pint glass is gnarled from a lifetime of heavy farmwork.

"Where in America are ye from?"

"New Jersey."

"Ah," he replies. "I've a cousin in New Jersey." He drains his glass, places it on the bar, and abruptly leaves the room. Justin looks at me quizzically.

"Suppose you can't expect much in the way of conversation from a man who's only got cows to talk to all day. Say, can you find us a place to sit?" Justin spots a free table at the far corner of the room and carries our drinks over while I'm paying for them.

A man sitting alone at a table by the fire leans over as Justin lays down our glasses. "Sorry," he says, "but ye can't sit there. It's reserved for the musicians."

I come over to the table as Justin's picking up our drinks again. "Ooh! So there'll be a session tonight?" I take a quick appraisal of the stranger: somewhere in his thirties, I'd say, and not altogether bad looking. Pleasant face. We could do worse for a drinking partner.

He nods. "Sit with me, if ye like. I'm not waiting for anyone." He tells us his name is Billy Byrne and Justin introduces us in turn.

Well, we soon find out why Billy Byrne is sitting alone: *the man will not shut up.* It's probably his curious penchant for ancient gossip that's keeping him at a table by himself even though the room is filling quickly. He seems to know all the dirt about every soul in the place, even the little old lady behind the bar who levels the head off every pint with a butter knife, then licks it on both sides as she hands over the glass. "That's Oonagh Coyne. *She* stole her sister's husband. Of course, they weren't married yet. But ye can't imagine the falling-out when it came time to divide the inheritance."

"How do you know all that?" I ask. "She must be well past eighty."

"A good scandal never goes stale," he replies with a shrug.

I tell Mr. O'Blatherty this is my first trip to Ireland. "Mine too," Justin says, piping up. "So I guess you're from around here, Billy?"

"Ballybeg." He clasps his mitts round his pint glass, though he doesn't take a sip. "It's just up the road."

At first glance I'd judged Billy Byrne youngish and harmless, but as I study him further the two-day stubble and the crags under his eyes give me pause. He turns his face to the fire, and his profile assumes harder edges in the flickering light. Then I look down at his fingers and realize he *can't* be in his thirties—it takes a long time to acquire such dark tobacco stains on one's fingers, even if he smoked his first at the age of nine. It isn't often I come across such a slippery one—I can't get a handle on him at all.

Soon the musicians arrive, their Gore-Tex jackets dripping rain onto the floorboards. They set down their cases and a barmaid arrives with a round of pints for the newcomers. There's a fiddler, a drummer, and an accordionist. They take a while tuning up, during which time Billy Byrne regales us with more odd tales that, by rights, should have been buried in the local churchyard along with the parties involved.

Billy Byrne zips his lips when the session starts. This isn't like most music I've heard in taverns, where the musicians are appreciated primarily for the sake of ambience. Nobody speaks while these windblown middle-aged men are playing; the whole room lapses into a companionable silence, and hands and boots softly keep the four-four time.

Then a pretty local girl treats us to an interlude of ballads, romantically grim in the tradition of this country. The seal woman, tamed by an island man, finds her coat and returns to the sea. A dead lover taps on her windowpane in the middle of the night.

Then she sings a song, unaccompanied, about her man going off to fight in the Easter Rising and how she'll never see him again. Someone so young really hasn't any business singing about things she knows nothing of, and yet the heart she pours into those lines is so uncanny that I have to second-guess my assumption of her ordinariness. She stands up from the table amid a round of warm, familiar applause, empty glass in hand, but when we meet eyes I see no flash of kinship, no glowing moon on my thumbnail.

Justin gets up to order us another round with the euros that have just materialized in his wallet, and Byrne glances after him. "Now, tell me one thing," he says, leaning closer and placing his paw on my knee. "Have I any chance at all?"

I choke back a laugh. "Certainly not, Mr. Byrne. Oh, no offense," I say quickly. "But you must know what they say about Irishmen."

He leans closer still, and I turn my head to avoid a whiff of his bog breath. "What's that?" he asks.

"All potatoes, no meat."

Billy roars with laughter. Must be even drunker than he looks.

I watch Justin standing at the bar, leaning in to listen to what the old farmers are saying and then tossing his head back in genuine amusement.

When he finally comes back to the table I flash him a teasing smile. "Look at you, hobnobbing with the locals."

He nuzzles my neck and doesn't notice that I've just spilled a bit of my Guinness in his lap. "I'll hob *your* nob."

The stout drips down my glass and I laughingly lick my fingers.

"Ooh, you dirty boy!" I glance over and notice Byrne's gone off to the loo.

The musicians pause for a sup, and the fiddler leans over and taps Justin on the knee. "Did no one tell you about that table?"

"Oh, was this table reserved as well?"

The man shakes his head. "It's bad luck to sit at that table."

"Why?"

Again the fiddler shakes his head. "Worse luck for me if I told you."

Justin gives me an uneasy look, and I shrug. He decides to answer with a laugh. "You aren't through yet, are you?" he asks the fiddler.

"We'll do a few more."

"Any more ballads?"

"There'll be ballads if you're up for singing 'em."

"Oh, not me," Justin says with a laugh. "But my girlfriend has a marvelous voice." (It's the first time he's ever referred to me as his girlfriend. I smile a secret, bitter smile at this. First times and last times should never be one and the same.)

A hush falls awfully suddenly on the crowd in this little room. "I don't know any Irish songs," I say, "but I can sing you one in German."

I turn to my right and see Billy's back in his seat, gazing at me with a rather unnerving intensity. "Do," he says, and the musicians respond encouragingly as well. "We'd love to hear it."

So I take a deep breath and sing a song they used to play at the cabaret at the end of the night, "Irgendwo auf der Welt":

> *Somewhere in the world there's a little bit of happiness,*
> *and I've been dreaming of that for a long, long time . . .*

Justin doesn't take his eyes off me—not once—and after the last line's passed from my lips I take a breath and revel in the enraptured silence. Then there is applause, cheers and whistles even. I begin to feel a little delirious with all the attention, laughing inordinately at the musicians' jokes and responding a little too warmly when Justin puts his arm around me. I need some fresh air.

I look to Billy Byrne. "Is there anyplace we can get something to eat at this time of night?"

"There's a chipper van just up the road. We'll leave by the back way."

So Billy leads us past the toilets, through an alley, and back onto the main street a few doors down from the pub's front entrance. To our right there's a row of thatched whitewashed cottages. To our left, twenty yards down the road, we see a big white truck with a side counter where a woman is handing out cans of cola and burgers in paper boxes. The cold fluorescent light casts a shimmer on the rain-slicked road. The image is stark as a Hopper, and the quiet on the street is broken only by the drone of a small generator on the ground by the rear tires.

Justin joins the queue and asks our companion if he'd like anything. "Nothing for me, thanks," Byrne replies.

"What do you think I should order? I want the real Irish junk food experience."

"If I were you, I'd have the curry chips."

So that's what Justin orders, along with a burger for me and a couple cans of soda, and the woman behind the counter hands him down a big box of French fries doused in brown muck. I give Justin a look—half doubt, half disgust—but he smiles and tucks in with good cheer.

I hop up on a stone wall facing the road—I never eat standing up; it isn't ladylike—and Justin hops up beside me.

We eat in silence as Byrne paces the sidewalk with his hands thrust into the pockets of his dungarees, looks up at the stars, watches the other locals place their orders at the junk truck. The burger isn't great, but I've had worse. On our way back Justin catches sight of a quaint little shop-front a few doors up from the pub. "Eve, look—antiques!"

Beyond the words HAHESSY'S ANTIQUES, OLD & RARE, hand-painted in Gaelic script on the window glass, we can just make out a display of dog-eared songbooks, an accordion and one of those old-fashioned wooden washboards, a set of end tables topped with panels of cobweb lace. "How fortuitous," he says happily. "We'll have to come back tomorrow."

Back at the pub, we're waiting to order another round when all the lights dim. People start shrugging on their jackets. "Last call," Byrne says.

"They're closing?" I cry. "But they *can't* close!"

"It's after midnight," the bartender replies as he pours our last pints.

"But it's a Friday night! Couldn't we have a—what do you call it—a lock-in?"

"Young lady," the bartender replies, "the last time we had a lock-in here, Shane McGowan still had all his teeth."

"Why deprive a toothless man?" I say. "Oh, please, sir? It would make our holiday—"

"No, it would make our *year*," Justin puts in.

It would make our lifetime, I reflect sadly. "We've only got one night here," I tell the bartender in a low, urgent voice. "We've got to make it count." He glances up at me—we make eye contact—he can see I'm not intoxicated. I am *not* going home before dawn, simple as that.

The bartender sighs. "All right, lads," he says. "Ye can stay. Put the money in the till and wipe the counter before you go, and don't be making any racket."

The two dozen or so folks left in the pub let out a huge cheer, and Justin takes me by the waist and nuzzles my neck. A couple of men pull down the shades in the front window, and we all resettle ourselves with our drinks, poised for further merriment. The fiddler plays another reel or two, and then, mindful of the bartender's warning, the musicians put their instruments away. A few men go up to the bar to refill their glasses and drop their coins in the till. Someone throws more peat on the fire and the overhead lights are switched off.

"Now you sing us a song, Mick," someone says to the man who's just put his drum back in its carrying case. The dialogue that follows seems to be an intricate system of entreaty and refusal, Mick the drummer telling the crowd it's too late, he's too tired, and so forth, but clearly *wanting* to sing. It's only a matter of how badly we'd like him to. Finally we manage to "convince" him, and the room settles down to listen.

"He's going to sing *sean nós*," Byrne says under his breath.

"What's that mean?"

Byrne seems to think we should already know this. "An air. Unaccompanied," he says shortly.

The man's voice is low and reedy—one might even call it fierce—and I can't help thinking he sounds like a human bagpipe. He keeps his eyes closed throughout, and he sings without seeming to care a fig for time or melody. It almost sounds as if he's making it up as he goes, ending each verse with a melismatic flourish. Had I any oomph to spare, I could understand his foreign lyrics; nobody volunteers an English translation afterward, but it hardly seems necessary. Where there had been vigorous applause at the close of other songs earlier in the evening, when Mick the drummer ends this one everyone praises him in low, sober murmurs, his fellow musicians clapping him on the shoulders.

Then come the stories. There are more tales of the selkie, and of the sea goat of Inishbofin—man-eating or benign? they can't seem to agree—and eventually somebody asks if I'd be willing to tell one, if I know any. So I tell a story Neverino told me once, about a young wanderer in the Harz captivated by a bashful, lovely chambermaid, and how ardently he begs her master for her freedom. The mysterious innkeeper sets him to three tasks, all of which he completes. Just as the young man begins to rejoice in his triumph he looks down and notices the innkeeper's cloven feet and realizes he's been tricked into marrying the devil's daughter. The young man flees the inn, but he is forever followed on the road by a dark misshapen figure, a queer sooty lump of a creature, who still has the silvery voice of the maiden with whom he'd believed himself in love. Every night, at every place he stays, she sits at the foot of his bed and weeps, whispering in that incongruously sweet voice, "I knew not that I deceived thee." And when I finish the fable with the words "I knew not what I was," Justin is gazing at me with such intensity that I have to look away.

SOON AFTER three o'clock old Oonagh Coyne appears in a plaid bathrobe and tells us the jig is up.

"What'll we do now?" I sigh as we put on our jumpers and jackets. "I'm not ready to turn in yet."

"I could take ye on a bit of a sightseeing tour," Byrne says. "Show ye all the local haunts."

I hadn't been talking to *him*. But to my dismay, Justin seems delighted at the prospect of a little late-night adventure, and for these last few hours I can't have him thinking I'm a stick in the mud. So I'll bide my time—we can always ditch our garrulous companion later on.

Ten minutes later we're walking out of town on a side road—a "boreen," Byrne calls it. The only sounds are our three sets of footsteps squelching along the muddy track and an occasional bovine groan from one of the stone-hemmed pastures on either side of the road. I spot an old clawfoot bathtub in one of the fields, the rainwater inside long since turned to slime. "Rather inconvenient spot for a wash," I say, and Justin laughs.

The unruly hedges obscure our view, but eventually the road dips and a view of the sea spreads forth below us, the moonlight glimmering on the water and a few lights twinkling along the far side of the harbor.

I keep stopping to admire the view, so after a few minutes Byrne and Justin are yards ahead. I catch a snatch of conversation here and there, and when I hear the words "ghost babies" I hurry up the road to meet them. I don't like the sound of this. "What did you say?"

"Oh, nothing," Justin says impishly.

"We're going to a graveyard, aren't we?"

"We're already here," Byrne calls over his shoulder, and suddenly I spot a rusted gate in the low stone wall that follows the road. Beyond I can make out the ruin of a small church. Byrne lifts the latch with a terrific creak and Justin follows him inside. Byrne turns and looks at me. "Aren't you coming?"

"I don't do graveyards."

"What do you mean, you don't 'do' them?" Byrne asks with a good-natured snicker.

"I don't go inside them."

"You'll be going in sooner or later," laughs Billy Byrne. "Might as well get used to the idea."

"I've got time," I reply with far more confidence than I feel.

"Suit yourself." So I wait at the gate while Byrne shows Justin the graves of all those men and women late of Tully Cross, reminding him of stories he'd told us earlier in the evening. The night's still enough that I can hear most of what they're saying, though they might be fifty feet or more from me. Past the graveyard the ground rises into a small headland, beyond which the sea is softly glittering. I can hear the breakers tumbling against the rocks somewhere below. I glance down at the rusty old gate and notice the metal nameplate turned toward the inside.

The metal screeches as I twist it round to read it:

BALLY . . .
GRAVEYARD

The rest of the name has worn away.

"Here we have a poisonous plant famed in folklore," Byrne is saying. "Belladonna—deadly nightshade. Also known as witches' berries."

Justin makes a sound of disbelief. "They let that grow here?"

Byrne shrugs. "Do you know anyone mad enough to go scavenging for wild berries in a graveyard? Shame, though. There are some useful plants growing here."

Justin sits on his heels and peers at the bush growing along the wall. "Only poisonous if you eat them, right?"

"Aye, that's right."

Justin plucks a nightshade flower, a purple star-shaped bloom, walks back to the gate, and tucks it behind my ear.

"Here," Byrne calls, and Justin trots back to his side. "See those blue bell-shaped blooms? That's comfrey. You put that into an ointment, speeds healing. Same goes for that royal fern over there in the corner. This place is more bountiful than Mrs. Molloy's kitchen garden. Of course, the auld wives have their own notions. Brew the spores of that royal fern into a strong tea, and they say you'll see the future in your dreams.

"But this isn't why I brought ye," he says, cutting short this curious lesson in morbid botany. He starts ambling toward the far wall of the graveyard.

"Eve, come on!"

"Where are you going, Mr. Byrne?" I call. "Is it outside the graveyard?"

"That depends," he calls back. *Depends?* Depends on what?

With a sigh I venture into the bog and brush round the perimeter of the cemetery, making my way to the grassy hillock beyond. The space is studded with broad smooth stones brought up from the shingly shore. "They'd swear on a Bible they'd seen 'em," Byrne is telling Justin as I stumble toward them. "Dancing along the cliff. Bones glowing in the moonlight. *Bones,* aye, that's what I said. Water table's awfully high in these parts."

Justin is staring at Byrne in amazed silence. "Ever seen them yourself?" I ask with a careless toss of the head.

Byrne stares at me. "Would I bring ye here if I hadn't?"

Justin and I look at one another, then up toward the cliff. Does he believe Byrne's story? Personally I can't say I doubt him; if I believe in myself then I can believe in anything.

Billy Byrne turns and walks a few paces, eyes on the ground, as if he's seeking one stone in particular. He finds it and stands over it with hands clasped and head bent. "Here he is," he says softly. "Here's my wee brother."

Justin and I trade nervous glances. He isn't about to cry, is he? We've only just met him, after all. He looks older than ever, and the change is so dramatic that I now feel certain it isn't just a matter of my misjudging his age. He *is* older. Suddenly I wish we were far away from this lonesome little graveyard.

"It's cruel," Byrne murmurs. "They never had the chance to live, and then they get buried out here beyond the wall just as if they'd done something wrong. Look over there." He points to the far end of this unconsecrated space, where the grass has grown tall around the simple markers. *"They're* the ones who did wrong. My brother, he doesn't belong here." Byrne pauses. "But where I'm from, in Ballywhatsit, folks believe these little ones are happy enough out here. Passing time 'til the Day of Judgment, just like anybody else."

"Ballywhatsit?" I ask. "I thought you said you were from Ballybeg."

"Fearsome good memory, this one," he says to Justin, jerking his thumb at me. "May you live to rue it."

I fold my arms. "So is it Ballybeg or Ballywhatsit?"

"Ballybeg, I think. Or maybe Ballyconneely. I can't say I remember for sure."

"How can you forget where you're from?" Then I feel a chill as I recall the sign on the graveyard gate. Bally*where?*

"Doesn't matter, so long as I remember how to get there," Byrne replies. "It's only a mile or two up the road."

It was a mile or two up the road a mile or two ago, but there's no point picking nits. I think back to earlier in the evening, when there was a pint glass in front of him, the stout disappearing by levels though he never seemed to take a sip. He didn't eat—he didn't talk to anyone but us, nor did anyone else acknowledge him with so much as a nod—and there's his ever-shifting appearance.

I ask him one more question now, though I think I already know the answer he'll give me. "Mr. Byrne . . . what was the name of your little brother?"

His back is still facing me, but judging by the sadness in his voice I'd bet he looks as old as his great-great-grandfather. "I can't remember that either," he says softly.

I lock eyes with Justin as I reach for Byrne's shoulder. Then I look away, toward the cliff. "Justin—I think I see something."

So Justin turns toward the cliff, just in case the ghost babies have come out to dance after all, and I lay my hand on Byrne's shoulder . . .

. . . Or would have, had he actually been there.

Justin turns back to where the mysterious Irishman was a second ago and gasps. "Where—what—where did he go?" He takes a few steps back toward the graveyard, turning this way and that. The night is still as ever. "How could he remember every detail of all those old scandals . . . but forget where he lives and the name of his own brother?"

I rub my arms to try to dispel the gooseflesh. "Perhaps for the same reason he's vanished without a sound."

"But that's ridiculous, Eve. He's got to be hiding in the graveyard."

"Go on and check, then," I tell him.

Justin strides to the wall and peers over it. He glances this way and that, waiting for any sign of movement behind the silent tombstones. "The drummer," he murmurs, half to himself. "He told us that table was bad luck." Now he gives me a look I know all too well—the look of a person who is on the verge of understanding but for sanity's sake would really rather not.

"We'd better go," he says.

Justin hops the graveyard wall and holds out his hand to help me over, and naturally I hesitate. But if there was ever a night I could be brave enough, tonight is it. I take a deep breath, grab his hand, and hop over the wall, and for a few moments I can hear nothing but our feet moving through the long wet grass. We're halfway to the grave-yard gate when I notice it: the darkest corner, which is on the side nearest the road, all the stones and grass devoured in shadow.

I've come this far; might as well kick it. It's only a silly story anyhow.

Justin pauses at the gate. "Eve? Where are you going?"

"I'll be just a minute!" I reach the corner and dip the toe of my boot into the shadow. Nothing. Thus emboldened, I aim a good sturdy kick at the old stone wall not two feet in front of me . . . *and miss.*

I let out the scream of my life, though of course I don't stick around to see if I've roused anybody. I sprint for the gate and Justin ducks out of the way to let me through, bless him. I keep on running up the boreen 'til my lungs hurt, and he soon catches up. "What was that all about?"

I shake my head, still breathless. "Don't want to talk about it." Then I realize that, through my own folly, we're already a good bit of the way back to the pub—that much closer to the end of everything. I stop and vigorously shake my foot, hoping to rid myself of that terrible sucking sensation I felt when my boot met nothing but dead space.

We keep walking back to the main road, glancing frequently over our shoulders, though I know full well we'll never set eyes on Billy Byrne again. So we stumble back toward Tully Cross, sour mouthed and shivering, light creeping back into the eastern sky so slowly that the sudden brightness of dawn comes as a shock.

"Wait, wait." I lead him by the hand toward the stone wall along the road. "Let's sit for a bit." We hop up on the mossy stones and swing our legs over so we can see the sun coming up over the hills. A few cows come lumbering toward us.

"Where did you say our B and B was?"

"I didn't."

"Huh?"

I sigh. "We have to walk back to town. It's, er, over the pub."

"But I didn't see any B and B over the pub . . ."

"It's a small sign."

"All right, as long as you've got the key." He puts his arm around my waist and nuzzles my neck as the cows approach, regarding us with blank-eyed curiosity.

I'd give anything to have that key in my pocket right now, to have a little more time. "I gave it to you."

Justin pats the pockets of his jacket, then his trousers. "I don't have it. Do you have it?"

"Uh-oh." This ruse is getting rather tiresome, but I can't very well tell him we're going home in twenty minutes. Besides, I don't want to go home any more than he does.

"I guess we'll have to knock. I hope they won't hate us too much. Man, I'm hungry again. How many hours 'til they start serving breakfast?"

"A few, I suppose." In a few hours he'll be having breakfast at home, without me. I wish I could pull a chocolate bar out of my pocket for him.

"You know something, Eve?"

"Hmm?"

"Sometimes I think I must be very old, sitting in a wicker chair someplace, and that all this . . . I'm reliving all this. My whole life, you know? Inside my head."

"That's the silliest thing I ever heard." I point to our bovine companions, who are still standing there staring at us. "See, they think so too."

"Is it silly?" A shadow passes over his face. "Lately I've been feeling like I'm fast-forwarding from one event to the next, and I have only the haziest memories of the things that have happened in between. Makes a guy wonder if there isn't some cruel twist coming up."

I glance at him sidewise, feeling a pang. Then I pull the nightshade blossom out from behind my ear and put it up to his nose. "Can you smell this?"

Cautiously he sniffs. "Yeah."

I point to the cows. "And can you smell them?" He wrinkles his nose in reply.

"That's good," I say gravely. "If this were all happening inside your head you wouldn't be able to smell anything."

"There's a point." He notices the Janus pendant round my neck and reaches out to finger it fondly.

I've had much too much to drink, and the greasy meal off the chipper truck hasn't done my insides any good either. Of course, my heart is even more mutinous than my stomach—I want nothing more than to give in to it, to run back the way we came, through the fields and down to the shore, so that we might fall asleep in each other's arms among the brittle swaths of dried seaweed.

But upon waking, caked in sand and cold to the bone, he would find quite a different Eve beside him. That very thought horrifies and sickens me. It's over, very nearly over—and because Justin can never know it, much less why, our last moments together are deprived of their rightful tenderness.

The sun is higher in the sky now, the air cool and sweet. Little birds flit in and out of the hedges as the cows plod back to the trough. It's the loveliest morning I've ever seen. I squeeze his hand and he turns to look at me. "What if something happened to me, Justin? No, I mean it. I'm being perfectly serious here. Life would go on, of course—but do you suppose you would remember me?"

"Don't be ridiculous." He pulls me to him and holds me tighter than ever, and I smile into the folds of his jacket. I suppose I'll have to content myself with that.

I'M QUIVERING with dread by the time we reach the alley that leads to the back of the pub. "Are you all right?" he asks, and what can I say? I give him a weak smile, a grimace more like. I undo the lock on the alley door with what little oomph I have left (just enough now to get us home and get me away before he can see what I am), and we go round the back. I gaze up into his bewildered face, lay my hand against his cheek, and when he opens his mouth to ask why the heck I've pulled him into the ladies' toilet, I press a finger to his lips. As the fog drifts into his head this last time he yawns and smiles, his eyelids growing heavy.

I say the words that will bring us back to Hartmann's Classic Toys . . . and that's when it all, figuratively speaking, goes to pot.

String 'er Up

27.

✹✹✹

THE FIRST thing I notice is that I feel awfully stiff in the limbs. I can't see very well either, though I can tell we're not in the bathroom like we should be. Then I notice my feet aren't on the ground; I feel myself flailing and realize in utter astonishment that I am actually *hanging* from something.

"Eve? Eve, what's going on?"

I turn my head at the sound of Justin's voice, and when I see what he's wearing—a jester suit, bells and all—the appalling truth becomes all too clear. *Lucretia!*

I tug and struggle, legs wheeling, but the crossbars are resting solidly on the flies and my hands feel as if they're glued to this stupid mouse-sized lute. My jaw hinge squeaks as I call out, "Justin? Are you all right?"

I watch Justin survey himself, shaking his arm so the bells jingle, and I see a flash of panic in his little glass eyes.

"You were right," I say. "We shouldn't have used her bathroom."

"What the hell is going on, Eve? Tell me I'm dreaming!"

"Oh, how I wish I could." I'm getting better acquainted with our surroundings now. It's a vantage never before seen by human eyes—that is, unless Lucretia makes a habit of turning people into marionettes, which wouldn't surprise me in the slightest. There's a row of kewpie dolls propped up against the bottom of the stage beneath us and beyond them the railroad track with its gleaming red locomotive. And beyond that is the window, where I spot a faint reflection of us in our new (and hopefully very temporary) bodies. I'm the Renaissance angel, of course: shimmering wings, dark flowing locks, my rosy cheeks dusted with glitter. Gosh, I *do* look lovely, don't I?

"Eve! What's happened to us?"

"Look." I nod at our reflection in the window. "See? We've been turned into puppets. And no, you really aren't dreaming."

He stares at his wooden hands. The bells on his cuffs give a pathetic jingle. "How the hell are you going to get us out of this?"

I turn to him sharply. "What makes you think I can?"

He can't answer me that—not yet, anyway. The cat will be out of the bag soon enough now.

I pause, taking in the eerie early-morning stillness. No shrieking kiddies, no Chatty Cathys, no jingling doorbell. It's still night here, and the only light comes from the streetlamp; we left Tully Cross sometime past five o'clock, so I guess it's a little after midnight. The loo flue may shoot us back and forth between continents in a twinkling, but it isn't a time machine. Would that it were.

I wait for something to break the silence, but all I can hear is the distant rumbling of a delivery truck. Where *is* the auld hatchet-face, anyway?

Then I start to panic. With Morven conked out, who's to notice I've been gone too long?

"Enough of this." I pull and pull and finally the lute comes loose out of my hands, and I cast it down with a discordant twang. Let's see how well these little wooden lungs work. "*LUCRETIA!* Show your face, you miserable shrew!"

"Lucretia? Lucretia Hartmann did this to us?"

"I *told* you you'd be sorry for taking that apartment."

The light goes on in the room behind the counter. So she's been in her office all along! We hear footsteps approaching and I can see her face in the window glass. "Ah," she says brightly. "You're back. I trust you had a pleasant trip?"

"Go to hell," I squeak as she reaches into the window, picks us up by the crossbars, and hangs us up again on a couple of hooks screwed into the wall above the display case. We're much higher up now, making our chance of escape even slimmer—not that I could make a run for it on these wonky wooden legs.

"Well," she says. "You've come to a pretty pass, now, haven't you?"

"You've got to know you'll be expelled, Lucretia."

She makes a show of considering this. "Perhaps I will," she says, tapping her forefinger to her lip. Then she points at me, and I feel awfully queer. "But it's a lot less likely now your sister's not running things."

I glance at Justin: his little wooden brow is warped with horror. "Oh, Eve! *What has she done to your face?*"

I struggle against the strings to turn myself so I'm facing the window again, but I can only catch a glimpse of my reflection. I gasp. The glitter slides down new runnels in my cheeks. She's turned me into a prune-head! "Now, really, Lucretia. I may not be a spring chicken, but don't you think this is rather overdoing it?"

"It's closer to the truth than the face you put on for this boy."

"It's my own face!"

"*Was* your face," she sneers. "It's been quite a while since you woke up looking like that, eh, hmmm?"

"What is she talking about, Eve?" The fright in Justin's voice is unmistakable, and I can't bring myself to look at him.

"It's not your place to judge me."

"Not my place!" Lucretia laughs. "Oh, but you do have me there, Evelyn. Our coven leader turns a blind eye because she's your sister, and not a peep out of anybody. Just imagine if I were to do the same as you, smoothing out all my wrinkles, cinching my waist, and making my hair grow nice and thick again just so I could have all the men drooling after me." (It's all I can do to keep from bursting out laughing; surely Lucretia was as homely in girlhood as she is in middle age.) "What would your dear sister have to say *then*?"

"I haven't broken any—"

"But you see, it doesn't matter that you haven't used any charms or philters. You refuse to abide by the spirit of the law, and it's time you were duly punished for it."

"Right," Justin cuts in nervously. "Lesson learned. Can you turn us back now, please?"

Lucretia looks him up and down. "I suppose you'll be wanting your deposit back."

I hear Justin's limbs clunking gently as he fidgets. "I think that goes without saying, ma'am."

"Lucretia, this is between you and me. I don't see why you should punish the boy."

"'*The boy*'?" Justin hisses. "Eve, who—*what are you?*"

"I'll explain everything," I whisper, as if she can't hear me.

"I suppose she was afraid you wouldn't want her anymore if you knew she was a hundred and fifty years old," Lucretia sneers.

He stares at me. "You . . . you told me you were a hundred and forty-nine. I thought you were joking because you didn't want to admit you'd turned thirty." He shoots Lucretia a look of defiance. "No. It can't be."

"See?" she says to me. "They always side with you no matter what rubbish you feed them. Evelyn this and Evelyn that. Evelyn, the pride of the coven. What a sorry lot we are, if you're the best of us! You and all your stupid war stories—"

"I never said I was a heroine," I cut in. "I did good work, and I don't see any harm in recollecting it."

"Hah! You 'never said.' What have you done that you haven't expected full credit for afterward?"

Quite honestly, I'm so taken aback at this that I can't even speak.

"*Coven,*" Justin is muttering to himself. "What the hell, Eve? When you said she was a witch I never thought you meant it literally."

"Justin, dear," Lucretia cuts in. "If I'm a witch, then what is she?"

I refuse to panic. After all, he understood once—I can make him understand again. He won't be angry for long. "I'll explain everything once we get out of here," I say. "I promise."

Justin shakes his head with childlike vigor. "She can't be a witch. She can't be."

"See!" Lucretia cries. "Everyone loves you. Everyone *believes* you, no matter what lies you throw at them." Now she seems to be gearing for a meltdown. "You think I don't notice how you all laugh at me? You and your snide laughter, always calling me a priss behind your hands—"

"Actually, we called you 'Little Miss Prissyknickers,' but I suppose that's close enough."

She leans in, and I get an unfortunately close view of her nose. For heaven's sake, what's the point of being a beldame if you can't dispense with your own rosacea? "Helena is guilty," she says fiercely. "You refuse to see it, but you will. She's damned by the evidence."

"Pah! The ravings of a lovesick schoolgirl hardly qualify as evidence."

"It didn't occur to you even when she closed the B and B? She might as well have painted the word 'murderer' on her own forehead!

Use your brain, for heaven's sake. Did you honestly think I would make that kind of accusation so lightly?"

I screw my little wooden prune-head into the fiercest grimace I can muster. What a stupid question! "I've had quite enough of this."

"But I don't see what the problem is, Evelyn. Go on and free yourself, why don't you?" She pauses. "Oh, but I suppose you've run out of oomph. Well. That *is* a pickle." She lifts me off the hook and carries me back to the puppet stage in the display case. I try to kick her but she's holding me at arm's length. "You can dangle here fifty years for all I care. Somebody will come along and buy you soon enough. Oops!" She attempts a girlish laugh but it comes out like a harpy's honk. "I'll have to change your face back first."

She walks away from the window case. "Not you, of course, Justin," I hear her say. "You're a nice boy, and I'm sorry to have put you through this. The baby sometimes goes out with the bathwater when you put a monitor on a loo flue. Not to worry, you'll wake up in your own bed." I hear her footsteps retreating back toward her office, but I can still hear her saying, "Honestly, though, I'd be a little more careful choosing my next girlfriend, if I were you."

Despair swallows me whole. The knowledge that I've just seen the last of him, and that it ended this way—I can't bear it.

Mind you, I don't care a fig what Lucretia says on that account. It's her talk of Helena that's needling at me underneath it all. Evelyn Harbinger, you foolish, foolish girl! Hah, *girl*. Silly old hag, more like.

I've never cared for the word "epiphany." Feels like a shard of glass in my mouth.

The jester puppet suddenly reappears at my side, inert. I hear Lucretia's footsteps coming back down the stairs. Then I see a sudden movement outside. There are faces at the window peering in at me, and my little wooden heart jumps for joy and relief. Mira and Vega! Then I hear the doorbell jingling, and Vega's hand looms above me. In another moment I'm freed of these stupid strings. Helena's here too, and Dymphna, and there are very harsh words spoken without the raising of voices. I feel jubilant in the knowledge that in the end it isn't me who's getting the comeuppance. Vega grasps me gently by the waist, the glitter from my dress spilling down her forearm. She taps me gently between the eyes and, mercifully, that's the last thing I remember.

Night and Fog

28.

1945–1946

She showed me mine, in crystal clear,
With several wild young blades, a soldier-lover:
I seek him everywhere, I pry and peer,
And yet, somehow, his face I can't discover.

—Johann Wolfgang von Goethe, *Faust*

CARRY ON and carry out, they tell you. But you feel quite sure the sun won't rise the next morning, and when it does you resent it for shining.

After he hid me in the milking shed, tucked the dagger in its sheath inside the curve of my sleeping form and his father's pocket watch in my hand, I like to think he kissed my lips and forehead and murmured a farewell in my ear.

He might have heard engines in the distance as he sprinted back to the stable and set fire to his notes. As the flames spread across the worktable, he would have drawn out the L-pill from a smaller bag inside his tobacco pouch and tucked it in his jaw before loading his pistol, all the while hearing the lorry grind to a halt outside, doors slamming, heavy footsteps but no orders shouted, not a word spoken. From one of the loft windows he'd have taken out four or five men before the rest could reach the door, but once they were inside the building . . . well.

I told you they killed him, and that wasn't strictly true. He didn't give them the chance.

I DROPPED THROUGH the trapdoor and came out of the milking shed to find both stable and farmhouse in cinders, the ruins still smoking in the wintry sunshine.

My first thought was that Albrecht Hoppe had betrayed us. It makes little sense in retrospect, of course; why would he cooperate with the men who were responsible for the death of one brother and would have taken any opportunity to do away with the other? But then again nothing made sense when it came to the German psyche in the grip of National Socialism, and I'm sorry to admit that in that first hour I put my whole heart into blaming Hoppe for Jonah's death and the collapse of the mission. His mother's behavior only added to my suspicion.

I hurried across the snowy fields between the abandoned farmstead and the Hoppes' place and tapped at the kitchen door. Frau Hoppe was genuinely surprised to see me—shocked, even. I caught a faint whiff of pine from the garland still tacked to the wooden mantelpiece and thought, *The holiday is finished, everything is finished.* She stood solidly in the door frame, as if to say I was no longer welcome inside. "We thought for sure they had captured you," she said. "Where did you come from?"

"I was hiding in the milking shed. Where . . . where is Herr Robbins?"

"Oh, but Herr Robbins is dead," she said. *Dead?*

"Tot," she said again, with an air much less sympathetic than I would have expected of her. "We heard gunshots. He killed some of their men before they got him. Albrecht could tell, because he saw more blood on the ground. But by the time my son got there they were all gone."

I didn't want to ask the next question, because in these paltry seconds I still had hope. I could bring him back. If it had happened less than three hours ago, I could bring him back.

"When was this?"

My heart sank when she answered me. Two days ago. Too late.

It took all I had left to hold myself together. "And . . . did they leave the body?"

She averted her eyes. "It is in the ice shed. But you cannot leave it there for much longer. *Verstehst du?*"

Frau Hoppe's manner had changed in a twinkling. With all the muttering and hand-wringing, her eyes darting this way and that as she spoke, I didn't need to read her mind to know she was eager to see the back of me. The aura of warmth and childlike mischief I had so admired in her was gone.

You see what fear does to people? Makes them small.

I swallowed my disgust as I said my last good-bye. I told her Jonah would be buried and I'd be gone before next morning. Albrecht and Addie were nowhere to be seen.

I WENT TO the ice shed and found his body under a tarpaulin in the corner. The Nazis had left him facedown in the snow, and my tears fell on his face as I brushed the grit from his nose and cheek. He looked almost as if he'd frozen to death. It's the cyanide—turns your lips blue. I kissed him again and again, wishing the poison on his lips could have some effect on me.

For a good long while I sat on the floor beside his body, mulling over the prospect of life without him. And there's no sense denying I thought of bringing him back just as the foolish young beldame had done at La Corbière.

But if I restored him—what then? He wouldn't have been the man I remembered, for one thing, and he might have resented me for the strange, numb half life I would have imposed upon him. He might very well have hated me for not letting him rest in peace. Nor could I argue that we couldn't complete our mission without him; Jonah would have been the first to tell me that a war can't be lost by a solitary failure.

And then I thought of Cordelia Wynne and her cold black heart. He was gone, and I had to accept that. I'd wait until nightfall, and then I would bury him.

Jonah had left me the crystals but there hadn't been time to hide the radio, and naturally the Nazis had retrieved it out of the smoldering ruin. I decided to find a loo and get back to London to deliver the intelligence in person, though the real reason for doing so was the good long cry I could have in Morven's arms. The thought of seeing my sister again was the only thing that would keep me going over the next ten hours.

I spent that time covering our tracks. I would finally have to find out what happened to Hans; I had to face the likelihood that he had talked, and also the possibility that I mightn't find a trace of him. They could have shot him weeks ago.

I flew back to Quedlinburg, to the roof of the town jail, and set about searching for our hapless radio operator. I didn't really expect to find him there, but perhaps I could locate his name in one of their bloody ledger books. Then I could say I had tried.

I poked my little bird head into each cell in the basement prison block, feeling sorry that I could do very little for the sleeping, broken men inside them. *I could free them,* I thought, *but what would become of them after that?*

But I did find Hans, in the last cell on the basement corridor. He was lying on a filthy pallet on the floor, staring sightlessly at the cracks in the ceiling. I hopped between the bars, resumed my womanly form, and he sprang up in horror. "Please, Uta," he gasped. "Please don't kill me!"

I stared at him. *"I'm* not the one you need to beg for your life."
I paused. "You talked to them, didn't you?"

He looked up at me in abject misery. "I couldn't stand it."

"What they've done to you here is nothing compared to what
would have happened to you in Berlin," I said. "But I suppose they'll
be sending you there eventually."

He clasped his hands together as if I were some terrible angel of
judgment. "I did it for my children," he said. "I said to myself, better a
traitor who provides for them."

I snorted. "Like you're providing for them now? Like you'll provide for them after they've shot you and thrown you in a hole?"

He didn't speak for several moments. "What are you going to do
to me?"

I was thinking of a sort of corollary to the beldames' oath, one that
said punishment for the genuinely penitent is a cruelty. And yet to leave
him here *was* cruelty when his execution was a foregone conclusion.

In the end I freed every last prisoner that night, in the hope that
they might find safe places to wait out the last few months of the war.

JONAH WAS one of the lucky ones. They hadn't worked and starved
him to death. He hadn't had to live with the shame of talking—not
that he ever would have, I know that much for certain—and unlike the
rest of his fallen colleagues, he would be given a proper burial.

Snow fell softly on the charred remains of the old farmhouse.
Earlier in the day I had spotted an old yew tree not far from it, and
I carried him over the fields toward it with a strength I didn't know I
had—a hideous inversion of a honeymoon night, but I could not
bring myself to fold him into a wheelbarrow. There were two inches of
snow by then and the ground was frozen solid, so I was obliged to
spend a little more oomph making the hole.

For the second time in my life I wished I could find a holy man, but as it was, I had to see him off in my own way. First I stood above him for a good long while, until I could no longer feel my fingers or my face. I cried for all the missions he'd never fulfill, the lives that would be lost because of the broken link—and for the children he'd never sire, the future perfect family who would never give him joy or comfort—and I cried in the face of my own selfishness.

Then I prayed to the only god I knew. It didn't take long; our burial rites are generally brief and to the point. I asked that Jonah's spirit be allowed to return to its maker and be at peace there. "And please," I said, "if it's not too much to ask—send him back to me someday."

The grave filled itself in as I took out Jonah's carving knife to mark the trunk of the yew tree with a Star of David and the letters JAR.

It hit me then that I would see and touch and kiss him no more, and I wept with renewed bitterness. I knew now that nothing was ever "for keeps."

O F C O U R S E, I had to use the Hoppes' water closet to get back to London. I looked for signs of life in the house, but all was still. I hesitated outside for a minute or two—I did so want to see Adelaide one last time—and suddenly she was standing in front of me, stealthy as a fox though she was wearing heavy rubber boots under her woolen nightgown.

"Addie!" I reached out a hand to stroke her silky hair, wet with melted snow. "What are you doing here? You ought to be in bed!"

"I snuck out the window." She looked at my soiled hands. "Oma says I can't talk to you anymore."

"Your Oma is right. I've got to go away now."

"But why?"

"Because if I don't, the bad men will catch me."

"Like they caught Herr Robbins?"

"No, Addie. They didn't catch him. He . . . he didn't let them."

"I heard guns," she said. "But me and Oma hid in the cellar and it was all right." Addie paused. "Frau Braun?"

"Yes?"

"Will I ever see you again?"

"I don't know, Addie. But either way, always remember me as your friend. Will you do that?"

She nodded, smiled, and threw her arms about my waist in a brief but snug embrace. "Tell Herr Robbins good-bye for me, and good luck." She ran off into the snowy darkness, toward the house and her warm bed, and I pinched my nose as I opened the privy door.

T HE REST hardly seems worth telling. I stayed in London for a few weeks, had my good long cry, and gave Morven Jonah's pocket watch for safekeeping. OSS London had received Jonah's transmission in its entirety, but the Allies had decided not to use the soap bomb to destroy the factory. The war in Europe would soon end by other means. But that night at the *Schloss* hadn't all been for nothing: another shipment of V-2s had been destroyed en route from Nordhausen on the fourth of January.

One night, while I was staying with Morven in Little London, I opened his pocket watch and my heart thrilled when I saw a folded-up bit of paper tucked between the gears and the brass casing, but when I unfolded it with trembling fingers, all I found was an old cipher.

And then I went back to Germany for one last mission. At that point, the end was in sight and the Allies wanted us to gather evidence for the trials. It was as dangerous as any other mission and yet the easiest by far. Now there was nothing to lose.

I met my sister in London after V-day and we took the flue back to Cat's Hollow, though my homecoming turned out to be temporary. I must have been insufferable those first few months—poor dear Morven! In Germany there hadn't been time for despair, but now I threw myself into it, hankies, booze, and all. Wasn't I perfectly entitled to breakfast with amaretto and praline chocolates every morning, and to sit around in my dressing gown all afternoon with piles of records all over the floor and coffee table, listening to the most depressing music I could get my hands on?

Other days I was restless and irritable and paced the city until sunrise. When we went out to eat I would inevitably drink much too much wine and start speaking of Jonah again. "And I don't even have a picture of him," I'd sob as we walked home through the warren, with me leaning heavily on my sister to keep me upright.

My sisters and aunties were sympathetic, yet there was a distant quality to their words of comfort; they didn't want to know any more about him than they had my other lovers. They'd seen it happen a hundred times already: the war transformed what should have lasted a couple of dates into something that felt like kismet. I could talk myself blue trying to explain that what I'd had with Jonah was different, it *was* kismet, but they only would have said *Yes, dear,* of course *it was special, dear.* Morven had declared long ago that all I really wanted out of life was one great love. Now that I'd finally had it, I didn't know what to do with myself.

Early that fall Neverino stopped to visit for a couple of days on his way to Argentina, where he planned to spend the next several years hunting for Nazis. He lifted my spirits and delighted my nieces with his own brand of magic, though Helena hardly knew what to make of him. We stayed up all night eating ambrosia cake and telling each other everything that had happened since we'd last met.

But as soon as he was gone I felt even lonelier than before. I'd had a portent, a dead pigeon on my windowsill. I would never see Neverino again either.

E VENTUALLY MORVEN suggested that perhaps I shouldn't retire just yet. I wasn't doing anybody any good sitting around singing my *Liebestod* over and over, now, was I?

So I asked the War Department to renew my commission and returned to Germany for the last time. I helped in the effort to compile and sort all the evidence against those who were to be tried at Nuremberg, and it was then that I came into possession of the ledgers from the prison at Fresnes, what my colleagues grimly referred to as the "book of lost souls." It wasn't one book, of course—there'd been many thousands of prisoners at Fresnes, and the records filled a room.

The book hadn't come into my hands by chance. I had tracked it down over a period of weeks, weaseled my way onto the team that was working through every last ledger trying to figure out precisely what had befallen all who were lost. I opened one of the books from early 1942 and flipped hurriedly through the pages looking for Jonah's alias. And when I found it—*Jean Renard,* then the details of his capture and his intended destination—there at the end of the line were two characters in neat red ink:

NN.

Nacht und Nebel: night and fog. He knew full well he would have been executed had he stayed on that train, but he couldn't have known this: there would have been no trace of him, no closure for his family and friends.

My next step was to find out who'd been in command at Fresnes in late 1941, early 1942. There were several candidates, not all of whom had been apprehended. I wasn't fazed at the prospect of tracking him down, whoever he was, but in the event I didn't have to. I caught my first glimpse of SS-Sturmbannführer Heinrich Engel from a back-row seat in courtroom 600, and I need hardly tell you he was wearing my father's face. I closed my eyes, saw Jonah's naked body in the darkness, his bare flesh mottled with round red scars.

The next morning the tribunal acquitted Heinrich Engel of three out of four counts of crimes against humanity. While grisly photographs of the executed Nazi ringleaders were released to the international press, Engel was being sentenced to ten years' hard labor in a Soviet prison camp.

I WAS EVEN more disgusted when I saw Heinrich Engel as he truly was. He was *fat*. Why did they have to feed these criminals so bloody well?

He was dozing when I let myself into his cell, and he sprang up and stared at me. "Who are you?"

"Doesn't matter." I conjured a card table and chair, bade him sit on the edge of his bed. "Cigarette?"

He nodded, no doubt believing himself still in the middle of a dream. I lit the fag, made as if to hand it to him, then snatched it away again with a cold laugh. I took a long drag. Then I leaned across the table and brought the burning end very near his hand; he tried to recoil and discovered he was unable to. He looked at me first with the panicked eyes of a caged animal, then with a sort of horrified recognition. We now understood each other perfectly.

"Now take off your boots."

"What?"

"You heard me."

He obeyed. Not such a bully now, was he?

"Socks too!"

He doffed his socks.

"Now lie back on the bed."

I gave him no choice but to obey me. I rose from the table, still smoking and eyeing him thoughtfully.

"What are you going to do?" he asked. I knew he was dying to cry out a string of expletives, *Fotze!* and *Schlampe!* and worse I'm sure, but he was much too afraid to.

"Tell you what," I said, as if I had changed my mind and decided to be merciful. "Sit up. Put your socks and boots back on."

As he did so he looked longingly at my cigarette, wincing as I stubbed it out on the card table with a taunting flourish.

"I'd love to watch you suffer as he did," I said. "But I haven't the patience."

So I did it in the space of a blink: the dagger came out of its sheath without any conscious effort, and I lunged forward and drew the blade across his neck in a neat red line. He clutched at his gaping throat, eyes goggling, blood spilling out from between his meaty fingers. I wiped the dagger on the leg of his prison-issue trousers.

You can't use magic to rob a man of his life, but nobody ever said I couldn't use my hands. He was still dying when I flew out the window.

Madness, Put to Good Use

29.

There were once upon a time three sisters, quite transparent, and very beautiful. The robe of the one was red, that of the second blue, and that of the third white. They danced hand in hand beside the calm lake in the clear moonshine. They were not elfin maidens, but mortal children. A sweet fragrance was smelt, and the maidens vanished in the wood; the fragrance grew stronger—three coffins, and in them three lovely maidens, glided out of the forest and across the lake: the shining glow-worms flew around like little floating lights. Do the dancing maidens sleep, or are they dead? The odour of the flowers says they are corpses; the evening bell tolls for the dead!

—Hans Christian Andersen, "The Snow Queen"

I WAKE UP in my bedroom at Harbinger House inside a warm patch of afternoon light. I lay the back of my hand—my crinkly liver-spotted hand—over my eyes and let out a groan. For a second or two I can't remember a thing; then it hits me and I scramble up on my elbows, struggling with the tangled bedsheets. "What's happened?"

Vega hands me a glass of a murky green liquid—tastes of rancid lemons and dirty feet—and though I feel better as soon as I've downed it, the stuff brings my panic into focus.

"Where's Morven? Where's Justin? He doesn't remember, does he?"

"He doesn't remember a thing," Vega replies. "He's back at Harry's house now." She sighs. "That was a cruel stunt Lucretia pulled. Who would've thought she had it in her?"

I give my niece an evil little smile. "She's in for it now, the old crow."

Vega shakes her head. "I'm sorry to tell you she only got a slap on the wrist. Dymphna's already called *that* meeting."

"What's this? How long have I been out?"

"Nearly a week."

I fall back onto the pillow with another groan. "How did you know?"

"Before she conked out, Auntie Morven told us you might run into a spot of trouble at the toy shop. Said she saw you in the View-Master." She pauses. "Incidentally, Granny's made her promise not to indulge you ever again."

"No need," I say crossly. "I already told her it would be the last time."

Vega suppresses a smile. "But in all fairness, Auntie, hadn't you said so before?"

"Why needle me? I'm never going to see him again. Mind you, I'd promised as much to Morven before I left. She'll tell you that. I meant to keep my word, and I will, without anybody else's intervention, thank you very much."

"Well, I hope you had a nice holiday." *I hope it was worth all the fuss you kicked up* is what she means.

"Best night of my life," I reply a little haughtily.

Vega stands up to go, and I only just notice she's looking far too weary for a girl of forty-six. "You'd better come downstairs, as soon as you feel up to it," she says. "Granny says she's got something to tell us."

. . .

I COME DOWN to find all the Peacocks and the Jesters assembled in the drawing room. When I greet them I try for my old brio, but I can't quite keep the quaver out. "Dymphna! How lovely to see you."

"Evelyn," she says, nodding somewhat stiffly. "I hope you've regained your strength."

"I *am* feeling better, thank you." I spot Lucretia seated at the far end of the room, but she avoids my eye.

Dymphna leans closer so she can murmur in my ear. "They're waiting for you in the kitchen." Glancing round confusedly at the room full of expectant faces, I back through the doorway and close the drawing room door behind me.

I find all the Harbingers round the table. Hieronymus is back in human form for the occasion, fully dressed for the first time in Lord only knows how long, and even Heck's come home. He's taken off his boots and the whole room smells of stale cheese. Nobody greets me. There's a terrible whiff of momentousness here, and with this second frosty reception in a row I'm fairly certain my comeuppance is at hand.

I stand on the threshold, hesitating. "Have I bought it?"

"Sit down, you goose," Helena snaps. "I have something to tell all of you."

Marguerite lays her hand gently over Helena's. "Mother?"

My sister takes a deep breath. "I am ready to confess."

Somehow we've all been expecting this, but I can't help sputtering out, "*What?!* But you—but you said—"

"Oh, I'm not denying I've lied to you," she sighs. "It was a lie of omission." She pauses. "I suppose it never occurred to any of you to *ask* me if I'd done it."

I believe the English have a word for the lot of us right about now, and that word is "gobsmacked."

"I wasn't very concerned at first. I thought she'd be easy to deal with. Then one night he told me he'd . . . *strayed* . . . and I knew it was too late. Hag knots or no, she hadn't needed any hocus-pocus to beguile him. She was young and obsequious. Told him he was a genius, made him feel virile. That was enough."

"Did he—did he tell you he was going to leave you?"

"Good heavens, no! He only wanted my forgiveness. After a period I told him he had it—but a wife can never actually forgive, can she?"

So it was just as the local chemist had suspected all those years ago, though he never could have proved she was behind it. "I tampered with his coffee that very Monday. Now that there are no more secrets between us, I must tell you that I felt no guilt, not even the slightest twinge. He promised to let Belva go right away, and I told myself that so long as he made good on his promise, I would never do it again.

"Well, you all know how it turned out. He began to make excuses for keeping her on. He swore up and down that he had ended it, that it had never really begun because it had only happened the once. I kept an eye on him at his office—"

"You *did* use that grimoire, for the fish-eye trick," Morven says. "We saw it in the View-Master."

Helena nods. "I'm sorry, dear, but I couldn't bring myself to admit that I'd ever opened it. The book itself was a token of *maleficium*— I told you I didn't know who'd sent it, but you all know well enough who it was—and I knew I could shake it off by actually using one of the spells. Anyway, I saw them together, day after day, sometimes working . . . and sometimes not.

"So I kept adding the methylene chloride, and he got a little sicker every day." She pauses to press her hankie to her eyes. "It wasn't that I wanted him to suffer; I only wanted to give him time to make good."

I picture Henry's life as an hourglass filled with coffee grounds instead of sand, his life slipping away cup by cup. I won't ever drink another coffee again as long as I live.

Tingles of horror creep down my neck when I think of what she's done—the cold precision of it and the apparent fact that in sixty years she's never once felt the need to ease her conscience. Why has it taken a public accusation for her to confide in her own family? Perhaps that's what sickens me most. After all, when *I* killed a man I came home and told her all about it. That's what sisters do.

Each of us, her daughters especially, must spend these few silent moments looking backward, reinterpreting every memory. Every home-cooked meal of the last sixty years was prepared by a murderess; every kind word, every embrace was bestowed by the mother who robbed them of their father. Rosamund finally says, "You didn't follow Clovis's instructions the night of the séance, did you, Mother?"

Helena's mouth twitches wryly. "The cufflinks and the other things were Jack's, not Henry's. Wouldn't do to have Henry coming through loud and clear, so I used Jack's things for interference. And I can't really blame Belva for hating me even in the afterlife. Yes, I suppose I should come clean on that too: I put a curse on her. Every man she ever seduced soon tired of her, and she never found true love or happiness. After all, she took mine from me—at the time it seemed only fair."

Vega clears her throat. "I need to know, Granny. Grandpa Jack . . . did you . . . ?" Jack, of course, was the only grandfather she could remember.

"Grandpa Jack gave me no cause," Helena replies. "Of course, it helped that the only pretty young things wandering about *his* place of business were to be made shortly into veal."

"What about Julius Mettle?" I ask.

Helena frowns. "What about him?"

"He came here to speak to you once—threatened you. We saw it in the View-Master. We . . ." But I can't bring myself to say it.

"You were afraid I'd done away with him, too? No, certainly not. Poor Julius . . . he had every reason to worry what his daughter was getting up to."

Mira gasps. "Belva killed her own father?"

"It's likely it was an accident, which is why the police never pursued it." My sister gives a rueful little smile. "If you ever dig her up again, you might ask her." Helena rises from her chair. "And now it's time I made my confession to the rest of the coven."

"Oh God." I hide my face in my hands. "How will we ever face Lucretia?"

She looks down at me sadly and puts her hand on my shoulder. "I am the only one who has to face her. I regret that my sin has tainted your reputations, and I am very sorry that you girls have come to grief over it."

We make a move to stand, but Helena motions for us to stay where we are. She takes a long, deep breath, turns heel, and marches into the drawing room. The door muffles her voice. We wait in agonized silence.

She comes back a few minutes later, sits down again, and takes the last sip out of her teacup. Always so composed, is Helena—far too composed. Would lead you to wonder if she's even fully human.

"I don't understand, Granny," Mira says. "Why did you wear his hair in a locket all those years?"

"Penance," she sighs. "I know better now, of course. My penance is only beginning today." We watch as she rummages through her sewing bag and pulls out another of Olive's marionettes, this one with a thick gray chignon, a tiny calico apron with a ruffle along the hem, and a relentlessly pleasant expression. She stands, props the marionette against the back of her chair, and loops the strings round the chair back. Then she straightens up, unties the strings of her apron, and hangs it on the hook by the door.

She stands in the middle of the kitchen, her eyes roving hungrily over our faces. "This is good-bye, my darlings," she says at last. "I can't say when I'll be back."

No pomp or ceremony here—there can't be any, I suppose, when you're departing in disgrace. It happens like a film reel with a missing frame: she's there, and then she's not.

We stay seated round the kitchen table for a long time, still in silence, as if we're waiting for the marionette to pick itself up and speak to us. From the drawing room we can hear the shuffling sounds of the rest of the coven preparing to leave, and eventually the noise moves into the hall, but nobody ventures into the kitchen. Can't say I blame them—it *would* be awkward, now, wouldn't it? The front door slams behind them.

Vega begins to cry then, and when her sister tries to comfort her she weeps even more bitterly. This is all very dreamlike, nightmarish I should say, and when the rest of us start talking again our mouths feel disconnected from the rest of our bodies. "Tea?" Deborah murmurs, and we say, "Yes, please," faintly, one echoing after another. The kettle boils, china cups appear on the tabletop, and the hot golden liquid rises to the brim of every cup.

But I need something to clear the fog from my eyes. "Time for a nip if there ever was." I get up and find the whisky bottle myself because it gives me something to do, and when I hold up the bottle everybody says, "Yes, please."

I pour a healthy glug into Morven's cup, and there's only the clink of her teaspoon stirring in the hooch and Vega still sobbing her poor little heart out. There's a freshly baked ambrosia cake on a china pedestal on the table in front of us, but no one has the heart to cut the first slice.

The Shadow at the Foot of the Bed

30.

The life that I have
Is all that I have
And the life that I have
Is yours.

The love that I have
Of the life that I have
Is yours and yours and yours.

A sleep I shall have,
A rest I shall have
And death will be but a pause

For the peace of my years
In the long green grass
Will be yours and yours and yours.

    —Leo Marks, SOE Codemaster

A GOOD TEN years after the war, a letter came for me at Black-abbey. I got a chill when I read the return address; I didn't recognize it, but somehow I knew to whom it belonged.

She had sent numerous requests for my address over the last decade, not surprising given that SOE was shut down right after the war. Such requests for information would be forwarded from one department to another and back again. She couldn't have found me otherwise; she didn't know my name.

But at long last some bighearted bureaucrat had found the right file and had taken the time to reply to her last letter. *I want so much to know the facts surrounding Jonah's last days,* she wrote me. *I would be so grateful if you would agree to meet me. Indeed, I am grateful to you already.* I stared at the perfect penmanship, telling myself I shouldn't go but knowing that I would.

Patricia Holt, formerly Rudolfsen, lived in one of those venerable buildings on Central Park East. She greeted me with a look of puzzlement, even dismay, and I asked her if there was something wrong.

"Not at all, I . . . well, you must have been quite young when you were recruited."

"Hardly more than a teenager," I replied, suppressing a smile.

She ushered me inside, and a maid appeared only to whisk my coat into the hall closet. Patricia had what was known as elegant taste, but I could tell as soon as I walked into her living room that every bit of porcelain, every plush surface, every canvas had been hand-selected for her and her new husband by someone they had no doubt paid handsomely. I lingered on a wedding portrait on the end table and realized she'd now been with her "new" husband twice as long as she was married to Jonah. No dress of parachute silk for Patricia Holt.

I looked at her, hard, and she gave me an uncertain smile as she fiddled with her diamond wedding band. She was just as Jonah had described her: plain but polished, capable yet awkward. Meeting her felt a little like coming face to face with the bogeyman.

"May I offer you something to drink, Miss Harbinger?" she said at last, and I asked for a whisky and soda.

"Thank you for making the time to meet with me," she said as she fussed about the tray on the sideboard. "I've been quite fraught these last few days—thinking of it, wondering what you would be like. I was so afraid there might be . . . well . . . some degree of tension between us."

For heaven's sake, why make it worse by speaking of it? "You said you were grateful to me," I began as she handed me the glass. "I wondered what you meant by that."

"You spent every moment with him at the end of his life, and that makes you important to me as well as to him." There was an awkward pause I filled with a healthy swig. "Won't you come inside?" She indicated the bedroom. "There's something I'd like to show you."

Patricia invited me to sit at her vanity table while she knelt to open the bottom drawer. The lamp beside her makeup mirror was completely out of step with the "tasteful" décor in the rest of the house: it was made of cast iron, a gnome crouching under a toadstool, with a pleated green lampshade.

"What an odd little lamp," I said, so that anyone else would have understood I loved it.

"Isn't it, though? It's the one thing of Jonah's that Alexander has let me keep. Keep out, I mean. Jonah had it on his nightstand in his boyhood."

She pulled out a broad wooden box, laid it on the table, and raised the lid with a reverent air. She'd been waiting ten years to share her memories with someone who'd known him, someone who would care. For half an hour she sorted through everything in that box, showing me photographs and small toys from his "boyhood," and told me anecdotes of their courtship. At one point she even asked if I, too, had lost someone dear to me. I said yes, and she seemed embarrassed. I caught a glimpse of a small packet of letters tied together with a bit of twine.

The whole thing was completely agonizing for me. I kept seeing flashes of his face in the darkness of the stable—white-whiskered in the shaving mirror—laughing as Addie's dirndl-skirted marionette hopped up on his knee and flirted and cooed—cold and still in the moonlight as I took one long last look at him before I drew the blanket over his face and climbed out of the grave. And his hands—even now I felt his hands on me, his breath hot on my ear.

"They told me a little of how it happened," she said. "But I think it would help if I could hear it from you."

I was careful to tell her no more than she already knew; I didn't even mention the *Nacht und Nebel* order. For what good? I only told her that we had gathered a great deal of intelligence, so much that Jonah spent too much time transmitting it in one go and that they were able to trace the signal to our safe house. He'd been warned only in time to destroy his notes and gather his arms.

"And where were you while this was happening?"

"We were quartered separately. It was the middle of the night. I didn't hear of it until morning."

She paused. "And by that time it was too late, I suppose."

I nodded.

"Alexander doesn't like me to speak of him," she murmured as she laid the box back in the drawer. "He says we must try to live in the present."

Right then something was welling in my gut—bile or bitterness, it tasted the same. Jonah deserved better than a cachet of photographs at the bottom of a drawer, and to hell with her second husband. Alexander Holt had spent the war behind a desk.

We ventured back into her living room, where she offered me another whisky soda.

"There's—a delicate matter—I've been wanting to bring up," she said once we had resettled ourselves in the leather armchairs.

I didn't flinch; I knew she wasn't brave enough to ask *that* question. "Yes?"

"Jonah's watch," she said. "I was wondering if you knew what became of it."

It was on my nightstand, still telling perfect time. "I'm sorry, I'm afraid I don't."

"It's just that, you know, it was a family heirloom . . ." She trailed off, gazing at me expectantly.

"Oh. An heirloom in your family, was it?"

She looked sheepish. "No, it was handed down from his grandfather to his father, who gave it to Jonah."

"He didn't give it to me, if that's what you're wondering."

"But you do remember him having a pocket watch?"

"Indeed I do."

"Perhaps the SS took it, then?" That she should phrase this as a question was only a small part of why she was irritating me now. Why shouldn't I resent her for taking a job in the Chairborne while her husband was parachuting behind enemy lines? The only Nazis she'd ever seen were the POWs on the film reels.

"Very likely." I paused for effect. "You know, I always wondered why you didn't follow Jonah into operational service."

She acted as though this hadn't stung. "I wasn't cut out for it." She gave a weak laugh. "Surely Jonah told you that."

"He did," I replied. "But men too often believe they are the better judge of our shortcomings."

She didn't smile at this. "He was right. I hadn't your fortitude, Miss Harbinger." I could see she meant that as an honest compliment. "That watch," she went on. The moment of goodwill vanished instantly. "He would have given it to his son, if we'd had one."

This I found most infuriating of all: she never so much as alluded to their impending divorce. In Patricia Holt's revisionist history, both she and Jonah had remained faithful to his death. (Now, I know what you're thinking—was Jonah being fully honest when he told me they both wanted out? She married Alexander Holt a scant two months after she got word of Jonah's death—it was in the papers—and that was all I needed or wanted to know.)

I wanted to tell her I knew she was a phony, but I decided I should be as dignified as I was able. Jonah would have wanted it that way. "But as it is," I said, "there's no one to give it to."

She hesitated, and I could see she was formulating a different tack—as if asking some other way might jog my memory. Why did she want that watch back so badly? It's not that she thought I might be lying, though of course I was; she just wanted every stone turned. Perhaps she assumed that any message that might have been folded inside was intended for her.

"Look, Patricia—the watch is gone. I don't know what else to tell you."

Another long hesitation, during which time I polished off my second whisky soda and considered going after my own coat. Finally she said, "I am sensing some hostility, Eve—may I call you Eve?—and I am wondering why. Have I done anything to offend you?"

I let out a little snort of incredulity—couldn't help it. She was so tiresome. "Just let me get this straight. You asked me here on account of a lousy pocket watch?"

"It's not—it's not just about the watch."

I waited for her to continue but gave up. "What is it, then?" In a way, I wanted her unspoken questions to come out in an angry torrent—*Just how close* were *you? How was it that you survived and he did not?*—but I knew she'd never get up the courage.

All brains and no guts is what he'd said. Very little heart, either.

I rose from my chair. "I think I'd better go."

She nodded and fetched my coat as I waited by the door. "Thank you for coming, Miss Harbinger."

I paused at the door, my hand on the knob. "Did you love him?"

She seemed even more taken aback than I expected her to be. "Why, of course I loved him."

"Not like I did." And I made sure to look her in the eye as I pulled the door shut behind me.

I NICKED TWO photographs of Jonah that day: his official SOE portrait, and another of him smiling and relaxed, shirt partially unbuttoned, sitting on somebody's patio with a cigarette poised between his long, slender fingers. I muttered a few words as I stepped into the elevator and *whoosh,* they materialized inside my purse. I got proper frames for them and keep them displayed prominently in Cat's Hollow. I wonder, did she ever notice they were missing?

I shouldn't have done it, I know. He didn't belong to either of us.

Pumpkin Day

31.

I T'S ALL over on the last night of October, just before five o'clock. A young man sidesteps a troupe of shrieking fairies on the front walk at Harbinger House, then rings the doorbell and holds his breath. Half a second later a young woman throws the door open and laughs a most maniacal laugh, and he sees now why the little girls were making such a racket. It's a night for superlatives, all right, because she is wearing the most disgusting mask ever made: slithering things in her brittle black hair, glistening yellow fangs, a jutting chin with squishy purple warts sprouting hairs a foot long—and all of it unsettlingly lifelike. The foyer is lit only by a candle inside a jack-o'-lantern, and he can't tell where the mask ends and her neck and eyelids begin.

"Hello," says the young man.

The leering witch beckons him inside with a flick of a razor-sharp fingernail. "Come in then, love, and give us a kiss!"

"I'll skip the kiss, if you don't mind," he replies with only the ghost of a smile. "Is Eve home?"

Vega sighs, stands up straight, and whips the mask from her lovely face in a single motion.

"You Harbingers are *really* into Halloween, aren't you?"

She shrugs. "We try."

He stares at the mask hanging limp in her hand. "So—is Eve . . . ?"

"She's not here," Vega says with another sigh. This time, when she beckons him with a plastic claw still stuck on her finger, he follows her in. "You'd better sit down. I'll put the kettle on."

I HAVE BEEN sitting in the gloomy kitchen all afternoon alternately weeping into my hankie and helping myself to far too much of the children's loot. I know he'll come tonight, but I just can't stomach the prospect of saying good-bye to him once and for all.

"At least there's *this* way," Morven says reasonably. "You can have your good-bye but he'll never know it's you."

I don't want to say good-bye. I want to keep on going as we are. But they tell me a girl's got to grow up sometime and that I'm lagging just a bit in doing so at the age of a hundred and fifty.

"Besides, someday he'll want to settle down," says my sister, "and the longer you let it go the worse you'll feel in the end."

"I can't imagine feeling much worse than this," I mumble into my teacup.

"I know how to cheer you up! We'll go to London tonight! You can travel all over the world again, just like you used to. We'll have the time of our lives."

I am fairly certain the time of our lives has passed long since, but I manage to refrain from saying so.

In good time night falls, the doorbell rings, and Vega answers it wearing that grotesque face that's only a mask when she takes it off. I can hear Justin's voice over the kiddies squealing on the lawn. Morven squeezes my hand before she gets up to brew us a fresh pot of tea. I hear two sets of footsteps coming through the dining room and I draw a deep breath.

To my surprise, his eyes light up when he sees me. "Mrs. Harbinger! How are you?"

"I'm well, thank you for asking, Justin. Will you—will you have a cup of tea?"

"Do sit down, Justin," Morven says as she cuts a slice of ambrosia cake. "Vega has made your favorite. You did say chocolate spice cake was your favorite?"

"Oh yes, thanks very much," he says, and tucks in with enthusiasm.

"It isn't as good as Granny's," Vega says, blushing, and while this is true the cake is still awfully good.

With eyes sore and stinging I watch him eat, and a change comes over his face as he remembers his original purpose. "You said Eve isn't here?" he asks once he's swallowed. "Where is she?"

My sister puts a steaming cup in front of him. "There's nothing in the world a cup of tea can't make right. Drink up, dear. It's cinnamon tea, very good for the digestion." The teacup Morven gives him is the cup Helena used to give all the girls who came here looking for solace in the midst of their crumbling marriages, but it has no such effect on him.

"Thank you," he says, "but you aren't answering my question. Where is Eve? I've been calling her for weeks."

"She's . . . she's gone away for a while."

"Gone? Gone where?"

"We—we're not sure, exactly."

"What do you mean, you're not sure? She just took off?"

"I—" I start to say, but Morven stomps on my toe.

"I'm very sorry, Justin, but she's always been a capricious girl. We can only hope that in time she'll grow up a bit."

He stares at the floor. "I just don't understand it. She's—she's broken up with me, without so much as an *e-mail*? Oh," he says, laughing bitterly. "I forgot. Eve doesn't have an e-mail account."

"Not an e-mail," I say as I push a small envelope across the table. "A letter."

> *Dear Justin,*
>
> *You may be quite angry with me for taking off like this, and I suppose you have every right to be. We've had a*

lovely time together over the past year, but it couldn't
possibly have lasted and I thought it best to end, as they
say, on a high note. I'm not going to try to explain my
reasons. All I can do is wish you a long and happy life
and hope that when you do think of me on occasion, it's
with as much fondness as I will remember you.

Love,
Eve

It took me three hours to compose that letter, and by the time I was finished I had fulfilled that classic cliché: a wastepaper basket brimming with crumpled stationery.

He tosses the letter aside and kneads the bridge of his nose between his thumb and forefinger. Suddenly he looks very tired. "How can she say she loves me and then do this? Explain it to me. You all know her better than anybody."

"She also left you this." I pull out a small box wrapped in brown paper and slide it across the table.

Without looking at me Justin tears off the wrapping, opens the box, and stares at the pocket watch. Then he drains his cup, sets it on the saucer, and fixes me with bright eyes. It's a queer look, a deliberate look, almost as if he knows that I am hiding something. Oh, he *knows* we're all hiding something; he's a smart boy, after all. But it's me he's staring at, me he's looking to for an answer. "Is she all right?" he asks me. "Is she safe, and happy?"

Happy—*hah!*

Every Harbinger holds her breath, and for one long moment the kitchen is still as a morgue. Finally I manage a nod, and in a blink his demeanor has shifted from imploring to angry. We are the aiders and abettors of the only girl who has ever hurt him.

"Thank you for the cake," he says stiffly as he tucks the letter and the box containing the watch into his inside coat pocket. Then he rises from his chair, pushes it neatly under the table, and walks out of the kitchen for the last time.

Once the front door has slammed behind him I lose all composure. I cry as if I've lost Jonah all over again. I cry and cry, and as they pat me on the shoulders my sister and nieces look at me with frightened eyes. Aren't I supposed to be the fearless one, the one to whom all sentiment is a show of weakness?

Never mind what might have been.

Carry on and carry out.

Nostalgia poisons the present.

What a load.

And All That Happened Afterward

32.

Fifty years later

OTHING FOR it but to bide my time, and mind you, I've taken extra-specially good care of myself. I still don't look a day over eighty—a very *spry* eighty. But I don't fool myself thinking I'll live much longer, and I know I'm lucky to have this one last chance.

When Justin married a second time I began to think perhaps it was all in the past and I'd do well to leave it there. I almost never ventured into the mews anymore for fear of seeing him, but I still heard about everything that happened at Fawkes and Ibis. Harry and Emmet passed on within a year of each other, and then the shop belonged to Justin. Under his ownership Fawkes and Ibis prospered beyond the founders' wildest dreams. There were profiles in all the big newspapers and magazines, Businessman of the Year awards—heck, they even gave him the key to the "city." I was afraid all the success would turn him fat and complacent, but I needn't have worried.

I've never forgotten him. How could I?

I saw him walking up and down Worth Street a few days after that horrible Halloween night. He was checking the numbers above all the bars and bodegas, frowning as he tried to recall just what address I'd given the cabbie the morning after the Astor ball. I stood just across the street in my overcoat with the ermine collar and sensible shoes and watched as he alighted upon the entrance to the warren. And when the gate opened and he peered hopefully inside, the man coming out of the ordinary alleyway gave Justin a dirty look before shutting the door behind him with a decisive clank.

He lingered a few minutes longer, trying to part the autumn-withered ivy with those slender pianist's fingers of his so he might see something. But doubt overcame him; he couldn't recall passing through that courtyard. He passed from gate to curb, glancing up and down the street with that same long face I'd first seen on a train through the Highlands so long ago. His gaze swept my way, I turned up my collar and peered into a dusty shop display of garbanzo beans and *jugo de piña*, and when I looked round again he was gone.

To cheer me up Morven went to Fawkes and Ibis and bought me the horned mermaid, and we hung it over the coffee table in Cat's Hollow. Not that we've seen much of it this last long while. We've had midnight picnics on the cold marble floor of the Louvre, watched the marriages of ordinary couples from the eaves of old stone churches. And yes, I've still indulged in the occasional randy-view, though I've never broken my promise. Lucky for me, European men seem to like their women as they do their wine.

We've spent a fair bit of time in Deutschland too. I took Morven back to the Romanisches Café, where you still couldn't see the ceiling for all the smoke. I kept jerking my head this way and that thinking I glimpsed faces from the old crowd, but nobody from the old crowd would pass through that doorway again.

And other evenings we would turn into ravens and fly to the top of the Berliner Dom, where the angels who passed the war at the bottom of the river have been restored to their rightful places. We sit on the ledge high above the Lustgarten, where all the punks and drunks are milling about among the potted fuschia, and when I snap my fingers a cold thermos and a pair of martini glasses appear on the ledge between us. The angels and cherubs loom over us, the copper gone corpse-green and black in the crevices, and from the shadows come the sounds of squeaking bats and cooing pigeons. We sit there sipping grasshoppers as we look down over the blinking lights of the new city, cranes paused at obtuse angles over every construction site. Whenever I open my mouth to speak of the past, Morven, in her gentle way, changes the subject.

We never stay away for long, though. We're in Blackabbey often enough to watch our nieces fall in and out of love, and bring a few new nieces into the brood while they're at it. Uncle Hy and Uncle Heck still come to all the coventions; we prop them up on armchairs by the fire so they can delight all the little ones, just as they used to, with their stories of war and adventure. We've got to oil their jaw-hinges regularly or else you can't hear them for all the squeaking.

Life goes on in Helena's absence. Morven decided we owed Lucretia an apology—one of those apologies contingent upon the other party doing likewise—and I grudgingly followed her lead. The truce isn't friendly, civil is the best that can be said for it, but with the mend the tension left our circle and we've been able to go on as we always have. It will be at least a hundred years, maybe two, before another Harbinger leads this coven, but our nieces are not so proud as we were.

In fifty years we haven't heard from Helena, not once. Her puppet doesn't come to life with the others at covention times, and none of the aunties can say what has become of her. I can't bear to think of our sister wandering endlessly through some cosmic wasteland, so much so that I've begun to imagine I can hear a solitary puppet traversing the darkened hallways in the middle of the night, limbs clonking softly, dragging the crossbar along the hardwood floors.

I want it to be more than just a groggy fancy of mine; I want to believe that her daytime silence is part of her penance. One of these coventions I'm going to catch that bespectacled puppet in the calico apron by surprise, and then I'll know she's all right. That's what I tell myself.

Auntie Em and the rest of the elders couldn't give much comfort.

I'd go over and over it with Auntie, rehashing the details and playing "what if," at every covention for years afterward—that is, until she finally stopped coming back and Mira had a baby girl. (Tetchiest kid I ever met.)

Anyway, I told Auntie before she left us that after all that had happened with Helena, I actually felt rather guilty that no one had ever punished *me* for what I did in the prison at Nuremberg. How could tinkering with a tin of ground coffee possibly be any worse than slitting a man's throat?

"This is silly talk," Auntie sniffed. "Henry wasn't a bad man, and *you* weren't the one who misused your magic."

I only let myself ask her about Justin on one occasion, and she wasn't any more help than she'd ever been before. "Why must you always insist upon asking the questions you can answer for yourself, when there are much more important ones you leave hanging?"

I'd cast a glance at the other Gibson girl still suspended from the mantelpiece—the one who had never spoken any scolding words to me because it had never spoken at all. "If you'll recall, Auntie, I've asked you for the truth more than once. I know you know more than you ever let on."

"I knew you didn't really care to know."

I rolled my eyes and threw up my hands. What tosh!

"Listen to me, Evelyn. A child's regard for her parent is a delicate thing. I didn't want to be the one to put the tarnish." Auntie paused. "She was my niece, and I loved her. I would have overlooked it."

"Overlooked *what?*"

Auntie Em fixed me with her beady little eyes. "You weren't the only one who saw your father in the carriage that day."

"You're saying . . . you're saying Mother . . ."

"She asked that none of us ever tell you girls the real reason for her disappearance." Auntie sighed. "But I think I've kept that secret long enough."

So I shivered all over again in that icy moment of revelation. You see, Helena had only taken after our mother.

ONE EVENING at dinner Mira was regaling us with all the fresh gossip from the mews—the shopkeepers were organizing a protest of the town council's plan to repave the old cobblestone alleyway, and there was talk of beldames from Little Hammersley opening a rival toy shop—and then my niece cleared her throat and said she'd heard something out of Fawkes and Ibis that might be of particular interest to me.

"Justin's wife has left him," Vega said excitedly, before her sister could continue. Mira kicked her under the table and all the glass and silverware clinked.

"It happened last week," Mira said. "His son told me all about it. Off to 'find herself' on some mountain in India, he says."

"Can't say I'm surprised," Vega put in. "She always did seem like a bit of a frooty-toot."

SO THAT'S how I find myself in front of the Fawkes and Ibis display window for the first time in who knows how long, heart thudding in my ears, all gussied up and trying not to look it. A man of thirty-five or so stands at the cash register—Justin's son, obviously, but the resemblance doesn't affect me as it did the evening I arrived with a toffee cake and a hefty appetite.

For a moment or two I pretend to examine a selection of mint-condition jazz records in the window, until I notice the back-room curtain moving out the corner of my eye. I haven't seen any recent photographs of him, so his appearance startles me. He looks almost just as Jonah did in the shaving mirror all those years ago: the lines of his face grown more angular, more noble; bushy brows but nary a hair left on his head. Still has his teeth though, and good for him.

My second thought is that with the way he carries himself anyone could tell his wife's just left him. He is seventy-five now, but his posture is terrible and there's a leadenness to his movements that makes him look at least ten years older. He busies himself writing something at the counter for a moment, but his son has noticed how I'm staring and I hear him say a few words.

In that first second, as he's looking up, I freeze in terror—what if he's still angry? Or worse, what if he doesn't recognize me and I have to go through the humiliation of reminding him? No, it won't come to that. If he doesn't know it's me I'll turn heel and never look back.

I needn't have worried. His face is positively transformed at the sight of me, if I do say so myself. So now I'm inside the shop with no memory of putting one foot before the other, and he is clasping both my hands, kissing my cheek, telling me he'd have known me anywhere. At a time like this people always say the years melt away in an instant, and how true it is! He hasn't even gotten a word out but I am back on the stairs at Harbinger House—dressed in white, and not so young as I looked—gazing down at him smiling broadly among the swarm of the coven. He's back in that moment, too, I can tell. It pleases me to notice that his son, still standing behind the cash register, looks rather shocked.

He introduces me, briefly, and then he gets his coat and we walk to the Blind Pig Gin Mill. (Yep, still around, though it's changed owners a hundred times since.) I order a whisky ginger and he says he'll have the same, and he insists on buying my drink.

He keeps the conversation safe at first. I tell him little vignettes of the places I've been, and he gives me all the mundane details of his life. Has two children from his first marriage, his daughter's in medical school in Boston, and his son is taking over the business.

"You've done very well," I say. "I've heard about all your successes from my nieces. Blackabbey Business of the Year for the twelfth year running, eh? Well done!"

"Thank you." He takes a pensive sip of his whisky. "Uncle Harry would have been pleased, I think."

"Oh yes, I'm sure he would have." He gives me a curious sidewise look; I was always too familiar with the auld gents, and he could never figure out why.

It's only a matter of minutes before he mentions the departure of Wife Number Two. "Married fifteen years and she up and decides she's got to find herself." He doesn't sound bitter, only sad.

"Went to India, did she?"

"How did you know?" he asks, and I just laugh. He polishes off his drink, pauses, and I can tell by the look on his face he's going to ask me something awkward. "How about you?"

"Me?"

"How many husbands do *you* have?"

I laugh again. "None."

"Really? You never married?" Behind that mask of reflexive surprise, though, I can tell he might have predicted as much. He's wondering how many other men got letters like the one I wrote him.

We finish our drinks in silence. He checks his watch and I feel a sharp stab of panic. "Tell you what," he says. "Stephen's gone home by now. What do you say we go back to the shop?"

The relief must be plain on my face, because he smiles and eyes me fondly for a moment before calling to the bartender. "Do you have any crème de menthe?"

The bartender smirks as he turns to fetch a dusty bottle from the top shelf. He goes to open it and Justin says, "That's all right, we'll take the whole thing."

BACK IN the ersatz parlor, the opera lights and red-velvet chaise lounge are long gone, but similar furnishings have taken their place. The flocked velvet wallpaper has been replaced as well, but the wall of door knockers is still there, and the room still has that queer homely air, as if some elderly eccentric actually lived here. No more clocks though. "All that ticking got on my nerves," he says.

He goes upstairs for the glasses—they use the apartment for an office and storerooms now—and in that idle moment, when my fingers and toes start to tingle, I know it's only the paresthesia flaring up again. It's a load off, having nothing to hide anymore.

Justin comes back with ice cubes in the cordial glasses, and for a moment we sip in silence. Then he notices the pendant round my neck. "You kept it?" He glances up, his face a mix of incredulity and pleasure. "All this time?"

I give a little nod, and the look on him now—I don't even want to describe it. A thrill of anxiety leaves me trembling so bad I nearly spill the crème de menthe in my lap.

"I looked for you for years," he says quietly.

I just sit there, saying nothing because I'm afraid of saying too much. I can't very well tell him that the lies I told are the same sort of lies that get the play written, acted, and applauded, that we'd have had no fun without them. No, Evelyn. No more excuses.

He reaches for the crème de menthe and refills my glass. "I need to tell you why my wife left me."

"No—Justin—honestly, I wouldn't want you to go upsetting yourself—"

He shakes his head, his mouth set in a grim line. "I wasn't sleeping well. That's how it started. Caroline said I thrashed around and cried out like I was dreaming of being tortured"—I wince as he says this—"and when she tried to wake me, she wasn't able. It got so bad I had to start sleeping in the guest room. That went on for a few months, until she had the notion to drag me to a hypnotist. Oh, he was a doctor and all, called himself a psychoanalyst specializing in hypnotherapy, but I only went because Caroline wouldn't leave me alone about it.

"The therapist, doctor, whatever—he asked what made her think

I could be remembering things from a past life, and she told him that whenever I had these dreams I was calling out another woman's name . . . not once or twice, but over and over throughout the night. She'd never told *me* any of this, she just sprang it on me in the doctor's office. So I turned to her there—I was none too pleased with her, as you might well imagine—and I asked her whose name it was."

"Whose?" I breathe, my heart thudding in my ears.

"She wouldn't tell me at the time. Anyway, I went along with the 'regression' only because the doctor told me Caroline would have to wait outside. After she left the room he put me through a bunch of relaxation exercises, and at the end of it I was back in the middle of one of those dreams . . . except it was much clearer than any dream I'd had so far. It had all the details of a real memory—faces, voices, rooms, textures—you know what I mean?"

I nod. "And . . . what did you see?"

"A lot of things. I was seated in front of one of those old-fashioned radio transmitters, in a dark little room with black curtains on every side . . . I saw places that I knew were in Paris but weren't at all like what I remembered . . . once I was on the roof of a barn looking out over mountains as the sun came up . . . once I was in a banquet hall wearing a uniform with a swastika armband, but I knew it didn't belong to me—I wasn't really a Nazi . . . and I saw myself in prison more than once. I couldn't feel anything sitting in that chair in the doctor's office, but I knew—I knew it had been horrible.

"But in almost every other place, *you* were there too. Just as you were when I knew you. You were beside me on the barn roof, and when I was packing up the radio you came up behind me, wrapped your arms around me, and . . . well. I told the doctor it didn't make any sense, that you were a girl I'd known as a young man, and that I was probably just mixing up old memories with scenes from movies I'd seen a long time ago. He didn't say much at the time, just said he wanted to schedule me for a second session the next week.

"In the second session he told me to go backward, to a time before I was in any danger. I found myself in an apartment, I couldn't tell where, but then he had me examine the ordinary objects around the room. I put my hand in my inside jacket pocket and pulled out a silver flask. It had a set of initials on it—JAR. And then I woke up, came straight home, and spent all afternoon looking for this."

Justin draws out the old pocket watch and holds it so the smooth gold lid catches the light: *JAR*. He looks at me. Then with shaking fingers he flicks open the lid and pries the watch-face out of its setting. The little folded bit of paper is still there, and he plucks it out from between the gears, hands me the watch, and unfolds the paper. "It's a cipher, isn't it?"

I nod.

"I wasn't remembering scenes from an old movie, was I?"

I shake my head. "How long ago was this?"

"Two months."

"Why didn't you contact me, Justin? Why didn't you come to Harbinger House?"

"I thought about it. Thought about it a lot. But how could I, after the way your family froze me out?"

"That was fifty years ago!"

"I could say the same for you and me, though, couldn't I? Fifty years can go by but it doesn't matter any less."

Oh, but it's been well over a century now, by my count. I'll tell you this—a gal's never too old to blush.

He takes the open watch from my palm, lays it carefully on the end table, and clasps my hands in his. "Tell me everything, Eve. Start at the beginning."

Deep breath, Evelyn. "First off," I say, "I'm a great deal older than you think."

But a woman *should* look for a man her junior. We live longer, you know.

Acknowledgments

I TURNED INTO a bit of a magpie while I was taking notes for this novel. Whenever anyone said something particularly funny, I told them on the spot that I was going to appropriate it—so thanks to Anjuli Fiedler, Diarmuid O'Brien, and Cathy Szalai for their witticisms. And Brendan O'Brien inspired me more than I can say.

Magic, Witchcraft and Alchemy by Grillot de Givry, *The Devil's Dictionary* by Ambrose Bierce, and *To Have and to Hold: An Intimate History of Collectors and Collecting* by Philipp Blom were all books that stoked my imagination. The shipwreck at Jersey is supposedly a true story, which I discovered by way of Anne Hartigan's play *La Corbière*. It was Schopenhauer who declared that marriage halves one's rights and doubles one's duties, George Santayana who said that "sanity is madness put to good use," and the novelist Thomas Wolfe who characterized the stranglehold of National Socialism on the German psyche as "some dread malady of the soul." And of course, I owe all the penis-snatching references to those sadistic monks (Heinrich Kramer and Jacob Sprenger) who wrote the *Malleus Maleficarum,* a witch-hunting treatise first published in Germany in 1487.

Most inspiring of all were, of course, the real-life spies of the Special Operations Executive (SOE) and the Office of Strategic Services

(OSS). Many smart and courageous women served as couriers and radio operators behind enemy lines, and their stories aren't quite so well known today as they ought to be. I loved reading *The Women Who Lived for Danger: The Agents of the Special Operations Executive* by Marcus Binney; *Resisting Hitler: Mildred Harnack and the Red Orchestra* by Shareen Blair Brysac; *A Spy at the Heart of the Third Reich: The Extraordinary Story of Fritz Kolbe, America's Most Important Spy in World War II* by Lucas Delattre; and *A Life in Secrets: Vera Atkins and the Missing Agents of WWII* by Sarah Helm. Joseph Persico's *Piercing the Reich: The Penetration of Nazi Germany by American Secret Agents During World War II* was especially useful.

A million thanks to my good friends and faithful readers: Kelly Brown (my partner in crime in Germany), Seanan McDonnell, Ailbhe Slevin, and Christian O'Reilly. Kate Garrick is the best agent a girl could ask for. Thanks to Sarah Knight for making this book all that it could be, and to Brian DeFiore and Shaye Areheart for their continued support. I am grateful to Sally Kim for believing in me, to Rico Zimmer for correcting my German, and to Mike McCormack and Adrian Frazier at NUI Galway for their ongoing inspiration and encouragement.

Thanks to my family most of all.

About the Author

CAMILLE DEANGELIS is the author of *Mary Modern*. She received an MA in writing at the National University of Ireland, Galway, in 2005, and her first-edition guidebook, *Moon Ireland*, was published in 2007. She lives in New Jersey.

Visit her at www.CamilleDeAngelis.com.

A Note on the Type

The text of this book was set in Fournier MT, a typeface created by Monotype in 1924, based on type cut by Pierre Simon Fournier circa 1742 in his *Manual Typographie*.